C000138633

THE LOST BLADE OF ZERIGOR

To Alasdair & Susan
With blessings from
Mill mead
love from Kevan

K K Sutton

Inscribe Publishing, Guildford, England

The Lost Blade of Zerigor

First paperback edition printed 2012 in the United Kingdom.

A CIP catalogue record for this book is available from the British Library

ISBN 978-1-909369-00-9

Published by Inscribe Publishing, Suite 232, Chremma House, 14 London Road, Guildford, Surrey GU1 2AG, England.

Cover Design and typesetting by Inscribe Publishing.
Printed and bound in Great Britain by IJgraphics, Guildford, GU2 9XW

THE LOST BLADE OF ZERIGOR

BOOK I

IN

THE RESTORATION

OF

THE CROWN OF LIFE

BY

K K Sutton

Dedication

To Gill my wife, Benedict, Genevieve and Francesca, my
children, without whose love, practical help and encouragement,
this book would never have been written

BOOK I

A COLLECTION OF WRITINGS

PART I

THE NAMING

Chapter One

Everyone ducked instinctively.

'What was that?'

'Hush, Beth,' Princess Lenyé held her sister closer and gently stroked the tousled hair. 'It's only an owl landing on the roof.'

'Owls wouldn't make a noise like that...'

Princess Lenyé glared at her cousin Quinn, trying to silence him with her eyes. She knew their enemies were closing in on them, but how had they been discovered here?

'Anyway,' Quinn was over to the window and struggling with the wooden shutter before she could stop him. 'Sounded more like an arrow to me.'

Princess Lenyé's eyes stung from the smoky atmosphere in the forester's cottage: a month on the run in various homes of refuge, but still she wasn't hardened to it. Suddenly she smelled a different kind of burning.

'There it is again,' Quinn had the shutter open at last.

They all knew that sickening whizz, followed by the scrunch of severed straw. Now they could see a ribbon of flame take hold in the thatch of the cottage opposite.

'Fire arrows,' squealed Beth. 'They're going to burn us out!'

There was a snick of the latch and the door burst open. Prince Kyros stood in the doorway, his tall figure and broad shoulders silhouetted by the crackling flames behind him. 'Quick. Uncle Morthrir's troops have found us at last. Everyone out,' his voice sounded tense, but still carried the weight of authority. He

1

glanced round the single downstairs room of the cottage at the huddled figures of his brother and sisters and cousins and the few courtiers that remained loyal: their pale faces turned towards him. 'Where's Rafé?'

Everyone looked at each other and then back to Prince Kyros.

'Already gone,' Quinn jerked the shutter to and fastened it. 'Not long after you left. Said he wanted to find an escape route in case the worst happened. About an hour ago, I would say.'

'He'll have to fend for himself and join us when he can. All of you. Make for our special beech tree at the Pool of Alesco.'

For an instant everyone remained rooted to the spot. Prince Kyros strode into the room and grabbed both his sisters by the hand and hauled them up. 'There isn't a moment to lose. Lenyé, take the girls and the women. You lads and men, come with me.' He pulled Princess Lenyé to her feet and whispered, 'If I am taken, you must save yourself.'

'Oh, Kyros, they won't hurt the younger ones will they?'

'There's more at stake than just our lives. One of us has to escape and bring Uncle Morthrir to justice, whatever that takes. Otherwise he will destroy the Krêonor and ruin all we stand for.'

'But Kyros.'

He held her eyes with his, 'You do understand, don't you.'

Princess Lenyé swallowed and nodded, reaching out to clutch his arm; but he caught her hand and lifted it to his lips. 'Take care, my Sweet,' he whispered, for her ears alone. And then he was gone.

Quinn and her two brothers followed Prince Kyros, while Princess Lenyé pushed the younger girls in front of her: the two cousins, with Beth clinging to her. Flames plumed along the thatch and leaped the small gap to the next cottage. Fire arrows rained down on the other cottages in the forest hamlet. Smoke poured off the roofs filling the single dirt track: the flames a dull red against the grey smoke and silver brightness of the moonlight. Princess Lenyé coughed and retched as the sound of hooves broke in amongst them, horses and riders swirling the smoke around in eddies that confused the eyes and muddled the brain: horsemen with swords and lances, riding them down, separating them and driving them further from each other.

Rough hands groped for them. Princess Lenyé felt her sister torn from her side. 'Beth,' she screamed. 'Where are you?'

'Here.' Beth's terrified voice was cut short as though someone had clamped a hand over her sister's mouth. Or worse!

Princess Lenyé tried to make for the sound, but was immediately cut off by two horsemen riding up out of the smoke, lances levelled, goading her, isolating her from the cries of the others, steering her out of the hamlet and away into the forest. She turned and fled, gathering up her skirts and darting in amongst the welcome trees. But the riders followed, chivvying her, harrying her, cutting her off whenever she tried to get past them and run back to the hamlet to save her sister. They were relentless.

She stumbled out of the trees onto a rim of rock that formed part of a great semi circle looking down on the expanse of Lake Sanchéso. Below her, and to the left, was the curious pinnacle of the Dangst Rock, like a warning finger leaning out slightly over the lake, where only a month ago she and Kyros secretly pledged themselves to each other: close cousins, destined to continue the Royal Line of the Krêonor. Even now the poignancy of that moment hung in the air, and she felt again the thrill of her love for him: nothing could ever extinguish that. For fun they dived the thirty feet into deep water at the base of the cliff and swam to the Eye of Hoffengrégor, the islet far out on the lake, named after the one-eyed seer who prophesied the rise and fall and Restoration of the Krêonor.

The same day they received the fateful news: both sets of parents had vanished; Uncle Morthrir had seized the throne, put a price on their heads and was hunting them as fugitives.

Princess Lenyé glanced back at the roaring flames now visible above the tops of the trees that screened the hamlet itself from view. The drifting smoke cleared momentarily to reveal Youdlh, Commander of her Uncle Morthrir's Household Guard, mounted on his fine charger. Holding his stirrup was the last person she expected: Rafé, the most trusted of the King's personal counsellors. How could he be involved with Youdlh? He was pointing down the tumble of rocks below his feet. Why had he betrayed them?

She was distracted by a figure lower down the rock face, leaping like a gazelle. By his strength and agility she knew it was Kyros. But what a state he was in: running for his life, his jerkin ablaze at the back, arrows skipping off the rocks around him as Youdlh's archers ran up to the ridge and tried to bring him down. He hurled himself across the short gap onto the top of the Dangst Rock using his momentum to spring far out, his arms coming up over his head as his graceful flight took him plummeting towards the lake, the flames on his back fanning higher as he hurtled into the water. He dived deep, arrows whipping into the foam around his point of entry. She held her breath for him, willing him to stay down as long as possible. If only his dive would take him far enough out, to where fingers of mist were creeping towards the shore, before surfacing, he could swim undetected to the Eye of Hoffengrégor and escape.

Princess Lenyé spun round at a sound from behind her. The two horsemen broke out of the forest and charged; the points of their lances levelled straight at her. Then she was running and stumbling and sobbing, 'Beth, I'm so sorry. I've failed you.' A pang of guilt shot through her heart as she thought about her real feelings towards her sister. 'What's happening to us?'

Chapter Two

Morthrir stood at the window of the private council chamber next to the throne room and watched intently as the thrush in the garden below seized the snail in its beak and dashed it on a large stone. He curled his lip in a sneer at the reminder. That's exactly what he had done with Dareth and Alkram, his two older brothers. How could they be foolish enough to think he wouldn't do it?

One month. Morthrir had been in the palace for one month, and was still ecstatic about his triumph. So far a successful and completely bloodless coup. This was what he had plotted for; this was what he had worked for; this was what he was born for!

The thrush hammered its quarry on the stone again and again. Morthrir was fascinated. He raised his hand in anticipation, and, as the thrush smashed the snail for the last time and the shell split away, he brought his fist down on the stone windowsill in exultant admiration for a fellow conqueror. The thrush pecked at the exposed flesh and swallowed its victim whole. He chuckled at the comparison!

Now he had to rid himself of his nephews, and high on his hit list was Kyros, the one man who could rally an uprising against him. Once his rivals were taken care of he could arrange the Coronation Day.

He slammed his fist on the windowsill again. Why was Youdlh taking so long?

He glanced out into the garden, hoping for more inspiration from the thrush, but it was gone. There was no sign of any life at all, only the shattered remains of the shell to remind him of the legacy of utter ruthlessness.

Reluctantly he pushed himself away from the window ledge and turned back into the room. He needed to think. His dark eyes swept the chamber taking in the rich wood panelling and heavy wall hangings as if for the first time. This was his favourite room in the whole palace. It was where all the significant details were discussed and the important decisions made. The throne room next door was for pomp and occasion and the endorsing of what took place within these four walls. He could feel the sense of power engulf him as he stretched out his right arm and clenched his fingers together, grasping it for himself.

He crossed the room to the exquisitely tooled parchment map stretched taut over its frame on the angled stand, and began tracing the outline of the Krêonor Kingdom with his finger. It was in this very room that Dareth conferred upon him the Princedom of Onadestra, the least of the regions carved up between the three brothers after their Father died, and the furthest away from the Royal Palace here at Terrazarema, the ancient capital and seat of real power. He placed his finger on the centre of the map and traced the hazardous journey by road to his own castle in Onadestra at the eastern extremity.

Morthrir swore aloud to the empty room at the reminder. He had accepted it with a smile and the expected words of gratitude, but inwardly he burned with anger and humiliation, recognising it for what it was, the unspoken condemnation of his eldest brother: you're no good, you're not wanted, stay away from us. What he really felt was the silent distance of both his brothers, blaming him for their Mother's death in childbirth. He screwed up his eyes as he felt afresh the intensity of the inner pain that still racked him deep within.

How could that be his fault?

Nothing was ever said, but he sensed he was always an intruder on the close relationship between Dareth and Alkram.

In wrath he departed for Onadestra, hating the mountain fastness, the ageing population in their ruined homesteads and the crumbling terraced slopes of a near-deserted province, despising the folklore that historically this was one of the richest domains in the whole Krêonor Kingdom.

That was sixteen years ago, when Morthrir was only nineteen.

He took a deep breath and forced himself to relax.

It didn't take long for his ire to cool and he could think straight again. Morthrir could wait to take revenge on his brothers, biding his time, increasing his wealth, and, more importantly, establishing his power-base on the back of that wealth. He smirked with pride at his strengthening inner resolve that had transformed him into what he was now. The high point of his achievements was to raise a standing army of foreign mercenaries loyal to him personally, and his generous payouts, but motivated more specifically by the prospect of richer pickings to come when Dareth and Alkram were overthrown.

He glanced back at the parchment. Almost against his will he felt his finger drawn down the map through the rugged mountain range across the grassy plateau to Mount Malkamet, nearly due South from his castle. Morthrir's mind continually feasted on a recurrent dream: a man raised up through the Royal Family to receive spiritual power for total dominion. The dream was never quite complete and always left him grasping endlessly for its fulfilment. Was this something you waited for till it came to you, or could you make it happen for yourself? He wrestled with that question for some time, his conscious mind warning him that you couldn't have that kind of power without paying a terrible price. But the dream kept repeating and there was never any mention of a price: only the rewards; his unconscious mind, his deeper self, continually pushing him to begin to make it happen by seeking out the mysterious mountain.

Finally he decided. He would make it happen.

Vividly he recalled that night in the ravine on Mount

Malkamet: the coming of the Four Summoners and the Ten Priests and his shock and horror and delight at the appearing of the Lord Abbérr... No, no. Even now, he couldn't bring himself to say that awe-inspiring name in full, despite the privacy of this room. That was when he knew he was invincible, and it was his right to conquer and subdue and stretch out his hand to seize all that he desired. Less than a year ago and now look how much he'd achieved since...

The clatter of horses' hooves in the central courtyard of the palace jerked him back to the present. That sounded like Youdlh. His express orders were to kill Kyros and capture Lenyé unharmed. He must have succeeded at last.

He rubbed his hands together in anticipation. With Kyros out of the way, it was Lenyé who now occupied his thoughts the most. His beautiful niece, Lenyé. At eighteen she was clearly available as a marriage prospect.

His own wife, Faria, remained barren over the years while Dareth and Alkram's wives bore them four children each. He smacked his fist into his open palm. 'Why them?' he shouted to the silent room. 'Why do they always have everything in life? And I get nothing!' In his sudden outburst of anger, he decided to have Faria disposed of. Then he could seize Lenyé and force her to marry him. Why not arrange the Wedding and Coronation for the same day and have a double celebration? With Lenyé he could strengthen and maintain the Royal Line of the Krêonor. Then he would be unassailable.

Whatever else he did, he was burning with desire for Lenyé. He had to have her as his bride.

Chapter Three

Princess Lenyé glanced back over her shoulder. The horsemen were gaining on her.

Kyros must have escaped from Youdlh. But she had to assume he would swim out to the Eye of Hoffengrégor. That meant he couldn't help anyone else. Even if he did turn back he wouldn't be able to get up to the hamlet very easily. The shoreline where he dived in would be crawling with soldiers by now. It was up to her to lose these two and double back to Beth and the others. She mustn't get caught.

Lenyé wiped her tears away roughly with the back of her hand. As she reached the end of the rocky outcrop, she crouched down with one hand on a gnarled tree root, gathered up her skirts with the other and jumped into the slot that ran down between high sides of rock back into the forest.

She knew every path, every track, every animal trail for miles around, from countless family holidays here. They would camp deep in the forest and live off the land for days, eating berries and roots and the game they brought down with their hunting bows. She could follow a trail, tell by every bent leaf and broken twig how long ago their quarry had passed, lie in wait like a stalking mountain lioness and remain completely concealed. Her woodcraft was well respected within the family; even Kyros was no match for her and he was two years her senior.

Her mind was racing: think, Lenyé, think. These men are on horseback and don't know where they are. I have to lead them through the smallest, tightest places, where their horses can't go and throw them off my scent. I know where I'll take them!

She ducked down under a low arch of yew branches and ran as fast as she could, her skirts still gathered up in her hand and tucked over one arm. The bright moonlight out on the rocks dimmed under the tree canopy, with an occasional patch breaking through here and there in the odd clearing. Then she was twisting and turning down smaller paths and trails getting deeper into the thickening forest, stumbling and almost tripping over as her eyes adjusted to the darkness amongst the trees.

An owl hooted in the distance.

She could hear the men behind her crashing through the undergrowth, cursing as the branches hampered their passage; the shrill neighing of their horses making her smile with grim pleasure that her plan was working as the soldiers forced their poor animals between the close-packed tree-trunks. She heard yells from both men as, presumably, their lances snagged and were torn from their hands. The ringing of steel as they drew their swords confirmed it, and she could hear them hacking away, trying to clear a wider path. But she was well ahead of them now.

Lenyé went to ground, hiding in a clump of briars and overhanging bushes. She lay there panting, her hand partly over her nose and mouth to break up the sound, and listened. The crashing of the men and their horses carried on for a while and then stopped. She expected them to resume any minute, but nothing happened.

Everything was quiet and still.

She could almost feel the silence as the forest held its breath: waiting. Even the owl had ceased its calling.

Cautiously she changed her position, easing herself up on her haunches so she could peer through the briar stems back the way she had come. Dimly she could make out both soldiers as dark smudges against the lighter patches between the trees: they had dismounted and were standing stock still, their drawn swords in one hand and holding their horse's reins in the other.

Then the nearer one started moving, hacking in front of him with his sword and pulling his horse along behind him; the other soldier followed suit, fanning out slightly to cover a wider tranche of ground. If they carry on like this, she whispered to herself, they're going to hack straight into my hideout.

What should she do? Run now, while she still had distance on her side? But then they'd mount their horses and be after her immediately. Or wait till the last possible moment, and hope that surprise would throw them long enough for her to make the one break that would get rid of them for good? She decided to wait.

If they mounted as soon as she bolted they would be concentrating on her rather than what was ahead. She needed that for her plan to work. If they saw beyond that thin curtain of bushes, she would lose the advantage of surprise.

Lenyé was distressed at the effect on the horses, but she couldn't help it. She must get away from these men.

Two years ago she and Kyros discovered this scree slope of loose, sliding stones, where the forest ended and the ground fell away so sharply, and spent a whole afternoon using the flat slabs that littered the area to slide down the steep slope. They went back to camp dusty and dishevelled, only to be given a right telling-off and forbidden from ever doing it again or trying to teach their brothers and sisters, as it was far too dangerous.

But there was an enormous difference between picking a choice slab, placing it carefully at the top of the slope and pushing off, compared to leaping over the curtain of bushes that hid the top of the slope, landing so as to pick up a slab in mid-flight and keep her balance as she slid down. She did it once when Kyros was chasing her back to camp: she made the leap and held her footing while Kyros was left stranded at the top in total surprise. She had to do it now. Her very life depended on it.

Lenyé watched the men as they approached, ready to make her move the instant they were in the right position. But the man in the lead veered off slightly to the left, and his companion moved over to close the gap between them. That meant the man in the lead would end up past her before the second man stumbled across her hiding place. Should she go now, before it was too late?

Lenyé hesitated.

They were almost on her and she was gathering up her skirts into the crook of her elbow and edging round slowly to dart away to their right when the men stopped.

'She can't be that far ahead now, Gronis.' The voice of the man in front startled Lenyé in the silence of the forest. 'We'd have heard her if she was still moving.'

'Listen, Patique. I could have brought her down with my longbow when we were back there, in bright moonlight. It's impossible to see anything in here more than a few yards ahead.'

'I know. But by the time you'd dismounted and notched an arrow, she would have disappeared completely. At least we know she's somewhere in these woods. Besides. Youdlh ordered this girl to be captured at all cost. No marks, no injuries, no wounds.'

Gronis didn't sound very convinced. 'And what happens if we didn't quite hear those orders properly?'

'Your life won't be worth living. The order's straight from Morthrir himself. Youdlh thinks he wants her as his bride.'

Lenyé stiffened at Patique's words. Uncle Morthrir wants me as his wife? What about Aunt Faria? Surely…

She was so distracted by her own wild thoughts that it took her a second too long to realise the men were moving again and hacking at the undergrowth. She ducked as the blade came crashing in amongst the briars.

'There she is,' Gronis yelled. 'Quick.'

Lenyé was up and running like a startled pheasant before the man could grab her.

She heard Patique shouting, 'After her.'

12

The moonlight was stronger here as the trees thinned.

Could she make it? The line of bushes looked further off than she remembered.

She heard the sound of horses' hooves gathering pace behind her; the men were in their saddles already and riding her down.

No time for any twisting or turning. This was a flat out race.

She heard Gronis' tense voice not far behind, 'You go that side and we'll catch her under the arms.'

She could feel the hot breath of the horses as they drew alongside her. Hands were already grabbing at her arms and shoulders on each side.

Now!

She leaped the thin line of bushes, through the last of the trees and felt herself hurtling over the edge into nothing, the sudden brightness of the moonlight almost blinding her.

She heard the screams of terrified horses as she landed, her legs braced and her feet sliding in the loose scree. Her momentum set off a veritable avalanche of sliding stones and flat slabs and stirred up a dust cloud that completely enveloped her.

She jumped sideways onto a slab, steered it with her feet to one side of the avalanche, and risked twisting her head round for a quick look behind her. The two horses were on their hind legs just over the brow of the scree slope, plunging and rearing and trying to regain their footing. Both men were thrown off backwards: Patique had his foot caught in a stirrup and was being dragged back up the slope; Gronis, already sliding down the scree slope on his back, was moving with her.

Lenyé zigzagged to slow her pace; and Gronis rocketed past her, screaming.

She steered to the right until she tipped over a ridge of rock onto another almost vertical slope. Neither she nor Kyros had attempted this bit before, knowing it was much too steep. But she had to end up as far away from the bottom of the main scree slope as possible. She couldn't just coast gently down into

Gronis' waiting arms.

Dust was in her eyes, up her nose, caking her face. She battled with every shifting angle and lurch of the slab, flexing her knees and twisting back and forth, her arms moving to counter balance her body: concentrating hard to stay upright. Above the noise of her own descent she could hear Patique shouting and cursing, the horses neighing in terror, and Gronis' scream cut short.

She glanced back again and was relieved to see both horses heave themselves up the bank. Patique's horse bolted: she caught a glimpse of him, with his foot still trapped in the stirrup, being yanked back through the bushes. The other horse followed.

Lenyé grinned with satisfaction. Her plan was working.

But she was going much too fast. She felt the strain in her thighs as she increased the length of each zigzag, and tightened the angle of each turn: every rough patch, rock protrusion, and downward slither on loose scree jarred up through her legs.

As she found a new rhythm, and gained in confidence, her thoughts went out to the others. If only they could escape to the Pool of Alesco, she would find them. If Kyros reached the island, she could risk a light to attract his attention. But then she might alert her Uncle's troops. Oh, Kyros. If only I could come to you...

Suddenly her slab caught on the edge of a rock splinter and was whipped out from under her feet.

Lenyé felt herself flying through the air before hitting the ground and bouncing on down the slope. She wrapped her hands round the back of her head and tried to protect her face with her elbows as she rolled over and over. Her back slammed into a hollow of rock. Instinctively she whipped her hands up to try and stop herself rolling any further. Her head jerked back and cracked against the ground. Everything went black.

Chapter Four

The six remaining Royal youngsters and their courtiers stood in a semi circle with their hands tied behind their backs and surrounded by a dozen guards, while other soldiers rounded up the villagers. Shouts and screams and curses came from the burning hamlet behind them, interspersed with the neighing of horses. The flames had died down now, but the acrid smell of burning still hung in the air.

Beth found herself standing next to her cousin, Quinn. She could see his face, white in the moonlight, with a nasty gash across one temple. She remembered him launching himself at the man on horseback who had gathered her up in one swift movement with his arm around her and his hand clamped over her mouth. Quinn took a kick on the side of his head with the man's boot still in its stirrup, and went down like a felled ox. She was pleased to see he was able to stand up unaided; and his lanky frame and cheeky grin were so reassuring, even though he was less than a year older than her.

Scudding clouds were beginning to cover the moon as a wind picked up and blew in amongst them, flapping their hair, and blowing the smoke away from them. Beth looked up and saw the cloud layer building far out over the lake and coming towards them, dimming the bright light of the moon.

She was distracted by the sound of hooves on dry leaves, and recognised Commander Youdlh as he walked his horse into the clearing and stopped in front of them.

'So.' His thick accent was hard for her to understand. 'What have we here?'

An officer stepped forwards and saluted smartly. 'Prisoners taken from the Royal Families and their courtiers, Sir.'

'I see.' Youdlh dismounted and walked towards them. 'But we don't seem to have all of them, do we.'

'Gronis and Patique went after the older girl, Sir. I saw them chasing her into the forest.'

'Good. And the older boy?'

'Not sure, Sir. I sent some of my archers after him, while the rest of my men rounded up these others.'

'He can't have gone far. Well done, Captain Elskin. A good night's work.' Youdlh walked right up to Beth and tilted her head back with his hand so she was looking him straight in the eyes. 'Pity to spoil such a pretty young face.'

Beth felt the hardened leather of his gauntlet grip tighter across her cheeks.

The man scowled at her. 'Where would your sister run to, if she was alone in the forest?'

'I...' she faltered. 'I don't know.'

'Come now.' Youdlh whipped a dagger from his belt and held it against Beth's throat. 'I'm sure I can be a little persuasive when I need to be.'

She choked with shock as the sharp blade pressed against her skin.

'No!' Quinn lurched forwards, and practically barged Beth aside. 'Not Beth. Whatever you're going to do, do it to me, but not Beth.'

Captain Elskin grabbed Quinn and pushed him roughly to his knees, right in front of the Commander.

'Oh,' Youdlh's tone was sarcastic. 'And who might you be?'

'Quinn. Younger brother of Prince Kyros.'

'Really? Well, for your information, Kyros is no longer a Prince, but an outlaw.' He paused to let his words sink in. 'So it's no good thinking you're second in line to the throne any more.'

'I don't believe you.' Quinn slid his left knee forwards, as he spoke, so that his foot was on the ground, and he could grip against it with his boot. Then he thrust himself upwards, straight at Youdlh. Even though his hands were tied behind his back, he caught Youdlh full in the belly with his head and they both went down together. Captain Elskin leapt into the fray and hauled Quinn off his Commander.

Youdlh staggered to his feet and yanked Quinn's head back by the hair. 'In fact,' he paused, still gasping for breath from the head-butt. 'You don't have to be second in line for anything now.' He stood poised, ready to drive his dagger into Quinn's neck. 'You can be first for a change.'

'No!' Beth screamed.

'Question is,' Youdlh continued. 'If we don't kill them now, what else are we to do with them?'

Captain Elskin frowned. 'We can't do that, Sir. The youngsters are from the Royal Household.'

'So?' Youdlh continued. 'Better to finish them off quickly, while no one notices.'

But before he could move, there was a commotion from behind. Several soldiers, led by their captain, came marching into the clearing. The two in the middle were half carrying, half dragging a man by the arms face down, with his hands tied behind his back and his feet trailing. They yanked him right up to Youdlh and dumped him on the ground.

Youdlh let go of Quinn's hair and turned to face the captain. 'Who's that, Harbona?'

'Not sure, Sir,' the officer answered. 'We found him in the water.'

Youdlh turned the man over with his boot.

'Rafé!' gasped Beth.

Youdlh grabbed the man by the front of his jacket and dragged him to his feet. 'King Dareth's own counsellor. My, my. The net is drawing tight.' He let go of Rafé, and the man lurched as if he was about to fall. His clothes were streaming with water, and blood trickled from the corner of his mouth. 'What have you got to say for yourself?'

'I was trying to rescue Prince Kyros. I saw him dive from the Dangst Rock, but your archers wounded him with arrows, one in the neck at least, and several others in his back and chest as he turned over.'

'Oh, Kyros!' Beth wasn't the only one to gasp at the shocking news.

'He was floundering in the water,' Rafé continued. 'I couldn't just leave him; but your men caught me and pulled me out before I could get to him.' He paused and sobbed. 'I saw him go down.'

A cry of dismay went up from Beth and the other prisoners.

'Excellent. One less for us to deal with.' Youdlh turned to Captain Elskin. 'I've changed my mind. Re-tie the prisoners' hands in front of them, secure them on horseback and place mounted guards either side. We'll ride out at dawn. I'm sure King Morthrir will want to talk to each of them.'

'He isn't King yet,' muttered Quinn under his breath.

Youdlh stepped over to him, stooped down and shoved his face right into Quinn's. 'But when he is, you'll be the first to know about it.'

Captain Elskin hauled Quinn to his feet and was about to thrust him back amongst the others.

'Oh, Captain,' Youdlh continued. 'Include Rafé with the prisoners. Morthrir will definitely want to talk to such an experienced counsellor. In private, of course.' He turned back to Rafé as if another thought had occurred to him. 'But what were you doing down at the water's edge in the first place?'

Rafé didn't answer.

Youdlh stepped up to him and slapped him hard across the mouth with the back of his gloved hand. 'I said, "*What were you doing down at the water's edge?*".'

'I slipped out of the cottage, not long before your men started loosing fire arrows, to try and warn Prince Kyros, and work out an escape route.' He glanced sideways at Quinn and Beth before continuing. 'I said nothing to the others at the time, as I didn't want to alarm them. None of us realised quite how close your troops were.'

Youdlh turned to the soldiers. 'Did your men find Kyros' body, Captain Harbona?'

'No, Sir.'

'Take a detachment with you and comb the shore. I must have proof that he's dead. If necessary, row out to the Eye of Hoffengrégor and check he didn't manage to swim that far. I want a thorough search.'

'No one could survive that distance. Not in the state he was in, Sir.'

Youdlh glared at him. 'Never take anything for granted.'

'They say the place is haunted, Sir.'

'You don't believe in those stupid stories about an old man lying at the bottom of the lake and watching our every move?'

Captain Harbona shifted his foot but didn't answer. He kept his eyes lowered.

'Well. Do you?'

'I…I don't know. Some people say they've seen a figure in white, walking out to the island on the water. I…'

'You're not scared are you?'

'No, Sir.'

'Get on with it, then.'

'We don't have a boat, Sir.'

Youdlh's voice was as cold as ice, 'Then find one!'

Chapter Five

Kyros hauled himself out of the water and collapsed on the grey shingle that surrounded the Eye of Hoffengrégor. He was exhausted from swimming and lay there feeling the cold mist engulfing him, chilling him to the bone. A slow numbness crept over him as he drifted into forgetfulness.

'Quick,' an inner voice jerked him back to reality. 'You cannot stay here. When the mist clears, you could be spotted from the shore once the sun is up.'

Kyros nodded, but he needed sleep more than anything.

'If you fall asleep now, all will be lost,' the voice was insistent.

At last Kyros roused himself. Lurching to his feet, he staggered across the rocks into the undergrowth and slithered down into a hollow. He lay there panting as his eyes closed.

He dreamed he was with Lenyé on the Dangst Rock. The sun was shining and he was down on one knee, holding her outstretched hand, telling her how much he loved her and asking her to be his bride. He could see the bright sparkle in her eyes as she looked down at him; feel the slight tremor in her fingers; almost hear her moist lips part as she answered, confessing her own deep love for him: how their lives together as cousins, as playmates, and as friends had changed to a love she never thought she could express fully; longing for the moment when he would ask her.

Then he stood up and drew her to him and kissed her full on the lips. They opened their eyes at exactly the same moment and there was the mischievous twinkle in her eyes that he adored, and he knew she wanted do something outrageous to mark this momentous occasion. So when she suggested diving off the Dangst Rock together and swimming out to the Eye of Hoffengrégor, he burst out laughing. 'What, with you in that dress,' he exclaimed. Then Kyros realised the solemnity of what they had just agreed, and the brooding sense of watchfulness of the ancient Prophet that hung over the islet. If they were serious about maintaining the Royal Line of the Krêonor, then he and Lenyé would become part of the fulfilment of the Restoration, and it was the most obvious place to be.

He remembered diving in, and going down so deep that he thought his lungs would burst before he came up for air; but then he seemed to be swimming in an impenetrable fog. He couldn't see anything or where he was going, and, to cap it all, he couldn't see Lenyé. He couldn't hear her either.

Something else was wrong. His sword kept getting tangled between his legs, and his dagger in its sheath kept slipping round on his belt and digging into his stomach. But he wasn't wearing any weapons that day. They were on holiday, and walked away from the pavilion together.

He felt rather awkward, sensing her awareness of some great import in the air, but he couldn't blurt it out here in case one of the others interrupted him. He wanted to hold her hand, but knew it wasn't quite the right time yet. Slowly they climbed to their secret tryst on the Dangst Rock: she, gathering her skirts over one arm, and he, tentatively grasping her outstretched hand in difficult places and helping her over the tumble of boulders.

Then there was a roaring in his ears, and his mouth and nose were full of water, and mere swimming was such hard work.

He felt absolutely exhausted.

This wasn't how he wanted to remember it.

Much worse, Lenyé was no longer there with him. He could see her as if in a blurred vision a long way off as she careered down their scree slope chased by riders on horses. Then the sparkle in her eyes when she challenged him to race her back to camp was gone, and her eyes were closed and there was darkness and dust and despair.

'Kyros.'

There was the voice again.

He awoke in a cold sweat, shivering uncontrollably, and knew it was only a dream.

'Lenyé,' he gasped. 'Where are you, my love?'

The day he proposed to her she was wearing such a stunning blue dress. From the puffed shoulders and long sleeves that accentuating her slender arms, to the plunging neckline and tight bodice that showed off her figure before billowing out into the many layered skirts below her waist. It made the blue of her eyes more vivid than he could remember. Even the pumps peeping out from under the fabric when a gust of wind suddenly blew the skirts against her legs, were the same hue. The continual whisper of breeze fingering the outer strands of her long golden hair, and the flushed glow of her cheeks against the light tan of her skin only served to make her look more beautiful than ever.

Breathtaking. Utterly breathtaking!

He knew instinctively she had intended that moment for his eyes only. She even wore a garland of early cornflowers in her hair as if to tantalise him. Had she remembered his whispered words of nearly four years ago? She must have. He recognised the emphatic shout of blue for what it was: she was saying, "Yes!" already.

'Kyros!'

He awoke with a start. Where did that voice come from?

Kyros sat and listened. There. Very faint. Coming from the end of the island where he dragged himself ashore. It sounded like a boat. The one thing he dreaded most. He couldn't possibly swim back to the mainland and out-distance a boat. He crept through the undergrowth down to the beach and peered out from behind a large tangle of thorns.

Just as he feared: a boat packed with soldiers, their weapons glinting dully in the moonlight. Kyros counted ten. His heart began to beat faster as he heard the scrunch of shingle and saw the men splash ashore. Should he attack now and take out as many as possible, or hide while they split up to search the island and creep back to the boat and escape?

He watched as two were left on guard and heard the commander say: 'If he overpowers us, torch the island and stand off in the boat. The flames will force him into the water and you can capture him.' The rest were detailed off around the shoreline at regular intervals. At a shout of command they drew their swords and started moving in towards the centre of the island, beating the undergrowth with the flat of their blades.

Kyros slipped away ducking down, keeping within the undergrowth, and taking cover behind trees. Still the men came on, and, as they climbed higher, the ring of soldiers drew closer together. Any thoughts he had of getting past them and down to the boat were useless now. They'd be on him straight away.

Now he was climbing in earnest, the sudden steep slope rising swiftly to the summit, leading to the crown of black rock where it lay hidden from the rest of the island by a ring of tree tops. The ancient writings called it the apple of the eye, the very centre of the island.

He knew, from his visit with Lenyé, that there was a small cave mouth at the top of the rock. They had found a ledge boring at an angle through the rock like a giant corkscrew, forming an almost perfect spiral staircase, except with no steps; and, where the central pillar should be, there was only a hollow centre that disappeared into nothingness. There were no handholds so they had to feel their way along the rock wall and try not to lean too far over into the hollow centre and fall into the void. According to folklore, the spiral wound its way right through the base of the island to the bottom of the lake and the very bones of the old Prophet himself. They began to climb down, but quickly gave up as they had no means of making any light. Also they both had a strong sense that they were needed back on the mainland with their brothers and sisters: that was when they found out about Uncle Morthrir's treachery.

The dull sound of blades beating the undergrowth and occasionally rasping on the rock made him quicken his pace and take risks flitting from cover to cover as the trees thinned.

'There he is!'

The yell to his right made Kyros hurl himself into a clump of bushes for cover. But it was too late. He heard the man immediately below him break into a run.

'Stay in line,' another voice to the left countered: a strong, self assured voice, accustomed to being obeyed. 'Keep him in sight and quicken your pace, but don't break the circle. That's just what he wants, so he can get down past us.'

Kyros glanced back over his shoulder.

The man was right. If they maintained that ever-closing ring there was no way for him to get through without a major fight.

He scrabbled for handholds to regain his footing. He must get to the top and find the entrance to the cave, before the men climbing the other side of the island could get above him. His hands were scratched and bleeding from the branches and exposed roots he used to haul himself up with, and his nose was full of the smell of crushed bracken. He was panting when he reached the top. Just a quick sprint up the flattening rock, then he could turn and draw his sword in that tiny cave mouth.

There was a shout from behind. 'Stay, Kyros.'

He whirled round.

Already the men were out of the tree line and stood below him on the bare rock.

'I am the officer, acting on behalf of Commander Youdlh. You are under arrest for treason against King Morthrir.'

'He is not King,' Kyros shouted back. 'If my Father is dead, then by right, I am King. You are in danger of high treason for laying hands on me. Take care what you do.'

'We have your brother and sisters and cousins.'

'If you harm them, I will take such vengeance on you.'

'We also have Lenyé. It would be a shame...'

'I don't believe you.'

Kyros heard a scrunching sound behind him. He glanced over his shoulder. Already the men climbing the other side of the island were visible above the crown of rock. He was as good as trapped. He whipped round and sprinted for the cave mouth.

'After him. A bag of prize money for the man who brings him down.'

So much for his brave stand in the entrance to the cave: he wasn't going to make it at this rate. The men were over the crown of the island and racing towards him. With a yell he fell upon their ranks hurling two men down in his fury before the others could rally and come at him; but he was past them and running for the cave mouth.

There was no time now to turn and draw his sword and make a stand. He would have to rush for the spiral immediately and grope his way down in the darkness. It was his only chance.

The instant he ducked down into the cave and thrust through to where he knew the beginning of the spiral was, a brilliant light flashed around him, brighter than the moonlight outside, brighter even than the sun at noonday. Despite the dazzling light, he was just able to discern the figure of a man coming towards him and blocking his path.

The man spoke, 'Few have dared attempt this hidden way, and none have ever returned to the Waking World. You cannot go past me.'

Chapter Six

Lenyé could hear a woman singing. It sounded very far away, as though coming down a long narrow tunnel. She recognised the words as part of the Lay of Hoffengrégor: the Song of the Prophet, but had never heard these particular words sung before, only spoken, and then always in hushed tones as though the words were too precious for common usage.

> '...not by the hand of any man
> shall the Ancient Blade be regained.
> Not by might or human strength
> shall the final victory be won...'

She felt locked in time, as though the words would never end, as though they were being quietly etched on her innermost being, her sudden clarity of mind opening up a vista of what lay ahead of her: that this was the time for her to reach out and find the lost Blade and so help to restore the rule of the Krêonor. For she was no man, but a girl on the threshold of womanhood, and great deeds lay ahead of her. With a quiet thrill she couldn't explain, Lenyé had an uncanny sense that these words were being sung over her because they were meant specifically for her and no other, and somehow they would form part of her destiny.

But then the moment was over and she was back to the raging thirst of reality.

'Water,' she murmured, her own voice sounding cracked and shaky in comparison.

The singing came a little nearer.

'Water,' she repeated.

The singing sounded closer still, and this time a faint scent accompanied it.

'Water,' she cried out in desperation, reaching out and clutching at where she thought the singing was coming from. 'I must have a drink!' Her hand gripped the wrist of... Of whom? She opened her eyes wide in alarm, but couldn't see anything. It felt like the wrist of a woman, slender and delicate, yet full of strength: a young woman. The wrist didn't jerk away. Rather, it came towards her and a hand covered the back of her own, eased it off the wrist and laid it gently on something soft and warm. Then she felt a hand under her head, lifting her up and something was held against her dry lips. Not the thick, crude pottery of a forester's cottage, but the cool smoothness of polished metal. The edge of the goblet tipped slightly in between her lips and she jerked an elbow under her to push herself more upright, trying to grab it with her free hand. Liquid splashed around her mouth and dribbled off her chin as she fell back coughing and spluttering.

'It's all right,' the voice was soft and comforting. 'Take your time.'

The hand was busy dabbing around her mouth and chin with a cloth, then it was back under her head and lifting her up and the goblet was placed against her mouth and tilted between her lips. This time she took a sip, then another and another till she was gulping the liquid down in great draughts, the goblet tipping at just the right angle to allow her to drink without spilling, till finally she drained it to the last drop.

But it wasn't water. It was too thick and too sweet and too satisfying. She let out a long sigh. Already she felt new strength course through her like fire.

'Good,' the voice came again. 'You have done well.'

'Who are you?' Lenyé's voice sounded much stronger now.

'I am Yanantha, of the line of those-who-see-the-end-from-the-beginning.'

Lenyé gave a gasp of surprise. 'I thought Hoffengrégor, the ancient Prophet, and all his kin died long ago.'

Yanantha laughed, a light tinkling sound, like water in a fountain. 'Always the line of the Prophets has endured, and will do so until the appointed time.'

Lenyé sat up and grasped at the wrist again. 'Where am I?'

'You are in the House of Consolation, such is my simple dwelling.'

'But how…'

'I found you at the bottom of the Mount of Sliding Stones.'

'No. How long?'

'That was early this morning. You must have lain there some time, for your brow was cold, and the dust was dry on your face. Perhaps you slipped at the top and fell all the way down.'

'No,' Lenyé tried hard to think. Everything was so hazy. 'I was running away from something that scared me. Or someone.' She gripped the wrist harder as though contact with another person would help her remember. 'Soldiers,' she exclaimed at last. 'Uncle Morthrir's soldiers.' Lenyé paused. 'But I can't remember why they were chasing me.'

'You said much about your fears while you slept, and I could piece the rest together from my understanding of the signs of the times. I think Morthrir was anxious to find his niece, Princess Lenyé.'

At the reminder of her name, Lenyé sat bolt upright, jerking Yanantha's wrist and hand against her. 'Kyros,' she screamed. 'Where's my Kyros?'

'It's all right, Lenyé.' Yanantha slipped an arm around her shoulders and held her close. 'I have been searching for him.'

'And Beth. What has become of my poor Beth?'

'Peace. Peace. Take one thing at a time and be at peace.'

'I'll never forgive myself if anything has happened to her.'

'Your sister and your other relatives have been captured by Morthrir's soldiers and taken to the palace. I hear news, for the birds of Sorentina fly from the finger of Yanantha to do my bidding. Your kindred are prisoners for the moment. It is you and Kyros that your Uncle particularly seeks.'

'Then I have to find Kyros and go and rescue them.'

'I do not say whether this is the right course of action, but I will help you all I can.'

'Why can't I see?' Lenyé raised a hand to her eyes, and felt the folds of cloth around her head and face.

'I was concerned for your injuries, and the effect bright light would have on your eyes till you were fully healed. But now that you have drunk a whole goblet of my cordial, I will risk removing the bandages. You are well on the road to recovery.'

As the final bandage fell away, Lenyé found herself looking at the most beautiful face she had ever seen: young, yet not young. No line or mark showed on the smooth white skin, framed by the raven hair; but there was an air of greatness about her, as though she had lived the span of countless mortal lives and read the secrets of many hearts. Then their eyes met, and Lenyé gasped in surprise and awe. She had never seen such captivating eyes: deep pools of wisdom, and yet such a soft violet sheen in the iris. Lenyé was the first to drop her gaze.

Yanantha reached out and smoothed Lenyé's brow. 'The bruising and the scars will be there for a while. Rest in bed for today and you should be able to get up tomorrow.'

'But what about Kyros?' Lenyé persisted. 'Did he make it to the island?'

'I think so. I saw him swimming into a layer of mist but he was heading in the right direction.'

'Then he did escape.'

'I can only assume he made it to the island. Whether he escaped or not I cannot say. Your Uncle's Commander will not rest until he's made a thorough search.'

'If they catch him, he's as good as dead.' Lenyé slumped back on the pillows.

'Do not despair. If he found the apple of the eye, the secret spiral that leads down to the Sleeping World, there is hope that he entered and so would evade capture.'

'I thought?'

'I know. It is forbidden for any mortal to tread that path.' Yanantha paused, with a vacant look in her eyes as though she was musing on something that remained hidden from Lenyé's gaze. 'But,' and her voice was barely a whisper, as though she was speaking to herself alone. 'The time is ripe for the Restoration.'

'Then I must go and seek him at once.'

'Stay.' Yanantha's voice strengthened as she glanced back to Lenyé, a warning blaze in her otherwise gentle eyes. 'If he does return, he will be much changed.'

'How so?'

'Do not be afraid for Kyros. He will return to you somehow. But in a way unlooked for and to fulfil a destiny that is still hidden from me.' She paused. 'Unless?' Yanantha faltered and her eyes were filled with doubt. 'Unless *he* is the one to…?'

'What is it?' Lenyé looked at her in alarm.

'The Ancient Writings tell of the Coronation Day for a young King who begins his reign while his Father is still King.'

'But his Father is dead,' Lenyé burst out. 'And mine, and our Mothers as well.' She felt tears pricking at the corners of her eyes with the sudden reminder. 'So that can't apply to Kyros.'

'No. It is nothing.' Yanantha hesitated. 'I am as yet unsure and will speak of it no further. He is beyond the help of either of us now, for I dare not follow him and the way is barred to you.'

'Then I am lost.' Lenyé turned away, wiping her eyes with the back of her sleeve. 'Without Kyros I can never hope to win through.'

'Do not distress yourself so much.'

'If Kyros is beyond my help, I have to rescue Beth on my own. But if Uncle Morthrir catches me, he will force me to be his bride. Only Kyros can save me from that.'

'When everything seems to be at its darkest point, you must have faith.'

'What do you mean?'

'You have three options: firstly, finding Kyros.'

'But we've ruled that out.'

'Correct. Secondly, rescuing Beth. But you have to be careful, for you are right. She is being used as a lure by your Uncle to lay a trap for you.'

'And thirdly?' Lenyé queried, not wanting to hear the answer.

Yanantha gazed at her for a moment before replying. 'There is a much harder path.'

'I don't understand.'

'Did you not hear the words sung over you in your sleep?'

Lenyé hesitated. Now that she was fully awake, the voice and the words and the singing seemed like a forgotten dream slipping further and further away from her, as if concentrating on them now pushed them to the very edge of her consciousness. 'I'm not sure.'

'Tell me what you heard?'

'I think,' she struggled with her words, as if an unseen force was even now trying to dislodge all memory of the singing from her mind. 'I think it was part of the Lay of Hoffengrégor,' her words came with a rush. 'About the Ancient Blade.'

'Good. You heard well.' Yanantha paused and looked her straight in the eyes. 'And what did your heart say in response?'

Lenyé looked up, sudden clarity returning to her. 'That I am the one to go and find…' she hesitated as the full import of her words came home to her.

'So, you *have* understood. Unless I am much mistaken, you are the one to recover the lost Blade of Zerigor.'

'But why me? I have no great ability to…'

'If not you, then who else? Lenyé. Be bold. Be courageous. And, above all, be strong. You are come as a Royal heiress to the Kingdom and in the flower of your youth for such a time as this. Unless the Blade is recovered, you can never free Beth and the others. For behind your Uncle Morthrir there sits a far greater power than any mortal can ever challenge unaided. That power is what you have to bring down and vanquish. But it is beyond mere human wisdom and strength to ever master. Without the lost Blade, even Kyros' return will avail little.'

'How will this lost Blade help me?'

'It is not a weapon of war. That was the folly of the ancient Krêonor and the reason why it was taken from them. It is an instrument of justice and peace. I cannot help you any more than that, for no one knows and it is hidden even from the line of the Prophets. If you are truly the one, then once you find the Blade, it is down to you and you alone to use it for its rightful purpose.'

'Very well.' Lenyé surprised herself with the sudden strength that seized her, and the power that rose in her voice. 'I do not fully understand all that you say, but this I know. I will seek the Blade of Zerigor, if you will show me the way.'

Chapter Seven

Kyros flung himself at the man and grabbed him around the waist, intending to wrestle him to the ground and get past him into the spiral before his enemies could attack.

But instead of being thrown by his weight and the impetus of his charge, the man stood firm, with legs slightly flexed and knees braced. Kyros felt like a battering ram hitting a wall of granite, and a searing pain shot through his left shoulder.

'Let me pass,' the words rasped in Kyros' throat. 'Don't you see? My enemies are upon me. There's no other way out.' He gripped the rock with his feet and thrust harder against the man's waist, but the man was immoveable.

'Unless you help me, you will be responsible for my certain death at the hands of my enemies.' Kyros heaved again. 'Who are you, that with all my strength I cannot prevail against you?'

'Kyros,' the stranger spoke at last. 'Why do you fight me and not know who I am?'

With a shock Kyros realised that it was the same voice he heard before when he was on the beach, and in the little dell where he hid, then waking him to warn of the approach of danger, and finally speaking to him in the cave mouth. He struggled to release his grip and stand back to look afresh at this man, but already the stranger had one powerful arm around his neck and was squeezing till Kyros was choking for breath.

'Was it not spoken of old,' the stranger gasped for breath as he struggled to get his words out. 'That no man shall gain entry to the Secret Spiral from the Eye of Hoffengrégor?'

Kyros grabbed the man's wrist, pulled the arm off his neck, and gulped great draughts of air into his seared lungs. Then he gripped the wrist with both hands, ran his feet up the man's shins till he could get a good purchase just above both knees, and whipped himself back in a powerful jack-knife movement, pulling his head out from under the man's arm and twisting the arm down and round, till his feet slipped off the man's legs and he regained his purchase on the ground, continuing to twist the arm round till he held the stranger in a back-hammer.

The man let out a howl of pain. But already he was twisting his arm back again. 'I will not let you pass me.'

Kyros wrenched with all his strength, sweat pouring off him, as he tried to regain the upper hand, but the man was too strong. Slowly, inexorably, the man's arm was moving round, lifting Kyros off the ground as he hung on desperately trying to pull it back. The man grasped one of Kyros' wrists, but the wrist was so wet from sweat that the man's hand slipped, and Kyros struck out with his foot, catching the man's leg and throwing him off balance and wrestling him to the ground with Kyros on top.

'Let me go,' the stranger struggled for breath.

'Not until you agree to let me enter the spiral unhindered.'

'Kyros,' the man was breathing more heavily now from exertion. 'You were born to be King of your people, but I will make you an even greater King.'

'Why would you do that?'

'Because you have prevailed against me, I will cause you to prevail against all those who oppose you.'

'How will I know this has been accomplished?'

'For the next hour, I will leave this entrance unguarded so that you may go through. But the price is this. I set before you seven tests that you may prove yourself worthy of being a King. You are free to face them, or walk away. Whichever you choose, you must stand before me when I sit on my throne and give an account of how you have used this freedom.'

'I still do not know your name. How will I find you if I do not know who to ask for?'

'Enough.' The man rolled over and lurched to his knees, dragging Kyros after him, and stood up with Kyros still clinging to the man's arm. 'Why do you seek my name, as it is hidden?

'I have to know who you are.'

'You shall know me better, for I will be with you. You must learn to trust in me and not your own abilities. As you came to the end of your strength after swimming through the water and needed my words to provoke you into action, so your first test is to continue to hear my voice and obey, even if you think you know better.'

The man placed one hand on Kyros' shoulder and held him at arm's length.

Kyros gazed at him, and saw such majesty in the face that he wanted to fall down before him in deference.

But the man lifted him up and said, 'Look at me.'

As he stared into the man's eyes Kyros felt power flowing into him.

'Be strengthened,' cried the man. 'With my strength alone, and not yours.'

The man thrust him away slightly.

That push was the most overwhelming force Kyros had ever known, like a fir tree lashed by a storm. As he bent backwards, Kyros felt he was frozen in time, unable to move, unable to defend himself; while this man held all power and all authority in his hand and no one anywhere could ever gainsay him. He watched in fascination as the man bent the elbow of his free arm.

In a voice that shook the rocks, the man cried out, 'Let your inner heart be opened.' Then, with the back of his hand, the man hit Kyros across both eyes blinding him instantly.

Kyros fell to his knees clawing at his eyes, but he couldn't see.

Chapter Eight

Beth watched Uncle Morthrir pacing up and down in the private council chamber through half closed eyes. She was dog-tired: a whole day and part of the night of forced riding between two warriors. They arrived at the palace a few minutes ago and were all locked in one of the reception salons to await her Uncle's good pleasure. She and Quinn were the first to be summoned.

She was relieved to be back in the familiar surroundings of the palace, but very wary of her Uncle. She would have been intrigued to be in here, a room normally out of bounds to all the youngsters; but she was too tired to notice, and too hungry to care. Besides, the staccato clicking of her Uncle's heels on the cold stone floor was getting into her brain and nearly driving her mad. She swayed on her feet and felt she would fall over any minute, but Quinn managed to clutch her despite his hands still being tied together in front of him.

'Steady, Beth,' he whispered, his voice rasping from lack of water. 'Don't let him get to you.'

'Ha.' Uncle Morthrir whirled round and pointed at them. 'So, my pretty one. Where would your sister hide in those woods? Hmm? You must know all the secret places up there.'

'Youdlh's already asked me that. I don't know.'

'Well even if he has. I'm asking you again.' His face contorted and he barked out, 'Where is she?'

'I don't know.'

'Very well.' He smiled at them and the expression on his face softened. 'We may have to try some more persuasive methods.'

'What's all this about, Uncle?' Quinn intervened. 'She's your favourite niece. Is this the way to treat her: hunted down like a criminal, strapped to a horse with guards either side, and hands tied together? What's going on?'

'Silence, boy.' He paused as if considering something. 'All right, I'll tell you. About a month ago I received intelligence that our ancient enemies, the Tsé-shâmé, had launched an attack on the Krêonor. I tried to warn your two Fathers, but they'd already gone to the Hunting Lodge with your Mothers. I sent messengers after them, but the lodge was empty and my men came back with a story of the hunting party being killed by lions.'

'Lions?' Quinn butted in. 'There are no lions in the woods up there. Nearer the mountains, maybe. But not there.'

'That's what I thought,' continued their Uncle. 'Gradually it emerged that your parents had been abducted by a raiding party, and the Tsé-shâmé were all set to sweep down on Terrazarema, seize power and take over the country. Of course I lost no time bringing my own troops in to defend the palace and guard the city, and try to find the rest of you as quickly as I could.'

'Then why chase us with your army?' Beth's voice was barely more than a whisper.

'What? Oh. They didn't *chase* you. We were desperate to *find* you. If the entire Family was captured, that would be the end of the Royal Line of the Krêonor.'

'Why burn us out with fire arrows?' Beth wasn't going to give in that easily.

'My troops thought the enemy had taken over that forest hamlet, and were all set to flush them out by fire. When you emerged and ran into their arms they were absolutely amazed, and delighted to have found you.'

'Then why did your men loose their arrows at Kyros?' Beth was fairly shouting with anger, all her tiredness gone in the heat of the moment.

'Loose arrows at Kyros? I think there's been some mistake.'

'That's what Rafé said,' Quinn interrupted.

'I see.' He paused, and glanced from Quinn to Beth, a sly expression on his face. 'Of course they chased him to start with: a big man with a sword rushing at my soldiers out of the smoke and flames. It must have been very confusing for everyone.' He hesitated. 'I'll question Youdlh and Rafé further. But so far neither Kyros nor Lenyé has been found. I must know where they are to protect them from our enemies. You do see that, don't you?'

'Then why did you have us tied to horses and ridden all the way home as if we were prisoners?' demanded Quinn.

'It was for your own good. I had to get you here as quickly as possible, under armed escort for your own protection.'

'So why are we still tied like this?' Beth shook her two hands towards her Uncle. She could feel her tiredness beginning to take over again, but forced herself to stay alert.

'How inconsiderate of me.' Uncle Morthrir picked up a small bell from the desk and rang it. Then he stepped towards them, pulling a dagger from its sheath on his belt. Beth cringed away from him, but he caught hold of her hands and cut the cords on her wrists first, and then Quinn's.

'There. Perhaps that will convince you I'm telling the truth.'

The door opened and a sentry entered. 'You rang, Sire?'

'Escort my nephew and niece back to the salon, cut every one's bonds and give them all some food and drink. Then have the other youngsters brought in. And tell Commander Youdlh I'll see him and Rafé now.'

The sentry led them down the passageway, unlocked the door to the salon, opened it and partly entered the room before turning round to usher his charges in.

'Now,' Quinn whispered in Beth's ear.' This way.' He dragged her off down the corridor away from the private council chamber.

'Hey,' the startled sentry poked his head out of the door. 'Come back,' and he started chasing after them.

But they were already round the first corner and racing towards the back of the palace.

'In here,' Quinn grabbed her by the hand and yanked her through a low arch, down a short flight of stone steps and stopped in the middle of a long stretch of straight wall. He pressed the edge of a tall stone block and immediately it swung open. He pulled her in after him and eased the block back into place. They leaned against it to catch their breath, their hearts hammering wildly.

'I'm so confused, Quinn,' Beth could hardly get the words out between her gasps for breath.

They heard the sound of approaching footsteps outside.

'I don't know what or who to believe any more.'

The footsteps stopped.

'Shhh.' Quinn waved frantically at her.

The footsteps carried on a few paces, then turned and went back up the corridor. 'Guards,' they could hear a note of panic in his voice as he shouted. 'Guards!' More footsteps sounded running up the passageway from the other end and passed them following the other man. Then there was silence.

'Whew,' Quinn let out a sigh of relief. 'That was close.'

Beth looked about her in the dim light. They were in a narrow passageway between two stone skins of the massive wall. 'Wow. I never knew this existed.'

'Kyros and I only discovered it recently. He caught me sneaking a pie from the pantry and chased me up the passageway we've just been in. I tripped and stuck my hand out against the wall, and caught my finger in the gap where the lever is.' Quinn pointed into the gloom behind her. 'That way leads down past the kitchens and out through a tunnel that comes up in the stables.'

'Does that mean we're going to get out of the palace?'

'Not yet. The other way leads to a gallery at the top of the throne room. You can watch all the proceedings while being totally hidden. But, best of all, you can look down the other side into the private council chamber.'

'Are you suggesting we go up there?' Beth clutched at Quinn and tried to pull him towards the kitchens. 'I want to get away now. Supposing someone hears us and works out where we are?'

'You said you were confused.'

'I just want to get away.'

'I don't believe a word about the Tsé-shâmé invading.' Quinn started pulling her up the passageway towards the private council chamber. 'In all our running and hiding no one has seen anything except Uncle Morthrir's men. We've got to find out what's really going on.'

Quinn and Beth crept along the gallery to a place where they could peer down through a vent and see and hear what was happening below.

Uncle Morthrir was leaning against the desk, partly sitting on it, with Youdlh and Rafé standing in front of him.

'So what really did happen to Kyros?' Uncle Morthrir tapped the point of his dagger against the edge of the desk while he quizzed the other two.

They glanced at each other and Youdlh took up the story. 'We saw him dive off the Dangst Rock. My archers loosed many arrows at him, but he hit the water and didn't come up. So I sent Harbona with a boat to cover the lake and check the island.'

'Did they find anything before you left with the prisoners?'

'No, Sire.'

'Hmmph. He could be anywhere by now.'

Quinn put his mouth right against Beth's ear, 'So they don't know for sure that Kyros is dead.'

Beth nodded. 'And we *are* prisoners,' she whispered back.

'All right,' Uncle Morthrir tapped the flat of the blade against his pursed up lips. 'Get a messenger back to Captain Harbona and find out what's going on.' He turned to Rafé and pointed the dagger at him. 'And your little play-acting sounded most convincing. So the youngsters still believe you're on their side?'

Beth started at what she heard, and Quinn grabbed her to stop her making any noise.

'He was magnificent, Sire,' Youdlh burst out. 'Even I was convinced he was one of them all the time.' He glanced sideways at Rafé. 'The young girl's terrified of me, so it's down to you to get her to talk. She's got to be the key to finding her sister.'

'Rafé,' whispered Beth. 'How could you?'

'Elskin and his men are searching for Lenyé,' Youdlh continued. 'As soon as the girl talks, we can get word to him of where to concentrate his efforts.'

'Excellent,' Uncle Morthrir tapped the dagger against his fingers as though counting off the points. 'Kyros is as good as dead, and Lenyé should be found soon.' He frowned, his eyes flashing and his mouth etched in a snarl. Then he hurled the dagger between Youdlh and Rafé. It turned over twice and stuck quivering in the wood panelling lining the wall. 'We just need to decide what to do with my wretched brothers and their wives.'

'Oh!' Quinn could hardly contain himself. 'They're still alive.'

'By my counsel, Sire,' Rafé spoke up. 'It would be prudent to keep them at your castle as a possible bargaining tool.'

'They're at Onadestra,' gasped Beth.'

'Shhh,' breathed Quinn, putting his finger over her lips.

'True.' With an effort Uncle Morthrir regained his composure. 'What do you think, Youdlh?'

'Once Kyros is dead, and the other young boys are here at the palace, there are no more contenders to the throne ahead of you.'

'So you're saying, "Have them killed."?'

'Yes, Sire.'

'Rafé?' Uncle Morthrir fixed his dark eyes on him. 'Still in the wait-and-see camp?'

'Yes, Sire.'

'Well. You always were the better strategist. I'll sleep on this and give you my decision in the morning.'

There was a hurried knock on the door.

'Come.'

The door opened and three soldiers entered, the leader being the same sentry who escorted the children out earlier.

Youdlh turned round to face them, 'Yes.'

'It is my duty to report the two younger children managed to escape while they were being taken back to the salon.'

'What?' Youdlh took a pace towards the soldiers.

'That's all we need,' Uncle Morthrir roared. 'Now we'll never work out where Lenyé's hiding. Catch those wretched children.'

Quinn grabbed Beth's wrist and started pulling her back down the passageway. 'Quick. We've heard all we need to know. We must get away and find our parents.'

As she followed him, Beth could just hear the soldier.

'We've combed the palace, but there's no trace of them anywhere. They've completely disappeared.'

Beth grinned to herself. Not only have those wretched children disappeared, they're off to Onadestra on a rescue mission!

Chapter Nine

'Right.' Morthrir paced up and down in the private council chamber after the soldiers withdrew. 'Youdlh. Get down there and find those children. Security is your responsibility. They must know every inch of the palace and have found a way to dodge the guards. Don't bother about hunting for them in the corridors. Check all the exits, especially the windows and the outhouses and double the guards on the stables. Look for any signs that they've got out. This is an emergency.' He smacked his open palm against the wall. 'Find those two children, or you're in serious trouble.'

'Yes, Sire.' Youdlh banged out of the doorway barking orders as guards came running to his urgent shouts.

'And make sure the other youngsters are totally secure,' Morthrir shouted after him. 'I don't want any more escaping. I need them here.'

Rafé was about to follow when Morthrir stopped him in his tracks. 'Shut the door, Rafé.' Morthrir's voice had lost the harshness of his anger and was almost gentle in comparison. 'There's something I want to talk to you about in private.'

'Oh?'

'Yes.' Morthrir waited for the door to be secured before continuing. 'I need to plan for an heir.'

Rafé paused before replying, as though the implications of what Morthrir was about to say were too distasteful for him to contemplate. But in reality he had seen this coming, and thought long and hard about how to help his new master. 'You want to rid yourself of your wife, Faria?'

'Naturally. After all these years she hasn't so much as given me a daughter, let alone a son.'

'And you would take another to fill her place?'

'Exactly.'

'Someone of the Royal Line of the Krêonor?'

'Don't be stupid, Rafé. There's only one candidate worth contemplating.'

'You mean, Lenyé?'

'Precisely. That's why I've come to you. We seem to be of the same mind on matters of strategic importance.'

'You cannot execute Faria openly, Sire. Your new subjects would be so horrified that it might just tip them over the edge and be the one final factor that would cause them to rise up in open rebellion.'

'I agree. Therefore we have to arrange a little accident for my wife. One that has reliable witnesses on hand. One that you could organise. Of course it would mean you riding out to Onadestra.' He paused and looked keenly at Rafé. 'What kind of accident should we devise? Hunting, perhaps? A stray arrow on a chase in the forest?'

'Wives don't usually go hunting without their husbands present, Sire. Perhaps you should leave me to work out the details when I'm there and seize the best opportunity that presents itself.'

'Very well.' Morthrir paused, and then began pacing the room as if to change the subject. 'Tell me. Is Youdlh loyal to me, or have you seen anything in his behaviour over the last month that would lead you to suspect he is playing his own game?'

'No, Sire. We have been very close in our counsels together and are of one mind in all that we do.' Rafé felt Morthrir's eyes boring into him: the man was clearly sifting his every word. 'Youdlh has posted his best troops and captains in search of Kyros and Lenyé,' he continued. 'We have the other youngsters and courtiers under our control. We…'

'Then why has it taken so long?' Morthrir's face was suddenly livid with anger. 'My closest counsellor and my chief officer, and those youngsters run rings around you. And now Youdlh's lost two of them.'

'With respect, Sire.'

'With respect. Nothing….' Morthrir left his sentence unfinished. 'Get out and do as you've been ordered. I want Faria dead within a week of your arrival, and no sentimental nonsense. Understand?'

'Yes, Sire.'

'And while you're there,' he continued, in a more conciliatory tone. 'Check up on my two brothers and their wives. Make sure their routines are secure, with no opportunity of escape. I'll deal with them shortly. You'll have full authority from me to oversee the security of the castle.'

'I would still counsel caution in dealing with your brothers. If too many accidents happen to key people at Onadestra in so short a space of time, then…'

'This won't be an accident, Rafé. This is going to be a public execution.'

'But Sire.'

'No buts, Rafé. I mean to go through with this.'

Chapter Ten

Rafé stopped at the archway, quizzing the soldier. 'You say the two youngsters ran in this direction and then disappeared?'

'That's right, Sir.'

'And you didn't hear anything before the other soldiers ran up this passageway and joined you?'

'No, Sir. That's when I raised the alarm and started calling for the guards. It was as though they vanished into thin air.'

Rafé looked through the archway at the narrow passage beyond. 'All right.' He glanced back at the soldier. 'Leave me.'

'Yes, Sir.' The soldier hurried off about his duties.

'So,' Rafé muttered to himself. 'Vanished into thin air, did they?' He made sure no one was watching. 'There has to be an explanation.' He ducked his head, crept down the flight of stone steps and began feeling along the wall of the passageway. 'It must be here somewhere.' He carried on to the end and worked his way back up along the other wall. Suddenly his hand found a slight gap between two of the stone blocks. He felt inside with his fingers and pressed a spring-loaded latch. There was a slight snick and a block of stone opened outwards. 'I thought so.'

He climbed through the doorway and pulled the block of stone to behind him.

'Interesting. That way must lead down to the back of the palace near the kitchens, but I wonder where this way goes to?'

He followed the narrow passageway within the walls, climbed a short flight of stone steps, but all the time found himself heading towards the centre of the palace. He gasped with amazement when he reached the end looked and down into the throne room. He was even more astonished when he checked a grill on the other side and could see right into the private council chamber. Morthrir and Youdlh were still there.

Youdlh was speaking. 'I don't understand why you're sending Rafé to Onadestra, Sire, when we still have to find Kyros and Lenyé. Surely you'll miss his counsel.'

'That's none of your business.' Morthrir paced up and down gesticulating with his right hand. 'Tell me. Will he go by road, or use our secret way through the mountains?'

'He never did like that way. He'll go by road.'

'Two weeks by road rather than one week the other way.' Morthrir drummed his fingers on the desk. 'He'll be out of action for quite a while. Lend him a couple of spare horses from your company. That should speed his journey.'

'Yes, Sire.' Youdlh turned to leave.

Rafé watched from his vantage point as Morthrir settled himself at the desk and began writing. He was about to turn back into the secret passageway when he was surprised by a knock at the door; not the main door leading into the rest of the palace, or the smaller one behind the map stand that opened out onto the balcony in the throne room, but the private one at the back that led, by a spiral staircase, to an entrance directly below the private council chamber and out into the gardens. The door that was only used for special visitors who wanted to pass unnoticed by anyone else in the palace.

'Come,' Morthrir sat back in his chair and sanded the ink on the document.

Rafé stiffened as he recognised the erect figure and sightless eyes of Eawen the Henosite. The man seldom came to big towns or cities; he was always out in his beloved mountains. And he never came at anyone else's bidding. So why was he here?

'Ah. Master Henosite,' Morthrir let the name roll around his tongue as though sampling a sip of vintage fire-juice. He slid the parchment into a drawer of the desk, 'This is indeed a welcome surprise.'

'My Lord Morthrir. I come in haste. You must call a convocation immediately to find Kyros and Lenyé.'

Morthrir nodded. 'You have the power to do that?'

'The Four Summoners are a law to themselves, Sire,' Eawen gestured with his hand. 'For they are not of this world, and only come at times of great need or great deeds or great appointments. I only have power to call up the Ten Priests. It will help if you have any clothing or personal effects from your kin.'

'I can do that for my nephew. But it would take a fast courier a week at least to get there and back for my niece.'

Rafé was quick to understand the implications of what Morthrir had just said. He must have clothing for Kyros to hand here at the palace, but all Lenyé's personal effects would be at her Father's residence a hundred miles away.

'Then the Priests will have to revert to other gifts of discerning your niece's whereabouts.' Eawen's quiet voice jerked Rafé's attention back to the conversation unfolding below him.

'They are able to do that?' Morthrir sounded surprised.

'Of course.'

'Excellent. Where would you hold this convocation?'

'Druis-cyf-rin, Sire.'

'The Great Oak Tree? That's a day's ride on the way to Onadestra.' Morthrir broke off, musing, before replying. 'How long will it take to gather the Priests?'

'Three days, Sire.'

'In that case, go ahead and call the convocation for midnight in three days' time, at the Great Oak of Druis-cyf-rin.'

Rafé smiled grimly. He would have to consider his next move very carefully.

Chapter Eleven

'What are you doing?' Lenyé came and sat at the table and watched Yanantha remove the cork stopper from its clay cylinder and ease out a rolled up cloth.

The sun streamed in at the open window, accentuating the delicate pictures of flowers on the pale lemon walls and casting shadows on the tiled floor from the ferns and other potted plants that filled one corner of the room. The whole atmosphere was alive with the scent of flowers wafting in from the garden.

'This is part of the original Writings of Hoffengrégor himself.'

Lenyé gasped. 'I've always wanted to see this. We only have copied extracts at home.'

Yanantha laid the cylinder and cork on the floor and began unrolling the cloth across the table. Lenyé leaned over eagerly to see what was inside, but the cloth was folded into the middle concealing the contents.

'If you really want to read what it contains, you'd better put these on.' Yanantha held out a pair of linen gloves and put on a pair herself. Then she carefully pealed back the cloth to reveal an ancient parchment within. 'Try to touch it as little as possible, it's very brittle.'

Lenyé stretched further over and read aloud, *'I, Hoffengrégor, called by the True King himself who is Lord over all the Realms, and appointed by him to receive the Peoples and instruct them in the way they should go; to all the sons and daughters who ever live to hear the voice of the True King and walk in his ways; do hereby set forth an account of the Comings.'*

Lenyé looked up at Yanantha. 'Does, *"all the sons and daughters"* include me?'

'Yes, as long as you *"hear the voice of the True King and walk in his ways"*.'

Lenyé paused, transfixed, as she recalled the day several years ago when she blew up at Kyros for not using her ideas as they played at being adventurers. He was always so pig-headed. She refused to speak to him for the rest of the day.

At bedtime Mother gently asked why she was in such a strange mood. Then it all came out in a rush of tears. Mother didn't scold; just said, *"sometimes when another person wrongs you it may be necessary for you to make the first move to put things right"*. Lenyé struggled with that. It was definitely Kyros' fault. Why should she have to do something about it? Finally she could bear it no longer and went to him and blurted out her feelings.

It was the hardest thing she ever did. Instead of the expected shouting match, he apologised for treating her so badly and said how much he missed her friendship, and would she be prepared to put the incident behind her. From that day onwards their relationship changed fundamentally. Kyros was still strong-willed and always so sure about what he wanted, but now he was prepared to defer and ask her opinion and include her ideas.

Lenyé touched the parchment with her gloved fingers as if seeking reassurance before she answered Yanantha. 'I've always tried to live by the code of conduct the ancient Prophet left to us. But I don't think I've fully arrived yet.'

'Good. If you were arrogant enough to claim you always lived as he asked us to, you would be disqualified. Read on.'

Lenyé skimmed through the Prophet's account, her lips moving slightly as she read to herself about the wonders of the new world and the Perfection of the Peoples on their island in the Western sea, with Zerigor wearing the Crown of Life. Then came the outbreak of war that destroyed the early civilisation.

'It's such old fashioned language,' Lenyé looked up then

focused back on the parchment. 'Yet it's so fresh and vivid; almost as though he was here telling us about it himself. But it must have been written at least a thousand years ago.'

'That's why I keep it in its cylinder and only let a few ever read it.'

'But I'm amazed he should go into such detail about the appearance of the different Peoples.'

'You shouldn't be. If every one looked the same, it would be a rather bland world.'

'That's always puzzled me about my family,' Lenyé glanced back to Yanantha. 'Uncle Morthrir has such dark eyes. Yet the rest of us have blue or green eyes.'

'Do not be too quick to judge outward appearances.'

'But when we received a visit from the heads of the Tsé-shâmé a few years ago, there were many men in the entourage who were clearly of Krêonor descent and looked exactly like Uncle Morthrir in colouring.'

'That may be the case, but then all the peoples of the world are descended from the *Bara-mâla-ké*, the first Peoples.' Yanantha smiled. 'There's been so much inter-mixing of races since, that certain physical characteristics are bound to merge with others.

'But it still doesn't explain why Uncle Morthrir looks so different to the rest of my family. After the visitors had gone, I asked Father about whether they could be related.'

Yanantha looked at Lenyé in surprise, 'So you thought he wasn't a true son of your Grandparents?'

'That was the very point I tried to make. But Father was furious with me: *"Don't you think we have more than enough problems with your Uncle, to be worrying about that!"* and he stormed out. He took me aside later and apologised for his gruff manner and told me that his younger brother was originally named Ibarno. I was surprised because it had never been mentioned by either of my parents before. I knew because Kyros told me years ago. Apparently I was only two at the time, but

51

Kyros remembers calling him Uncle Ibarno by mistake and being terrified by our Uncle's reaction.'

'I don't suppose he ever did that again.'

'No.' Lenyé sat back and folded her arms. 'And another thing. Father told me his brother was always so demanding as a child, and would pout and scream if he didn't get his own way till people gave up in desperation; it didn't seem to matter what my Grandfather did, he ruled the whole household from the nursery upwards. In the end they all had to accept him as a son and a brother and learn to live with it.'

Yanantha looked steadily at Lenyé. 'Do you know what the name "*Morthrir*" means?'

'No.' Lenyé frowned. 'It never occurred to me that it even had a meaning.'

'Literally, it means *death-laugh*.'

'I don't understand.'

'Someone who mocks at death.'

'I still don't understand.'

'Did I not say to you, "*behind Morthrir there sits a far greater power than any mortal can ever challenge unaided*"?' Yanantha shuddered. 'Your Uncle has met with that power and received his life back from the grave to do terrible deeds in the future.'

'But he's doing them already,' Lenyé jerked her hands out, gesticulating in anger. 'Uncle Morthrir is behaving now as he did as a child. Grasping hold of things that aren't rightfully his and refusing to let go. If my family had faced up to the implications then, we wouldn't be in this mess now. My Father and Uncle Dareth have paid for my family's tolerance with their lives.'

'You have a very real grievance, and no one can easily put that right, but it is still too early to judge your Uncle Morthrir.' Yanantha turned back to her work as though signalling an end to the conversation.

Lenyé resumed her reading about the three people-groups as they went their separate ways on the mainland. She continued reading out loud, *'A cloud of anxiety covered my meditations for I had forebodings of evil yet to come. Through the vision and discernment given to me I was able to see from afar and discover the intent of the Tsé-shâmé, and it was after this fashion.'*

'Yanantha,' Lenyé's agonised cry made the Seer jerk her head up.

'What is it?'

The shadows danced on the floor-tiles in agitation as a gentle breeze blew in through the window and set the ferns rustling.

'The parchment's been cut off. Where's the next section?'

'Alas. It was done by Hoffengrégor himself.'

Lenyé frowned, 'Where is it now?'

'No one knows. Presumably it vanished with him.'

'Surely you've tried to find it? What is the evil he speaks of and the intent of the Tsé-shâmé?'

'I can only guess this must concern the secret knowledge which the Tsé-shâmé sought from the Beginning.'

'How does that affect me?' Lenyé persisted.

'If I am right, then I believe this secret knowledge releases the Hidden Power into the Waking World.'

'What is this Hidden Power?'

'It is the very Power that seeks to control your Uncle.'

'And how do the missing Writings relate to this?'

Yanantha hesitated. 'I think the Writings of Hoffengrégor about the rest of the Comings are the key to releasing the Lost Blade for its proper purpose.'

'So even if I find the Sword, I still have to locate these Writings?'

'No. That is not your task. You have to trust that others will come to your aid.'

Chapter Twelve

Kyros was in despair until he heard the voice.

'Get up.'

He lurched to his feet and stuck out a hand to find something to touch that would guide him, but his hand grabbed thin air.

'Walk straight ahead.'

He shuffled forwards, very conscious of the gaping void in the middle of the spiral that fell away into nothingness, but breathed a sigh of relief as his hand touched the side of the cave.

'Start walking.'

Kyros obeyed, and found it was easier than he thought. He quickened his pace.

He heard the zip of arrows as, presumably, his pursuers had reached the mouth of the cave behind him. There was an occasional ping as one struck a rock ahead of him, then an arrow shaft caught between his feet and nearly tripped him.

Kyros felt something sweep past him down the void and stuck out his hand instinctively to grab whatever it was. From the feel he realised it was a man on a rope.

The voice said, 'Just keep walking.'

He felt three more go past him, but tried to block them from his mind, concentrating on his hurried pace and the feel of the rock on his right hand side. Kyros heard a shout of command from above. He could hear footsteps behind him, and panicked. How was he going to fight them off if he couldn't see?

The voice said, 'Throw your left hand straight out in a punch.'

Immediately he did so and connected with the jaw of a man.

The man gave way before him, his cry changing to a scream as, presumably, he fell away into the void.

'Throw yourself forwards with your arms out in front of you.'

Kyros launched himself and connected with two other men, his impetus throwing them to his left. Their gasps of pain also quickly changed to long drawn out screams.

'Jump back against the rock wall and swivel to your left.'

Kyros obeyed. His hand connected with another soldier and he used the man's momentum to hurl him into the void.

He heard the shim of a drawn sword above him, and the voice said, 'Duck to your left and use your shoulder.' The man went over his back quite easily and Kyros heard the clash of helmets banging together followed by two screams. Good, he thought to himself. That must account for the fourth man below me as well. Now there can only be two behind me.

Before he could move he felt hands grabbing him.

'Thrust yourself backwards,' the voice came again, and Kyros obeyed feeling a man go over the edge of the spiral as he did so.

'Carry on going down, but this time as fast as you can.'

Kyros staggered to his feet, groping for the rock wall, and broke into a run.

Kyros paused in his headlong flight and leaned against the rock wall on his right. He was gasping for breath and his chest heaved with pain. The fingertips on his right hand were rubbed raw from feeling his way along the rock.

The spiral appeared to have no end. He'd been running and running but, apart from the sense of going steadily downwards, nothing changed. Worse. He could no longer hear the voice.

He squatted down on the narrow ledge to rest and wondered how many of his enemies entered the spiral behind him. An hour, the stranger said. He'd accounted for seven by the guidance of the voice. That meant only one more could have got in, unless the captain had signalled the two guards by the boat to join them. He cocked his head on one side to listen. At first he thought he could hear stealthy footfalls, but even his own breathing echoed and was magnified in the close confines of the spiral. He wasn't sure of anything his senses told him any more.

As his breathing returned to normal he began reviewing recent events. Why was Uncle Morthrir hunting them down like this?

He had disturbing memories, when he was only four, of his Uncle's Coming of Age Parade in Terrazarema. Kyros had always known him as Uncle Ibarno. But when a herald trumpeted and proclaimed his name to announce the start of the ceremony, his Uncle refused to step forwards and motioned with his hand for silence, before speaking: *"Brother Dareth. As you are King, I have written to you in private about my wishes, which you appear to have ignored. Now, in the hearing of all the people gathered today, I formally declare that I am no longer Prince Ibarno. I reject the memory of him utterly. As I am twenty-one today, this is the first act as my own master. From now on I will only be known as Morthrir."*.

No one knew where he got that name from or why he did it. Maybe that had sparked his Uncle's actions now.

He cocked his head to listen for approaching footsteps but still there was no sound of pursuit.

Kyros couldn't forget that his Uncle had the same dark eyes as a few leaders of a foreign delegation which visited the palace some years ago, instead of the lighter-coloured eyes of the Krêonor he had always known. He thought then that his Uncle must be related to them somehow, rather than his own family.

The men were Tsé-shâmé, but clearly of Krêonor descent.

That reminded him of the Writings of Hoffengrégor going back to the dawn of civilisation.

He started at a sudden sound, but nothing happened

The ancient Prophet talked of the Krêonor, the Tsé-shâmé and the Harmoth dwelling on an island, far out in the Western sea. Zerigor ruled in perfect unity, giving light to all the Peoples from the *Krêon of Tulá-kâhju*, the Crown of Life, placed on his head by the True King, who dwelled in the Realm of the Blessèd Throne.

But the Tsé-shâmé sought after a secret knowledge to gain power for themselves, which enticed some Krêonor to side with them, and resulted in war between the Peoples. Because of the physical likeness, Kyros was convinced there was a connection between that secret knowledge and his Uncle Morthrir.

He cocked his head again to listen, but still nothing.

The war culminated in great waves that broke upon the island and destroyed the Kingdom and the Crown of Life was swept from Zerigor's head by the flood.

Kyros sighed. From his boyhood up, he had always wanted to hold that incredible crown and see the light that radiated from it. That was how the Krêonor got their name: the Crown of the Peoples of the Waking World to rule all the others.

The spiral was playing tricks with his hearing. He thought he could hear stealthy footsteps approaching, then absolute quiet.

Even as a grown man, he harboured the dream to lead a ship of adventurers to locate the sunken island and find the *Krêon of Tulá-kâhju*, and bear it in triumph to the mainland. Surely that would re-unite all the Peoples again as it did before.

A sudden movement of air jolted him out of his reverie. He ducked as something went over his head and felt a noose jerk tight around his neck and yank him forwards onto his face.

The next thing he knew a man was on him, grappling his arms behind his back and binding his wrists together. Kyros felt a hand grab him by the hair and yank his head up and a dagger was pressed against his throat.

'Kyros. You're under arrest. I'm taking you back with me.'

He lashed out with his leg, but the man hauled Kyros to his feet and forced him to march ahead back up the spiral.

Chapter Thirteen

Morthrir sat at his desk musing on his recent meeting with Eawen the Henosite and fingering the small gold medallion on its fine chain that hung around his neck. He had it engraved years ago with the inscription:

Morthrir
Lord of Onadestra

It was not long after he took over the Princedom that he first met Eawen, *"Man of the Mountain"* as the locals called him. No one was willing to tell him where Eawen lived: they were obviously terrified of the Henosite and his powers. But Eawen was often seen at the southern end of the high grassy plateau that stretched all the way from Onadestra to Mount Malkamet itself, as though he had some secret affinity with the place. Morthrir was out riding alone one day when the man appeared out of nowhere, ran alongside his cantering horse, caught hold of the reins and pulled the horse to a stop.

'My Lord Morthrir,' he cried in a loud voice. 'I have a message for you.'

'I think you must be mistaken. My name is Prince Ibarno.'

'Not so, my Lord. For that is but a name given to you by your Father. Your real name is Morthrir, and you have been spoken of before your birth as the *Coming One*, for that is your title. Those with eyes to see have been waiting expectantly for you.'

From the glazed stare of his eyes, the man was clearly unable to see, but he moved his head as though he knew exactly where everything was and what anyone was doing.

'How can I take a name like that to myself? I am not yet of age and my brother, King Dareth, still has authority over all that I do.'

Eawen the Henosite stretched out his hand and grabbed the horse's mane. 'Why not wait until your Coming of Age Parade? Write to your brother beforehand, notifying him of your intention to make a name change. If he refuses you in private, then challenge him in public. Even your brother will find it hard to deny you then, and you can begin to assert your authority.'

He sat still on his horse, pondering all the man's words; then roused himself. 'You said you had a message for me?'

'Yes.' Eawen released the mane as the horse snorted and jerked its head away from the Henosite's hand. 'A message from the Hidden Power that is arising in our times. Listen, and listen well. For the Hidden Power says: "*I have called you from birth and given you your name as an heir in the Royal Family of the Krêonor, for you are mine and will walk in my ways and know my power. At first you will only know me darkly through dreams. When you have proved yourself worthy, a time will come when you shall know me face to face and all things will become clear and my power will be upon you to do great deeds*".'

'And who is this Hidden Power?' Morthrir pulled the reins tighter as his horse thrust its head up and began to move forwards. 'Tell me so that I may come to know him better?'

'It is not easy to know him,' the Henosite frowned. 'Do not make light of such deep matters, for you can still be rejected if you fail to fulfil your potential. He will make himself known to you at the appointed time.'

With that the man was gone.

PART II

THE OPEN DOOR

Chapter Fourteen

Lenyé accepted the boots gratefully: they would be so much more practical on the run than her own badly frayed slip-on shoes. Yanantha knelt down and helped her put them on. But what boots. Lenyé had never felt such soft, supple leather: from the strong sole and flat heel, to the cunning array of eyelets that allowed her to lace them right up the back of her leg to the middle of her thigh.

'Done,' said Yanantha, tying the final lace. 'There's a box of wax to go in your travel bag. That'll keep water out for about an hour if you have to wade in any rivers to confuse your hunters. But you must wax the leather regularly. There's nothing worse than cold wet feet when you're on the run.'

Lenyé opened the box and examined the slightly worn cube of wax. 'Hmm,' she sniffed appreciatively at the scent of roses.

'And now for the belt and dagger,' Yanantha held them out to her and Lenyé secured the belt around her waist.

'I don't know how to thank you for all your...' Lenyé began, but Yanantha cut her short.

'I haven't finished yet.' Yanantha took a small knife from the table and pierced the front of Lenyé's dress, slightly below the top of her boots. 'Can't have you hampered by these great big skirts when you're trying to run.' She sliced all the way round till the layers of fabric fell away and dropped at Lenyé's feet. 'It seems a shame to spoil such a lovely dress; that blue looks stunning on you, even if it is a little faded.'

'Thank you.' Lenyé mouthed the words, but her thoughts were suddenly elsewhere.

Vividly she recalled that day in late summer, nearly four years ago, when she and Kyros were working with the harvesters on her Father's estate. The sun had already set, but there was still a little light left in the sky. They were tired out and covered in dust and dawdling together some way behind the others as they headed back to the farmstead for the evening meal. Kyros kept stopping and picking cornflowers and presenting them to her, but she wouldn't take them.

'I don't like cornflowers. They mean...,' she hesitated.

'What do they mean?' he caught her by the hand and pulled her towards him.

'I don't know. I don't want to say.' She made a moue at him with her lips. 'Why can't you pick me poppies instead? There are more of them and they're a much prettier colour.'

'Only one man can ever pick you cornflowers.'

'Who says you're a man yet? And what makes you think it's going to be you anyway?'

But he held her hand and continued to pick cornflowers till finally she broke away from him and raced off down the lane.

'I don't want your silly cornflowers!' she shouted over her shoulder.

He chased after her and caught her and they fell, laughing, in a heap amongst the long grass between the lane and the ditch. She lay there panting with her head on his stomach and felt his breathing slow to normal. She could tell by the intermittent movements of his arms that he was doing something.

'What are you up to?' She tried swivelling her eyes to see, but as she moved her head he covered her eyes with his hand.

'Keep your eyes closed,' he ordered, in that rather serious way of his when he was engrossed in something, that made her burst out laughing, and almost missed the rest of his sentence.

'And then you'll understand.'

'Understand what?'

'You'll see.' He carried on for a little while, and she was about to open one eyelid and take a peep, when he said, 'Keep you eyes closed and sit up.'

Without pausing to think about what he was planning, she obeyed.

Then he was putting something on her head.

'What are you doing?' her hands went instantly to her hair, and she could feel a circlet of flowers.

'Don't open your eyes yet.'

She could tell by the feel of his breath on her cheek that he was very close to her. Next minute he kissed her on the lips. 'Kyros.' She jerked her face away from his and her eyes snapped open. 'How could you. We're cousins!'

She tried to slap him, but he caught her hand and drew her back towards him and kissed her again. She remembered how she struggled to break away. But the third time, her resistance vanished and she melted into him and returned his embrace.

They walked slowly, hand in hand, along the lane to the farmhouse. But she let go before they arrived so that no one else would know. There were shouts of derision through the open kitchen door about being back so late; but before they entered, Kyros whispered in her ear, 'One day you will wear cornflowers for me because you really want to.'

She hung that garland on a hook in her bedroom till the petals began to wilt. Then she pressed it between two folds of linen till it had dried out and gone hard and she hid it in a drawer under some clothes so that no one else would see.

Lenyé kept her thoughts to herself, but her feelings for Kyros deepened over the swift years: there was something so special about him. It was almost as if they were destined for each other.

She had the dress made in secret earlier this year: apart from the seamstress only Beth had seen it, and helped in its design.

She took it away with her to the pavilion at Lake Sanchéso, and had worn it for the very first time that morning when Kyros invited her to take a walk with him, just the two of them on their own. The stunned expression on his face when she stepped out of the pavilion and he saw the dress, said it all: she was trembling with anticipation.

But the dress was completely soaked when they swam out to the Eye of Hoffengrégor and back again, and she'd worn it ever since, she had to; there was no chance to change before the others stumbled across them on the Lake shore with the terrible news about their parents. Then they were all running for their lives: a month in all weathers, but particularly the blazing sun, until the intensity of that blue had faded.

Now the dress was ruined and she never wanted Kyros to see her in it again, in case he thought the old wives tale had come true: that if the picked cornflower faded too quickly it was a sign that his love would never be returned. But she had returned his love; her heart was brimming over for him. And she knew he loved her. She would always hold the love of Kyros close in her heart and…

'Help me with this.' Yanantha's quiet voice jerked her back to the present.

'Oh. I'm sorry,' Lenyé stammered. 'I was thinking of something else.'

Between them, they cut through the seams and sewed the layers of cloth into a lined cloak and hood. 'That'll help keep the worst of the cold out. 'Now for your hair.' Yanantha gathered up both of Lenyé's plaits and pinned them at the back of her head. Then she passed her a soft, cream-coloured cloth cap with a peak. 'Come and see,' and she took Lenyé by the hand and led her to a mirror standing against the far wall.

'Lenyé pulled a wry face as she settled the cap on her head at a jaunty angle. 'I hope Kyros never sees me like this. I look more like a page boy than a...,' she faltered.

'...Princess?' Yanantha smiled at her in the mirror. 'Hardly. Your pretty face and your figure give the game away far too easily. And I'm sure Kyros would still recognise you and love you the same. Remember. This isn't a disguise. Every soldier in the land will be looking for you, and out to get the bounty money for himself. You need speed and freedom of movement and protection from thorns and stings.'

'How am I ever going to win through?'

'You'll have to rely on your wits and courage. Why don't you go and try out those boots while I finish off here.'

Lenyé climbed up the steep path that would lead her to the top of the scree slope, keeping a low profile against the sky line. Yanantha's warning about the soldiers seemed all too real away from the House of Consolation where it lay hidden in the woods. But she was glad to be out in the open and enjoy the feel of sun and fresh air on her face. She found the gash in the line of bushes where the horses regained their footing, and the smooth trail in the scree itself where Gronis slithered down past her.

That's odd, she thought, as she noticed a branch a few yards down the slope, partly covered with stones. It's far too curved and the shape's too regular to be a branch at all.

Lenyé climbed down sideways, digging the edge of her boot soles into the scree to stop herself from slipping. She reached the branch, squatted down, and began picking the stones off it, and then gasped as the outline became clear. A longbow. It must belong to Gronis. Of all the weapons he could have dropped. She eased it out from under the last few stones and twanged the bowstring. Perfect. He must have been a specialist marksman to have one like this. She knew a warrior on horseback only used a small bow for close quarters; a longbow would be too unwieldy. Lenyé held the longbow sideways in her awkward squatting position and drew the bowstring back as far as possible. She could feel by the resistance that it was much more powerful than any hunting bow she had ever handled before, and would pack an enormous punch when she actually loosed an arrow. She glanced around expecting to see his quiver close by. Idiot. A horseman like Gronis would probably have it attached to his saddle. When he dismounted to use the longbow, he'd unhook the quiver and take it with him.

She returned to the House of Consolation with the longbow and twenty slender stakes cut from a nearby ash grove. Yanantha had a store of feathers and a cloth pouch full of arrowheads. Lenyé shook a few out into the palm of her hand and was pleased to see they were made of polished steel, with a well formed tang to receive the arrow shaft, and not the crude flint she was expecting. While Lenyé cut stakes to the right length, notched one end and bound the feathers and tips in place, Yanantha sewed a leather quiver for her.

'You'll need to head North,' Yanantha cut off the last thread to complete the quiver, and began slotting each arrow in as Lenyé finished it. 'That much I *can* tell you. And it'll throw your enemies off your trail for a while. They'll expect you to head East and try to rescue your sister.'

'And when they do work out their mistake?' Lenyé let her words hang in the air between them.

'They'll waste even more time retracing their steps. By then you'll be well away and your trail will have gone cold.'

'Don't you believe it. Youdlh won't trust his warriors to track me in the forest. They're horsemen from the plains. He'll bring in hunters to follow me, and they won't miss a thing.'

'Then have faith in your destiny. You will get through.' Yanantha slid the last arrow into place. 'That's everything completed.' She helped Lenyé attach the quiver to the belt. 'Take the rest of the arrowheads and some feathers.' She held out the pouch to Lenyé. 'Twenty arrows won't last long.'

'Thanks.'

Also, I prepared this while you were out.' Yanantha held up a leather satchel. 'Food and drink for some days: mainly dried meats, fruit, fresh bread, honey cakes, a flask of wine and one of water. Ready for instant flight.'

'But I thought I would be staying,' Lenyé interrupted.

'Don't worry,' Yanantha laughed. 'This is just in case the worst happens. I'm sure we still have a few more days together before they find my home. Before you set off, you must learn more from the Wisdom of the Prophet, and receive my help in the maturing of yourself as a person. Also, I need time to be still and listen to seek words of guidance for your journey. And you need time to fully regain your strength.'

They had finished clearing up from the evening meal and were settled in chairs to talk through the relevant sayings of the Prophet when there was a whirring of wings in the doorway.

Yanantha held out her hand and a tiny bird, no bigger than a wren, settled on her finger and began singing.

Yanantha frowned. 'Are you sure?'

The bird sang again.

'Quick!' Yanantha was up in an instant and pulling Lenyé to her feet. 'You must go at once. They are on us already.'

'But what about…?'

'No time now. Here take these.' She pulled open a drawer in the table and thrust a parchment, a glass phial of ink and three quill pens into Lenyé's hands.

Lenyé blindly shoved them in her satchel, buckled on her belt and grabbed her longbow.

'Out the back way,' Yanantha was pushing Lenyé ahead of her. Wade up the stream to conceal your scent, and then pick up the path to the left of the river to head North.'

'What about the words you promised to seek for me?'

'Each day I will send you one of the birds of Sorentina to instruct you. Write everything down on that parchment and guard it with your life for it will become your guide.'

'But how can I?' Lenyé turned back towards Yanantha in dismay. 'I don't understand their language.'

Yanantha laid one hand on her head and the other on her shoulder. 'Receive the gift of speaking and understanding the language of all creatures.' She leaned forwards, kissed Lenyé on the brow and then embraced her. 'Go in peace, and may the blessing and protection of Hoffengrégor himself be upon you.'

Lenyé could hear footsteps running up the path to the front door.

'Head for Mount Nastâri, in the far North,' Yanantha whispered urgently. 'Inside is a labyrinth of inter-connecting caves. A very ancient race of giants lives there. I hear rumours that one of them wears a sacred sword strapped to his back and protruding over one shoulder. I believe that is your lost Blade.'

'But who are they?'

'The last remnant of the Nastrim: a race the Krêonor should have despatched to the Realm of the Departed long ago, but failed in their task. Much evil has come into this world as a result.'

Lenyé shuddered.

'My thoughts will go with you to cover and protect you and blind their eyes to your purpose. And I will send you what help I can,' Yanantha continued. 'But be careful. Do not stir up the Nastrim, for they are deadly in battle and sell their lives dearly. But my heart tells me your destiny is closely bound up with them. Look for the...'

A crash against the front door halted her in mid sentence.

'Fly, Lenyé. Fly!'

Chapter Fifteen

Kyros stumbled up the rock ledge of the spiral, at the mercy of his enemy.

With his hands tied behind his back he could no longer feel the rock wall to guide him. Instead, he had to keep bumping his left shoulder against the rock wall just to make sure he hadn't strayed too far from it; but only gently, in case the rebound made him overbalance to his right and fall into the void.

What had happened to the voice?

What had he done to be deserted now?

His captor was in such a strong position, driving him remorselessly back up the way he had just come and into captivity to await his Uncle's good pleasure. He knew what that would ultimately mean. All his hopes of escaping and getting back to free the others were now gone.

The rhythm of his pace and his shoulder against the rock wall settled him and he was able to think more clearly. 'If the voice won't help,' he muttered. 'I'll have to do it myself. I can't go back up to the top with all those soldiers waiting for me. That will be the end. I have to act now.'

The rope around his neck was the problem. He had stumbled forwards earlier only to find the rope was tied around his captor's waist. So even if he could somehow jerk his enemy out into the void, the sheer force of the man coming up short at the end of the rope would throttle Kyros, bringing him to his knees and dragging him over as well, before he could do anything to counterbalance the man's weight.

'Faster.' The man behind him flicked the rope against his back. 'Faster.'

The feel of the rope down his back gave Kyros an idea. 'The next time you do that, my friend,' he murmured to himself. 'I'll be ready for you.' He deliberately stumbled and slowed his pace so that the rope would start to fall slack between them.

'I said, "*Faster.*"'

When Kyros felt the rope smack him lightly on the back again and brush against his fingers he stopped altogether.

Then he exploded into action.

Grabbing the rope with both hands, he spun round and squatted down, dragging the rope taut. Then he jerked the rope as far out over the void as possible with his foot. He braced himself, thrusting his feet against the rocky ledge and leaning backwards. The weight of the man stumbling into the void, made the rope whip tight under him, burning his hands and dragging one foot over the edge before he could stop it.

The man screamed.

There was a scrabbling sound from below, and then silence: just the dead weight of the man's body pulling against him.

Kyros leaned back against the rock wall, gasping for breath, relieved that he'd managed to prevent the rope from tightening around his neck.

He tried calling, but there was no answer. The man must have banged his head as he fell and was probably unconscious. He jammed one foot on the rope to act as a brake, let go with his hands and tried to feel far enough round on his belt to reach his dagger. He would have to cut the rope and let the man fall if he was ever to get free himself.

Kyros heard an inner voice, but not the one he was hoping for. It sounded more like himself speaking: how can you send another man to certain death to save yourself?

He struggled with his inner voice. This man's after me to take me back and hand me over to Uncle Morthrir who intends my

72

execution. What good does my death do anyone? And how is the rule of the Krêonor to be restored then?

Again his own inner voice responded: supposing it was you on the other end of the rope. Would you want him to let go?

Of course not, but…

Who is able to decide? Whether to take life or spare it?

I don't know.

Which one of you is deserving of death? Deserving of life? You have to decide: his life in exchange for yours?

And so the debate went back and forth in his mind.

'Very well,' he muttered out loud.

His searching fingers just managed to reach the pommel of his dagger and he was able to inch it out carefully till the haft fell into his hand. But instead of cutting the rope under him and letting go so that he could stand up, he worked away with a saw-like action against the rope binding his wrists. He had no idea how much progress he was making, and it seemed to take forever before the rope parted and he was able to free his hands.

Kyros slotted the dagger back into its sheath. Maybe there is a better way.

He hauled on the rope between his feet to make some slack so he could loosen the noose around his neck. But instead of slipping it over his head and letting go as he originally intended, he thrust one arm and shoulder through, so he could hold the dead weight of the man below him. He rammed himself backwards into a squatting position until he could stand up, hauling on the rope until he felt the man's body ease over the edge of the rock ledge. When the line went slack he stooped down, reached forwards and pulled the man as far back towards the rock wall as he could.

He felt the man's face, but there was no flicker of response: his hand came away wet.

He lifted his fingers to his nose and sniffed: blood.

He tried feeling the man's chest. There was a slight

movement of breathing, but very shallow.

'What am I supposed to do?' he muttered to himself. 'I can't take him to the top, just to be caught by the other soldiers. I can't take him with me; he'll slow me down too much. I'll have to leave him here, and hope he comes round fairly quickly.'

He pulled his jerkin open, ripped off a strip of his shirt and bound it round the man's head and face where he thought most of the blood was coming from. He loosened the noose around his shoulder and under his armpit and eased it over his head. Then he fumbled with the knot at the man's waist and pulled the rope away.

Kyros pushed himself to a standing position with one hand against the rock wall, and set off going steadily downwards.

But his inner voice wouldn't let him rest: what if he dies before he comes to? Whose fault would that be?

Mine.

He carried on feeling his way down the spiral.

And if he rolls over in his sleep and falls into the void?

That would be my fault as well.

Kyros slowed his pace. He's my enemy and he's been ordered to kill me.

Does that make it right?

Kyros stopped. What am going I do?

He's still a man and deserves to live and needs all the help he can get.

Surely there'll be other soldiers climbing down. They'll find him.

Supposing only eight got through in time. You finished off seven in that fight back up there. So, apart from this man, you're the only person left.

He sighed, turned round and retraced his steps: he knew what he had to do.

Even though he was going slowly and feeling his way he still tripped on the man's body.

Kyros felt for an arm and pulled the man into a sitting position, then levered him across his shoulder and staggered to his feet. He jerked the man into a more comfortable position and set off, but the odd shape across his shoulder and the extra weight made him weave a zigzag down the rock ledge. He couldn't tell how close he was to the rock wall any more and went more slowly feeling his way with his feet alone.

He was dog-tired with a raging thirst, but he set his will to the task of getting to the bottom and being able to put down his burden.

Kyros lost all trace of time. It felt like he'd been carrying this dead weight all his life, going deeper down the spiral into the unknown. His legs began to sag and he crumpled to his knees. But even then he wouldn't give up. He re-positioned the man on his back and crawled forwards on all fours.

He must get to the bottom.

He eased his hand forwards for one last move thinking he would collapse any minute, but instead of coming down on rough rock, he felt soft sand. He moved his other hand forwards and found sand again. Then his knees were off the hard rock and sinking into sand. Better still, the sand was flat instead of falling away before him in a steep descent.

He lurched forwards again and again and again, the prospect of reaching the bottom filling him with renewed energy.

Kyros reached forwards with his hand one more time and touched something warm. He closed his fingers around it wondering what it reminded him of and where he had felt something like that before. Then he jerked back with shock tipping the man off his back and they fell in a heap together. His hand had closed around a human foot in a leather sandal.

Chapter Sixteen

Rafé slipped back down the secret passageway, hurried past the block of stone where he entered, and descended towards the back of the palace. He wasn't surprised at what he overheard: he was always guarded when dealing with Morthrir and Youdlh.

He hurried on. He would leave for Onadestra tonight. But the convocation was going to cause problems. If he waited for the convocation, it would delay him getting to Onadestra. If Morthrir sent more soldiers, and they arrived before him, they might carry out the execution order before he could intervene.

But the convocation itself was his main focus. He smiled grimly. Morthrir was clearly out of his depths. Beware the honey pot you are putting your hand into, Sire. One day you will wake up and find the honey gone, and your hand stuck in the jar.

He paused to get his bearings and was distracted by a scuffling noise through a small grill in the wall at his feet. He crouched down and put his eye to the bars and found himself looking into the smallest of the kitchens leading to the pantries. A candle was bobbing about towards one end, and he was able to make out two figures filling a couple of bags. Then the candle came towards him and he was able to see their faces in the glow. 'Beth and Quinn,' he muttered to himself in amazement. 'What are they doing here?'

They came right up to the wall, and, before he could move, there was a slight snick and a block of stone opened out into the kitchen, right by his hand. Then Beth and Quinn were in the passageway and pulling the block of stone to behind them, before they turned round and saw him.

Rafé lunged forwards stifling Beth's scream with a hand over her mouth and pinning her against the wall. In the scuffle the candle was knocked out of Quinn's hand: it fell to the ground and went out. Immediately they were plunged into darkness.

'Shhh.' Rafé whispered, urgently. 'Or you'll give us all away.'

Quinn grabbed Rafé's arm and tried to pull him off his cousin. 'We don't want anything to do with you. Not after what we overheard. You're working for Uncle Morthrir and Youdlh.'

'No I'm not,' he hissed back. 'It may look like that if you overheard our conversation. But I am a King's man: loyal to both of your Fathers. You have to believe me.' He eased his hand off Beth's mouth. 'There. We're all a bit calmer now.'

'We have to get Onadestra and find our parents,' Quinn began to drag Beth by the hand down the passageway.

'So you heard that bit of the conversation, did you?' Rafé clutched at Beth's arm to stop them. 'You'll never make it on your own. I am also setting off for Onadestra under cover of darkness. Why don't you come with me? I can get you some cloaks and blankets to keep warm as we journey. I know a man who can give me a couple of horses. If I ride one, you can both use the other. Wait for me at the clump of trees just beyond the stables; I'll get the horses and meet you there.'

'But how *can* we trust you?' Beth was still shaking after the shock of running into him.

'Because I, too, have been along your secret passageway. I, too, have looked down into the private council chamber. And I, too, have overheard your Uncle Morthrir and Youdlh plotting together. If we don't hurry and get to Onadestra and save your parents, your Uncle is going to have them all executed.'

Chapter Seventeen

Lenyé awoke to the sound of birdsong and the half light of early dawn throwing the tree canopy overhead into silhouette. She shivered, despite the cloak wrapped around her. She lay there listening intently to the singing, and then marvelled, for the interweaving pattern of whistling, chirping, piping and chattering blended together in a composite tapestry of moods and meanings that formed an impression in her mind of overwhelming joy and thankfulness at the rising of the sun and the beginning of a new day.

She was startled by the whirring of wings, and a bird alighted on a twig almost next to her face. It was slightly bigger than the one which came to Yanantha yesterday with the warning. The bird cocked its head on one side and began singing to her. As she listened, Lenyé could make out distinct words and phrases. Of course. The bird of Sorentina.

'Wait.' Lenyé rolled over and fumbled in her satchel for the parchment and writing implements. 'Slow down.'

Lenyé deliberately left a space to write the words of Hoffengrégor that Yanantha had sung over her. The bird began to repeat the message and Lenyé wrote it down as fast as she could:

If for vision, be an eagle

She paused, waiting for the bird to continue. 'Is that it?' She looked up from her writing, but the bird had already gone.

Lenyé frowned as she puzzled over the words. I certainly

need vision, but Yanantha can't possibly mean me to become an eagle.

The same thing happened for the next three days as she headed North through woodlands towards the mountains by day and camped by night: a different bird and a different line, but still the sense that Yanantha was watching over her and teaching her the things she must learn:

> *Soar beneath the heavens above*
> *Looking down, discerning all things*
> *Maid of honour, bring new life.*

On the fourth day she pondered on all four lines, realising that the quatrain was a complete saying in itself. These must be some of Yanantha's words of guidance, she whispered to herself; as I don't recognise them from the Lay or the Writings of Hoffengrégor. I guess the attributes of the eagle are supposed to be "*the maturing of myself as a person*" that Yanantha spoke about. She probably thinks I'm still just a child.

But the more she reflected on the words, the more a great desire to display those virtues filled her heart and mind: to truly become a person of such deep vision and discernment that her character would change for the better and so begin to fulfil her Royal destiny.

Also on the fourth day she came across two sets of tracks, cutting across her path at right angles and heading East. They were the marks of heavy boots, like the ones Youdlh's warriors wore. But no hoof prints. Why would warriors be around and not riding their horses? It could be hunters; but then they wouldn't leave any tracks at all.

She followed the tracks to check no one was watching her, but they carried on for some distance, then abruptly ended at a huge tree whose lower branches swept down almost to the ground before rising up again. She crept right round the tree to see if the footprints re-appeared, but there was no sign of them.

Those men must have climbed into the tree, and were probably still there.

The first four days without sighting anyone made her a little too complacent, thinking she had completely thrown everyone off her scent. But why would these two be heading East so far up the trail? Surely they would have started from Yanantha's House or the scree slope at least. Why come all the way up here first?

She shaded her eyes and scanned the foliage of the tree, but there was no sign of any men.

She retraced her steps, and carried on heading North. But the sense of unease grew stronger all day, and she spent more time doubling back and checking her trail, and using running water again, wherever possible, to cover her scent. Maybe there *were* hunters out there after all. That's what worried her the most. Her words to Yanantha, in the safety of the House of Consolation, were far more unnerving out here. Perhaps those footprints were a blind to tempt her out into the open. Maybe they were already watching her, waiting, knowing exactly where she was heading: preparing a trap from which she couldn't escape. Fear gripped her innards, and she crept through the undergrowth, starting at every sound and staying stock still at the slightest rustle of a bird or the noise of an animal darting away from her.

She camped more carefully that night, choosing a place amongst rocks, but sheltered overhead by the branches of a huge tree.

Lenyé still felt uneasy as she fell asleep.

Chapter Eighteen

'Welcome, Kyros.' A voice echoed around him. A strong voice. A cheerful voice. But not a voice he recognised, and certainly not the one he was listening for. 'Give me your hand.'

He felt someone seize him by the hand and drag him to his feet. As he gripped in return and felt himself rise, the voice rang out in a clear command: 'Receive your sight.'

Immediately something like scales fell from his eyes and he could see.

Kyros staggered at the brightness around him, and clapped his hands over his eyes to protect himself. Gradually he opened his fingers as his eyes grew accustomed to the light.

In front of him stood a man as tall as himself, with long white hair and a white beard. He was clothed in white robes that reached to the ground around his sandaled feet, and in his hand he held a staff with a crook at the top. The man carried no torch, but light emanated from him and Kyros was able to see beyond the figure to the rocky walls of a cavern, which arched away into darkness above their heads. The light blazed in the man's hair and eyes.

No. Not eyes. For one eye was closed, but the other held him with a piercing gaze.

Kyros gasped in amazement. 'I know who you are. By your one eye you must be...' Already he began to bow his knee in deference, for there was such a sense of presence about this man.

But the man stopped him. 'It is not right for the Prince and future King of the Krêonor to bow before a mere Prophet. For we are fellow-labourers in the Restoration.'

'So you *are* Hoffengrégor. I thought you were dead.'

'I may have passed from your Waking World, but you cannot destroy the life of a man that easily.'

'What about the old prophecies?' Kyros continued.

'It is true. I lie on the bed of the lake and watch with my one good eye, waiting for the fulfilment.' He chuckled. 'Isn't that what they say in your Waking World? Yet most people dismiss it as an old wives' tale.'

Kyros dropped his gaze. He had always believed in the Prophet-of-old and the ancient writings yet to be fulfilled. But some of the tales about a man in white walking on the water around the island and watching through the spiral to ensure his prophecies came true always seemed a bit far fetched to him.

He tried to cover his confusion. 'I presume this is the Realm of the Departed?'

'Not quite. When that arrow hit me in the eye and the spiral opened up to swallow me alive, I was set upon by spiritual enemies who claimed unfinished business against my prophecies. I was permitted by the True King to recover from the wound and descend to another Realm and so continue the struggle. This is the Realm of Travail. I may have ceased from my trials in your Waking World. But here the long battle is all the more intense and the true labours of men come to fruition.'

'But I thought once you passed from the Waking World all things became whole.'

'Even here my eye is closed,' Hoffengrégor continued. 'For we remain as we entered and carry the scars of battle from the Waking World. But all will be put right in the Restoration, when the bed of the lake is raised and the Eye of Hoffengrégor is no longer needed. For then I shall see as I was always meant to see.'

Chapter Nineteen

Beth hugged Quinn round the waist. They were riding through open heathland, past clumps of birch trees interspersed with swathes of heather, and unexpected boggy patches ringed by tussocks of grass which they had to avoid. But they were keeping up a good pace and rapidly approaching the darker loom of firs ahead which rose towards the heights of Onadestra.

She gripped the horse with her legs and eased herself up. They'd been riding for three days, taking turns in the saddle while the other perched behind on the horse's back. But the cantle of the saddle forced her to sit away from Quinn so it wouldn't rub, creating an awkward angle that made her back ache as she leaned forwards to hold on. And she was still sore all over from their forced ride to Terrazarema.

She glanced behind. 'Slow down, Quinn. Rafé's miles away.'

Beth felt the motion change from a light canter to a walk as Quinn checked the horse's pace, brought him to a halt and eased him round so they could both look back down the trail.

'Why's Rafé going so slowly?' Quinn flicked the flies off the horse's neck with the loose end of his reins.

'I don't know. Surely he would want to get to Onadestra as quickly as possible if our parents' lives are at stake?'

'Don't think much of his loyalty,' Quinn pulled the horse's head up to stop it eating grass.

'Pity Rafé didn't steal three horses,' Beth shifted slightly. 'Then we could ride one each and I wouldn't feel so sore.'

'Rafé didn't steal these horses.'

'What makes you say that?'

'They're war horses. He must have been given them.'

'Quinn. He was just as much a prisoner as you and me. Who would give him war horses?'

'Uncle Morthrir, of course.'

'But why?'

Quinn twisted round to look at her. 'Think back to that conversation we overheard. He wasn't a prisoner then. And Youdlh was congratulating him for play acting and fooling us.'

'But what about in the secret passageway by the kitchens? You believed he was on our side then. We both did. Eventually.'

'True,' Quinn flicked the reins as he pulled the horse round, dug his heels in and eased him back into a light canter. 'But I'm not so sure now. Whatever he said then, I reckon he's been sent to Onadestra by Uncle Morthrir.'

'Sent?'

'Yes. Don't you remember? He said, *"I'm travelling to Onadestra as well"*. But he never said why.'

'You're right,' Beth was thinking hard. 'But then he said, *"I know a man who can get us a couple of horses"*. That sounds very underhand. He must have stolen them.'

'But if he was ordered to go, the man he referred to might just as easily have been Uncle Morthrir. In which case, he's not telling us the whole story.'

'But why would he be given two horses?' Beth persisted.

'Speed. Uncle Morthrir wanted him there as quickly as possible. He could ride one and lead the other and then swop over when the first horse got tired.'

'So we're back to your question: *"why's he going so slowly?"*.'

'I don't know,' Quinn turned his head to look at her over his shoulder. 'Something's happened since he was given those orders. We'd better keep alert and find out.'

Chapter Twenty

The fifth morning was different. At first Lenyé didn't know what was wrong. Of course. She woke up to the dawn chorus as usual, but there was no bird of Sorentina to sing to her. She searched the immediate vicinity of her camp, but saw nothing. Then she scanned the sky through the branches of the overhanging tree.

What was that?

She could see a tiny black speck floating high above her. The more she watched, the more she realised it must be some bird of prey, soaring on the air currents. Then she saw it wheeling and sliding down lower, and the rising sun caught the golden feathers under the wings and on the body and she knew it for what it was: an eagle, circling in all its majesty.

Lenyé gave a little gasp, and her heart skipped a beat. Could this be a sign for her: part of the fulfilment of Yanantha's message? Maybe it was coming to teach her the meaning of those words. The eagle continued to circle and drop lower as if it was searching for something.

Or someone.

Of course. It really was looking for her.

She gathered up her satchel, slung the longbow over her shoulder and made sure there was no trace of her camp to alert others. Then she crept out into a small clearing and waved. She wondered whether the eagle was actually interested in her or merely out hunting. But then she saw it dip to one side and straighten, almost in salute, and Lenyé knew the eagle had spotted her.

The great bird was much lower now and wheeling right overhead. It appeared far more threatening at such close quarters. Maybe its intentions weren't quite so honourable towards her as she first hoped. Lenyé began edging back into the forest to put some protection between her and the eagle. She looked up again and saw with horror the enormous wings folded into the body and the bird dropping like a stone straight at her with its talons extended. Lenyé didn't wait to find out: she turned and fled.

She was vaguely aware that her flight was taking her down a track that plunged deeper and deeper into a darker part of the forest with great boughs overhead and thick tree trunks each side, leading her further into a narrow slot that had all the makings of an ambush. She didn't care. She desperately wanted to put as much cover between her and that dreadful bird as possible: she could only hope the tree canopy would foil its dive. She kept glancing up over her shoulder and still the great bird came on right underneath the branches now, and, with wings outspread again, was speeding towards her. It was nearly on her when she felt hands on either side groping for her and pulling her up short, almost wrenching her arms out of their sockets. Men leaped out in front with drawn swords. 'Get her, lads,' one of them cried. 'Captain Elskin will make us rich men if we take her alive.'

But even as he spoke, Lenyé felt a rush of wind overhead and the massive bird hurtled past, hitting the row of men at head height with its wings outstretched and they all went down in a flurry of feathers and flailing arms. 'Run, Lenyé!' the cry from the great bird left her ears ringing with the shrillness of its warning. In the confusion, Lenyé yanked her arms free, leaped over the pile of bodies in front of her and raced on down the path.

Chapter Twenty One

Kyros heard a groan from behind him and whipped round in alarm. He stood staring at the man he had carried down the spiral.

Hoffengrégor broke the silence, 'Who is your friend?'

'I don't know,' Kyros scowled. 'He is no friend but an enemy, who will even now seek to take my life.'

'But you have borne him here through much hardship. Surely that lessens the enmity between you?'

'How can I ever trust him? He serves my Uncle Morthrir. Now that I see him in the light I recognise him from a time when I stayed at my Uncle's castle and watched him wrestle a huge man to the ground and practically kill him. It took five strong men to break his grip and get him off his opponent. His comrades called him the Constrictor. Ironic that I should wrestle with some stranger back there and prevail, when close behind me was this formidable man. I'd stand no chance against him.'

'Kyros,' Hoffengrégor's voice was gentle, but there was a stern note in it that made Kyros look up at him. 'If you prevailed at the entrance to the spiral, then you have a strength that maybe you are unaware of.'

'I don't agree. I was just desperate to get away from my enemies.' Kyros stooped over the prone body and pulled a fine chain necklet out from under the man's collar. Fastened to the chain was a gold medal. 'I thought so.' He mouthed the name engraved on one side with distaste:

'Captain Harbona.'

He glanced up at the old Prophet. 'Next to Youdlh, he must be one of my Uncle's most valued officers.'

He turned the medal over and read the inscription on the other side:

'*Medal of the Highest Honour*
For Valour in Arms and feats of strength
In recognition of Services Rendered
as Personal Bodyguard to
Morthrir,
Lord of Onadestra.'

He thrust the necklet back inside the man's collar. 'See what I mean,' exclaimed Kyros. 'This man is even worse than I first thought.'

'Do not judge too quickly. A man may be forced to serve the wrong master through ignorance or circumstance or folly. Only when he is obliged to choose between him and a genuine alternative can the man truly be judged.'

'Does that excuse him when he tries to kill me?'

'Of course not. But wisdom will always triumph, even if we have to lay down our lives in the Waking World.'

'That's a high price for anyone to pay.' Kyros stood his ground and folded his arms in front of him, a question still troubling his mind. 'Why has *my* sight been restored and your eye is still closed? You said we remained as we were and bore our scars from my world.'

'You still walk in the Waking World and are preparing for Kingship. You have not yet passed over as I have. Let us say you are just a temporary visitor here.'

'I don't understand.'

'Remember, you wrestled with the True King at the entrance to his Kingdom.'

'The True King, you say.' Kyros was stunned. 'Is that who he was?' He turned away, musing on the strange meeting, which now seemed a lifetime ago. 'I have wrestled with the True King,' he muttered to himself. 'Yet I still live.' Kyros turned back to Hoffengrégor. 'He never told me who he was.' Kyros looked directly into the old Prophet's face. 'Will you not tell me his full name?'

'It is not for me to say, if the True King himself remained silent. You will only be able to call him the True King until you come to know him by direct revelation to your inner being. Did he not give you the gift of hearing his voice and choosing to obey?'

'There was no option. I couldn't see. If I hadn't obeyed that voice, I would have been taken by my enemies.'

'Exactly.'

'But why did he desert me when I needed to hear him the most?'

'The True King never deserts those he has chosen to accomplish his purposes. Rather, he has given you the greatest gift of all. For you still hear his voice, but now it sounds like your own. You have passed the first test, and your inner voice is now guided by Him.

Kyros stood in silence thinking over what the old Prophet had just said.

But Hoffengrégor hadn't finished. 'Because you learned to obey the voice of the True King and showed mercy to an enemy, you have also passed the second test that he set you, and have learned to value someone else's life above your own freedom. Therefore I have been sent to you that your sight might be restored.'

Kyros glanced up at the old Prophet's face. 'I didn't even know that was a test. How am I supposed to aim for something if I don't not know what the test is in advance?'

'Any man can set his will to achieve an objective. It is not what you accomplish that is important so much as what you become. The True King is far more interested in you developing a relationship with him and the effect that will have on your character, rather than what you do.'

'But what about my own hopes and aspirations?'

'Do not despair. These are closely linked to what the True King is seeking to achieve in you. I suspect there is some passion you have always wanted to pursue in life, and never been able to. Am I right?'

Suddenly Kyros felt an overwhelming desire to open his heart to the old Prophet. 'I know this sounds ridiculous, but I have always dreamed of recovering the *Krêon of Tulá-kâhju* from the ancient site of Bara-mâla itself.'

'The Crown of Life?' Hoffengrégor paused and gazed at Kyros. 'No. I don't think that is ridiculous at all. For every King in the Waking World is but a picture of the rulership of the True King that is yet to come, and every Crown in the Waking World is but a foretaste of the *Krêon of Tulá-kâhju* on the King's head to give light to all the Peoples.' He placed his right hand on Kyros' shoulder and looked keenly into Kyros' eyes with his one good eye. 'May the restoring of your sight be a sign for the Restoration that is yet to take place. For the mark of the True King is upon you, otherwise you could not have prevailed against him. Neither would you bear such a great dream. Let me affirm you in that, for an anointing rests upon you and will carry you.'

'I'm not sure how this is all going to happen, but I feel it deep in here,' Kyros placed his hand over his belly. 'Sometimes I'm doubled over with pain just thinking about it.'

'You mean, like a woman in childbirth?'

'If that's what women go through; but I'm not sure I like the analogy.'

'Perhaps not. But it's a good sign. What you are saying is not a mere idea, but something that has been growing inside of you, and needs to come to birth. Maybe you do not understand fully now, but you will. For the present, it is your task to come to know the True King for yourself and to take that knowledge back to the Waking World. For am I not correct in thinking the knowledge of the True King has almost disappeared or is treated as amusing legends of a bygone era, and those who do maintain his honour are disregarded in the main?'

Kyros didn't say anything; he was thinking back over his views about dismissing most of the Writings of Hoffengrégor as irrelevant for today's needs. But here he was, standing in front of the old Prophet himself.

'Well?'

'I suppose you're right.'

Hoffengrégor smiled. 'That is often the way. Sometimes you have to lose things before you realise their value. Do not worry. You have to learn how to operate in the Realm of Travail. The most important thing you need to know is that weapons from your world have no effect here, except for the Sword of Justice which Zerigor once bore. But that is now lost in the Waking World. Your best means of defence and attack is to call on the name of the True King.'

'And he'll come running at my beck and call?'

'No,' Hoffengrégor chuckled. 'His name, uttered by someone from the Waking World, who knows him and walks in his ways, creates a bridge directly to the True King himself. It's as though he is right there with you in that situation and allows the En-luchés, the Guardians of Light, to break through any opposition you encounter and come to your aid. You asked me what his name was. When you come to know him better, he will reveal his full name to you. When he permits you to use *that* name, he will release far greater power through you. Any victory gained through his name in the Realm of Travail releases further victories in the Waking World on behalf of the True King. Similarly, any setbacks here create setbacks in the Waking World. So it is up to you to walk closely with him, to call upon him in your times of need, and to release the power of his name in your life. You have the choice: either to use that power or rely on your own abilities. In fact, that is your third test. And it's the best advice I can give you in so short a time.'

'That's a lot to take on board and understand so quickly.'

'I know,' the old Prophet put his hand in his pocket and pulled out a roll of cloth sealed with bindings. 'Here,' he passed it to Kyros. 'Take this; it will help you understand your journey. It contains two scrolls from the Book of Beginnings, which were lost to the Waking World when I fell down the Spiral. After all, if you do not know your origins, how can you discern the right path for what lies ahead? One is sealed and can only be opened by the right person at the appointed hour. The seal on the other one can broken at will. Do not try to read them now for there is no time, but keep them safe till you return to the Waking World.'

Kyros weighed the roll in his hand: it felt heavy for its size. Then he thrust it into a pocket of his jerkin.

'Come,' Hoffengrégor held out his hand to Kyros. 'For you have much to do and the time is short.' He gestured to the man on the ground. 'Bear your friend a little further and bring him to my dwelling where we can tend him. There are many things I need to instruct you in.'

Reluctantly Kyros stooped, lifted Harbona in his arms and followed Hoffengrégor in silence through the cavern, his feet kicking up the loose sand as he walked.

'Stay close,' Hoffengrégor called back over his shoulder. 'Our troubles will start when we reach the entrance to the cavern. I saw many Maljaros, the Birds of Darkness, gathering, but none of the En-luchés, the Guardians of Light, who should have arrived to help us.'

Chapter Twenty Two

Lenyé stumbled out of the forest onto a mound of tumbled rocks that began to rise to the skirts of the mountains. She slumped down on the ground, gasping for breath; then looked up in disbelief. Sitting on a rock, facing her, was the eagle, calmly preening the feathers in one of its wings. She glanced at the way she'd just come, and then back to the bird. 'I thought you were still behind me.' She faltered as the eagle looked up and gazed at her intently.

'Why did you run away from me?'

'You looked so threatening, coming straight at me like that.'

'I was trying to get between you and those men. Did you not know they were near, and waiting to trap you?'

'No...Yes. Something was definitely wrong. I felt uneasy all of yesterday.'

'Good. You should learn to trust your intuition more often. Then you will become like an eagle someday; rising up and seeing what others fail to notice. Also, you must believe the words from Yanantha. Did she not promise that I would be with you?'

Lenyé frowned. 'I'm not sure she meant an actual eagle. But I'm very glad you came. I've had no one to talk to for four days. The birds of Sorentina came and delivered their message and then they were gone. You're not going to leave me, are you?'

'Do not fear being alone. Sometimes it strengthens your resolve for a great task. But comfort comes in comradeship, and the wings of wisdom are greater when shared.'

'But I don't have any wings.'

The eagle threw back its head and uttered a chuckling sound. 'You don't need wings on your arms, but in your spirit: you must learn to rise up and see in the spirit realm, and then all things on the ground will fall into place.'

'Is that from Yanantha? Do I need to write it down?'

'No. I, Chuah-te-mok, tell you this as an eagle. For I hover between the heavens above and the Waking World below. I bring down what is not visible in the Waking World and when I shed my feathers at springtime to make way for fresh plumage, then my youth is renewed, and I mount up with wings outspread and rise to take up the desire of mortals to be free once more. Learn to do that, and you shall indeed be honoured, and wherever you go, you will bring new life.'

'So you *do* know Yanantha's words.'

'Maybe. It would help if I knew what they were.'

Lenyé recited the words from memory.

'All I can say is Yanantha knows the way of the eagle, as she knows every creature. I have been sent to help and instruct you. Yanantha's words will enter the very depths of your being and feed and sustain you. The more like an eagle you become, the stronger you will be to accomplish your goal.'

'It's easy for you, but I find this a hard saying to put into practice.'

'Come. We have talked much,' the eagle craned his head round before turning back to Lenyé. 'Those warriors were overwhelmed, but not totally destroyed, and many more are gathering. Their commander will soon learn that you have evaded their net, and lay his plans accordingly. You will not escape them so easily another time.'

She spent most of the morning scrambling higher and higher into the foothills of the mountains, the hovering eagle guiding her around great fissures and the gorges of tumbling rivers. At last Chuah-te-mok descended on a great rocky outcrop and

Lenyé climbed up to find a place to rest next to him, taking care to sit amongst a jumble of boulders that broke up her shape on the skyline. She fumbled in her satchel for some dried meat and figs. Her wine was all gone, but she filled both flasks earlier with water from a clear stream. She offered him some of the meat, but Chuah-te-mok shook his head saying he preferred his food fresh and raw.

'While you eat, look towards the plains below and tell me what you see.'

Lenyé shaded her eyes with her hand and looked out over a rugged plain that stretched westwards away from the forest towards the sinking sun. 'I see dust on the plains moving towards these mountains, but I cannot see what is causing it.'

'You see well, but your eyes are not as mine. Even from here I can make out what is in the dust. Do you not see more now?'

Lenyé screwed up her eyes against the glare of the sun on the rocks. 'Little black specs. But I cannot tell what they are.'

'Then make a guess.'

'The only things able travel at that speed would be horses, galloping. But why so many and so tight together?'

'Think, Lenyé.'

'A herd of wild horses?'

'Then you have nothing to fear. What else, for I see that the horses are not alone?'

'Youdlh's warriors?'

'Which means?' Chuah-te-mok raised his wings slightly to balance himself as a sudden updraft of wind swept over them.

'They know where I am heading, and are trying to cut me off.' Lenyé rubbed the dust out of her eyes with her knuckles. 'But why send that lot to catch one woman? It looks like half his army. What does it mean?'

'They must fear something else.'

'Like what?'

'If they've worked out you're heading North,' the eagle

turned his head and looked intently at her. 'Who would you meet up with?

'Yanantha mentioned the Nastrim. But they sound terrible. Why would I want to be involved with them?'

'True. But what would your Uncle Morthrir think you were intending to do by going to them?'

Lenyé hesitated. 'Persuade them to attack him?'

'Exactly. He must be terrified you're going to raise an army greater than his before he has fully established himself. That's what he fears most about you. The one person left who can defy him by force.'

'But those riders are at least two days away, even if they ride through the night as well.'

'Which means the immediate threat to you is from where?'

'Behind us.' Lenyé jerked back to the forest in alarm, and squinted as her eyes adjusted to the darker loom under the trees.

Nothing stirred, but again she felt the same sense of unease: that hidden eyes could be watching her, even now, and making their plans against her. 'We need to be moving,' Lenyé was about to put her water flask back in her satchel when Chuah-te-mok stopped her.

'Get your writing things. I have something to pass on to you from Yanantha.'

'How did you receive it? You can't possibly have seen her since we met.'

'No. But I needed to be sure you learned your lesson well and are ready for the next one.'

Lenyé pulled out her parchment and quills and began writing as Chuah-te-mok spoke:

'If for ruling, be a lioness
Bright the huntress, crowned in splendour
Let your courage match your virtue
With great strength now be endowed.'

'I don't suppose you're going to tell me what that means?'

'Certainly not. I never mix with lions. That is for others to play their part. I must return to my eyrie for a while.'

'I thought you were going to stay with me,' there was a slight tremor in Lenyé's voice. 'I don't want to be on my own again.'

'You are never alone if you have faith in your destiny. Do not fear. I will watch over you and return when you have need of me.' With that he was gone, circling to find the thermals that would lift him high up the mountainside, but, before he was totally out of earshot, he called down to her his final words of wisdom: 'Remember, nothing happens to you without significance.'

Lenyé sat watching him in admiration. I wish I could scale the mountains that easily. Still. I guess I'll have to do it on my own two legs. I can't exactly send Chuah-te-mok in there to find the Sword for me. She rolled up her parchment and re-packed her satchel, securing the two buckles. Then she slung it on her back, hitched the longbow over her shoulder and set off.

She continued walking up the sloping rocks and climbing where necessary and found a place to camp for the night under an outflung shelf of rock. The next day she set off early and was about to climb through some tumbled boulders when she instinctively froze. Out of the corner of her eye she caught the movement of something above her. She crouched behind a large boulder and peered round the edge.

There it was again.

Some large creature was perched on a rock shelf ahead of her.

Chapter Twenty Three

'Beth,' Quinn shook her by the shoulder. 'Wake up.'

It was only a half moon but enough to bathe the clearing in its silvery light, casting dark shadows under the trees around them.

Beth grunted and turned over. 'What?'

He shook her harder. 'Beth, wake up. Rafé's gone.'

Beth was wide awake now. 'Which way did he go?'

'Through those trees.' He pulled Beth's blanket off her. 'If we're quick, we might just catch up with him.'

They raced across the clearing where they'd camped for the night and plunged in amongst the trees; then slowed down to pick their way through the tangled undergrowth.

They came out into another small clearing.

Quinn pointed ahead, 'There's a proper path to follow.'

'Shhh.' Beth grabbed his arm and pulled him down with her. 'There he is.'

'Where?'

'There, on the other side of that tree. But what's he doing?'

Both children strained their eyes to see in the dim light. Then they saw a dark figure emerge from behind the tree.

Beth gasped, 'That's not Rafé.'

'How can you tell? The hood's right down over his face.'

'Rafé hasn't got a cloak like that.'

'Are you sure?'

'There's only one way to find out,' Beth was already up from their hiding place and creeping over to the beginning of the path. 'We'll have to follow him.'

Chapter Twenty Four

Morthrir lay tossing and turning in bed that night. He slept fitfully and woke every so often, the pressures of the day nagging at his mind. But more particularly he brooded over his experiences on Mount Malkamet. He greatly desired to journey back there, for he felt his power waning and was desperate to be renewed in his spiritual strength. He got up and opened the shutters so the fresh night air could permeate his room, before settling back in the comfort of his bed. He felt a light breeze against his face as he drifted off to sleep at last.

But he was falling, falling, falling: falling into nothingness. The gentle breeze strengthened to a violent wind whipping his hair forwards, almost dragging it out by the roots. He leaned back against the gusts and gazed out over the rock strewn ravine, his eyes drawn inexorably along the path of the wind to the dark bluff of the mountain peak at the head of the steep-sided valley. This must be the right location.

Ever since he came to Onadestra there were whispers of a secret place high in the mountains. Especially when Mount Malkamet was mentioned, the local people would fall silent and a look of fear would come into their faces. Once the process of rebuilding his domain was well under way and he could give his attention to other matters, he took a team of soldiers to seek this infamous mountain. At last they found it and explored every inch of the ground and he and his men stood on the curiously flattened summit scanning all around for some clear sign. Personally, he was convinced the ravine had the answer: from the sharp cleft of the valley itself, pointing towards the summit of the mountain like a giant marker, to the fire blackened pile of stones at its very centre. They must have been built into a cairn at some stage, for they were too regular in shape and too close together compared with the random boulders elsewhere.

Morthrir and his team had been here twice before on separate expeditions, but only during the full light of day. No one wanted to be anywhere near this peak when the sun went down. So Morthrir left the men at base camp well back on the grassy plateau, and he was now entirely alone. Sunset was already several hours ago and the ravine was darkening as the last streaks of daylight faded from the sky. He was determined to see if solitude and the hours of darkness would reveal anything. He found a nook in the rocks where he could watch over the whole of the ravine, and waited.

It was a relief to be out of the wind. He felt exhausted from battling against it. Gradually his eyelids began to droop.

In his mind's eye, Morthrir could see lights: torches planted in a ring around the cairn. But something was wrong. He wracked his brain to work out what it was. Of course: the cairn was no longer a ruinous mass of stones, but built up again as it must have been in ancient times. Surprisingly it was long and narrow and flat on top, like a bed. He shuddered: or an altar of sacrifice. Then it struck him like a blow. The torches burned without a flicker in the violent wind. He could hear it whistling past his rocky hideout; even see tufts of grass, on the outer extremity of the torch light, buffeted by the wind. But everything within the ring of torch light was utterly still. Surely the flames would have been blown out by now? For some strange reason his eyes felt so heavy and finally his lids closed.

Morthrir snapped his eyes wide open, his attention riveted on a time-candle in its glass sleeve supported on an iron pole. Of all the bizarre things to have in a place like this: what was it doing here? A metal cross-piece was thrust through the wax about half way down, with the number **12** emblazoned on the candle in front of it. About an inch above the cross-piece was a horizontal black line. If the cross-piece marked the midnight-hour, then the time-candle had about twenty-five minutes to burn.

Suddenly he was aware of four figures approaching the torches from each point of the compass. The loose folds of their long robes whipped around them, and the hoods over their heads nodded and danced in the howling wind. As the figures moved in amongst the torches, their robes fell limp around them and their cowls drooped further over their faces casting their features into deep shadow.

This was no dream after all, but a living reality.

He could see each figure was dressed in a different colour: white from the North, black from the South, red from the East and grey from the West. As they reached the altar they bowed, as if in greeting to each other, and raised their right hands in salute: their palms showing pale against the glow of the torches.

Then the figure in white turned towards him and beckoned. Morthrir crouched down, rooted to the spot, unable to move. The figure in black also turned towards him and raised his right hand high in salute. Morthrir cowered deeper into the nook of rock: how did they know he was there? The red figure, which was practically facing him, raised both arms in a gesture of embrace. Again Morthrir was unable to move. Then the grey figure turned right round to face him, dropped to its knees and held out both hands in an attitude of adoration.

At last Morthrir stirred as though some will, greater than his own, was releasing him to respond. He climbed out of his hideout and was instantly aware of the power of the wind surging around him, trying to lift him off his feet. He stumbled down the rocky slope and stepped into the ring of torch light. Immediately the wind ceased raging around him, and he was aware of voices chanting in harmony; but he couldn't understand the words.

All four of them pointed to the altar between them. Morthrir felt himself dragged up onto the stones. He struggled violently, but it was as though unseen hands gripped him and were thrusting him forwards against his will. He heard each figure speak in turn, but this time he understood their words:

'You have come alone.'

'You have come at last.'

'You belong to us.'

'In darkness, you will do our bidding.'

Then in unison they began to chant: 'Hail to the Lord Abbérron. For he is Great. His dominion shall cover the whole Waking World. And he will seize the Wealth of Nations.'

Morthrir's mind swam in confusion so that he failed to notice the cords being bound around his wrists and ankles.

The chanting ceased, his mind cleared and he twisted his head sideways to look at the time-candle. The black line was just burning away: a quarter to twelve. He tried to sit up, but felt, instead, the cords biting deep into his skin. He jerked his head to the other side to see what was going on and became aware of more figures in brown robes and cowls forming a circle between the four figures and the ring of torches. Instinctively he began counting them: ten in all. He struggled in panic, but they laughed at him, their voices sounding harsh as they mocked him. The four figures began circling around the altar, and the brown-robed figures circled the other way, then they changed direction two or three times.

The four figures stepped towards the altar, the figure in white bearing a silver chalice. The others raised Morthrir's head while the fourth eased the rim of the chalice between Morthrir's lips and made him drink. It was strong red wine, but tasted bitter, as though it had been drugged. Morthrir coughed and spluttered and wine trickled down his chin, but they forced him to drink more until the chalice was drained. His head swam and he lost all sense of time. The chanting began again, and, even though he could not understand the language, he felt fear grip him for he recognised the dirge they were singing for what it was: a death chant. In one last desperate effort he roused himself and tried to burst his bonds, but they were too strong for him, and he fell back panting and sweating from exertion.

He glanced at the time-candle again, just as the metal cross-piece fell away: midnight.

As if in answer, he heard the sound of weapons being drawn and the bright dagger blades shone and flickered in the hands of the four. With a cry they rushed forwards and plunged their daggers straight into his heart.

As Morthrir screamed, a bright flash engulfed him, his bonds dropped from his wrists and ankles like charred candlewicks, and immediately he was on the flattened peak of the mountain. The strong updraft of wind behind him thrust him forwards onto his hands and knees. He raised his head and saw a great figure standing before him, clothed with light: brighter than the sun. Morthrir fell on his face, but as he did so, he was aware of others with him on the summit. He looked to his left and dimly he could see the two circles of figures from the ring of torch light; but they weren't circling now: they were bowing low before the awe-inspiring presence in front of them.

Then the White figure from the North stood and raised its hands. 'Hail, Lord Abbérron,' it cried. 'We have found the man. Through death we have brought him to you.'

'Morthrir,' the Lord Abbérron's voice was deep, and the mountain top shook at the sound of it. 'The sentence of death over you for trespassing on Mount Malkamet has been rescinded. You are brought back from the dead to serve me, and me alone. I have appointed you as my Regent in the Waking World. You shall reach out your hand and take all that you desire. On one condition: that you worship me only. Now go. Destroy all those who oppose you, and therefore stand against me. Do not fear, for death shall not come near you.'

Chapter Twenty Five

Lenyé breathed a sigh of relief: it was only a young stag. She crept forwards and squatted behind a wizened tree growing out of a crack in the rock, keeping the stag in focus. She didn't need to hunt for meat, so could easily pass it by and carry on with her journey. But something was wrong. She checked the air currents to make sure she was still down wind, but the stag was obviously distressed by something. All her experience and skill at hunting confirmed that one of the best indicators of danger was another creature's reactions.

She eased herself across to a smaller rock to get a better view and then gasped. The poor thing. It must have got one of its hooves caught in a crevice or something, for she could now see it bucking with its rear legs, trying to free itself. What should she do? Leave it, or try to release it?

She waited, motionless, scanning the rocks above the stag's head; and then saw what was causing the distress: a lioness, her tawny coat bright against the rocks in the sunshine. Why would such an experienced stalker expose herself so far away from her quarry? She wasn't even crouching or slinking: just standing there in all her magnificence, surveying the scene below her. If the stag wasn't hampered by its leg it would have bolted for cover by now. Maybe there was a whole pride of lions out on the hunt and this one was the decoy, distracting the victim while the others crept into place for the kill.

The stag shied round to face the assailant, its ears pricking and flicking for sounds and its nose up, snuffing the air. Again it bucked with all the power of its haunches to try and release its hoof.

Lenyé slipped the longbow off her shoulder. She wasn't going to kill the lioness, just give it a warning arrow: show her there were other predators that were interested in the quarry. She eased her right hand across to her quiver inch by inch so as not to startle the stag or alert the lioness.

The stag shot round to face her, its ears twitching.

How could it have sensed what she was doing? Lenyé had the arrow in her hand now and was about to notch it on the bowstring when there was a movement of air behind her and something hit her between the shoulder blades, throwing her forwards and making her drop the longbow and arrow. She landed face down with all the wind driven out of her by the weight on top. She felt the breath on the back of her neck and heard a man's voice close to her ear, 'Got you at last.'

She felt him grab her right wrist and begin twisting her arm up behind her, while someone else hauled at her left arm.

'No!' Lenyé kicked out with her legs and tried throwing her assailant off, but the men were too strong for her. They held her arms behind her back while someone tied her wrists together; then her ankles. At last she felt the weight of her attacker shift as he heaved himself off, grabbed her by the shoulder and rolled her over.

She glared at them. Four men dressed in the garb of Youdlh's warriors and one dressed like a hunter. Lenyé tried to thrust herself up into a sitting position; but her boots slipped on the rock and she fell back, helpless.

Two of them reached down, caught hold of her by the shoulders and hauled her to her feet.

She stood there swaying slightly, trying to stare them down. 'You'll never get away with this.'

The men laughed at her empty threat.

One of them, clearly the leader, separated himself from the

others and swaggered up to her. 'Who is there out here to save you now?' He stooped down and hefted her onto his shoulder. 'Elskin's going to be pleased with this. Come on lads. Someone grab that longbow. It looks like one of ours, anyway.'

The men were very agile, part running, part slithering down the rock face she spent so long climbing up. She was jolted around on the man's shoulder and at one point felt herself slipping off, but he hitched her up with his other arm over his head and settled her weight more evenly across the line of his shoulder.

They reached the top of a particularly steep cliff. Lenyé recalled the painstaking scramble it took her to climb up to the top. She was still wondering how they were going to get her down this bit when she was aware of a tawny blur to her right, and suddenly the lioness was in amongst them, rearing up on her haunches and lashing out with her heavy forepaws. Two of the men were pitched straight over the edge of the cliff; two more tried to draw their swords to fight her off, but were also hurled over the edge.

Lenyé heard the roar as the lioness rounded on the man carrying her. She could feel him flex his knees slightly and shift her weight forwards on his shoulder while he drew his sword and turned to face the lioness. Lenyé was thankful she was on his left shoulder and a little further away from that dreadful drop down the cliff face. He edged forwards and swung his sword at the lioness but she batted the flat of the blade aside with her paw and launched herself at the man's chest.

Lenyé screamed as she felt the man thrust away from under her, but her fall was broken by the back of the lioness, and the creature's powerful legs, planted firmly on the rock, prevented her from sliding over the edge. Once Lenyé stopped rolling, the lioness sprang past her. Lenyé was face down and couldn't see what happened, but there was a scratching and growling sound followed by a long drawn out shriek.

She heard the claws on the rock, felt the whiskers brush her face and smelled the lioness' breath as it sniffed at her hair.

'Thank you,' Lenyé was almost too stunned at the speed of the attack to fully appreciate what happened. 'You saved me from those men.'

'That's what Yanantha sent me to do.'

Lenyé jerked her head round to focus on the lioness' face. 'Yanantha? Oh my goodness! I nearly loosed an arrow at you back there.'

'I know. I was watching and I'll explain later. But first I have to get you out of here.'

'Are you the one mentioned in the last words from Yanantha?'

'I don't know about that. My name's Ariella.' The lioness growled slightly. 'Firstly, how do I get you further away from the edge to safety, seeing as you can't move? And secondly, how do I get those ropes off you?'

'If you can get the dagger out of the sheath on my belt and put the haft in my hands, I can at least work at cutting the ones on my ankles.'

Ariella managed to roll Lenyé over on to her back, and pull the dagger out with her teeth. Lenyé held the haft and drew her legs up so she could move her feet backwards and forwards to cut through the rope on her ankles. Then she wedged the dagger in a crack in the rock and moved her hands up and down to saw through the rope on her wrists.

Lenyé rubbed her arms and massaged her ankles through the leather of her boots to get the circulation going again. Then she sheathed the dagger, grabbed her longbow, which one of the men must have dropped, and the two of them retraced their way back to where the stag was still trying to free its hoof.

Lenyé recovered the arrow and shoved it back down into her quiver.

'Take a closer look,' Ariella slunk away to the right.

Lenyé climbed up the rock, calling gently to the stag. When she was within a few paces she could see the stag's leg was tied to the stump of a knarled tree trunk by a short length of rope. Lenyé approached, still calling gently and cut the rope with her dagger. The stag raised its head and sniffed at her and licked her hand. But at the sight of Ariella approaching round a rock, the creature started and bounded away.

'Did you see that?' Lenyé was indignant. 'The poor thing was tethered by a piece of rope.'

'Which means?' Ariella prompted.

'Those men must have done it.'

'And why would they do that?'

'I don't know. It seems a pretty cruel thing to do. Did they know you were there? And why would they be hunting you?'

'They weren't hunting me. It was you they were after.'

'What?

'I watched the whole thing, from the trapping of the stag to their careful stalking of you. I've often seen plainsmen ranchers hobble one of their buffalo to entice a predator out of cover. They used the unusual sight of the tethered stag to catch you off your guard.'

'Then why didn't you try to warn me?'

'The paw burned in the bush fire teaches the best lesson. You'll be a more wary lioness next time.'

Chapter Twenty Six

Kyros reeled, thrusting out his arm as if warding off a blow and blinking at the shock of brilliant light that broke in upon him as he stepped out of the cavern.

'Ah, my friend,' Hoffengrégor reached out a hand to steady the body of Harbona as it nearly slipped out of Kyros' arms. 'I should have warned you about the Guardians of the Spiral.'

For a fleeting moment Kyros saw two beings like men wrapped in light, one on each side of the entrance. They had drawn swords in their right hands as they turned ceaselessly to watch: firstly, over the entrance to the cavern; secondly, at each other; thirdly, out into the Realm of Travail; fourthly, away from each other and back again to the entrance, in a continuous circle.

'Who are they?' Kyros gasped.

'The True King set them as guards to prevent any unauthorised person gaining access from the Waking World, or any creature escaping from the Realm of Travail into to your world. They continuously turn to watch the entrance to the Spiral, each other to ensure neither of them is tempted to relax his guard, out into the Realm of Travail, and, finally, at what happens behind them, in case an enemy catches them unawares.'

Kyros stumbled past and his eyes cleared so he could focus again. The air was filled with light, far brighter than sunlight in the Waking World, but after the shock of the Guardians of the Spiral, his eyes adjusted to it and he was able to see properly. He felt the intensity of the light on his face and the back of his hands, as if it was burning into him.

The ground dropped away at his feet as he gazed out over a vast plain, broken in places by clumps of trees and outcrops of rock that stretched away to mist-clad ridges in the distance. Immediately below them was a forest, the topmost branches on a level with them as the ground sloped steeply away, the grey trunks and limbs peeping through the leaf canopy.

He shifted the weight of the man in his arms and took a deep breath. As he did so he felt a surge of new strength go through him, as though the very atmosphere of this place was charged with power. All he had to do was step forwards, walk over the sea of leaves in front of him, leap across the plain, scale the highest ridge and swarm up the mountain range behind it.

'Come.' Hoffengrégor's voice brought him back to reality as the old Prophet caught him by an elbow and led him to a steep path at one side that plunged down a series of flat rocks, and zigzagged away below them to disappear amongst the trees.

Even as he followed the old Prophet, he caught sight of something black out of the corner of his eye hurtling towards him. It hit him in the left shoulder and, with a cry of agony, Kyros spun round almost dropping the man he was carrying.

He glanced up and saw five birds like crows, only much larger, and gasped as his eyes were riveted on them, almost against his will. He could see no mark or indication of feathers; rather they drew all light to themselves and gave nothing back, not even a glint from their eyes: black holes in the air, as though they were sucking the light away from him. They hovered well above his head with the ease of hawks: the downdraft of their wings stirring up the dust around his feet and momentarily blinding him. A sixth bird swooped up to join them.

'Maljaros,' the old Prophet muttered. 'Don't stare at them for too long.' He grabbed Kyros by the arm. 'Six. A complete detachment. That's bad news.' He led Kyros down a couple of the rocks, like huge steps. 'Quick.' his voice was hoarse with urgency. 'Down in amongst the trees. It's our only hope.'

Kyros blinked the dust out of his eyes and followed hard after Hoffengrégor. But the Maljaros dived in formation whirling around him, harrying him, trying to tip him over the edge of the steep path: their wings fanning his face, their claws tearing at him as they flew past, and their hooked beaks snapping and grabbing at his hair and clothes in the their relentless attack. Their harsh cries rent the air, filling him with fury, for, with his arms full, he couldn't stand and fight them off.

He ducked instinctively at a whistling sound as the old Prophet turned back towards him and started whirling his staff above his head and laying into the birds.

'Be gone, foul Maljaros,' the old Prophet yelled, smacking one full in its breast and then turning as another hurtled past, lashing out at it with the crook of his staff and catching it in the tail.

The birds screamed at him and flew up to resume their hovering and watching: glaring with malevolent eyes. As the old Prophet ran in amongst the trees, they dived again, two birds hitting Kyros hard in the backs of his knees as he stumbled towards the shelter of the trees. He fell backwards with the dead weight of the man sprawling across him, and pinning him down.

Immediately the birds were on them, tearing with their claws and pecking at them. Kyros instinctively covered his eyes with one hand and the eyes of Harbona with the other. Even if he had the Blade of Zerigor instead of his own, there was no time to draw a sword and fight them off. The birds pecked ferociously at the backs of his hands till Hoffengrégor waded in amongst them with his staff clearing the birds out of the way.

'Remember to call upon the name of the True King.' Hoffengrégor seized Kyros by the wrist and hauled him out from under his burden. 'These are enemies beyond your own abilities to deal with.'

Kyros grabbed the man by one arm, swung him up on his shoulder and struggled in under the trees while the old Prophet acted as rearguard with his staff.

PART III

A HEART EXPOSED

Chapter Twenty Seven

Lenyé and Ariella found the men's horses still tethered to trees in the woods below them. Lenyé cut the ropes and let them go, but as she came to the last horse she unbuckled a strap on its saddle and pulled the axe out. She hefted it in her hand, feeling the point of balance as she pretended to throw it.

Immediately she was back with Beth, the morning of the high feast day when her family and Kyros' were staying with Uncle Morthrir and Aunt Faria to celebrate the beginning of Spring. Lenyé smiled to herself at the memory: such happy days. Beth was only five and had a pretty blue ribbon in her hair for the special occasion. Then she felt a stab of jealousy at the reminder of her sister. Beth was the youngest in the family and had a way of attracting everyone's attention. Somehow the two brothers in between were never a serious threat, but a sister was different. And Beth was such a gifted musician; she was always in demand to play whenever the families came together. Lenyé felt she could never compete with that.

She tried hard to thrust her thoughts aside and refocus on the high feast day. The previous evening Lenyé unwrapped a late present from her Uncle and Aunt for her twelfth Birthday: a bird-kite, with a long brightly coloured tail. She was desperate to try it out, and could hardly sleep that night, she was so excited. Next morning they were both up before the boys and hurried out into the park through a gate in the garden wall. A warrior was sitting outside one of the barrack blocks waxing boots. He seemed very friendly so they stopped to talk and watched him work some beeswax into the leather.

'Have to be especially careful of the movement behind the toes and the bit above the heel at the end of the stitches,' he looked up at them and grinned. 'If they go hard and crack and split here,' he pointed to the deep crease behind the toes, 'or there,' he sliced across the back of the boot with his finger. 'Then the whole boot's ruined. Once you start patching them you're on a slippery slope downwards. You can usually tell the state of an army just by looking at their boots.'

'Is that for chopping wood?' Beth darted forwards and tried to pick up the odd shaped axe. It had a longish handle, and the head was straighter and thinner than a normal axe, but the blade curved up to a sharp point at the top. On the other side of the haft from the blade was a thick pointed spike.

The man laughed. 'I have chopped wood with it when we've been out at camp, but it's a warrior's axe. I need to polish it for the festivities this afternoon.'

'What's that spike for?' Beth ran her finger along the bright steel and touched the tip. 'It's so sharp.'

'If you're fighting other riders and you've got that in your hand, you go for them with the spike. That'll pierce through chainmail as easy as anything and wound or even kill them. You could do it with the point of a sword rather than slashing across the mail rings with the blade, but you would have to be incredibly accurate. Or just plain lucky. Besides, with the spike of an axe, you can pull them off their horses so they fall under the hooves of those riding behind them.'

'Ugh,' Beth screwed up her face. 'That sounds horrid.'

'Not half as horrid as being pulled off yourself. But more importantly, it's for throwing.'

'Like this?' Beth tried to lift the axe but found she needed both hands even to pull it along the ground.

The man laughed, 'See that old tree stump over there?' He

leaned forwards and picked up the axe.

Lenyé glanced across the dusty forecourt to where the park began. The stump was about the height of a man and a good thirty yards away.

'You're left-handed,' Beth was still watching the man in fascination. 'Like me.'

The man grinned. 'Not left handed. Just ambidextrous.'

'What does that mean?'

'I can use either hand as well as the other. When the warriors charge at an enemy line, they throw an axe with their left and follow up with a lance in their right. There isn't time to use one hand for both. We all have to learn how to use our left hands.' With that he stood up and, hardly pausing to take aim, threw the axe.

Lenyé watched it spin several times in the air before hearing the dull thud as it imbedded itself in the stump.

Beth was already running over to see and Lenyé chased after, holding the kite out so that its tail swooped and billowed behind her. She slowed down to make sure Beth got there first.

'I can't move it,' Beth turned as Lenyé caught up with her.

Lenyé put the kite down carefully on the ground and they both tried. But still it wouldn't budge.

The man strolled over and grasped the end of the haft. 'That would have spilt an enemy's shield from top to bottom and I would have got him with my lance on the follow through.' He jerked upwards and the axe came away easily in his hand.

'Does it hurt,' Beth looked up at the man with such a solemn expression on her face.

'Does what hurt?'

'When you dig that spike into another rider.'

'I'm sure it does. That's what it's designed to do.' The man obviously saw the tell-tale signs of distress in Beth's eyes, for he knelt down, dropped the axe on the ground, slipped one arm around her waist, touched her gently on the tip of her nose with his forefinger and said, 'I've got something for you.'

'Really?'

'Close your eyes and hold out your hand. Here,' he dug in his pocket, pulled out a stump of beeswax, placed it carefully on Beth's palm and closed her fingers round it. 'That's yours to keep.'

Oh Beth, Lenyé screwed up her eyes, as thoughts came tumbling into her mind: where are you now? What's happening to you? Why has Uncle Morthrir done this to us? If I discover he's treated you badly or done anything to you, I will never rest until he's brought to justice and made to pay for all this mess. But I'm going further away from you. I have to. You do understand that, don't you? I can't challenge him yet. I have to recover this Sword. Then I'll be strong. Then I'll come and find you and we can get our own back. Beth, you will be all right and wait, won't you? Don't do anything silly till I'm there to look after you. She knew she was overprotective towards Beth to make up for her real feelings. But she couldn't help herself.

Lenyé smacked the haft of the axe into her hand as if Uncle Morthrir was standing in front of her and the blow was intended for him. Then she smiled grimly. No. That wasn't the way. Anger and revenge? She would end up like her Uncle. Reluctantly she slid the axe back and fastened the buckle on its strap. It was too big to take with her, and she would hate to use such a vicious weapon against anyone, including her Uncle.

She untied the horse's tether from the picket and let it go. Poor thing. She could take it with her, but it would be useless on the rocky crags of a mountain. 'I only hope it escapes any wandering predators,' she muttered aloud, glancing at Ariella and giving the lioness a warning look.

Lenyé picked up her longbow and set off with Ariella to find a camp for the night.

Chapter Twenty Eight

'Look,' Beth pointed from their vantage point concealed amongst a clump of trees. 'There are more of them.'

'Ten,' Quinn finished counting the figures as the last one entered the clearing, carrying a lantern. 'All in the same brown cloaks and hoods.'

'Quinn. I feel really uneasy about this.' The night breeze touched Beth's face with chill fingers and she saw the leaves tossing in the surrounding trees; even the hoods and cloaks of the robed figures were bobbing and billowing. 'It looks really creepy.'

'But we have to know what's going on.' Quinn squeezed her hand. 'And we've got such a brilliant view from here.'

They watched as some of the figures built up a pile of stones into an altar to the left hand side of a massive oak tree, almost directly in front of their hiding place. Others were inserting large iron candleholders into the ground on the tree-side of the altar, while another figure came behind lighting long fat candles by holding the door of his lantern open and shoving the wick into the flame. He thrust each candle into a holder, the flame dancing and fluttering in the breeze. At last the candles were all in place.

Beth was distracted by the tenth figure as he rammed an iron stake into the ground, fitted a thin time-candle in its holder and then checked the position of the moon. She glanced up and knew from her camping experience that it was very close to midnight. She watched him thrust the metal cross-piece through the wax, light the candle from the lantern and slot the glass sleeve into place around it. Beth could see the flame was very close to the metal cross-piece. That would be about right: any minute now, the candle would burn down and release it, presumably to indicate midnight to the rest of the group.

'What's happening?' Beth pointed to the massive oak tree. All the branches and leaves were still moving in the breeze, but the hoods and cloaks of the robed figures hung motionless around their wearers. 'Look at the candles,' Beth clutched Quinn's arm. 'The flames have gone absolutely still. I don't like this. I want to go back.'

Quinn put his arm around her. 'We can't. They'd spot us if we move now.'

She shivered against the comforting warmth of his body. 'This is so weird.' Beth glanced back to the time-candle and saw the metal cross-piece fall away.

Immediately a figure emerged from the other side of the oak tree and walked right round to the front of the altar.

'Uncle Morthrir,' gasped Beth. 'What's he doing here?'

'I don't know,' Quinn whispered back. 'Don't move. If he sees us, we've had it.'

They watched as their Uncle knelt in front of the altar while the robed figures formed an arc on the other side.

A robed figure at the far end of the arc stepped forwards. 'You have summoned us to Druis-cyf-rin. We need proof of who you are and your authority to call this convocation and what it is you require to know from us.'

'I, Morthrir, Lord of Onadestra, Crown Prince of the Krêonor, hereby call you together and offer this token of proof.' He pulled the signet ring from his little finger and cast it upon the altar. 'This is my personal seal and guarantee of who I am.'

The robed figure picked it up and examined it, then passed it to his neighbour and so on up the line. The final figure tossed it back onto the altar. 'We see, and confirm you are who you claim to be.'

They saw their Uncle stand up and approach the altar. He retrieved the ring and slid it back on his finger, then pulled a garment from under his cloak and held it aloft.

'That's Kyros' dress uniform,' Quinn whispered in Beth's ear. 'I can see his coat of arms on the shoulder.'

Their Uncle laid the garment on the altar. 'I seek the whereabouts of my nephew, Kyros,' he paused as he smoothed out the creases. 'Find him for me, and tell me how I am to triumph over him.' He stepped back and folded his arms.

The ten figures came forwards and each laid a hand on the garment. One of them spoke: 'It is some time since he wore this. The connection is very faint.' They each held up their other hand towards Morthrir and began to chant. The spokesperson continued, 'We will put forth our combined will to try and...' Then with a cry they all leapt back from the altar, blowing on their hands as if they'd been burned. The figure spoke again, 'This man is covered by a greater power than ours. One which we dare not challenge. He has the greatest level of protection we have ever encountered.'

'So.' The children heard their Uncle's voice full of menace. 'Are you saying I have to go to your superiors, or that I cannot overcome him?'

'We are unable to call up the Four Summoners. They only appear at their Master's bidding. Only they can answer your questions.'

'Very well,' he gathered up the garment and tucked it back under his cloak. 'I have no personal effects for my second request, but I need to know the whereabouts of my eldest niece, Lenyé.'

The robed figure spoke again, 'We will have to perform certain rites to establish a connection in our minds. If you would kneel on your side of the altar with your palms together, that will complete the Ring of Maliché.'

The children watched as Uncle Morthrir knelt and placed his

palms together in front of him, while the robed figures reformed their arc on the other side of the altar. The figures began to chant before breaking into a slow shuffling dance, weaving in and out along the arc. The chanting rose to a crescendo, stopping abruptly on the climax.

Again the spokesperson stepped forwards. 'She is far away and surrounded by rocks.'

'That's not very helpful,' their Uncle's voice cut through the air like the crack of a whip. 'She could be anywhere. Can't you be more specific than that?'

'No, Sire. The rocks give off vibrations that interfere with her aura, and our combined thoughts cannot touch her.'

'By that argument you wouldn't be able to find anyone.'

'We are normally very successful, Sire. However, on this occasion it is beyond our arts to locate her.'

'So!' The children recognised the mounting anger in their Uncle's voice as he rose to his feet and shook his finger at the robed figures. 'You're nothing but a pack of charlatans, masquerading as Priests of the Hidden Power. I may not know your identities in the Waking World, but if I ever do discover who you are I will hunt you down and take my revenge upon you without mercy. I had intended to ask you to confirm the Hidden Power over me. For already I find it grows weaker the longer I am away from Mount Malkamet. But doubtless even that simple feat is beyond you.'

A voice interrupted him, not the previous spokesperson but the figure at the other end of the arc. 'You speak against things beyond your comprehension, and blaspheme against beings far superior than your own simple wit can even begin to imagine. We will perform this rite, not because you ask us, but because it is our duty to obey the Master. But beware: the consequences of what you seek are deadly serious and once you have fully entered in there is no going back.'

'Very well.'

Quinn watched intently as his Uncle sank to his knees and placed his hands together, while the robed figures reformed the arc and began their chant and dance. This time Quinn could hear the name Abbérron at the end of each phrase, and then the name was taken up and repeated over and over and over again. He could feel something begin to engulf him, like a huge hand squeezing the breath out of him. He tried to move but his legs were unwilling to obey him. The grip tightened till his chest hurt and it took a lifetime to gasp each precious breath into his lungs. Just as he felt he could endure it no more, there was a shout from the robed figures: 'You are the one. You are the one.' And they all pointed at his Uncle. All except the figure in the middle, who raised his arms straight out at shoulder height and brought his hands together, pointing directly over Uncle Morthrir's head. A bolt of power shot from the figure in a widening semi-circle expanding as it filled the clearing and emanating into the surrounding trees. Even though Quinn was squatting on his haunches he felt it like a physical blow to his chest and he staggered backwards, his mind whirling in a maelstrom of confused voices and bright bursts of light.

How long it lasted he couldn't say, but when he did come to, his Uncle was gone and the robed figures were busy snuffing out the candles and pulling up the candle holders and knocking over the altar and scattering the stones.

'Quick, Beth,' he whispered. 'We must get back before Rafé knows we've left the campsite.' He turned towards his cousin to grab her, and then froze. Beth wasn't there.

Chapter Twenty Nine

Lenyé sat in the cave mouth, with Ariella, drinking in the beauty of the landscape: the ethereal moonlight transforming the greys and browns, and bathing the rocks in a mystical sheen. She could see a huge mountain ahead, separated from the others and sweeping down to the plain below where she and Chuah-te-mok saw the galloping horses. Ariella agreed it was Mount Nastâri.

They talked over the events of the afternoon and Lenyé's journey to locate the Nastrim domain and find the Sword.

'They're giants, Ariella. You saved me from five men, but what can one lioness do against a mountain full of giants?'

'Don't worry. We'll think of something. That's why I'm here.'

'Thanks. I just wish it was all over, and I had the Sword in my hand and we could sort out my Uncle.'

'What happens after that?'

'I have to free my family and find Kyros.'

'The King's son?'

'Yes. He's my cousin. I miss him so; and my sister, Beth.'

'Where do you think Kyros is now?'

'I don't know. Yanantha said something about the spiral on the Eye of Hoffengrégor. But she wouldn't let me go out to the island. She said Kyros was beyond my help and I needed to concentrate on what only I can do.'

'I have a message for you from Yanantha.'

Lenyé whipped round to face the lioness, 'She's seen him?'

'Alas, no.'

Lenyé heard the slight growl before Ariella continued.

'She found traces of him on the island and signs of a struggle in the cave mouth at the centre. She tried again later, but the soldiers had set fire to the island and it was completely wasted. Nothing was left but ash and ruin and charred tree stumps.'

'He's dead.' Lenyé slumped back and buried her face in both hands. 'No one could live through that and escape unharmed.'

'If he made it that far, he must have gone down the spiral.'

'I will have to hold on to that and live in hope,' Lenyé raised her head and looked at Ariella. 'For I will not believe he is dead.'

'You're close to him, aren't you?'

'I'm in love with him,' she hesitated, her voice thick with emotion. 'We're pledged to be married.'

'You mean engaged?'

'No. It isn't official. Kyros tried to ask my Father's permission before we went to Lake Sanchéso, but Father and Mother had left for the Hunting Lodge and he missed them. He went ahead and proposed to me assuming he could ask my Father when he was back from holiday. Then we found out about Uncle Morthrir seizing power and both of our parents had disappeared.'

'You don't know where they are either?'

'They're dead,' Lenyé choked back a sob. 'I'm sure of it. I didn't realise before, but Uncle Morthrir is absolutely ruthless.' She rubbed her eyes with her knuckles. 'There's always been something funny between my Father and Uncle Dareth on one side of the family, and Uncle Morthrir on the other. Nothing was ever said in front of us youngsters, but there was always a cold atmosphere whenever he was around. He must have been planning to get his own back for years.'

Ariella nuzzled her face against Lenyé and waited till the sobbing died down. 'So Kyros asked you without your Father's permission.'

Lenyé swallowed before answering. 'He couldn't wait any longer. He said he'd burst if he didn't tell me of his love.'

'And you felt the same way?'

'It had been growing in me for some time. I didn't even have to think. It was just the right moment to say, "Yes".'

'But until your Father gives his consent, it can never become a proper engagement, can it?'

'How can he if he's dead? I don't know what happens now. Maybe we have to make up new rules for a situation like this. But I know one thing that won't change: Kyros will never break his word to me, or me to him.'

'And Beth?' Ariella looked at her.

Lenyé stiffened. 'Why do you ask?'

'You mentioned her earlier.'

'Ariella, I'm so confused. I'm trying to learn the lessons of an eagle and a lioness, but deep down inside I feel really hurt about Beth being the centre of attention and so good at music.'

'Surely your feelings aren't Beth's fault. Wouldn't it be easier to focus on the kind of person you are and the things you do well? Isn't that what Yanantha's sayings are trying to do.'

'I suppose so. But I still feel it deep inside.'

They fell silent and Lenyé wiped a sleeve across her eyes. Ariella's gentle probing brought all her hopes and fears to the surface and helped to release her feelings. She'd never felt quite so close to an animal before, not even Daivat, her horse back home. She put her arm around the lioness' shoulders and Ariella leaned against her. Lenyé could hear the great cat purring.

'What time do you think it is?' Lenyé broke the silence.

'It must be well after midnight.'

Lenyé glanced up at the moon, 'You're right. We loved using the moon to tell the time when we were camping as a family. It meant we could sit up late round the fire and listen to stories.'

'You ought to turn in and get some rest.'

'But I'm much too wide awake to sleep,' Lenyé stretched her arms above her head. 'And the moon is so beautiful tonight. It feels as though something significant is about to happen.'

'You feel it too?' Ariella moved her head to look into Lenyé's eyes. 'Good. You're becoming more like a lioness every moment.'

'What was that,' Lenyé was up on her haunches ready for action, and pointed. 'It came from over there.'

'I didn't hear anything.'

'It wasn't a noise. More an intense feeling of some kind of energy being released.' Lenyé stood up. 'You stay here, and I'll take a look. I could do with some exercise.'

'Take care,' Ariella lay down, stretching her paws out in front of her. 'Night-time is more filled with danger than the day.'

Lenyé slung the longbow over her shoulder, skirted the tumble of boulders below their cave and began climbing towards a large flat rock. That's where the energy came from.

The rocks were still warm to her hands from the heat of the day, but a chill wind had picked up and ruffled the stray strands of hair escaping from under her cap. She crouched down and leaned forwards to take her weight on her hands and arms as she straddled a small fissure in the rocks, when suddenly she was aware of a blur of tawny movement from her right. She thrust out her arm to protect herself, but something lithe and heavy hit her on the shoulder and bowled her onto her back.

With a twist of her hips she used the momentum to roll right over and end up on her haunches, her left hand under her shoulder for balance, her right hand instinctively going for the hilt of her dagger. She squatted, dagger poised to strike as she turned to face her assailant. 'Is that you, Ariella?'

But there was nothing there.

Lenyé slipped the longbow off her shoulder and laid it carefully on the ground, so it wouldn't impede her movements. Then she slunk down onto her forearm and slid the dagger into the tufts of grass that hid the top of the flat rock in front of her. As she parted the grasses and eased herself forwards to peer through them, she found herself staring straight into the eyes of a fully aroused cobra.

Chapter Thirty

Rafé was astonished. He found himself looking through the eyes of some creature, straight at Princess Lenyé. So the emanation he channelled had worked. He found her immediately.

But where exactly was she?

And what kind of creature was he using?

The answer to the second question was easier: a cobra.

He always acknowledged Lenyé's physical beauty and lively personality. But the eyes that stared back at him were filled with such a strong sense of intelligence that he recoiled in surprise.

She was much too good for Morthrir. If only Kyros had stated his intentions, but it was too late now. Morthrir had beaten Kyros to it. And Morthrir was relying on him to make it happen.

So where was Lenyé?

He tried to exert his will over the snake and force it to focus beyond the girl's face and give him some clues, but the snake resisted him and moved its head.

Suddenly the connection was broken, and Rafé couldn't even see Lenyé anymore.

He tried calling to the snake in his mind, but didn't even have a name to focus on.

Then his mind cleared and he was back at the convocation. One of the Priests was trying to placate an incandescent Morthrir and usher him away from the oak tree towards his horse, while the others hastily cleared everything away.

He shook his head and decided to try again later.

Chapter Thirty One

'What's wrong with him?' Kyros watched Hoffengrégor as he stooped over the inert figure lying on the tufty grass in the clearing amongst the trees. 'I thought he banged his head when he fell and was only unconscious, for I felt blood on his face.'

'That is true. We can tend those wounds quite easily. But,' the old Prophet stood up and turned to face Kyros, 'he has braved the spiral unbidden and has therefore broken the law of passing over from your Waking World to here. The Maljaros know that and will do all in their power to capture and destroy him.'

'Is that why they attacked our eyes?'

'They hate all creatures that see with the light of life. They tried to render you as they are: blind to the light of any world and consumed by darkness. But even they are only a faint shadow of the Dé-monos. You only felt those birds sucking the light out of this world. The Dé-monos are much worse. Do not look into their eyes, for they will suck the very life out of you.'

'Where do they live?'

'It is not so much a case of live: more one of waking death, the very absence of life as we know it. Where the Maljaros hover, the Dé-monos are never far behind. For they hunt together, and are bent on our destruction. Only the En-luchés, the Guardians of Light, can protect us from them.'

Kyros leaned further over the figure on the ground. 'What can we do for him?'

'Because he entered illegally, his life is forfeit. He remains forever cursed to wander in the Realm of Travail at the mercy of all the powers ranged against us. Make no mistake. If they capture him they have the right to sacrifice him.'

'Is there no hope for him?'

'None. Unless...' Hoffengrégor paused deep in thought.

'Unless?' Kyros prompted.

'The True King himself can pardon him.'

'How can that pardon be obtained?'

'If another human stands in his place and pleads his case.'

'It's that simple?'

'Simple. But very costly. Firstly, he must have the express permission from the True King to enter this Realm. And secondly, he must do it of his own free will.'

'Who is there in the Realm of Travail to do that?'

'Kyros,' the old Prophet turned on him and fixed him with his piercing gaze. 'You are the man.'

'How so?'

'You are the only one from the Waking World to enter the Realm of Travail, and who can yet return to your own world and take him with you. Do not doubt. You are here, not by accident, but by design. On you now rests the fate of the coming Restoration. The destiny of both yourself and this man are bound up together. If you fail here, you have failed completely.'

'But if he remains my enemy, what chance do I have?'

'Kyros. This man already serves a master. That is proof of his capacity for faithfulness. But we both know of Morthrir's treachery. Did I not say a man can only chose between two masters when he is shown a genuine alternative? He must see another master who displays the genuine virtues of wisdom, fidelity, mercy, forgiveness, justice, judgement and love. The very opposites of what your Uncle Morthrir stands for.'

'I can never be all those things? You make my task too hard.'

'Are you not a Prince of the Krêonor, and destined to become their King? You will be the most exalted King that has ever lived. But only if you choose to serve the True King.'

'How can I do that?'

'You can either establish a Kingdom for yourself, or become an Ambassador of the True King and usher in his Greater Kingdom in the Waking World. For that is the Restoration.'

Before Kyros could answer there was a crashing sound through the leaf canopy above them and five Maljaros burst through, knocking Kyros to the ground. One of them pulled the roll out of his pocket and flew off. The others seized Hoffengrégor by the shoulders of his garment. The old Prophet dropped his staff as a sixth Maljaros flew screaming straight at his face. The downdraft from their wings was like a tempest as they began to drag Hoffengrégor out of the clearing.

'In the name of the True King...' Kyros hesitated, for the words sounded strange to him. How could there be any power locked up in a name? Then he spoke with more conviction. 'Be gone, in the name of the True King.' The Maljaros flew away screaming, but to his horror he saw they were dragging Hoffengrégor with them.

'Help us, En-luchés,' cried the old Prophet. 'Kyros,' he yelled, as he disappeared amongst the trees, but his cry was cut short.

Kyros scrambled to his feet and slapped his pocket. 'The roll. Hoffengrégor, they've stolen the roll.' He was about to run to the old Prophet's aid, but as he looked up, there, standing directly in front of him was a dazzling figure: white light pouring from him, lighting up the whole glade.

'We meet at last, Kyros,' the voice was rich like flowing molten honey, allaying all his fears with its musical rhythm of running water. 'I am Vashtani and have come to conduct you to our citadel, where you will be protected against any further attack. Lift up your companion and follow me.'

The scuffling sounds of Hoffengrégor still struggling with the Maljaros grew fainter, but before they completely died away, the old Prophet's voice drifted back to his ears. 'Kyros. Beware the eyes of anyone who stands against you.'

Chapter Thirty Two

Morthrir kicked hard into the sides of his horse spurring him on faster. He was in such a rage at the failed outcome of the convocation that he only just managed to rein the horse in as a cloaked figure leaped out of the trees in front of him. The man pulled his hood back and Morthrir recognised Eawen.

'Master Henosite,' Morthrir's voice was sharp with anger. 'Explain to me what went wrong. Your Priests said Kyros was protected by a higher power that they couldn't challenge; and Lenyé was too far away and surrounded by rocks, so they couldn't find her.'

'Sometimes these meetings of the night do not always produce the desired result.'

'Then why didn't you warn me?' Morthrir banged his fist on the pommel of his saddle. 'What's all this about higher powers and being too far away? Surely rocks don't stop their combined thoughts from reaching their target?'

'You have to understand, Sire, that there are two spiritual powers eternally at war with one another in the spirit realm.'

'Which one is the more powerful?'

'The Lord Abbérron, of course.'

'I see,' Morthrir studied the other man's face. 'And how does he display his power?'

'He seeks to bring change through those who will rise up in his name to subdue the Waking World so it can be a better place for his servants to live in. He does this secretly, behind the scenes, never imposing himself on those who reject him, but always seeking converts to his noble cause. He will keep on working tirelessly until he gains the ascendency, and his great labour is carried forwards to completion by a rising tide of popular expectation of better things for everyone.'

Morthrir frowned. 'Am I right in thinking that anyone who desires to receive his power has nothing but the right motives?'

'Exactly, Sire. But there is another power, masquerading as the Supreme Authority in all Realms, and referred to by some misguided fools as the True King. That power seeks to prevent all these admirable goals and keep the peoples of this world subject to petty regulations on how to live.'

'Are you suggesting I take any notice of these regulations?'

'Oh no, Sire. You and I, and many others secretly strive to overthrow this tyranny, so we can hasten the great and awe-inspiring day of the coming of the Lord Abbérron himself. Then all rule and power will be turned over to him, and all people will finally be free to worship him and serve him alone.'

'If the Lord Abbérr...,' Morthrir stumbled over completing the name, '...is greater, why did the Priests refer to a *higher* power?'

'They probably meant they would need the additional power of the Four Summoners to support your request, Sire.'

'Their exact words were: "*This man is covered by a greater power than ours. One which we dare not challenge. He has the greatest level of protection we have ever encountered*".'

'I can understand your dilemma, Sire,' the Henosite gestured with his hand.

'And what about this rock penetration nonsense for Lenyé?'

'It might be due to the same cause.'

'Really? So the convocation was a complete waste of time.'

'On the contrary, Sire. It has helped identify what you are up against.'

'Hmmph,' Morthrir slumped back in his saddle. 'I really don't care about powers in the so-called spirit realm fighting it out. I just want answers here and now.'

'Will that be all, your Majesty?'

'No. When I asked them to confirm the Hidden Power over me, so that I could use that power in this present crisis, nothing happened. Their collective power seemed to be diverted by one of the Priests for his own ends. The power that came from him completely missed me.'

'In that case, I would suggest these three issues will take the direct intervention of the Lord Abbérron himself to resolve.'

'And just how do you propose to arrange that?' Morthrir sneered at the man. 'As I understand it, you cannot even call up the Four Summoners, let alone the Lord himself.'

'You are correct, your Majesty. But I can set up a Grand Convocation for one of the more auspicious dates in the year. Your requests are certainly of significant enough import to arouse the interest of all the chief participants.'

Morthrir sat staring at the man.

'It should be when night is at its shortest,' the Henosite continued, 'so that anything transacted at midnight is condensed into as brief a time as possible, and therefore more power can be released. And it should be when fertility is being celebrated as you are looking for new power to be conferred afresh on you. That's right, isn't it?'

Morthrir studied the man's face, 'Correct.'

'Then the next major opportunity will be in thirteen days time: midnight at the Summer Solstice.'

Chapter Thirty Three

Lenyé felt a movement of air as she leaned against the flat rock.

'Don't move,' there was a hint of a growl from behind her.

Lenyé froze. What do I do? That cobra looks at least eight feet long. I daren't move. But if that's not Ariella behind me.

'Why?' The hiss from the snake was unmistakable.

Lenyé blinked in surprise.

'Why are you so frightened of me?'

'I thought that...'

'I'll do the talking.' Lenyé recognised Ariella's growl. She could now pinpoint the source of it slightly to her right.

'Keep absolutely still,' Ariella continued.

Lenyé glanced sideways and glimpsed the outline of the lioness crouching low and slinking further to her right.

The cobra twitched its head away from Lenyé and swayed to and fro as if testing the air for a new adversary. Then it turned back to Lenyé and stared straight at her.

Lenyé felt mesmerised by those eyes. It was as if someone else was using them to stare fixedly at her.

Suddenly the snake moved its head and broke the spell. 'You still haven't answered my question.'

'I've always thought that snakes,' she hesitated.

'Struck first and asked questions afterwards?'

'Yes.'

There was a series of hisses, as though the cobra was laughing at her. 'But I, Ra-Na-Jiri, have done nothing to frighten you.'

'Then why the raised head and flared hood?'

'Something disturbed me on the other side of the rock.'

Lenyé was fascinated by the cobra. He was only a few inches away from her. She just gazed at him in awe: those intense eyes, in his pale creamy, scaly face; and that forked tongue, forever flicking in and out as though he was sniffing at her. And the perfect curves of the flared hood with its intricate pattern of dark markings against his paler colouring. She'd never been this close to a snake before and thought he was the most beautiful creature she had ever seen. She was just reaching out her hand to touch him when a movement away to her right distracted her.

She glanced sideways as Ariella appeared over the top of the rock. Lenyé could see the bunched muscles of the shoulders behind the lowered head as the great cat prepared to spring.

'Wait,' Lenyé's whisper was hoarse, but it was enough to stop the lioness. 'This is Ra-Na-Jiri and he's a friend.'

Lenyé was relieved to see the muscles relax, as Ariella slunk warily onto the top of the rock and approach the snake.

'A friend?' This time the growl was more like a purr.

Ra-Na-Jiri lowered his head, the hood deflated and he moved towards Ariella. Suddenly he reared up, with his hood flared, but this time the cobra was facing away from Lenyé. She gasped at the beautiful pattern on the back of Ra-Na-Jiri's hood, and the curious markings like a pair of eyes. Ariella also whipped round, crouching for a spring, her haunches taut with anticipation and her tail lashing almost in Lenyé's face.

Ra-Na-Jiri struck at the far edge of the rock. Ariella followed up with blinding speed and sprang past the cobra.

Lenyé sensed the tension of the other two, grabbed her longbow, whipped an arrow from her quiver and notched it on the bowstring.

There was a shout and two men dressed as warriors broke cover, running off and splitting from each other so that the chasing lioness was momentarily confused.

'Whew,' Lenyé let out her breath. The men raced down a

gully, with the lioness chasing after them and roaring. 'That was close.'

'Told you,' Ra-Na-Jiri slid back across the rock and faced Lenyé again, his hood now totally deflated and his head seeming quite small in comparison.

Ariella climbed back onto the rock and lay down on her side, panting. She glanced over to Ra-Na-Jiri then patted at him.

Instantly the cobra rose up in an attacking stance, hood fully inflated, and accused Ariella of not guarding Lenyé properly. The lioness thrust herself up on her haunches growling.

'One bite from me,' Ra-Na-Jiri hissed, 'and you would keel over and die a very painful death. You do realise we're talking about a creeping paralysis that eventually leads to suffocation as you can no longer breathe.'

'One swipe of my claws and your precious hood would be in taters. Don't forget, my reactions are much faster than yours.'

Lenyé dropped her longbow and arrow and seized the lioness by the scruff of the neck. 'Stop it.'

But Ariella wrenched herself away and crouched down, the muscles in her haunches flexing for the spring.

Ra-Na-Jiri swayed to and fro, his tongue flicking in and out.

Lenyé sat down on the edge of the rock, grabbed Ariella's head and began stroking her. 'Can we stop arguing, please? If you've both been sent to help me, at least agree to be friends. And if those men are still around, we need to be moving on.'

'Well said,' Ra-Na-Jiri hissed at the lioness and settled down in his coils.

Ariella's low growl changed to a purr as Lenyé's gentle stroking began to have effect. Then she sat up and looked at the cobra. 'How do we know you've been sent to help? If that's why you're here, you must have been given some special words from Yanantha.'

'Words. What words?' Ra-Na-Jiri's head was up, and the hood partly inflated.

'They're supposed to lead Lenyé to her goal.'

'That's right,' Lenyé interrupted. 'I had to flee from Yanantha before she could tell me everything I needed to know. She's been sending me messages so I can catch up. The birds of Sorentina brought me words of how to be like an eagle. When I learned that lesson, Chuah-te-mok told me how to be like a lioness. You say you've got more words for me?'

'After you,' Ariella growled at the cobra.

'Let's hear yours first,' Ra-Na-Jiri hissed. 'Unless you've forgotten them.'

'I haven't forgotten them,' Ariella growled. 'But my words are for Lenyé's ears only.'

'You haven't got any.'

'Yes I have.'

Lenyé frowned at them both. 'I don't know why you keep arguing.'

The lioness sighed. 'All right. Are you ready for this?'

Lenyé nodded. She repositioned her longbow to lean against the rock, slotted the arrow back into her quiver, and pulled the writing things out of her satchel; the early morning sun just giving her enough light to see what she was doing.

Ariella continued:

> 'If for waiting, be a she-bear
> Incubate from death to life
> Guard your offspring, guard them fiercely
> Use your power, rich in mercy.'

Lenyé finished writing and left the parchment flat on the rock for the ink to dry while she put the writing things back in her satchel.

'A she-bear?' Ra-Na-Jiri settled down into his coils again. 'I just hope she doesn't come lumbering along to join the party right now.'

'And why not?' Ariella yawned, showing her fangs. 'It's not

up to you who Yanantha chooses to help Lenyé.'

'Stop it, you two.' Lenyé cast a handful of sand across the parchment to dry off the last of the ink, rolled it up and stashed it in her satchel. 'I've never heard so much bickering in all my life.' She glanced up at the sound of birdsong greeting the dawn. 'It's morning already. You two have argued the night away.'

She grabbed the longbow and was just about to stand up. 'What was that?' She spun round and faced back down the mountainside, then vaulted over the flat rock and ducked down the other side for cover.

She peered round the edge in time to see two lines of soldiers hurrying into place on the rocks below her. The nearest line was kneeling, bows in hand, arrows notched; but the bows were pointing to the ground and the bowstrings were not pulled back yet. The row behind was standing, bows raised and ready for action. Lenyé had seen the *offset-box formation* before. The back line loosed their arrows, walked through the front line, knelt and re-notched, while the other line stood and loosed. They could move forwards quite quickly, and the tactic was deadly. But she'd only ever seen it done with longbows before. These were the small bows all the warriors used while on horseback. She smiled grimly to herself: they would be in range of her longbow well before their arrows could even reach her.

A man stepped forwards and raised his voice. 'Princess Lenyé, we are here to escort you back to the King in peace. Anyone who takes up arms, or fights on your behalf will be killed by my soldiers. There is no escape. It will go well for you if you come quietly.'

139

Chapter Thirty Four

Vashtani, the leader of the cohort, leaped lightly into the saddle and took the reins from his attendant. Kyros stood watching, somewhat bemused by the size of the steeds. He eyed the creature selected for him, and wondered whether the tiny wings between each fetlock and hoof served any purpose, other than to act as a fan and keep the animal's legs cool when it was galloping. Kyros climbed onto a rock, thrust his foot in the stirrup and swung himself up into the saddle. He leaned forwards and down to take the unconscious Harbona from another attendant, and lifted the man to his saddle-bow.

Then the whole entourage was moving, the horses' hooves slipping and grinding on loose stones as they picked their way down the slope through the forest. They gathered pace amongst the thinning trees, till at last they thundered out of the cover of the forest and were pounding down the remains of the hillside to meet the plain that lay stretched out before them.

Kyros found himself at Vashtani's side. 'Should we not try and find Hoffengrégor and rescue him?'

His companion threw back his head and roared with laughter. 'Rescue Hoffengrégor? Don't be absurd. He's more than a match for those Maljaros.'

'But he was very alarmed at their numbers and seemed concerned to get away from them till help could arrive.'

'Don't worry. He'll be free of them by now and heading back to his dwelling. His time of service to you is over. It's your companion I'm more concerned about. For we are few and

140

cannot repel a concerted attack out here in the open. We must hurry to our fortress in the mountains beyond that nearest ridge if we are to get him beyond the reach of our enemies.'

Kyros heard the note in the horses hooves change as the ground began to level off and give way to coarse sand, but the expected thudding from fast galloping never came. Instead there was total silence, except for the creak and jingle of harness. He looked down to see the legs of each horse locked as though in full gallop, but the hooves didn't touch the ground: the power came from the tiny wings which beat so fast they were a blur. He was astonished at the rapid approach of the distant ridge of rock: their speed over the plain was far greater than any horse in the Waking World could ever achieve.

Just then six detachments of Maljaros flew overhead chattering. Vashtani skewed round in his saddle and barked commands to the rest of his cohort in a language Kyros couldn't follow. Then he raised his hand palm outwards to the densely packed black shapes above them. Standing up in his stirrups, he cried out with a loud voice, and, with a great screeching sound, the Maljaros broke formation, circling and wheeling above them in disarray before breaking off and flying away fast in an southerly direction.

Vashtani called out to his second in command, 'I will not have those troublesome birds fly so close in future. Make sure they do not return within range.'

His officer saluted, and looked away, but Kyros caught a fleeting glimpse of a wry smile playing at his lips.

Vashtani turned back to Kyros. 'Please forgive that momentary interruption. As you can see, they appear terrifying, but have no real power.'

'Do you have any control over them at all?' Kyros felt relieved the Maljaros were dealt with so easily.

'In a manner of speaking, yes. Why do you ask?'

'It's just that one of them stole a roll which Hoffengrégor gave me. I thought you might be able to get it back.'

'Did they? How interesting. I can certainly try.' Vashtani turned to his second in command and issued another order.

This time Kyros noticed a distinct smirk on the officer's lips, and felt a cold shiver run through him. If these were the Guardians of Light that Hoffengrégor spoke of, why was this one laughing at him behind his back? Oh, True King, he whispered to himself. If ever I need your wisdom to help me, it is now.

Vashtani turned back to him, 'I think we can safely say that will definitely be followed up and the roll recovered.'

Kyros was about to reply, but then noticed, as if for the first time, that whenever Vashtani spoke to him, he would never look Kyros in the eye. He cast his mind back over that encounter in the clearing, his comments about the Maljaros being no match for Hoffengrégor, and the conversations since. Had Vashtani ever looked him in the eye? He wasn't sure. But if not, then why not? Hoffengrégor's last warning troubled him.

Who exactly were Vashtani and the rest of his cohort? Far from being rescuers, they could be enemies. But then surely enemies would be recognisable as such. Vashtani himself, at their first meeting, shone with such a bright light. That light was veiled now, as though Vashtani wanted to remain hidden from watching eyes as they journeyed. But it was still there: reassuringly there. And Vashtani said he had come in answer to his call; and that was when he used the name of the True King. Surely these were the En-luchés? They couldn't be anything else, could they?

But the doubts kept nagging at his mind and a strange foreboding came over him.

Chapter Thirty Five

'Want me to slither down and bite the soldier with the big voice?' Ra-Na-Jiri was already beside Lenyé in a tight coil, his head raised as if peering over the rock.

'Don't be ridiculous,' Ariella slunk round the rock and came up behind them, growling in anger. 'There are far too many men to take out like that.'

'Why can't he?' Lenyé was fumbling to pull an arrow out of her quiver. 'Ra-Na-Jiri. You get down there and distract them. They've got bows and arrows in their hands and can't get their swords out easily, so you won't have any weapons to fear. Ariella, you slink through that gully and take them from the side.' She glanced up and saw a black speck hovering in the sky above her. Lenyé grinned to herself in anticipation: they won't know what's hit them.

The man shouted out again. I'm going to count to three, Princess Lenyé, and if you haven't come out of cover by then, I'm going to order my men to loose their first volley of arrows.'

Lenyé knew she had to delay things while the others found their places. 'What guarantee do you give me that you will treat me well?'

'I am responsible for this section of Captain Elskin's company.'

'Where is Captain Elskin? It seems I need to talk to him.'

'He is elsewhere with the rest of his man. You'll have to talk to me. I give you my word, as an officer of the King, that we will treat you well.'

'As far as I'm concerned, you're serving the wrong King. So I don't believe you. You've been chasing me for five weeks now. I call that an act of aggression.'

'I'm only following orders.' The man broke off, jumping back as if startled by something.

Lenyé notched the arrow on her bowstring, chuckling to herself. Ra-Na-Jiri must be down there already and surprising the soldiers. She watched in amusement as the archers in the front row sprang to their feet, jumping backwards and colliding with the row behind them, throwing them into confusion; some even loosing arrows wildly into the air as their fingers slipped off their bowstrings.

With a roar, Ariella was on them from the side, the momentum of her charge bowling several of the men over. Then she was up on her haunches, her powerful front paws knocking men down. Then she sprang at a knot of soldiers and chased them across the rocks as they fled in terror.

But the officer kept his head, and rounded up a handful of men. They charged up the hill, stopping every now and then to aim their small bows and loose their arrows. They still weren't properly in range, and their arrows fell short by several yards.

Lenyé settled in a crouching position with the small of her back against a rock; she wanted as much support from the flex of the longbow as possible once she loosed the arrow. She held the longbow sideways as she'd done on the scree slope, but this time eased the power of her left shoulder and the weight of her body into the bow as she drew back the bowstring to the full extent of the arrow, her hand just brushing the lobe of her right ear as she cocked her head to one side and squinted along the length of the shaft. Her face was set and grim: she'd never loosed an arrow at men before in her life. The soldiers came charging up the rocks towards her. She waited until they cleared a jumble of boulders and there was nothing in the way of her target.

There was the characteristic whizz as she loosed the arrow

and the man at the front went down as though he'd been hit by a charging buffalo. She had to thrust the awful sight from her mind, but her hand trembled on the handle of the longbow, as she began to draw the next arrow. *Them or me, them or me,* she repeated over and over to herself. It became a desperate round of draw and loose, draw and loose, as quickly as she could, before the startled soldiers realised what happened to their comrade and could take shelter from her powerful longbow. That, at least, drove the terrible thoughts from her mind and gave her something to focus on. Already several archers further down had regrouped away from the lioness and the cobra and had the *offset-box formation* working properly. They were loosing arrows over the heads of the charging troops, and were beginning to find the range.

She caught a familiar sight out of the corner of her eye as the black speck overhead dropped out of the sky. Chuah-te-mok came out of his dive and spread his wings to fly underneath the arc of the soldiers' arrows. Then he was in amongst them, his talons extended and his fearsome curved beak attacking the eyes of the troops.

With a roar, Ariella fell on their scattered ranks from the rear, and Ra-Na-Jiri was clearly still at work amongst them as several soldiers kept jumping back unexpectedly.

Lenyé felled her last man, and darted over to a rock further down. Then she was loosing arrows into the *offset-box formation* with deadly effect, bringing them down as quickly as she could, moving from rock to rock to confuse her enemies. She was just notching her last arrow, when a roar of triumph went up from Ariella. Every man was accounted for and the battle was over. Lenyé stood up to survey the scene of devastation below her. The four of them had wiped out an entire troop of some twenty-five soldiers, all of them hardened warriors.

She glanced up at the sun and realised it was well past midday. Her eyes were drawn to Chuah-te-mok and she watched him circling over the battleground. A movement on the ground distracted her, and she saw Ra-Na-Jiri's head go down as the cobra began slithering back up the slope with Ariella padding behind her.

Lenyé felt all the tension of the battle drain away and her legs began to tremble, before she collapsed onto her knees and sank down at the side of the rock, dropping her longbow and curling herself into a ball, her whole body shaking like a leaf. She was sobbing uncontrollably, her mind suddenly in shock as all the thoughts came flooding back in over killing her first man.

Ariella came bounding up the slope, still roaring in triumph; and then stopped. She nuzzled her face into Lenyé's side, trying to open out the tight ball. 'It's all right, Lenyé,' she purred. 'You've just won a great victory. You're a true lioness now.'

But Lenyé continued shaking as Chuah-te-mok settled on a nearby rock and cocked his head in alarm, while Ra-Na-Jiri slithered up the rock face to join Ariella.

The lioness nuzzled her again, then spun round, snarling as a great shadow loomed over Lenyé's shuddering body.

Chapter Thirty Six

The day after he arrived back from the convocation Morthrir sat at his desk in the private council chamber.

He slammed his fist amongst the ink phial and the box of sand. *Why does this power keep on eluding me?*

Firstly, they couldn't find Kyros. Some nonsense about a higher power protecting him! What power? Surely Abbérr...? Even now he was unable to fully form that name in his mind.

Secondly, they couldn't find Lenyé. Said she was far away and surrounded by rocks. As if that should limit their powers. All that rubbish about rock vibrations interfering with her aura. They're incompetent. If they were my ministers, I'd have them executed by now.

Then when they came to confirm the Hidden Power over me, they worked themselves up into such a frenzy, but at the vital moment when they all pointed at me, nothing happened. All except the Priest in the middle. He didn't point to me at all. Maybe he redirected all the power of the convocation away from me onto something else, or used it for his own purposes.

What's going on?

There was a knock at the door.

'Go away.'

The door burst open and Youdlh thrust himself into the room in great excitement. He marched straight up to the desk not even waiting for the guard to close the door behind him.

Morthrir didn't look up. 'I said go away. That includes you.'

'But Sire. I have word from Captain Elskin.'

Morthrir raised his eyes and scowled. 'Have they found her?'

'They've sighted her in the forests, heading North.'

'North. Why would she head in that direction? Surely she would head East and come to Terrazarema and try to rescue her siblings and cousins.'

'That's the assumption we've been working on up till now, but it hasn't produced any results. This is a definite sighting.'

'Doesn't prove anything. She may be trying to mislead us.'

'But why would she head North, Sire? There's only rocks and mountains and...'

'Rocks and mountains?' Morthrir was up from his desk and over to the map on its stand. He traced a line from Lake Sanchéso. 'Not quite due North, but near enough.'

'What is it?'

'Mount Nastâri, home of the Nastrim.'

'I don't understand.'

'Surely you've heard of the giants. Some of the bitterest foes of the ancient Krêonor. Even your warriors would be hard pressed in a conflict with them. They're deadly in close combat.'

'So you think she's heading North to enlist them against us?'

Morthrir laughed. 'Don't be ridiculous. Get more men up there and head her off. Put Elskin in charge. Don't let her even make contact with them. If she does, you're in deep trouble.'

Chapter Thirty Seven

'Allow me.' The huge shape stooped over Lenyé and picked her up as though she weighed no more than a feather. 'You three may be great at winning battles, but not so clever at restoring those wounded in spirit.'

Lenyé felt herself cradled in the softest fur she had ever known, and heard soothing words in her ear.

'It's all right,' the voice was deep but very reassuring. 'You can tell old Mamma Uza-Mâté your troubles.'

Lenyé opened her eyes and gasped. She was looking into the furriest face of the largest female bear she'd ever seen, with warm brown eyes that were so dark they were almost black.

Lenyé was still doubled up, as if in pain, but managed to get some words out through her sobs, 'It's just that… I've never killed a man before. Well, several men, but the first was the worst.'

'It's all right. Take your time. You need to let it all come out.'

'He…, he…, he just collapsed,' Lenyé sobbed again. 'As though all the life went out of him in an instant. Like a candle blown out by the wind. One minute he was running up the rock face. Next minute he was flung back as though… as though he'd run into a stone wall. And it was my hand that did it.'

'I can't help what you've done. But sometimes we have to do things that afterwards, if we thought about them, would drive us crazy. I remember my first litter, and a hunter got between me and my cubs. And suddenly I went berserk. I punched that man so hard, he was dead before he hit the ground.'

But you had a proper excuse: you were protecting your cubs. Every Mother has the right to...'

'You don't understand. If it's bad for *you* to kill a man, it's far worse for *us creatures*. To us, all humans are Royal. And to take their life in anger...,' She let her voice trail away. 'It's like a curse on us.'

'But we can't help how the world is,' Lenyé persisted. 'Everyone has an enemy of some sort.'

'Ah. But it wasn't always like that. We creatures remember, even if you humans have forgotten.'

'Remember what?' Lenyé sat up, wiped her eyes with her sleeve, and instinctively put her arms around Mamma Uza-Mâté's neck to steady herself.

Humans and creatures originally dwelt together in peace and harmony. That was before the great Breaking-in.'

'Breaking-in?' Lenyé sounded puzzled.

'There was a time when the Dé-monos broke into this world from their existence in the spirit realm.

'Who are the Dé-monos?'

'They come from another Realm altogether and appear like men, only bigger,' Mamma Uza-Mâté paused and looked Lenyé in the face. 'They have tremendous power and can clothe themselves in light, and so deceive the unwary. But they have always taken what is not rightfully theirs.'

'What happened when they did break into this world?'

'They were captivated by the beauty of the daughters of men and took some of them to be their wives, and had children by them. Their offspring were enormous: nearly twice the height of an ordinary man, with six fingers and toes on each hand and foot.'

Lenyé frowned. 'How did that change things between humans and creatures?'

'The Dé-monos brought a curse into this world. It took the intervention of the True King himself to expel them and seal up the entry point. But their offspring remained. The Krêonor were commanded by the True King to despatch them from the Waking World.'

'Wait a minute,' Lenyé tilted her head to one side as she thought this through. 'You must be talking about the Nastrim.'

'That's right. They carry the taint of the Dé-monos. They cannot be killed by ordinary weapons: only the Sword of Justice has power over them.'

'What's that?'

'It's the very Sword you're looking for. It was given to the Krêonor by the True King.' Mamma Uza-Mâté went quiet for a minute or two as if thinking, before continuing. 'It's his Sword. Don't you understand? Justice is locked up in that Sword, not for this world only. The Waking World is the proving ground of Justice for the entire Universe.'

'So why did it go missing?'

'Some of the Krêonor became corrupted by the Dé-monos before the entry point was sealed. They wanted to know how to get hold of and use the power of the Dé-monos for themselves. In exchange, the Dé-monos demanded that the Sword was to be delivered into their keeping: then they could escape the judgement the Sword would inflict on them. That led to the big war and the downfall of the Krêonor civilisation, and the death of Zerigor, fighting to put the Sword beyond their reach. That was his fatal error: using the Sword as a weapon of war.'

'But it still doesn't explain how the Sword went missing.'

Mamma Uza-Mâté looked around and lowered her voice as though she didn't want anyone else to hear. 'The Sword was snatched from Zerigor's hand. Then Hoffengrégor spoke the words of the Restoration. He held the Orb and Sceptre out of reach of the Dé-monos for as long as possible: the two emblems of Kingly rule saved from the wreck of the island of Bara-mâla and committed to his care. Rather than let them fall into the wrong hands, he threw the Sceptre of Authority to the East

151

where it remains buried in the ground to this day. Some say a great tree sprung up to protect it. And he flung the golden Orb of Universal Rulership far into the North where it smote the mountains and made most of the landscape collapse to form the hanging lakes, of which Lake Sanchéso is the greatest. Some say another mountain grew up over the Orb to hide it. Hoffengrégor fell away down a long spiral in the rock that leads to the Realm of the Departed, or so we are given to understand. But effectively, the Sword was lost, and no human has set eyes on it since.'

Lenyé shifted slightly in the she-bear's arms. 'Yanantha heard a rumour about one of the Nastrim with a sacred sword strapped across his back and protruding above his shoulder.'

'Maybe that's true.'

'She thinks it's the missing Sword.'

'But it won't do him any good.'

'Why not?'

'Hoffengrégor spoke over it and decreed that no man could ever draw that Sword again because Zerigor used it as a weapon of war.'

'But are the Nastrim really men?' Lenyé persisted.

Mamma Uza-Mâté looked long and steadily at Lenyé before answering. 'You know, you might just be right there. After all, they're partly of the seed of women, and partly of the seed of the Dé-monos from the spirit realm.'

'And do the Nastrim still have any contact with the Dé-monos?'

'No. The entry point was too well sealed. If the Dé-monos find another route into our world, then, who knows?'

Lenyé went quiet for a moment, thinking over what Mamma Uza-Mâté said. Not even Yanantha had hinted at any of this. Maybe it was going to come later, by the birds of Sorentina. Or maybe the creatures really did remember when all others had forgotten. She frowned as she looked up into Mamma

Uza-Mâté's eyes. 'And finding the Sword is going to restore all that's been lost?'

'I can't say for certain. But it's a start.'

'Yanantha thinks I'm the one spoken of to do that.'

'There you are. You also have something as precious as children to guard.'

Lenyé stared at Mamma Uza-Mâté with a puzzled expression on her face as the she-bear continued.

'Those soldiers stood between you and your baby.'

'My baby?'

'Yes,' Mamma Uza-Mâté sounded excited. 'You have to enter the womb of all beginnings, and incubate the outcome of your quest in your inner being. That is bringing your deepest desire to birth. We bears do that in winter. It's not lost time, but preparation. Then we emerge into the bright light of the spring world. That's what you need to do. You may have a time of waiting and preparation to go through, but when you do emerge, nothing can stop you. Not even your Uncle Morthrir's soldiers.'

'But I still feel so bad about killing them.'

'Like you said. If someone comes between me and my cubs, or you and your baby, then they're asking for trouble. No one can deter you from your quest.'

'I've never seen it like that before.'

'Listen. The task of finding the Sword and bringing about the Restoration has been laid on you. Do that, and we'll make a she-bear out of you yet.'

'Will I have to kill anyone else before all this is over?'

The she-bear sighed. 'Not even Mamma Uza-Mâté can tell you that.'

Chapter Thirty Eight

Quinn was in a panic. 'Beth,' he whispered, his voice hoarse with emotion. 'Where are you?'

There was no answer. He felt his way back through the undergrowth towards the path and stumbled over her body.

'Beth.' He knelt down beside her and ran his hand down her arm. 'Beth. Whatever's the matter?'

He grabbed her by the shoulder, but her body felt as rigid as a board when he tried to move her. He stroked the hair out of her face and shrank back in horror: there was just enough moonlight in amongst the trees for him to see her eyes wide open and staring fixedly. He leaned over her again. 'Beth. Wake up. It's all right, they've finished. It's all over.' He smoothed her brow and then tried slapping her cheek very gently, but nothing happened.

'I've got to get you out of here. They might find us.'

He tried rolling her from side to side. 'Beth, please wake up. We have to get back to camp before Rafé.'

Still no response.

He slid his hands under her shoulders and the backs of her knees and lurched to his feet. 'Come on. I must get you back.'

He half staggered, half ran down the path, clutching her to his chest; still calling her name and trying to rouse her. He found himself sobbing: 'This is all my fault… if I'd listened to her… she didn't want to stay… if only we'd come away when she said, she would be all right now… and we still don't know if Rafé's mixed up in all this…it's all my fault.' He broke through the undergrowth and out of the trees into their camp site, bundled her over to the remains of their fire, and laid Beth on a blanket and covered her with his.

She was moaning now, 'Lenyé…danger…snake…'

'Where's Rafé?' Quinn was talking to himself in desperation as he glanced wildly round, but there was no sign of him. 'Whew. At least he doesn't know we've been gone.'

He tried patting her face and rubbing her arms but she continued moaning: her eyes unblinking and still staring.

'What am I going to do?' he muttered to the silent campsite. 'I can't leave her like this to go and find Rafé. Where is he?' He was about to slap her face again, but was distracted by a movement under the trees where he had broken out of the undergrowth.

'Rafé,' he shouted as he raced across and grabbed him by the arm. 'Something's wrong with Beth. I tried to find you, but thought you must have gone for a walk in the woods.'

Rafé caught him by the wrist and prevented him from running back to Beth. 'How long has she been like this?'

'I don't know. Not long. I've only just woken up and found her. You must come.'

'I thought I heard a noise in the woods earlier and went to investigate.' Rafé wasn't in any kind of hurry. 'You didn't see anything did you?'

Quinn hesitated. 'No.'

'Good. I'll take a look.'

Quinn raced over to her and looked round for Rafé but was surprised to see the man stop by his own bedroll first and slip his bag under the blanket. What's he doing? Quinn muttered to himself. He must know this is an emergency?

Chapter Thirty Nine

Lenyé looked over Mamma Uza-Mâté's shoulder and was startled to see how far away from the others they had wandered while they were so engrossed in their conversation.

'Hey. We need to get back. Put me down. I think I can walk again.' Lenyé stroked the rich fur on the she-bear's neck. 'And thank you. I feel completely at peace inside now.'

Mamma Uza-Mâté's deep booming laugh caught Lenyé by surprise. 'I'm so glad. I was beginning to think we had another casualty of the battle when I showed up. Tell you what. Why don't you climb up on my shoulders, and I'll run you down to the others?'

Mamma Uza-Mâté raced down the slope, while Lenyé held onto each forepaw and bounced up and down on the massive shoulders, laughing from sheer pleasure. The she-bear came to an abrupt stop in front of the others, lifted Lenyé effortlessly into the air, and placed her gently on the ground. 'One restored Princess,' Mamma Uza-Mâté chuckled. 'Returned to lead her great army,'

Ariella growled, 'Took you long enough. We've got other things to be getting on with, rather than hanging around here while you two have some private joke.'

'Like what?' Mamma Uza-Mâté stood there, arms akimbo and bent over slightly to look the lioness directly in the eyes.

'I've got cubs that need me, Chuah-te-mok has his eyrie to go to and Ra-Na-Jiri has a nest somewhere he needs to get back to.'

'And you're saying I'm too old and past it to be interested in a litter this year?'

'No,' there was a note of a growl in Ariella's voice. 'I didn't mean that.'

'Well let's all be absolutely clear. This is the biggest thing any of us has ever been involved in. We bears don't forget as easily some others,' she scowled at Ariella. 'I feel it in my bones every day: a deep longing for the Restoration. Do you know what that means? No more watching your back. No more enemies. When all creatures are friends again, and we live in perfect harmony with the whole of mankind. If that isn't worth giving up one season of rearing young to achieve, I don't know what is.'

'No one told me that was what we were trying to do,' there was a plaintive note in Ariella's growl.

'The she-bear's right, you know.' Chuah-te-mok finished preening his feathers and turned his bright eyes on them all. 'I sensed the importance of what Lenyé is doing when I was circling above the mountains, before the battle. We have to see this through.'

'And you?' Mamma Uza-Mâté fixed her gaze on Ra-Na-Jiri.

'All this knowledge is too wonderful for me. But this I can say. I'm for Princess Lenyé. Wherever she tells me to go and whatever she tells me to do, I'm going to do it. So count me in.'

'You two as well?'

Chuah-te-mok and Ariella both nodded.

Mamma Uza-Mâté turned to Lenyé. 'Then command us.'

'First we must attend to the dead.' Lenyé glanced over the scattered remains of the soldiers and then turned back to the others. 'I cannot leave them lying here. Help me gather their bodies together and cover them with stones.'

She walked down amongst the men who fell to her arrows, and, as a mark of respect, went to the one she brought down first. She knelt beside him and tried to pull the arrow out of his chest, but it was embedded too deeply, so she broke off the protruding shaft and threw it away. She did the same for the

157

others. Between them they heaved the bodies into a group and covered them with a pile of stones. While the others gathered up the discarded weapons and debris of war into a pile, Lenyé replenished her quiver with spent arrows, and filled three more quivers to sling over her shoulder for spares.

It took them the rest of the afternoon. Dusk was already falling as they stood around the mass grave. Lenyé held up her right hand and spoke over the dead: 'Here let these fallen remain in peace, and may this be the beginning of the end of all enmity between the Peoples and Creatures of this world. So let it be.'

Lenyé led the way as they climbed to higher ground and found a cave to rest in and made preparations for the night. She risked a fire at the back, concealed from the entrance by a spur of rock, to cook some fresh rabbits for herself that Chuah-te-mok caught. The others preferred to eat theirs raw.

Lenyé lifted the remainder of the roast meat off the flat stone she used for cooking, with the point of her dagger, and laid it out on a nearby rock to cool. At last she could replenish her dwindling stock of dried meat.

The others settled themselves down for the night: the lioness stretched out in front of the fire, enjoying its warmth; the eagle perched on a lump of rock, with his feathers ruffled; and the she-bear slumped in a sitting position with her back against the rock wall.

Ra-Na-Jiri coiled himself in one corner, but raised up a sleepy head to talk to the she-bear. 'I suppose you've got one of these special messages from Yanantha as well?'

'Yes I have,' Mamma Uza-Mâté replied. 'But I think Lenyé and I talked about most of it earlier on.'

'You'd better let Lenyé have it in writing. She's keeping a record, you know.'

Lenyé turned her parchment to the light of the fire and wrote while Mamma Uza-Mâté spoke:

'Beware the Executioner
Sword of Justice is his prize
You must pierce his last defences
Seize the Sword as you arise.'

Long after the others fell asleep, Lenyé continued to ponder the words inscribed on her parchment as she lay wrapped in her cloak and huddled by the dying embers of the fire. Could she really become like an eagle, a lioness and a she-bear in time to fulfil her quest? She seemed to have made some progress today: at least the others encouraged her to believe so.

And what of her conversation with Mamma Uza-Mâté earlier, and the most recent words from Yanantha? She had no idea who the Executioner was. And what were his last defences? The whole thing was so much bigger than she originally thought. Was she really going to be able to outwit the Nastrim and steal the Sword from them?

Then she found herself thinking about those warriors riding towards the mountains. The four of them had taken on a company of twenty-five men and utterly destroyed them. But then they had surprise on their side and the power of her longbow against their much smaller bows. How would they fare against half an army?

Her head began to spin with it all.

She thought about her new friends, savouring the effect they were having on her. Chuah-te-mok was really terrifying at first, but then he brought down those warriors when they grabbed her in the ambush, and re-appeared just in time for that battle. He was so wise, and able to discern things she couldn't see and very friendly towards her, but somehow seemed a little aloof to the others. Ariella was great: so powerful and lithe, and full of concern for her when they started talking about Kyros and her parents. She felt such a strong bond with the great cat. And Mamma Uza-Mâté was so big and her fur so soft and warm, and those eyes, so deep and yet so full of humour; she just loved having the she-bear around with that reassuring presence.

What about Ra-Na-Jiri?

Where did he fit into all this?

Why was he so argumentative towards Ariella? And he completely ducked the issue of having any words from Yanantha, when Ariella challenged him. Even when Mamma Uza-Mâté recited the words she had, Ra-Na-Jiri still didn't volunteer any of his own. Had Yanantha really sent him? And what was that release of energy that heralded his arrival? Lenyé definitely felt something, even if Ariella didn't. Yet now he was committed to helping her. What was it Chuah-te-mok said when he left her earlier? *'Remember, nothing happens to you without significance.'* Did that mean Ra-Na-Jiri? She thought he was going to strike at her when she first saw him, and he turned out to be one of her most loyal friends. Yanantha must have sent him.

But then she was back to the conversation with Ariella about Beth. The lioness was right. She now had far more skills that were becoming apparent to others concerning herself. It was as though Ariella's words were beginning to free her from those awful thoughts about Beth.

Chapter Forty

Kyros watched the clumps of trees and outcrops of rock come and go as their swift progress over the plain continued unchecked. Already they were half across and the ridge of rock rose ahead of them, dominating the horizon as it swept upwards and was lost in the higher mountains behind it.

The nagging doubts continued in his mind till he realised that Vashtani and his cohort may not be the En-luchés after all, but were potential captors, luring him by deceit into their power.

He wondered whether he and Harbona could survive the impact of hitting the ground. But there was no other way. If he slowed his steed, or manoeuvred his horse away from the centre of the group, Vashtani would guess his intentions.

Help me, Oh True King, he whispered to himself.

He waited till the next approaching clump of trees, whipped his right leg over the saddle, gathered Harbona up more closely in his arms, freed his other foot from the stirrup and leaped.

He twisted in the air, landed on both feet, and flexed his knees to take the impact. His momentum bowled him over and Harbona crushed him to the ground, as the other horses sped by.

With a cry, Vashtani wheeled his cohort round, but Kyros was up, slinging Harbona over his shoulder and running for the shelter of the rocks and trees. He heard the drumming of hooves on the coarse sand and realised that now the steeds were actually galloping on the ground: the trees were clearly too close for any more flying. But Kyros cried aloud to the True King and felt new power surge through his limbs and out ran them, reaching the shelter of the trees in time to lay Harbona in the hollow of an ancient trunk before drawing his sword and turning to face his enemies.

The cohort reined in their great steeds only a few feet away from the first of the rocks, and Vashtani slid to the ground in one fast movement, before running in amongst the trees to confront Kyros. The rest of his cohort followed and fanned out in a horseshoe behind their leader.

'You cannot escape from us, Kyros,' there was a menacing tone in Vashtani's voice. 'Besides. We mean you no harm.'

'I've heard that before,' shouted Kyros. 'From the lips of the man I carry. It means the same thing, whether my enemies are human, or come from this world.' He raised his sword and took a step forwards. 'In the name of the True King, I will not yield.'

Vashtani faltered and stepped back, before recovering himself. 'The True King, you say. What do you know of him?'

'That he is with me wherever I go and will come to my aid.'

'Really,' there was a touch of sarcasm in Vashtani's voice. 'I do not see him. Where is this King that he can come so suddenly to your rescue?'

Kyros was about to respond when he was forced, almost against his will, to look at Vashtani's face, and, more specifically, the eyes. Then, just as the Maljaros drew all light to themselves and gave nothing back, so too, he felt something vital being drawn out of him, as though all his strength was ebbing away. Not just his physical strength, but his hopes, dreams, aspirations and all the things he held dear and made life worth living were disappearing from him. It was like a thick fog enveloping him and threatening to snuff out the light of life within him. His sword arm drooped and the tip of the blade dug into the coarse sand in front of him. Hoffengrégor's words came to mind and he tried to hold on to them in his despair, as if thoughts of the old Prophet were the only thing that could help him now: *"The Dé-monos are much worse. Do not look into their eyes, for they will suck the very life out of you."* What did he say would counter this? Kyros tried hard to recall anything that would help. But nothing came. Then the thought flashed in his mind, as though planted by another, that Vashtani was a leader of the Dé-monos and therefore a deadly enemy, and there really was no escape.

With a great effort he cried out, 'Enough.' But it sounded feeble to his ears. The usual ring of conviction in his voice had totally deserted him, and, instead, he seemed to be mumbling meaningless platitudes to a powerful opponent who would give him no quarter. With a hand that felt like a lead weight he slowly raised his sword and sliced through the air between them as though to cut off the power in Vashtani's gaze.

Vashtani roared with laughter. 'You come against me with a sword from the Waking World?' He paused, trying to get the better of his amusement. 'There is no blade from your world that can harm me, save one.'

'You mean, the Blade of Zerigor?' Kyros was astonished to find himself making the connection so quickly, despite Hoffengrégor comments.

'Correct. That blade was taken from the Krêonor and hidden, and now has a very safe keeper. You will never get it back.'

Vashtani raised his hand and pointed at the sword. Kyros felt the balance of his weapon change, and, to his horror, saw the blade bend downwards as though it was melting. The blade continued to twist and turn till it dissolved in a billow of smoke before his eyes, leaving only the hilt in his hand.

Before Kyros could move, Vashtani and his cohort were upon him. 'Fool.' He heard the mockery in Vashtani's voice close to his ear. 'It's not you we want. It's your companion. Without him, your so-called True King will never let you leave this Realm.'

'Oh, My King,' Kyros cried in anguish. He cast the useless hilt away and threw himself forwards amongst the rushing shapes of the Dé-monos. 'Save me from my enemies.'

Chapter Forty One

'What's the matter with her?' Quinn was relieved to see Rafé reach out his hand and gently close those terrible, staring eyes. He watched closely as Rafé held his finger tips to Beth's upturned wrist and moved his lips as though counting, then ran his hand over her brow.

'Get me some dock leaves.'

Quinn ran across to the other side of the clearing to obey. Even now he had to be careful not to let Rafé see he knew where that path was. He found some dock leaves and raced back with them.

Rafé rubbed the leaves between his palms and then wiped his hands over her brow and down her temples.

Beth moaned again, 'Lenyé... danger... snake...'

'Has she said anything else?'

'No. She needs help. Can't we take her back to Terrazarema? What about the Apothecary? He'll know what to do.'

'Doctor Nostrea is under house arrest and his apartment is constantly watched. It is too dangerous for any of us to go back. Besides. She's beyond the help of an Apothecary now.'

'But we can't leave her like this. We must do something.'

'I know where to take her. The cottage is not far out of our way and is completely isolated. You'll be safe there for a while. We'll head for the home of Ishi-mi-réjá.'

'That's a strange name. Who is this person?'

'She's a very wise old woman,' Rafé was already covering Beth with a blanket. Her name means *Miraculous Stone*.'

Chapter Forty Two

'Three times.' Morthrir stamped up and down in the private council chamber waving his arms about. He paused in front of Youdlh. 'Three times! What kind of an army do you call yourselves? Three times and she gets the better of you each time. And half of Elskin's men wiped out. What kind of an officer is this fellow? One girl. I don't believe this.'

Youdlh stood with his hands clasped behind his back. 'She must be getting help from someone.'

'Who?'

'I don't know, Sire. Elskin's scouts are trying to make contact with her. She seems to have gone to ground for some time now.'

'She appears out of nowhere, overpowers a group of soldiers with a massive feathered missile that injures and wounds most of them, then disappears. Only a giant could have thrown that. Five men found dead at the bottom of a cliff and one of them your best tracker. Only a giant could have done that. Then a company of twenty-five crack soldiers gets wiped out and buried under a pile of rocks. Only giants could have done that. Use your head, Youdlh. She's infiltrated the Nastrim, trained them up and used these opportunities to see how well they perform against our soldiers. Then she's going to mobilise the whole lot against us. I want you up there with all the troops you can muster and quash this threat before it gets properly started.'

'I've already sent Elskin some reinforcements round by the plains some time ago. They should be there by now.'

'I want more men up there. Call half the army out. Don't just stand there.'

'With respect, this is not a time for splitting up our forces. We need to consolidate power here and establish you as King.'

'You've had six weeks and you still haven't caught her. One girl and the whole of Youdlh's mighty army is made a complete laughing stock.' He paused to gulp some air. 'Get out.'

'But Sire…'

'I said, *"Get out"*.'

Youdlh paused with his hand on the door handle. 'I think you should recall Rafé, Sire. After all, he is your strategist.'

Morthrir was standing in the middle of the floor. He raised his arm and pointed straight at Youdlh, his whole body trembling violently. 'Don't you dare tell me how to run my affairs! We both know the importance of Rafé's current mission. And we both know why he's not here for the present. If you think Rafé's the only one who can strategise and plan and get results, you're very much mistaken.'

'Sending the army is more likely to start a war, not prevent it.'

'Rubbish, man. If you go and sit on their doorstep with a big enough force and demand they hand over my absent bride-to-be, they might just agree to do it. After all, there hasn't been a war between the Krêonor and the Nastrim for centuries. They may still want to avoid an open conflict.'

'And if they don't agree to hand her over?'

'Then you're in the right place at the right time with the right number of men to make them give her back.'

'Very good, Sire.' Youdlh turned to the door again, but Morthrir stopped him.

'Oh, Youdlh. Make sure there are enough soldiers here to guard the palace while I'm away. I need a bodyguard to accompany me to Mount Malkamet.'

'Why are you going there at such a key moment?'

'Never you mind!'

PART IV

THE PREPARATION

Chapter Forty Three

Lenyé led the way up the lower slopes of Mount Nastâri and stepped onto a big flat rock to check if there were any caves that might lead into the heart of the mountain. As the others joined her, she felt the rock move slightly with their combined weight. She turned and shaded her eyes with her hand to look out over the plain before speaking to the eagle. 'No sign of that dust cloud any more. Maybe the army was heading somewhere else.'

'That dark patch down there,' Chuah-te-mok pointed with his beak. 'I can see horses tethered. 'Shall I go and check it out. It might be their camp?'

But even as he spoke, several plumes of blue smoke arose as if from numerous campfires, and Lenyé could see for herself the extent of the army.

'Why not? We need to know as much about them as possible and what they intend to do.'

Chuah-te-mok flew off and was quickly descending on the thermals. Lenyé marvelled at his graceful flight as he dropped lower towards the campsite.

She turned back to the others. 'Where's Ra-Na-Jiri?'

'He was lagging behind quite a way,' Ariella growled. 'I knew he'd have difficulty keeping up with the rest of us.'

'Please can you go back and look for him.' Lenyé glanced from one to the other. 'Mamma Uza-Mâté you go too.'

'What about being left here on your own?' Mamma Uza-Mâté's voice was full of concern.'

'I'll be all right. I need to be alone for a while to think.' She jumped up and walked to the edge of the flat rock for a better view of the plain, just as the others stepped back onto the rock face. The flat rock shifted again as their weight changed and suddenly there was a tearing, grinding noise and the whole rock tilted backwards and downwards. Lenyé screamed as she felt herself sliding down the steep angle of the rock before plunging into a chasm below. The grinding noise continued as the whole rock crashed down on the top of the chasm, cutting out all the light. Small stones and an occasional boulder came pattering and thudding down around her and then everything was still.

'Lenyé, where are you?' Ariella's roar was full of anxiety.

'Can you hear us?' Mamma Uza-Mâté heaved a loose boulder aside. 'Ariella. Help me shift this rock. She must be underneath it.'

Lenyé shook her head and sat up. Their voices were muffled, but she could still hear them, and there was a chink of light in one corner. 'I'm all right. Can you hear me?'

'You're very faint.'

'There's no way we can shift this rock.'

'I can see daylight in the top right hand corner. Can you get anything down to me?'

'Where's that snake,' Ariella was almost beside herself with concern. 'The one time he'd be really useful and he goes and disappears.'

'There he is,' Mamma Uza-Mâté pointed. She beckoned to the cobra. 'We need you to slide down this hole to Lenyé.'

Ra-Na-Jiri slithered up to them and examined the fallen rocks. 'If you think I'm wriggling into a tight little hole like that, you're greatly mistaken.'

'If you don't do it voluntarily,' Ariella growled at him. 'I'm sure Mamma Uza-Mâté can poke you through the opening and keep on shoving till you come out the other end!'

Chapter Forty Four

Kyros awoke to the sound of voices: some murmuring quietly close at hand, others singing softly. He was in a grassy glade ringed by trees. But more importantly he could smell cooking. He sat up and groaned, realising just how ravenous he was.

'Kyros.' The voice behind him was strong and vibrant, and as Kyros turned to see the speaker he was dazzled by a blinding light. The stranger had the appearance of a man, but of greater stature, and a light shone from him.

'Well met, at last, my friend. I am Stellatus, Herald of the Eastern Principality, sent by the True King himself to grant you safe passage in all his Realms. But Vashtani, a Prince of the Démonos, withstood me and delayed my coming for several days.'

Kyros bowed low in awe before him, but Stellatus reached out his hand and raised him up. 'Do not bow before me for we are more like brothers than you think, and we both serve the True King according to our own abilities.'

'I'm really confused,' Kyros hesitated before continuing with his question. 'Why do you and Vashtani look so alike? Surely, if he is an enemy, I should be able to recognise that.'

'To the unwary, or the untutored, Vashtani and his cohort can mimic us and make themselves look like us for a short time.'

'I don't understand.'

'They were once as we are: En-luchés, filled with living light. Now they can only briefly recall what they once had, for their inner light-source was shattered and they no longer shine with the light of life. For they have become Dé-monos, a corruption of

Dé-mono-chromés, meaning *those-of-one-colour*—in their case, the complete absence of living light which weaves strands of many colours together. They are therefore nothing but darkness; that is their real manifestation.'

'How did this happen?'

Long ago they tried to deceive the True King of their intentions to seize his throne and install their own leader, Abbérron, as supreme, and were confined to the Realm of Travail as a result. We were sent here to watch over them and prevent them entering the Waking World again.'

Kyros frowned, 'Hoffengrégor warned me about their eyes.'

'Quite right. But when they seek to use another for their purposes, they will never look you directly in the eye; they will only use that as their final weapon against you.'

'Now I understand Vashtani's strange behaviour. He never once looked me in the eyes.'

'You did well to work out what was going on and break away from them when you did.' Stellatus smiled at him. 'But you will need to continue training your senses in order to discern the difference between us in future, for they will appear in other guises.'

'Tell me what happened. I thought it was the end for me.'

'You have to understand that the Dé-monos are ruled by Abbérron and do his bidding. The name of the True King has immense power throughout all his Realms. By invoking his name, you called directly on that power, as though the True King himself was present with you. Even Abbérron is subject to that name.'

'What does using his name actually do?'

'As soon as you cried out, the air was rent and all Vashtani's resistance melted before us and we were able to overpower him and his cohort and rescue you. In fact, you have now passed the third test the True King set you; for when all other weapons failed, you were prepared to trust in the power of the Name of the True King despite great peril to yourself.'

Stellatus led him over to one of the groups where they were served with fine bread and roast meats and strong wine.

Kyros sat in silence for a while thinking over the things he had just heard. Then he told Stellatus of the theft of the roll and his mistake in telling Vashtani about it.

'That's unfortunate,' Stellatus passed Kyros some more bread. 'We will have to try and recover it before they learn the value of its contents and seek to destroy it.'

'Why would they do that?'

'The Writings of Hoffengrégor are the key to understanding what is going on and how to accomplish the purposes of the True King. If we recover the roll, you must guard it with your life.'

Kyros shrugged. 'They still managed to grab Harbona from me despite my efforts.'

'I know. That is very serious. Vashtani and his cohort have escaped with him and will be secure in their own fortress by now. That man's life hangs in the balance and you are the only one who can free him. That is your fourth test.'

'How am I to get there in order to do that?'

The En-luchés gathered around Kyros and began to sing, and he was lifted up on their song and carried away with them at great speed over the plain towards the mountains. As they crossed a huge ridge of rock, Kyros could see an enormous fortress, on the plain with a high mountain behind it. But even as they cleared the ridge, he felt an enormous release of energy. The En-luchés were scattered and the power of their song was broken. Kyros felt himself hurtling towards the ground, and cried out in the name of the True King for help. He looked up and saw Stellatus speeding towards him, and the strength of the single En-luchés' song began to slow Kyros down till he touched the ground, rolled over several times and came to a complete stop.

Chapter Forty Five

'Lenyé,' Ra-Na-Jiri whispered. 'Are you all right?'

'I think so,' Lenyé's voice sounded shaky. 'Just a little dazed, that's all. Where are we?'

'Apparently a rock tipped and you fell down some kind of chute. There's no way out the way you came. Mamma Uza-Mâté tried shifting the rock but it was too heavy for her. She was going frantic by the time I got there.'

'Yes. Where were you? I was getting a bit worried.'

'That last rock face was too steep for me to keep up with you.'

Despite the fall, the longbow was undamaged, and Lenyé still had all the quivers of arrows and her satchel intact.

The chute went straight ahead and downwards. Ra-Na-Jiri led the way as his eyes were more accustomed to dark places and he could sense vibrations in the ground. Lenyé stumbled behind him with one hand on the rock wall.

They came to a small passage on their left. Ra-Na-Jiri reared up to test the air. 'Shall we risk it?'

'This must lead out to the face of the mountain,' Lenyé felt round the opening with her hands. 'It has to be worth a try.' She followed Ra-Na-Jiri only to find it ended in a rock wall.

They retraced their steps and carried on down, trying a few more passageways off to their left, but with the same result. The main passageway turned abruptly to their right. They were several paces into the bend when suddenly Ra-Na-Jiri rose up hissing. 'Don't move another step. Someone's there.'

Chapter Forty Six

Rafé and Quinn started out not long after dawn, with Rafé carrying Beth in his arms as he rode. Quinn followed behind as they held their course, weaving in and out of the trees as best they could, keeping the line of the rutted roadway in view to their left as it wound East towards Onadestra. The horses walked or cantered gently in the last remaining bits of open heathland, before they entered the forest that lay between them and the rocky range that swept up to Onadestra.

But Rafé couldn't carry her like that indefinitely. They paused briefly in a small dell at noon and took some refreshment. Quinn propped Beth up with an arm around her shoulders and tried to get some water into her mouth, but she choked and it dribbled out between her lips.

'We'll have to make better speed than this if we want to get there by sundown,' Rafé finished packing away their provisions. 'Why don't we cover the pommel of your saddle with a blanket and she can ride in front of you?'

Quinn found it easier than he expected. Beth stayed in place with one of his arms around her waist hugging her against his chest, or sometimes allowing her to droop forwards till she was practically lying along the horse's neck.

They moved further away from the road into the heath, and cantered for long stretches over the cropped grass and heathers. But by late evening they were still several miles from the cottage they sought and camped again for the night. Quinn was desperate to get some water into her, but still Beth choked and the water dribbled away down her chin.

It was dusk the next day when they saw a thin column of blue smoke drifting lazily up amongst some trees away to their right.

Rafé reined in his horse and stopped. 'Take your bag and bedding rolls and carry her for the last part of the way. I'll take the horses and find somewhere to camp further ahead in those woods.'

'Aren't you coming with us?'

'No. Ishi-mi-réjá will recognise you and Beth. We can't help that. Don't worry, she won't betray you. But if she sees me with you, it could be dangerous.'

'Don't you trust her?'

'I trust no one. Your Uncle has spies and informers everywhere, so I treat everyone the same. The fewer people who see us together, the less chance there is for news to slip out. If your Uncle ever catches wind that we've been travelling together, he'll hunt me down till there's nowhere left to hide.'

Chapter Forty Seven

Stellatus cupped his hands around Kyros' ear and whispered, 'Behold the gates of Malvi-Quîdda, stronghold of the Dé-monos.'

Kyros stood next to him and surveyed the huge fortress. Each tower, each pinnacle, each turret was etched in black as the rays of the setting sun caught it in stark silhouette from behind. The ramparts rose fifty feet to the parapets. A single arched tunnel at the front led to a portcullis, and behind that were two massive gates shut fast. In the failing light he was just able to discern innumerable arrow slits that pierced the walls and turrets. The outline of trebuchets, great engines for casting rocks, could be seen behind the parapets.

Kyros sighed. It looked impregnable.

'There is only one way to overcome the Dé-monos,' Stellatus' voice was soft in his ear. 'You have to begin by destroying Malvi-Quîdda. But my heart warns me that even as you do that, Abbérron will be preparing a masterstroke in retaliation.'

'I can only handle one thing at a time. Tell me what to do.'

'By passing the third test, you are well on the way to accomplishing this goal. Your use of the name of the True King, as his Ambassador from the Waking World, releases his power against them. But this time you have to focus that power and physically mark out where you want it released. You must circle the fortress six times, calling on the name of the True King at regular intervals, and on the seventh time circle in silence, then shout in the name of the True King. Even if the Dé-monos try to disrupt that, you must finish the seven laps. That is your fourth test.'

'What happens then?'

'I do not know for certain. But the strength of the Dé-monos will be laid bare and you can seize the opportunity to free your companion.'

'Am I to do this by myself? What about the other En-luchés? Are they not able to help?'

'They were scattered by a trick of our enemy. You must act now while the Dé-monos are unprepared for any assault. But I agree. You shall not be alone in this. First we must summon the Sacred Pilgrims of Lohr.

'Why are they called Pilgrims?' Kyros sounded puzzled.

'They were Krêonor who dwelled in the Plains of Lohr when they lived in the Waking World, but considered themselves to be only passing through that Realm, as Pilgrims, waiting for the True King and his rule to be established amongst the Peoples.'

'And why, Sacred?'

'They set themselves apart to honour the True King.'

'Why are they so important to us now?'

'They barred the way against the Nastrim and the Tsé-shâmé while the rest of the Krêonor fled to safety in the wars at the Beginning. They refused to use any weapons, holding fast to the name of the True King instead. They were butchered by their enemies and reserved as martyrs in the *Place of Rest* for such a time as this. Your arrival here has triggered the unfolding of the True King's purposes concerning them. But we must be quick.'

Stellatus resumed his song and Kyros was lifted up with him and borne away across the mountain range heading East, and then down towards a cave mouth at the foot of one of the mountains.

When they were standing on the ground again, Stellatus laid his hand on Kyros' head, 'Go in peace, for this is our gateway to the Realm of the Departed.'

Chapter Forty Eight

Lenyé eased the longbow off her shoulder and notched an arrow. She could hear heavy footsteps and see a light approaching in front of them from their left. She also noticed that their passageway ended straight ahead in a rock wall, but another passageway crossed it and disappeared to their right.

Suddenly a line of soldiers appeared carrying flares and marching across the end of their passageway without even a glance in their direction. Each was protected by a round helmet with a nose guard, a chainmail hauberk that reached down to the middle of their thighs, and polished greaves on both legs. Strapped slantways from the left shoulder down their backs was a long, double-handed sword, which was partly covered by a round shield. Lenyé could just make out a shorter, fighting sword hanging from the left side of their belts.

It took a while for the line to march past them and gave her enough time to register the various weak spots in their armour: throat, eye and possibly thigh. She would have to aim with care in the flickering torch light and hoped fervently it would never come to that. Fortunately none of the soldiers looked round in her direction. Finally the light from the flares died away.

Lenyé let out a long slow breath, 'Whew. They're massive.' Not even Mamma Uza-Mâté's description had given her any idea of what they were really like. 'How am I going to decide which one of them has got the Sword I'm looking for?'

'I don't know,' Ra-Na-Jiri's hiss startled her in the sudden silence. The cobra continued, 'It's no good turning right. We might bump into those soldiers.'

'But there might be more troops following from the left,' Lenyé pointed out. 'Perhaps they're mustering their army against Youdlh's warriors. They must have seen the camp by now.'

'In which case, it's better to meet them head on, than get squashed together in the middle of two companies.'

Lenyé hesitated. 'Let's head left.' She slid the arrow back into her quiver and slung the longbow over her shoulder. 'It's more the direction we need to take.'

They carried on in silence, with Lenyé feeling her way carefully along the rock wall to her left, and the cobra alert for any more vibrations.

They hadn't gone far when Lenyé saw a light growing round a corner ahead. From the sound of marching feet there could be no doubt that more soldiers were approaching, and this time they were in the same passageway. There was no time to run back and hide like last time and hope they weren't spotted.

Lenyé removed the longbow from her shoulder, calmly notched an arrow and took aim at roughly the head height she estimated from seeing the previous company. The light came on, now brightening as the leading soldier and the front rank appeared from round the bend, marching directly towards them, and the loom of light washed up to her feet and moved beyond her. In that instant Ra-Na-Jiri raised himself up, slightly in front of Lenyé, weaving this way and that with his hood flared. Out of the corner of her eye Lenyé noticed that the light from in front threw him into stark silhouette, the usual markings on his hood hidden by the blackness, his moving shadow streaming out behind him.

The company stopped abruptly. Before she could loose her arrow, the leader at the front dropped to his knees and bowed his face to the ground, with the rows behind immediately following his example.

Lenyé was trying to find a gap in the armour of the leading soldier to aim at, but his prostrate position only offered her the top of his helmet and the chainmail on his shoulders. The more she searched, the more astonished she became at their behaviour. They were raising themselves up on their knees and then bowing down again gracefully and chanting in unison: '"Ra-Na, Ra-Na".'

'What are they doing?' Lenyé glanced down at Ra-Na-Jiri. 'And why are they using your name like that?'

Instead of the usual aggressive stance of an attacking cobra, Ra-Na-Jiri was swaying, almost in time to music only he could hear, the hood alternately collapsing as he leaned forwards, throwing the small head into sharp relief, and then rising up so that his hood would inflate back to its characteristic wide curve.

'Ra-Na-Jiri,' Lenyé leaned forwards and touched the back of the cobra's hood with her arrow tip. 'What are you doing?'

'Can't you see? They're worshipping me.'

The soldier at the front, who appeared to be the captain of the company, raised himself up and shuffled forwards on his knees, alternatively bowing with his head to the ground and raising up so that he could move towards them. When he was a few feet away, he pulled the round shield off his back and cradled it in both hands, proffering the hollow inside part to the cobra.

'What is the meaning of this?' Lenyé drew her longbow and aimed the arrow directly at the captain's eye.

'Most noble one,' he sat back on his haunches to address her. 'Our forefathers worshipped the great god Ra-Na, the serpent who fell from the sky and taught our ancestors knowledge of all things and how to attain wisdom. He has been venerated ever since by the Nastrim, although the god himself has not appeared for many centuries. And now, not only has the great god, Ra-Na, appeared before us, he has brought with him the goddess Saida, Huntress of the Heart and Bestower of Divine Love. You have only to loose your arrow, fair lady, and I will worship him and follow him to the death, if needs be.'

'I see,' Lenyé lowered her longbow. 'It is true that Ra-Na-Jiri and I travel together.'

'I know not what this "*Jiri*" means. No doubt it is a name of affection you have for him, which is a sign to me that you are the Huntress of whom I speak.'

'What's he saying, Lenyé?' Ra-Na-Jiri interrupted. 'I can't understand a word of it.'

'You can't understand?' Lenyé paused, thinking hard.

'That's right,' Ra-Na-Jiri swivelled round to look at her. 'I can't understand what people say. Or even giants. Only you.'

Lenyé gasped in astonishment. Of course. Yanantha bestowed on her the gift of speaking and understanding the language of all creatures. She could understand them, and they could understand her. But they couldn't understand ordinary human speech. The captain's accent certainly sounded strange, and she had to focus carefully to follow him, but she could still understand what he said. Clearly, Ra-Na-Jiri could not. She was going to have to act as his interpreter.

Lenyé turned back to the captain. 'Will all the Nastrim show such dedication if Ra-Na,' she paused slightly to emphasise the shortened name, 'appears before them?'

'Only King Ogandés can confirm that. Maybe some in high office will feel threatened by the physical appearance of our god; but most will be overjoyed. I, Captain Turvil, will convey you to the King and his court and we shall see. But first, the great god Ra-Na must always be above the heads of those who worship him. My soldiers and I have been trying to make ourselves lower by bowing down, but alas, we cannot sink below the ground. Therefore I must raise him up.' He bowed forwards again and offered the open side of his shield to Ra-Na-Jiri. 'I would invite the great god Ra-Na to be carried in my humble shield.'

'I think he wants you to climb on his shield, O great Ra-Na.' Lenyé smiled to herself as she tried to get used to his new name. 'Looks like you're going to travel in style from now on.'

Without a word, Ra-Na-Jiri slithered onto the shield, coiled his body round and raised his head up facing Lenyé.

Immediately Captain Turvil stood up, holding the shield high above his head, and the rest of the company stood with him. Then they marched forwards, ushering Lenyé in front of them.

Before long, the passageway broadened out and was well lit with flares fixed in brackets on the rock walls. Lenyé walked ahead of them, still unsure of how she was going to handle the situation. She could hardly believe what had just happened. This must be Yanantha blinding their eyes. But she could be walking deeper into a trap, and kept the longbow in her hand and the arrow on the bowstring just in case.

Lenyé passed under a tall archway and gasped at the throng of giants assembled as she stepped out into the great chamber of the King. As the captain passed through the archway behind her he shouted: 'Make way for the great god, Ra-Na and his consort, the Huntress Saida.'

There was a sudden hush as all eyes turned to them. Captain Turvil ushered Lenyé forwards in front of him and they mounted the steps to the dais of King Ogandés.

The King stood, and all his courtiers with him, then he descended to the foot of the steps and turned. Captain Turvil placed the shield and Ra-Na on the empty throne and indicated to Lenyé to stand on the right hand side. Once the Captain descended the steps the King bowed low before the throne and the whole assembly prostrated themselves at the same time. A chant of, "Ra-Na, Ra-Na", swelled up around them and Lenyé noticed Ra-Na-Jiri swaying from side to side, his eyes staring straight ahead as though he was in a trance. She also noticed a huge giant bowing down on the other side of the throne who had not descended the steps with the King. But what caught her attention most about him were the two swords strapped across his back. They were much smaller than the double-handed swords she'd seen on the backs of the Nastâr soldiers: more like short stabbing swords in a Nastâr's hands. They would still be full-sized swords for a human. Whenever the giant moved or turned, both swords shone and glittered in the light from the intricate pattern of gems embedded in the scabbards.

'What is your command, O great god Ra-Na?' The King sat up on his haunches. 'Your coming is most timely. For even as we speak, an army of men,' he paused as though the word itself was distasteful to him, 'is camped in the plains outside our lower gates. Such a thing has not happened for centuries. Not since the wars with the Krêonor. Now your advent will assure us of victory.'

Lenyé leaned over towards Ra-Na-Jiri. 'You're going to have to think of something to say.'

'What?' Ra-Na-Jiri was startled by her voice. 'You think of something. I'm too busy enjoying myself.'

'Very well.' She turned back to the King. 'Ra-Na requests that your throne be moved to the bottom of the steps. Exchange this captain's shield for a platter of pure gold, suspended by gold threads, with golden ropes hanging to the floor for access. And let no one, other than his consort, ascend these steps.' She glanced at the prostrate giant on the other side of the throne, and noticed the King's eyes following her gaze.

'That is Acwellan, my Lord High Executioner,' King Ogandés gestured towards the prostrate giant, 'and second only to me.'

'Then the Lord High Executioner can descend with your throne. There will be no lessening of his power and authority.'

She watched as the orders were carried out. The Lord High Executioner followed the throne and bowed before the golden dish. He glanced at Lenyé, and she felt his eyes boring into hers with the haughty look of someone who does not believe in gods, and is convinced that those who claim divinity are imposters.

Chapter Forty Nine

After Youdlh had gone, Morthrir paced the length of the private council chamber thinking over their conversation earlier, *"Why would she be headed North, Sire? There's only rocks and mountains and..."*. The mountain must be Mount Nastâri. But rocks as well?

The Priests said, *"She is far away and surrounded by rocks. Our combined thoughts cannot touch her"*.

Perhaps it was not the rocks that were impenetrable, but something to do with the Nastrim themselves. Some power they wielded that countermanded the power of the Priests.

Maybe Lenyé was trying to use that.

In which case, if she was hiding with the Nastrim, he needed something to entice her out and come to him of her own accord.

Morthrir flung open the door and shouted for Youdlh. When the man entered hurriedly and out of breath, Morthrir barked, 'How quickly can you get word to Captain Elskin and the Field Commanders up at Mount Nastâri?'

'Within five days, Sire. Maybe six.'

'Tell them to get a message to Lenyé if she's hiding with the Nastrim. Tell her to come to the palace of her own accord within seven days of receiving this message, or I start executing the other youngsters, one a day, starting with Beth, then Quinn, then the next youngest.'

'But Sire. We don't have those two in captivity any more.'

'Exactly. We can always say we went ahead with the executions. If your soldiers ever find those two, they are to be killed immediately. Is that understood?'

Chapter Fifty

Quinn staggered to the door of the cottage with Beth in his arms and banged it with his elbow.

The door opened and he was greeted by a lively old woman with rosy cheeks and a beaming smile. 'What can I do for you, young Master?'

'Please. Can you help my cousin? We're lost and she's in a terrible state.' He held out the rigid body to her.

'Oh, the poor lamb. Give her to me.' The old woman carried Beth into the cottage and laid her on a bed at the side of the room. 'How long has she been like this?'

'Night before last.'

'Too long by all accounts. Still. You came to the right place. If I can't cure her, my name's not Ishi-mi-réjá.'

Chapter Fifty One

After a week in the wilds since Yanantha's House, Lenyé was enjoying the comfort of the apartment they'd been given, revelling in the sheer pleasure of laying aside her weapons and satchel and being able to relax. She wallowed in a hot bath and washed her hair; then sat in front of the fire in the main salon, plaiting her hair while it was still damp. Ra-Na-Jiri was coiled in his golden dish supported on a tripod on the other side. The smoke from the fire drifted up against the wall and escaped through an angled shaft above. The rest of the salon was richly furnished with very large armchairs, thick rugs on the floor, a writing bureau and plenty of flares on the rock walls to light the chamber. But there were no windows or curtains. Lenyé longed for sunlight and the feel of fresh air on her face and the joy of seeing her friends left outside, which brought her full circle to completing her quest and getting away as quickly as possible.

There was a knock at the door.

Lenyé glanced at Ra-Na-Jiri, 'Come in.'

A messenger entered accompanied by four soldiers and invited them both to dinner with King Ogandés.

Lenyé sat opposite the King at a square table in his private dining room. Acwellan sat on her right. Ra-Na-Jiri's golden dish was positioned on a tripod to her left. The cobra was fed by some female servants, while the three of them talked.

She was surprised to see Acwellan still wearing his two swords and asked if this was his usual practise.

'Indeed, O Mighty Huntress,' Acwellan wiped his mouth on a serviette and took a sip of wine. 'I am never without them. I constantly swap them around, so no one knows which is which.'

'They look so alike, and yet you imply they differ some how.'

'You do not know the history of these swords?' Acwellan sounded surprised. 'I thought the gods know all things?'

'If that was the case,' Lenyé paused, 'then you would only need one God. But as there are many, there is a specialising in activity and knowledge. I am merely the Huntress.'

'Hmmph,' he grunted, but sounded unconvinced. 'Then I will tell you. The Sword of Justice came to me at the end of the wars with the Krêonor. It is the most precious possession of the entire Nastrim race. With this Sword, I am able to despatch any of the Nastrim to Elasis, the resting place of the true dead.'

'And the other sword?' Lenyé persisted.

'Is an exact copy,' Acwellan took a large mouthful of food.

'In case the original gets lost?'

'Hardly,' King Ogandés chuckled. 'The Sword of Justice has absolute power in my Kingdom. The other sword cannot despatch a Nastâr in quite the same way. Death by that sword plunges the victim into the *Death of the Undying* and they are forever trapped between this world and the next.'

'How fascinating,' Lenyé was probing for more information about the Sword. 'Is that because the Nastrim are jointly descended from the Dé-monos and the daughters of men?'

'Exactly,' Acwellan paused to take another sip of wine.

'Any other weapon of this world would have the same effect,' King Ogandés continued. 'That was why the Krêonor longbows were so greatly feared during the wars. Many thousands of Nastârs were killed and are now trapped.'

'Is there no way out for them?' Lenyé felt really concerned.

The King and Acwellan glanced at each other.

'Not until the secret way is opened up,' Acwellan resumed, 'and the Dé-monos re-enter our world, can they return here.'

'What happens then?' Lenyé was intrigued.

'They can never be killed again in this world by ordinary weapons. Only the Sword of Justice would have any power over them. But as it is in my possession that will never happen.'

'Why not?'

'With an army like that, the Nastrim would be invincible.'

Lenyé was distracted and glanced at Ra-Na-Jiri. He was staring fixedly at her with eyes that made her feel uneasy. She shivered slightly, before turning back to King Ogandés, trying to concentrate on the conversation again. 'But I understood the True King himself sealed up the entry point.' She felt out of her depths. 'Surely no one can re-open it. '

'The Dé-monos won't give up that easily,' King Ogandés paused with a forkful of food half way to his mouth. 'Our greatest hope is they will join with other spirit-beings and force a point of entry somewhere else.'

'All it needs is a word of power from a human being with the right authority in this world,' Acwellan looked long and hard at Lenyé. 'Then the Breaking-in will begin.'

'But the two swords must act as a formidable deterrent to the Nastrim,' Lenyé was keen to bring the conversation back to her immediate objective.

'Precisely,' King Ogandés finished his mouthful. 'They are fiercely loyal to me personally, but they're held in check by the terror of the *Death of the Undying*. When the Lord High Executioner draws both his swords, no one but him alone knows which one will fall on his victim.'

'But, Acwellan' Lenyé turned to him. 'Surely you have a means of knowing?'

'I have. But it is known only by me.' He looked at Lenyé, his intelligent eyes closing slightly as he studied her face. 'No one else will ever find out.'

Chapter Fifty Two

Rafé was pleased with his campsite and how well the horses had settled to their pickets under the trees. And more importantly, he was free of Beth and Quinn for a while.

He sat cross-legged on his blanket, rested his elbows on his knees, placed the tips of his fingers against his forehead and temples, and started to control his breathing and calm his mind. He focused on the snake and was able to reconnect with it almost straight away.

The first thing he did was to think, "Name". After several attempts, the thought arose in his mind, "Ra". He didn't try probing; rather he let his mind wander away as if he wasn't particularly interested. The name began to chase after him: "Ra-Na". As he re-focused, the name moved away, almost playing a game with him, as though it didn't want to reveal anymore of itself. He let his mind wander and refocus two or three more times, but without any result.

Rafé sighed. He knew it wasn't the full name, but it was better than nothing.

Then he commanded the snake to reveal what was going on around it.

Immediately he was able to see through the snakes eyes.

Rafé gasped. There was a blaze of lights and he could hear muffled voices. The snake was jerking its head around and presently Rafé worked out it was swallowing food that was passed to it by several females. But the females were enormous.

He willed the snake to stop its jerky movements and tried to study someone to its right. Dimly he could make out the features and realised it was Lenyé. Then he forced the snake to move its head and he could see two more faces one directly opposite and another to its left. But they, too, were enormous, and completely out of proportion to the size of Lenyé's face, even though they were no closer. Where could she be? And more importantly, who was she with?

The only conclusion he could come to was that Lenyé had infiltrated the Nastrim. Giants would certainly fit with the images of the large females and the other two faces. Now he could see the whole scenario, he realised that he was witnessing a dinner party. In which case, Lenyé must be a favoured guest. Maybe she was trying to persuade the Nastrim to attack her Uncle. Maybe...

Suddenly the snake jerked its head to grab a morsel of food, the connection was broken and Rafé's mind went blank.

Chapter Fifty Three

Morthrir was going frantic. With Rafé away he had no one intelligent enough to talk to. He could only shout at Youdlh or berate him for ineptitude. At least Rafé could always be relied on to give some sound advice.

But some news from Youdlh was good. The advance force was in place and the army was camped behind them and contact had been made with the Nastrim. The Executioner was their chief negotiator and seemed to be quite amenable to Morthrir's request. Youdlh was hopeful of a speedy settlement. The Nastrim hadn't actually admitted Lenyé was there, but where else could she be? Clearly the Executioner was a man he could do business with.

Man? Morthrir smacked himself on the forehead.

Giant, then.

If all the stories were true, he'd be ten feet tall with six fingers and toes. Some opponent. A few hundred of those would be a formidable force to contend with. But legend had it there were thousands. And if they did have some secret power, that would make a confrontation even worse.

There was still Kyros who had completely disappeared, as far as Morthrir could make out. What if he did escape down that so-called spiral on the island? The returning troops certainly seemed to think that was the only place he could have got to. What about Captain Harbona and his men? Surely someone should have emerged from the charred wreckage of the place to report back by now. But nothing.

He was in two minds about travel arrangements to Mount Malkamet. If he went via Onadestra he could never make it in time. The mountain was a good two days from the castle. Besides, it would be like blowing a fanfare and sending out the wrong message. The fewer people who knew about this Grand Convocation the better. He would have to go by the secret way through the mountains after all. Should he order up some pack animals? There were always plenty for hire on the other side of the River Rubichinó. Horses were useless at climbing those steep paths, but would make good time on the grassy plateau at the top compared to mules.

He paused, deep in thought.

No.

Stick to horses.

Speed was essential, and mules on those mountain paths were no faster than going on foot and leading the horses. He had to time it right: six days to the head of the pass, and another day to Mount Malkamet itself. That wasn't leaving any room for error. As long as the ford across the River Rubichinó was still passable he would be in time. But it was high summer and the weather was fine and there was no hint of any rain. The ford was the least of his problems.

Chapter Fifty Four

Lenyé shivered in the moonlight and wrapped the cloak around her. Ra-Na-Jiri was next to her, coiled on his golden dish and supported on the shoulders of four giants. They were both on a large flat rock that stood about twenty feet above the plain and fifty feet from the foot of the mountain. To her right was a similar rock, known as the Execution Rock. On the ground between her rock and the Execution Rock was a metal dish supported on a tripod with a fire burning on it. Steps were cut into both rocks on the sides facing each other allowing easy access to the fire from the top of the rocks.

The King and his courtiers sat below her vantage point on a wooden dais in the middle of a semicircle of rock that enclosed that part of the plain like an enormous letter "D". A huge company of spectators was gathered around and behind the dais, spreading out and filling the "D". She noticed there were about twenty breaks in the semicircle of rock, where soldiers spilled out onto the plain to form a protective guard ring for the whole ceremony. On the Execution Rock to her right stood Acwellan, with his sword hilts protruding above his shoulders. Kneeling in front of him with his wrists and ankles bound was a giant: his neck resting on a block of wood.

King Ogandés stood up and addressed the crowd. 'Fellow Nastârs. Last night, this traitor, Decatur, crept into the private chamber of Acwellan, the Lord High Executioner, to steal the Sword of Justice. But Acwellan was too quick and the dog escaped with his treacherous hand severed from his wrist.'

Lenyé glanced at the victim again and noticed that the bloodied stump of his right arm was indeed wrapped in a cloth and lashed to the other wrist. As the Nastâr raised his head, she realised the pallid face wasn't so much the fear of death, but the loss of blood that made him look so awful. Even so, there was a defiant glitter in his eye, before he lowered his head on the block.

'That was how he was found out this morning,' the King continued. 'And so, by moonlight, as is our custom, he is presented here to suffer the penalty of his crime. I hereby charge the Lord High Executioner to fulfil his duty and strike off his head. But before we proceed we would like a final judgement on this criminal from the great god Ra-Na.'

All eyes turned to Lenyé.

She whispered up to Ra-Na-Jiri on his golden dish, 'Do you have any words for them?'

'Words, words,' he muttered. 'All you ever want from me is words. You think of something.'

Lenyé tried to smile as she turned back to King Ogandés, but inwardly she was thinking furiously. 'The great god Ra-Na commands you to turn this execution into a sacrifice to the gods.'

There was a shout of approval from the crowd.

'Very well.' The King nodded to Acwellan, 'Proceed.'

Lenyé's attention riveted on Acwellan as his hands went up to the two sword hilts protruding over his shoulders. One of them was definitely the Sword she was looking for: but which one?

Her thoughts went back to Ariella and the others and she started longing to be away from this awful place with her prize. She glanced up and saw a familiar shape hovering high above them: a black speck against the moon. Her heart skipped a beat. Chuah-te-mok. The eagle was always there when she needed him. But how could he work out which of the swords was the right one and direct his dive to snatch it?

There was a blur of movement and the sword blades were

shimmering in the Executioner's hands. In a loud voice he proclaimed, 'Now let justice fall.' But before he could strike, the prisoner wrenched his arms apart, the wrist with its missing hand slipping through his bonds. As one sword flashed down, he grabbed the Executioner's wrist and twisted hard. With a cry of pain Acwellan flipped over, releasing the blade in his fall. The prisoner threw himself on it, drew his feet up and cut his bonds, slipped the loop of rope off his wrist and stood up, sword in hand. Acwellan regained his footing, switched the remaining sword to his right hand and turned to face his opponent.

Lenyé couldn't help siding with Decatur, the intended victim. He'd caught Acwellan completely by surprise, but now it was down to sheer strength and speed and quick thinking.

They circled round on the top of their rock, the cut and thrust favouring first one and then the other. Lenyé found herself trying to outwit Acwellan. If she was in Decatur's place, she would have followed up that series of hacking moves that drove Acwellan back, by leaping on the block of wood and using the height advantage. Then she smiled grimly to herself: if she was fighting Acwellan, she still wouldn't be tall enough to strike the winning blow. As Acwellan responded and drove his victim back, she would have used the momentum to drop down off the rock and draw him towards the fire, then run back up the steps onto the rock again: that would definitely give her the height advantage. When Acwellan tripped on a chain that appeared to be secured to the rock itself, she was amazed how he used it to his benefit by parrying his opponent's stroke and throwing his victim off balance.

There was a roar from the crowd as Decatur caught the down stroke of Acwellan's blade on his cross-guard. For an instant the two were locked together, glaring into each other's faces. Then Lenyé saw Acwellan flick his wrist and thrust upwards heaving Decatur's sword away and driving his opponent back. Decatur stumbled, lost his footing and slithered off the rock. Acwellan leaped down the steps, three at a time, to the ground below and waded in with a series of blows before Decatur could stand up.

Despite her personal sympathies, Lenyé couldn't help admiring the prowess of Acwellan: his precise strokes, the speed of his reactions and the sheer finesse of his sword play. It was as well to be aware of her enemy's ability.

She realised the victim was weakening. Acwellan clearly had the upper hand, almost playing with Decatur: the swiftness of his strokes and parries beginning to confuse the other giant. She started measuring heights and angles of the rock with her eyes and gauging the distance between the two rocks and the fire in the middle. If she really was going to kill Acwellan, she would have to tempt him down onto the ground much earlier in the contest, regain the height of the rock before he could respond, and then launch herself at him. She would need some way of catching him by surprise.

Lenyé was so occupied with her own whirling thoughts that she nearly missed the final moment. With a sudden sweep of his blade Acwellan sent the sword spinning out of his adversary's hand. Then he drove his own blade deep into his opponent's heart. A cry of anguish escaped from his victim's lips: 'Not the *Death of the Undying*.' Decatur dropped to his knees, then collapsed onto his back and breathed no more.

The Executioner leaned over his victim and pulled the blade out of Decatur's chest. Then he held it over a bowl while others poured water from a jug to cleanse it, before drying it on a piece of cloth and sheathing it. To her horror, Lenyé saw Decatur's body sink slowly into the ground, as though pulling out the sword released him from this world. A low moan came from the assembled crowd: 'Not another one trapped in the *Death of the Undying*. How many more must suffer?'

Lenyé's eyes flicked to the sword on the ground and she stared at it, her heart beating wildly. If Acwellan's sword had only despatched Decatur to the *Death of the Undying*, Decatur's

Sword must be the one she wanted. She watched as Acwellan walked towards it. It was too far away for her to get there first. If only she could attract Chuah-te-mok's attention, he could do it. Had he seen? Lenyé looked up searching the sky, but the great eagle was still no more than a speck in the moonlight. Not even he could dive that quickly.

Very calmly Acwellan retrieved the Sword from the ground and sheathed it. Then he unfastened both swords from his back and swapped them over so quickly and so many times that Lenyé was now completely muddled. She had no way of telling which sword was which any more.

King Ogandés was about to speak, when Acwellan cut in. 'We have sacrificed our victim to Ra-Na,' he turned to Lenyé and his face was grim. 'What petition will he grant in return?'

Lenyé hesitated and then conferred with Ra-Na-Jiri before turning back to Acwellan and addressing him directly. 'Because you have freely sacrificed to Ra-Na, great blessing will flow to your King and all his subjects.'

A shout of approval went up from the crowd amidst chants of "Ra-Na, Ra-Na", and it took King Ogandés some time to quieten them. Even then a low murmur of "Ra-Na, Ra-Na" continued.

A smile played at the corners of Acwellan's mouth. 'Your Majesty,' he turned in mock contrition to King Ogandés. 'Forgive my asking so bold a question but I believe it is your place to petition the great god Ra-Na for a sign to confirm his blessing.'

'Very well,' the King's voice rang out over the crowd. 'What sign will you give us?'

Lenyé conferred with Ra-Na-Jiri again and explained their request.

'You know. I've always wanted to fly,' Ra-Na-Jiri was swaying to the sound of the chanting. 'Why don't you give them some story about me going up into the sky? That would be such a spectacular sign. Nobody could miss it.'

'And if it doesn't happen, as it's never likely to?' Lenyé let her words hang in the air.

'We keep spinning it out for as long as we like, saying the time isn't quite right yet. I'm enjoying myself too much to care.'

Lenyé turned back to the King. 'Your Majesty. Ra-Na fell from the heavens at the Beginning. If you see him lifted up in the same way that he came, your request will be granted.'

The chanting rose to a tremendous crescendo.

She glanced at Acwellan and was disconcerted to see his eyebrows raised in genuine surprise.

Lenyé didn't feel as confident as Ra-Na-Jiri in what she had just done. If they failed to satisfy this crowd there was no knowing what might happen to them.

The packed ranks surged forwards in a tighter knot, cheering and shouting. Acwellan walked over to her rock, drew both his swords and knelt before Lenyé and the golden dish. He bowed his head to the ground and touched the tip of each sword on the ground in front of him. 'O great god Ra-Na. You have heard our petition. Grant our request.'

Before he could finish, Lenyé glanced up and saw the familiar shape falling out of the moonlit sky. 'Chuah-te-mok,' she gasped. 'How could he possibly know which sword to go for now?'

Acwellan slid the sword in his left hand slightly forwards in the direction of the golden dish. Lenyé peered over the edge of her rock to get a better view. Had he unwittingly disclosed the true sword? If only Chuah-te-mok understood. Even as Acwellan retracted the sword, a dark shape broke in amongst them. Lenyé closed her eyes and held her breath in anticipation, and heard a clang of something hard striking against metal.

Lenyé expelled her breath: he's done it!

She opened her eyes and was surprised to find Chuah-te-mok practically level with her on the rock. As the eagle spread his wings and flew off, Lenyé was horrified to see, not the gleaming sword she was expecting, but the thrashing form of Ra-Na-Jiri gripped in his talons.

Acwellan stood up, then turned and bowed to King Ogandés. 'Your Majesty, and all loyal subjects of the King. Now we have seen with our own eyes the sign of confirmation. The great god Ra-Na has been taken up from us,' he paused to let his words sink in. 'But he has seen fit to leave his consort here to assure us of his further good pleasure.'

There was a roar of approval from the crowd and chants of "Ra-Na, Ra-Na, Ra-Na".

Lenyé was appalled. What was Chuah-te-mok thinking of? And what's going to happen to me now that Ra-Na-Jiri's gone?

In the ensuing hubbub and confusion, Acwellan held Lenyé's gaze as he faced her again and called up to the four startled guards on her rock who still held the empty golden dish. 'Escort the Huntress to my chambers for her own safety.' He partially climbed the steps and beckoned one of them to lean down so he could whisper in his ear, but Lenyé distinctly heard his words as they carried on the breeze: 'Relieve her of her weapons and post a guard till I come.'

Chapter Fifty Five

Kyros bade farewell to Stellatus and turned to enter the gateway. As he passed through, a chill blast caught him by surprise.

He shivered. An uneasy feeling crept over him that was more than physical cold: it was the fear that grips all who pass from the Waking World to the Realm of the Departed.

Stellatus' warning still rang in his ears: 'Do not stray from the path or engage with another being as you pass through the first two regions: the *Death of the Undying* and *Those Awaiting*. The Sacred Pilgrims of Lohr are beyond these, in the *Place of Rest.*'

Kyros was soon engulfed in a dim glimmer, not the total darkness he was expecting, but there was no source of light that he could make out, and the atmosphere began to weigh down on him as though it would snuff out his very life.

'Oh, My King,' he cried out against the awful gloom. 'Give me strength to come through this place and reach my goal.'

There was no discernable landscape, no hills or valleys or trees, not even a horizon; everything was a dull grey with no break in the monotony. But his feet had found some kind of path.

Then he realised what had been growing on him for some time: utter silence. Not the mere cessation of intrusive sounds that helped to create a sense of peace and wellbeing in the Waking World, but the complete absence of anything that could ever make a sound of any kind. Even his feet on the path hardly made any noise at all. It was as though his ears were covered by thick, fluffy material that blocked out all noise.

He thought about Lenyé, as if the reminder of the one he loved would help dispel this gloom. He began murmuring her name, his voice strengthening to counter the sense of despair:

'Lenyé, Lenyé
Where are you, my sweet Lenyé?
How I long to see your lovely face
And the sparkle in your eyes
Captured now only in dream and my memory of you
Reflected in the Pool of Alesco...'

'Who goes there?' a hoarse voice shouted at him in the gloom He stopped. 'Who's that?'

The voice came again, 'Why do you seek to pass?'

Kyros hesitated, and then whispered to the True King for discernment so that he would know what to do. As if in response, the thought flashed through his mind: but I haven't entered either of the first two regions yet. Stellatus' warning about not engaging with another being doesn't apply here.

The voice was more urgent this time. 'What is your answer?'

'Pass what?' Kyros shouted back.

'You have come to the River Lammista-ké, the place of trial for those who enter the Realm of the Departed.

'What trial?'

'This is your last chance to review the words and deeds of your life and make amends before being consigned to your fate.'

Kyros laughed. 'I always thought it too late by then. Surely that is dependent on the quality of person you are in the Waking World. Tell me how I may pass and so come to my goal?'

'You have to cross by boat. Those who fall into the river and try to swim are stripped of everything: the thoughts of their minds and the very recollection of their names.'

'Where is this boat? I have to pass over.'

'Who are you to speak so boldly?' the voice was suspicious.

'I am Prince Kyros of the Krêonor, heir to my Father's throne in the Waking World.'

'When you say, "*Heir in the Waking World*", do I understand that you are not yet dead?'

'That is correct.'

'Good. I am Decatur of the Nastrim.'

'The Nastrim!' Kyros felt a hot anger rising within him. 'Then we are enemies. Your race was responsible for slaying the Sacred Pilgrims of Lohr, whom I seek.'

'Let us put aside our differences over an ancient war; for I must speak to you.'

'Very well. You may take me across.' Kyros heard a boat approaching and could see the outline with a figure rowing over the stern with one oar. There was a scrunch as the prow ran onto the bank. Decatur dropped the oar and reached out his hand.

Kyros was surprised at how tall the figure was: ten feet at least. He took the proffered hand, intensely aware that he was gripped by five fingers and a thumb as he stepped into the boat.

'We are well met.' Decatur pushed off and began rowing.

Kyros soon realised why Decatur only used one oar: the hand of his other arm was missing.

'We have much to discuss and only on the passage over the river can we talk,' Decatur spoke rapidly. 'For once on the other side all talk ceases and we are constrained to wait in silence. I tried to rouse the others of my kin, but they are locked in endless inactivity, and only open their eyes and glare at me and mutter and fume in hushed squeaks that are incomprehensible.'

Kyros felt the boat lurch as he sat down on the middle thwart. 'Then why are you still in command of your faculties?'

'It is the duty of the last entrant to remain alert and ferry the next incumbent across before joining his brethren in the descent into forgetfulness to become a mere shade. That is why I must talk to you now; for as soon as I reach the further shore, I have to surrender the boat to you and join them.'

'So what is it you want to talk to me about?'

'You need to know that the Nastrim were born of Fathers from the Spirit Realm and Mothers from the Krêonor in the Waking World. And because of the mingling of two completely different beings, one spiritual and one mortal, we were never able to procreate.'

'Is that like the pack animals we breed?' Kyros' mind was racing. 'A donkey and a mare produce a mule which is infertile.'

Decatur paused in his stroke and glared at Kyros. 'The principle may be the same, but I don't like the comparison. We're talking about Lords of the Realm of Dominion as our Sires, and the Crown of the Peoples of the Waking World for our Mothers.'

'I'm sorry,' Kyros felt the motion of the boat pick up as Decatur continued rowing. 'I didn't mean to insult your forebears.'

'For though we have the enduring life of our Fathers, our Mothers gave us the desire to increase in numbers and so have a hope for the future. But as that is denied us, our labour under the sun has become grievous and we find all things are mere folly.'

'But surely you would find fulfilment in sharing your skills and crops with the Peoples of the Waking World?'

'No. We have been an ever dwindling race. Many were slain centuries ago in the wars with the Krêonor. That is why you haven't heard about us for a long time. We have chosen to remain in our mountain fastness and not run the risk of any more of us being killed in open warfare. Mingling with the Peoples was never an option.'

Kyros heard the swirl of water against Decatur's oar. 'So how did you come to be ferryman?'

'I was despatched here by Acwellan, the Executioner. I was his last victim.'

'How did he do that?'

Decatur sighed. 'All weapons forged in the Waking World do not have the power to fully kill us, but despatch us here to the *Death of the Undying*, where we descend into forgetfulness. There is a *Place of Rest* where we are entitled to go, which we call Elasis; but we can only be sent there by someone wielding the Sword of Justice. Acwellan, the Executioner, has that Sword, but for some reason he uses an exact copy of it, forged in the Waking World, to execute any Nastârs that come before him incurring the death penalty.'

'So why are you interested in me?'

'The Sword of Justice belongs to the Royal House of the Krêonor. When Zerigor lay dying all those centuries ago, Acwellan snatched it from his hand.'

'You mean the Lost Blade of Zerigor? Our ancient writings talk of recovering it; but no one knows where to even begin the search.'

'You would not recover it easily with Acwellan guarding it.'

'So why doesn't Acwellan use it in his executions?' Kyros persisted.

'I recently discovered the reason for that. He is seeking to amass all the slain Nastârs here, in the *Death of the Undying*, and attempt a re-entry of our Fathers into the Waking World. That will raise us from our slumber and drag us back with them. Acwellan's plan is to form an army for one final onslaught to avenge our ancient defeat and wipe the Krêonor from the face of the Waking World and rule in their place. He, of course, will make himself King.'

Kyros heard the surge of water as Decatur unexpectedly dug his oar in deeper. 'Why are you telling me all this?'

'Because if you really are from the Royal House of the Krêonor, that Sword is rightfully yours and you can use it to despatch the Nastrim to our true resting place. I don't think any of us, having tasted the emptiness of the *Death of the Undying*, want to return to the Waking World with that hopeless sense of futility. We only ever want to be sent to Elasis.

'So you would openly oppose Acwellan to gain that chance?'

'That's how I lost my hand,' Decatur raised the stump of his right arm. 'Trying to steal the Sword from him one night. He was too quick for me, and had me arrested and brought before him for execution.'

'But if Acwellan has this Sword, how do I fit in?'

'You must promise me that, when you return to the Waking World, you recover this Sword from Acwellan and release us.'

'I cannot make such a promise. Nor can I undertake such a task. For I am on a mission here in the Realm of the Departed, and seek the *Place of Rest*.'

He heard the slap of water as Decatur pulled up the oar and threw it into the bottom of the boat.

'What are you doing?' Kyros cried out in alarm.

Decatur stepped over the stern thwart and stretched out his good hand towards Kyros. 'If you will not help me, I must cast you into the river. For I will not give up this boat until I, and all my brethren, have been released from this accursèd place.'

Kyros was astonished at the speed of the Nastâr as Decatur lunged forwards and gripped him by the throat.

He felt himself choking and unable to breathe and his head was forced back as Decatur pressed the grizzly stump of the handless right wrist under his nose and heaved.

Kyros whipped his hands up between Decatur's arms and thrust hard. The stump slid off his face and the Nastâr released its grip on his neck.

The boat rocked with their sudden movement and Kyros lurched backwards, caught the thwart between his legs and stumbled, flinging out a hand to catch the gunwale and save himself. The boat lurched violently as Decatur sat down. Kyros' hand went wide, completely missing the side of the boat and he pitched over the gunwale into the river. 'Oh, My King,' he cried. 'Only you can help me!'

Chapter Fifty Six

Lenyé was ushered into Acwellan's private chamber between two soldiers, and stood glaring at him.

'Why are you treating me like a prisoner?'

'I have seen snakes like that before when travelling in the South,' Acwellan paced up and down, 'where they are often killed as pests or eaten as a delicacy. So they are not always divine. One appears on Mount Nastâri for the first time in many centuries, and the Nastrim welcome him as their god, Ra-Na.'

Lenyé's mind was racing: where did Ra-Na-Jiri come from? And why were there no words about a snake from Yanantha? She must get the truth out of him.

'That eagle-snatch was most convincing,' he continued. 'The Nastrim believe it was proof of his divinity, and his blessing will start the great Breaking-in. When I tell them they've been fooled, they will tear you apart in their fury.'

Lenyé felt a tightening in her stomach. If she escaped from the Executioner, a mob would be after her.

'It was a stunt to trick us, and win our friendship.'

'Rubbish,' Lenyé was indignant. 'Captain Turvil saw Ra-Na.'

'And you pretended to be his consort.' Acwellan pointed at her, 'There's an army out there seeking the renegade bride-to-be of their new King, Morthrir.' He paused in front of her. 'Then I find out he's King of the Krêonor: our sworn enemies.'

He rounded on her. 'You appear in our midst as some divine being or a runaway bride. You may look like a Huntress with your clothing and weapons, but your longbow is exactly like the ones the escorts had when they delivered their message.'

Lenyé was almost deaf to what he was saying as she concentrated on thinking of a way out of this. Even Chuah-te-mok's suggestion to seek aid from the Nastrim against Uncle Morthrir would seem ridiculous now, and…

Acwellan cut across her train of thought as he continued. 'In which case, we have been harbouring a Krêonor all this time: a deadly enemy, for whom our law imposes an immediate death sentence.' He stooped down and thrust his face close up to hers. 'Tell me who you really are, and why you're here.'

'If you execute me,' Lenyé challenged him. 'That army will avenge my death. But if you hand me over to them, and I am forced to be a bride, then as Queen of the Krêonor I will exact a terrible revenge upon the Nastrim.'

'So I was right. You are human after all.' He paused. 'I have another proposal. The Dé-monos are very close to breaking into this world again. Vashtani, my Father, is one of their most powerful lords. I'm going to keep you as a gift to be his new bride, so we can begin to restock the Nastrim with youngsters.'

Lenyé struggled with the implications of what he said. This would be far worse than a forced marriage to her Uncle. She tried to deflect his remark. 'When will I get my longbow back?'

'I have taken it so my crafters can test the power of the weapon and come up with a suitable defence against it.'

He snapped his fingers at the soldiers. 'Take her away, and place a guard over her rooms.'

As they led her out, she felt the anger in his parting remark. 'I have challenged your precious Krêonor army to fight for you. In three days time, I chain you to the Execution Rock. If they win, they take you. If I win, I keep you for my Father. Before the week is out, you will be a bride either for Morthrir or Vashtani, whether you like it or not.'

Chapter Fifty Seven

Quinn was worried about Beth. The cottage was warm from the stove in the kitchen, but Beth had been shivering violently ever since he woke up that morning. He was doing his best but Ishi-mi-réjá's probing questions were beginning to reveal the gaps in his story. When he finally admitted that two nights ago they were close to the great oak tree of Druis-cyf-rin, the old woman rounded on him in amazement.

'Either you're as strong as an ox, or someone else helped you. There's no way you could've brought her all that way in two days on your own.'

Ishi-mi-réjá continued to bustle about her kitchen making Quinn fetch water from the well to boil in a huge pan, while she cut up some old sheets and stirred them in the pot with a large wooden spoon. 'You carry on stirring and I'll get Beth out of her clothing. I'm going to have to wrap her up tight in these hot cloths to stop her shivering.'

She disappeared into the other room and he could hear her moving about and muttering to herself.

'Squeeze out the cloths and pass them through to me.' Ishi-mi-réjá shoved a large wooden tray round the door frame and Quinn began loading the hot cloths onto it. 'That's enough,' and the tray disappeared.

He could hear more movements.

'You can come in now.'

Quinn gasped when he saw Beth. She was encased in white sheeting from head to toe. Only her face and hair were left uncovered. He was horrified to see steam rising from the hot cloths. 'Are you sure you know what you're doing?'

The old woman laughed. 'If you don't like it, you can take her elsewhere.'

'No. No. It's just that I don't know…'

'… what the matter is with her?' she finished his sentence for him. 'Midnight. At Druis-cyf-rin. That can only mean one thing.'

'I don't understand.'

'That oak tree is a doorway. One of the thin places between this world and the spirit realm. Did you see anything or anyone near the tree?'

'No,' Quinn hesitated. 'Not really.'

'But you had help getting Beth here, that's plain enough. I don't want to know who, because that same person may be involved and you're trying to protect them. The fact of the matter is she's been hit fair and square by an emanation. Someone has sent out a summons for a very specific purpose.'

'How do they do that?'

'They would have to harness the collective power of a group focused on a specific outcome, and re-direct it to their own purpose. If it was at Druis-cyf-rin, we're talking about a convocation; and that means real power.'

Quinn frowned. 'What's that got to do with Beth?'

'Your cousin appears to have been very sensitive to it.'

'Is that why she's…'

'Gone into trance?' Ishi-mi-réjá chuckled. 'That's her natural protection. It shows she's able to ward off any wrong influences and remain true to herself. Tell me. Have you ever noticed anything different about your cousin?'

'Different? In what way?'

'Well. Which hand does she write with, for example?'

'Her right hand, same as the rest of us.' Quinn paused. 'No. Wait a minute. She's left handed.'

'Are you sure?'

'Yes. When she learned to play the lute, she made such a fuss that they restrung it the other way round and her tutor had to work out the chord shapes for her right hand so she could pluck the strings with her left.'

'So she had the strength of character to make it work for her left-handedness?'

'Yes. She's a brilliant player now.'

'Interesting. Anything else?'

Quinn hesitated. 'Beth and I used to mess about with my brother's practise swords. Once she learned how to use one I could never get at her to strike properly because she held the sword in her left hand and protected her body in a completely different way than most opponents.'

'Did she pick it up quite quickly?'

'Yes.'

'I think I'm beginning to understand.'

'Are you saying there's something wrong with left-handed people?' Quinn sounded indignant.

'No. Of course not. They just see things differently and experience things differently from us right-handed people. It also means that she's probably more spiritually aware than most people, or rather, she's more able to make the inner connection than most people. That's why she reacted so strongly to the emanation.'

'And you can cure her?'

'I can bring her out of the trance. Curing her is as much down to you and how you help her from now on as it is to me.' She passed him a stone from the mantel shelf. 'Here. What do you make of this?'

Quinn turned it over in his hands. The stone was an odd shape, like a piece of dough someone intended to mould into a bread roll, but gave up part way through leaving strands sticking out like spines all down one side. There were odd little indentations down the other, as though the baker stuck his finger tips in the dough and the dimples hadn't risen and disappeared. The bottom curved inwards like a sea shell. But the whole stone with every projection and every cavity was worn smooth, as though the sea had washed over it for aeons. He held it up to the light of the window. Its grey colour was solid enough. Even the curious yellow and white swirls and veins that mingled with the grey appeared to go right through the stone itself and weren't just surface colouring.

'It's very heavy for its size,' he ran his finger along the dimples. 'Did you carve it?'

'The old woman chuckled. 'Not likely. That thing is so ancient there wasn't anybody around to carve it when it was formed. That's my miraculous stone. That's my *ishi-mi-réjá*. That's me.'

She took it from him and held it between her two palms, then began stroking, almost caressing the stone. 'Here. Try again,' and she passed it back to Quinn.

'Ow.' He dropped the stone. 'It's so hot.'

She was surprisingly quick and caught the stone before it hit the floor. 'Ah. Not everyone feels that. You're not so far behind your cousin in these things after all.' She laid the stone in one hand and caressed it again several times. 'Come. You can watch while your cousin is set free.'

Chapter Fifty Eight

Lenyé sat in her apartment stunned at what the Executioner said. She was painfully aware of the threat of Uncle Morthrir desiring her in marriage.

But Vashtani: Acwellan's Father!

She'd never heard of anything so awful.

There had always been the scary stories they were told as children about beings from another world breaking in and carrying off the fairest of the Krêonor women to be their wives and giving birth to a race of giants. But when you get to a certain age, you stop believing things like that. She always tried to shield Beth from the horrors of those stories when it came to her turn to read from the scrolls before bedtime. Yet here she was amongst a race of giants that only ever hovered on the edge of reality in her world. So the stories must be true after all.

How could Acwellan be so sure the Dé-monos were going to break back in? What was it Mamma Uza-Mâté said? *"They brought a curse into the world. It took the intervention of the True King himself to expel the Dé-monos and seal up the entry point"*. She tried to argue that at dinner, but King Ogandés quashed the idea, saying, *"Our greatest hope is they will join with other spirit-beings and force a point of entry somewhere elsewhere"*. And then Acwellan capped that by saying, *"All it needs is a word of power from a human being with the right authority in this world, and the Breaking-in will begin"*. King Ogandés was right, she thought to herself, it doesn't sound like the Dé-monos are going to give up that easily. But who is this human being with the right authority? They can't mean me because they think I'm the Mighty Huntress. Maybe that's why Acwellan pushed me so hard to reveal who I am. If he knew I was a Princess in the Royal House of the Krêonor, perhaps he would recognise that as the right level of authority, and force me to speak this word of power.

But then her heart went out to Kyros. If only he was here, he would know what to do. He had a far greater claim on her than Uncle Morthrir or Vashtani. They might try and use force, but Kyros was her choice and her love for him was freely given.

But then she thought of the things she'd come through and caught a glimpse of her cut down dress and boots in the mirror on the wall and thought of her page-boy jibe when she was with Yanantha. 'O Kyros,' she spoke aloud in the silent room:

'How can you love me as I am?
For the dress I had made for you is ruined
And I am tired through travel and many labours
But always to You and You alone may my beauty be,
Hidden from any other mortal eye,
A maiden in waiting
Kept solely for You
Come to my arms, my Prince
For I am waiting for You

Sweet Kyros,
If ever the ether can convey my thoughts to You
So let them carry,
Like a sparrow darting from her nest
Like a lark on the wing in carefree abandon
Like a swan spanning the skies
And an eagle falling on its prey
May my words find their rest
Let my love come to You.'

Chapter Fifty Nine

Ishi-mi-réjá rested the stone on Beth's forehead, and placed her hands on the girl's shoulders. 'Beth. Tell me what you see.'

Beth jerked against Ishi-mi-réjá's hands, her mouth wide open in a silent scream. The stone shot forwards onto her stomach.

'It's all right,' Ishi-mi-réjá eased her down onto the bed. 'Take your time. You have to speak this out.' She replaced the stone.

Beth jerked up again, and gulped out some words. 'Snake... big head... swaying ... about to strike... Lenyé... look out!' Then she fell back on the bed shaking under Ishi-mi-réjá's hands.

Quinn saw the stone replaced, and heard the old woman sing, 'Be free, be free, be free,' over and over and over again.

At last Beth shuddered and went limp. She opened her eyes. 'Where...?' She struggled against the swathes of sheeting. 'Where am I? Quinn where are..:?' she broke off. 'Who are you?'

'It's all right, my dear.' Ishi-mi-réjá's voice was soft. 'Your cousin's here.' She stood up to let Quinn sit on the bed.

'Quinn. Is it really you?'

'Beth. I'm so glad to see you back to your own self again.'

'Where's Uncle Morthrir?'

'Shhh. Quinn put his finger to his lips.

The old woman laughed. 'Thought I recognised you. King's youngest son, and Lord Alkram's youngest daughter.' She looked from one to the other. 'Escaping from your Uncle, are we? Don't worry. Your secret is safe with me.' She turned to Quinn. 'Why don't you run along outside and chop some wood, while I help Beth dry off and get dressed?'

Chapter Sixty

The surface of the River Lammista-ké appeared to be totally calm when Kyros was being rowed across, but underneath there was a great turbulence that sucked him down and a strong current swept him rapidly from the boat. He tried grasping at anything that would slow his progress and was horrified to find the bottom of the river filled with faces that appeared out of the gloom and shrieked at him with silent mouths, before disappearing as the current dragged him away.

Kyros clawed upwards till his head burst above the surface. 'Save me, Oh My King,' he cried out in despair. 'Do not let me suffer the afflictions of this accursèd river!'

But he couldn't fight the current. It pulled him under and rolled him over and swept him further away from the ferry.

With a shock his whole life flashed before him as though he'd swallowed a hook and a fisherman was reeling in the line and stripping his life away: his attitude to people he knew and things he'd done and hasty words he'd spoken which he was now thoroughly ashamed of. He didn't have time to decide whether the thoughts were good or bad, he just tried to hold onto them as his identity began to vanish.

Then Kyros recalled his best memories. He could see his Father lean forwards and stir the embers of the fire on that precious evening when the two of them were alone for a few days on a hunting trip. He was twelve, and they talked far into the night about things only a Father and son can discuss. That was when he really bonded with his Father and knew he had crossed the threshold into manhood. He could see his Mother's hair silhouetted against the sunset under the pear trees in the orchard as she played her lute and sang to them, while the rest of the family feasted on freshly picked fruit. And he rejoiced at the profound effect her love and gentleness had on him. He could see Lenyé's beautiful face and fair hair and sparkling eyes, and hear her laughter. O, Lenyé. Where are you now? Never let me forget your loveliness. If only I could come to you and hold you in my arms and tell you of my love.

But it was no good; even these thoughts were stripped away.

How long he fought and tumbled and surfaced to gasp a breath before he was swept under again, he never knew. It felt like he had been doing this all his life and gradually the mere repetition of it was filling his mind as though there was nothing else he could think about anymore.

Finally, there was only one thing left he could cling on to: 'My King,' the thought welled up within him like a tiny spring of sweet water bubbling out of the ground. 'Come to my aid!'

Then he saw a picture of himself, as clear as the day it happened. He was with Lenyé and their two Fathers and his brother and sisters and the rest of his cousins on a walking trip high up in the mountains. He slipped and fell into a crevasse; and only the rope secured around his waist, and lashed to the centre of his walking stick, saved him. The stick jammed across the opening of the crevasse and the rope brought him up with a jerk, leaving him dangling over a long drop. He was pretty shaken by the time the two Fathers had pulled him up, but he was all right.

This time, it wasn't a walking stick but a large boulder his rope was attached to. The boulder was caught in the jaws of the crevasse above his head. The other end of the rope wasn't tied around his waist: he was holding it in his hand. There was no one else to help and he was left to his own efforts to pull himself out. But the more he tried to climb up the rope, the weaker he became, and kept slipping back. Then he noticed that the rope wasn't tied around the boulder, but seemed to come right out of the boulder itself. As he watched, the boulder got bigger and bigger until it was the size of a huge rock, so big that it eased itself up within the jaws of the crevasse. Then the rock started to roll along the crack of the crevasse, winding the rope around itself and hauling him up till he was lying on top of it.

Kyros heard a voice, which he recognised instantly. 'Do not fear, for I am with you. When everything else has been stripped from you, I am your rock. I will never let you fall.'

Then he was in the orchard, under the pear trees, lying on his stomach but leaning on his forearms, and laughing. And there, only slightly in front of him and facing him, and also lying on his stomach, was the man who wrestled with him in the mouth of the cave. And he was laughing, as though they both shared a great jest together. Even though Kyros knew this was the True King, he felt no sense of fear or awe: just sheer delight at being in his presence.

'Come,' the True King chuckled and reached out his right arm and placed his elbow on the ground and held his hand out towards Kyros. 'We have wrestled before, and you prevailed. Let us try arm wrestling to decide the winner.'

Kyros, still laughing, stretched his arm forwards and they grasped hands.

They were evenly matched. First one, then the other would push his opponent's hand down, only to find the resistance increasing and have his hand pushed back again.

'Last time we met,' the True King smiled at Kyros. 'You prevailed against me. This time you are prevailing *with* me. Now I will elevate you in the eyes of those whom you lead, so they may know that I am with you.'

As the True King finished speaking, his face blazed with brilliant light. Kyros instinctively screwed up his eyes, but the light seemed to penetrate his whole being till he was full of light himself. Then he blinked in surprise for the brightness no longer blinded him.

'You asked me my name when you were not ready to receive it,' The True King's eyes narrowed as he became serious. 'Now you are ready.' He lowered his voice and whispered, 'I am Luchianó-bé, Lord of Light. I entrust you to carry my name with you. You have my authority to use my name in any Realm, but especially when you return to the Waking World. You must gather my people and speak my name to them, for they have largely forgotten it or scoff at it.'

Something entered into Kyros, more than the light he had already received, more than the reassurance of that rock saving him when he was powerless to help himself; it was as though something new and vibrant coursed through him, not just his body, but his mind and his inner being as well. He felt strengthened and enriched as though the light that now entered him had turned into the light of life to sustain him.

In that moment he was engulfed with an intense feeling of peace, and a deep love was kindled in his heart for Luchianó-bé. It was more important for Kyros to go on loving this man, this King, this…, how was Kyros supposed to describe him?

Who was Luchianó-bé?

He was more than a man, more than a King, more than any other being Kyros had ever encountered.

Suddenly Kyros knew, not because he had cast aside his ability to think things through and come to a rational conclusion. Something deeper than reason had laid hold of him. He just knew, intuitively: not even by the whispered words of the True King's voice, but by a deeper revelation to his inner being, as though knowing the True King as he did now had opened something in his consciousness to receive the full truth about Luchianó-bé.

Kyros had never felt so alive as he did at that moment: he was bursting with it. He wanted to shout!

Luchianó-bé was Lord of Light, not because he ruled over it or controlled it, but because he was the very source of light itself. And Kyros had seen it and felt it and been filled with it. Kyros began making the connections in his mind: if he was the source of light, that meant he was the source of life. And, if the deep feelings stirred in Kyros' inner being were anything to go by, he must be the source of love as well!

In response to that revelation, Kyros only wanted to be continually in his presence, and to love and serve him in return, whatever the cost.

Immediately Kyros was faced with a choice: to recover the Crown of Life and unite the Peoples of the Waking World and rule over them, or to voluntarily lay down his desire as an offering to Luchianó-bé instead. Kyros wavered. He could either cling to his boyhood dream and try to make it happen by his own efforts, or accept that his whole life paled into insignificance in comparison to the greater life of Luchianó-bé. Kyros struggled with what he would lose; but then his mind cleared and he realised of how much more worth the knowledge of Luchianó-bé was, compared to anything he could ever do with his own life. It wasn't about achieving; it was all about being in a relationship with the True King: of receiving his love and giving back the love in his own heart. Without a moment's hesitation he let go of his dream.

He felt a tightening of the hand that still gripped his, and a wave of joy rushed through the other man's fingers up his arm and flooded his whole being, as though Luchianó-bé himself was overjoyed at what had just happened. For Kyros sensed that a great transaction had taken place: he was at one with Luchianó-bé, and he could never live for himself again; but only to serve the True King. In that instant Kyros knew he had ceased from all his own strivings and had come to a place of utter rest.

He recalled the words of Hoffengrégor, "*...wisdom will always*

triumph, even if we have to lay down our lives in the Waking World."
Kyros winced as he remembered his strong reaction against that statement at the time, but it made sense now. If he had to lay down his life for the honour of serving Luchianó-bé in the Waking World, then it was a small price to pay. Also, he understood the light that blazed in Hoffengrégor's hair and the old Prophet's one good eye: it wasn't anything special about Hoffengrégor himself; rather, it was light that came through the man's relationship with the True King.

Then he heard the True King's voice whispering to his inner being: 'I plant a dream in the heart every child born into the Waking World, which only they can accomplish. Sometimes the dream comes to fruition, but often the adult is pulled away by other desires, or the dream gets twisted by people who want to take advantage of it, and the original dream withers and disappears when the person dies. Even if a boy like you achieves his dream, it is only a shadow of what it could have been if he would only give his dream back to me. But you have held on to your dream, and it has become the driving force in your life. Now that you have given it back to me, it has become my dream. Did I not say, *"You were born to be King of your people, but I will make you an even greater King"*. Because you have surrendered your dream unreservedly to me, we will prevail together to fulfil it. Any dream that becomes my dream must come to pass in the Waking World.'

Kyros stretched out to grasp Luchianó-bé more firmly, as if he never wanted to let go, but found himself thrusting against water instead. With that, the light was gone, the hand withdrawn, and he was being tumbled again in the River Lammista-ké.

He was vaguely aware of the course of the river winding in great curves, first to the left and then to the right, and then a sweeping curve to the left that went on and on and on as the current swept him round closer and closer to the bank. He tried reaching out to grasp anything hanging over the edge, but his

221

hands came away empty. Then he was swept to the other side of the river as it curved away to the right.

He came up for what he thought would be his last breath, all his strength was gone and all hope of ever getting out of the river had left him. 'Even if this river claims my life,' he spluttered as he spat out a mouthful of water, 'Yet I will still trust in My King!'

Instantly he heard Luchianó-bé's reassuring voice speaking directly to his inner being: 'Everyone born into the Waking World has to face Lammista-ké, King of Death. And the meeting point is here, at his river, where you are either ferried over, or plunged into its depths. You can meet this river in your own strength and suffer the consequences. But if you face it in my strength and are prepared to die for me, then I will give you back your life. You have now passed through death ahead of your appointed time. Because you trusted in My Name, you no longer need to fear this river for it cannot hold you down or destroy you. Arise, Kyros, for your old life has been washed away; behold, all things have become new.'

Kyros was dragged down again by the current, but he struck out with renewed strength, and, as his arm broke the surface, he felt his wrist gripped by a hand. He kicked with his feet and found himself being hauled up onto the bank.

He opened his eyes and saw a figure dressed in white.

'I am Osâcah, leader of the Sacred Pilgrims of Lohr,' the figure spoke with such a gentle voice. 'Welcome to the *Place of Rest*.'

Chapter Sixty One

Quinn finished chopping the wood Ishi-mi-réjá wanted and sat thinking things over. His Uncle lied about finding Kyros and Lenyé to protect them. Clearly he wanted Kyros dead, but what about Lenyé? His Uncle had only asked those robed figures to find her. And what was this Hidden Power his Uncle referred to?

He was feeling really confused. What was going on?

Where did Rafé fit in? Was he at the convocation, or had he only gone to investigate a noise he heard? And now the delay with Beth needing to recover; they were never going to find their parents at this rate. Should they keep track of their Uncle instead and prevent him finding Kyros and Lenyé? There was too much happening and he didn't know what to do any more.

He was startled by Ishi-mi-réjá coming out of the cottage.

'I'm just off to gather some more herbs,' she called out to him. 'Why don't you get some fresh air for a while; Beth's going to be pretty drowsy all day. There's a package of food on the table for your mid-day meal. I'll see you at supper time.'

Quinn entered the cottage. Sure enough, Beth was fast asleep on the bed. He gathered up the wood, stacked it neatly by the stove and stuffed the package of food in his bag before grabbing his cloak and setting off to find Rafé.

He reached the wood and crept through the undergrowth before spotting Rafé saddling one of the horses.

'Where's he going?' Quinn whispered to himself. Once Rafé had disappeared amongst the trees, Quinn saddled the other horse and followed at a distance.

Chapter Sixty Two

Morthrir tossed and turned in bed, sat up with a jerk and slumped back on his pillows, muttering: 'Something's wrong.'

He was staring at the tapestry behind his desk. It was a depiction of the True King setting the Crown of Life on Zerigor's head at the Beginning. How he hated that picture with its reminder of the Krêonor heritage. Why couldn't the Krêonor accept the Crown of Life was lost forever, and the True King was unlikely to turn up after all these centuries to do anything about it? He always meant to tear it down and have it destroyed now that he was in control, but somehow there had always been more pressing issues to attend to. Besides, once he was sitting at his desk and facing out into the room, he didn't really notice it.

So why did it seem to be so significant now?

And why am I on the wrong side of the desk?

What's the Henosite doing in my chair, on my side of the desk? And why am I standing when important visitors are normally invited to sit? What's going on?

'I need to take possession of your offering,' the voice was low and measured.

Morthrir's eyes flickered from the tapestry to the Henosite's face. 'I don't understand.'

'We're talking about the price.'

'Price? What price?' Morthrir clutched the edge of the desk to steady himself. 'I didn't know there was any price involved.'

'*"Didn't know there was any price involved?"*' there was a hint of a sneer in the Henosite's tone. 'What you're asking for isn't free.

Maybe, in your haste to seize the rewards, you overlooked the small matter of a just recompense.' The Henosite pointed his finger directly at Morthrir's chest, 'The price is you.'

'Wait a minute.' Morthrir's eyes riveted on the Henosite's grim face in shock. 'I could never agree to that.'

The Henosite's scowl softened slightly. 'Not the physical bit that you lose when you die. I mean the part of you that lives on.'

'I'm not going to die.'

'Not yet. But one day you will.'

'But the Lord Abbérr...'

'The Lord Abbérron said, "*You are brought back from the dead to serve me, and me alone.*" That only applies to the rest of your life in the Waking World. Not for ever.'

'But surely he will watch over me?'

'Possibly.' The Henosite stared at Morthrir with his unseeing eyes. 'It is conditional, though. Remember his exact words, "*I have appointed you as my Regent in the Waking World. You shall reach out your hand and take all that you desire. On one condition: that you worship me only*".'

'I fully intend to worship him.'

'Fully intend?' The Henosite frowned. 'That's not enough. Do you understand what is involved?'

Morthrir shook his head.

'Worship means you have completely surrendered yourself to another. We have to finalise the transaction to make that happen. Your price is absolute power, is it not?'

'Yes...,' Morthrir hesitated, his attention focusing back on the tapestry. It was almost as if Zerigor himself was staring at him with a warning look in his eyes.

'So when will you agree to my terms?'

'Give me three days while I consider.'

'Three days?' The Henosite shook his head. 'What will you give to justify the extra time?'

'Money. I'll empty the entire Royal Treasury.'

The Henosite threw back his head and laughed. 'The miniscule amount you have in the treasury wouldn't satisfy the least of my servants. Let's make it a bit more than that shall we. What else do you have to offer?'

'My palace…, my country…, my people.'

'Your palace? Is it true then that you have been crowned in secret and no one is aware of it?'

'Yes. No. Well, it's going to happen. Soon. When I locate the girl I intend to marry.'

'I think you'll find you're already married.' The Henosite leaned forwards with his elbows on the desk. 'You are trying to bargain with things and people that do not yet belong to you. Maybe we could reduce the time you need to consider.'

'Two days.'

'What little extra would you give for that?'

'Lenyé.'

'Lenyé?' The Henosite sat back with a puzzled expression.

'My wife-to-be.'

'When you have her in your clutches and are able to make the transaction, I might be tempted to agree.'

Morthrir's attention flicked back to the face of Zerigor, as if for inspiration. Everything he wanted and dreamed of was slipping from his grasp. Beads of perspiration stood out on his brow and he shivered. Almost against his will his focus was drawn back to the Henosite, and he felt the man's eyes boring into his own as if the sightlessness had gone and…

Then he recoiled in horror.

The familiar face and vacant eyes disappeared to be replaced by the vision of a great figure seated across the desk from him, its radiance hidden by a cloak and hood.

'What else?' The voice was no longer the Henosite's but it sounded the same, only in a far deeper register.

'I have nothing else.'

'Then we'd better make it today.' The figure held out its hand to shake on the contract. 'Now.'

Morthrir whipped has hand off the edge of the desk as he backed away. 'You drive too hard a bargain.'

The figure before him smiled and extended its hand further across the desk. 'That's life. It depends on whether you want something badly enough. Like power.'

'No. No. Not here. Not in Terrazarema. It has to be…'

'On Mount Malkamet?' The figure paused as if considering the proposal. 'Very well. But when we do meet again, I shall require your answer: absolute power in exchange for you. I will have the documents drawn up. Make sure you sign both copies.'

Morthrir swayed on his feet as the full import of the consequences swam before his mind.

'If I need you again before that date, where can I find you?'

'Here. In my private council chamber.'

'*Your* private council chamber?'

Morthrir felt as though he was standing naked before his inquisitor, that nothing was hidden from its eyes, that everything he had ever said or done or thought was known to…; no, no, even now he couldn't bring himself to whisper the name.

'Do not assume that any of this,' the figure indicated the room with a gesture of its hand, 'is yours, until the transaction is completed. If you want it badly enough, then go ahead with the Grand Convocation you've called. But make sure you only come before me again with the right answer.'

The figure disappeared, and Morthrir was left staring at the tapestry.

But something was wrong. Zerigor was no longer looking in Morthrir's direction, as though he had deliberately turned away in complete rejection.

With a cry of anguish Morthrir collapsed in a crumpled heap on the floor.

PART V

THE LONGBOW

Chapter Sixty Three

Lenyé was surprised by Captain Turvil's knock on her door. He was on his way to test her longbow and arrows for their penetrating power against the Nastrim armour. Acwellan wanted bigger shields made to protect his soldiers. But she was even more amazed at his unfolding story of a well-supported conspiracy to overthrow Acwellan. Decatur was a ring leader.

'There are many more who will side with us,' Captain Turvil continued. 'But in three days time we face an army in battle. Acwellan won't change his tactics, but we need your longbow and many more like it if we are going to defeat them. We are prepared to defy him and make ready in secret.'

'So why didn't the Nastrim develop longbows of their own?' Lenyé was genuinely interested.

'We have only ever been allowed to kill our foes by direct hand-to-hand combat, using swords and javelins.'

'Why's that?'

'The Executioner believed that killing an enemy from a distance prevented us from entering Elasis, the proper resting place for our dead. As he's been the long-term guardian and keeper of the Sword of Justice, we have always had to obey him.'

'I see,' Lenyé picked up her longbow and drew back the bowstring. 'I can handle a six foot longbow and thirty-seven inch arrows. If you're going to copy it, I suggest using exactly twice the dimensions. Make up a few test models to see if doubling the size will work for the average Nastâr.'

She talked him through what woods to use and how to

straighten and seal the arrows.

Captain Turvil glanced up, 'Is that it?'

'Not quite,' Lenyé held out her hand for one of the arrows. 'Do you have anything that burns well?'

'We use a mixture of pine tree resin and seed oil for lamps and flares. Is that any good?'

'Perfect. Can you make up some soft ribbons of flax or hemp?'

'That's no problem. Is there a reason behind all this?'

'Fire arrows,' she crooked her finger just behind the tip. 'You soak the flax ribbons in your mixture and tie them round here. Before the arrows are loosed the archer sets fire to the ribbons.'

'And the effect of such a weapon?'

'Confusion and panic.'

That night Captain Turvil reported back to Lenyé in her apartment. A team of crafters had made six longbows and enough arrows for some serious testing. They were staggered at the result. The new longbows increased the performance by far more than a factor of two in terms of arc range and penetrating power at the point of impact.

Now that the frames and jigs for the longbows and the arrow clamps were ready, many sympathetic Nastârs were making the weapons. Captain Turvil had selected one thousand Nastârs for secret archery training, and organised them into companies to focus on the two basic tactics needed: loosing arrows in a high arc to take out advancing horsemen; and aiming, with a lower trajectory, directly at a specific target.

Although Lenyé was eager for his news, part of her mind was elsewhere trying to work out the tactics to use against Youdlh's warriors. Her thoughts drifted back to the day the warrior threw his axe at the tree stump. Funny how little things stick in your mind. Beth treasured that piece of bees wax ever since, keeping it in a special box in one of her drawers.

After the feast they were treated to a spectacular display of horsemanship by Youdlh's warriors. Over the next few days, she and Kyros learned some of the basic skills they had seen and were able to use a lance to pick a peg out of the ground, but only at a slow trot. They also learned how to use a bolas made of weights tied on the ends of interconnected cords, for throwing at animals and entangling their rear legs to bring them down.

They begged their parents to let them stay longer when it was time for them all to go home, and their Fathers agreed, somewhat reluctantly, she recalled as she thought back to that scene in the courtyard. Why was there always this cold feeling between her Father and the King, and Uncle Morthrir? It had to be more than just their Mother dying in childbirth, while the baby survived. Oddly enough their Uncle had welcomed the idea, and Aunt Faria was delighted at the prospect of having some youngsters around the castle for a little longer.

In four days their riding skills improved dramatically and they were able to lift a peg at full gallop. They also learned the more dangerous versions called *lana-dan* and *lana-din*. Both involved three riders and a rope with hoops in it, stretched across the course before you reached the pegs. In *lana-dan* you rode in wedge formation, and the leading rider in the middle had to thrust his lance through a hoop and lift the rope so that the two flanking riders could pass underneath it and pick a peg each. In *lana-din* the flanking riders were in the lead and lifted the rope for the central rider to go underneath and pick his peg.

It was hard enough at a slow trot. You had to focus solely on your role, either lifting the rope or going for a peg, shut all else out of your mind and trust your companions to do their part. If someone failed to lift the rope... The consequences didn't bear thinking about. But the teachers knew their business, and she and Kyros were soon doing both techniques at full gallop.

By the end of the week they were through with their training and took to riding further afield with a food hamper and staying out till evening. One day they rode down a lane they hadn't used before and were startled by shouts and the thunder of hooves. They tethered their horses and crept through a line of trees to see what was going on and were surprised to find a complete training camp for Youdlh's warriors. They could see the horsemen doing *lana-dan* and *lana-din*, not just three riders picking pegs out of the ground as they had learned, but whole squadrons organised to charge at an enemy's ranks.

At one end of the practice area was a row of shields on wooden frames with each squadron taking it in turns to ride straight at them. The *lana-dan* formation translated into a wedge of warriors that burst through the line of shields at one specific point. The *lana-din* formation looked like an inverted wedge that enabled the outriders to hit the line of shields first on either side by veering off at divergent angles and taking out a much longer line of shields as the central riders hurtled through the gap.

The shields were re-set while the commander regrouped his squadrons and positioned his longbowmen behind them in an *offset-box formation*. That was the first time she'd seen it used. Lenyé held her breath as they began loosing arrows over the horsemen while two columns of warriors galloped down either flank and wheeled across the front of the shields, loosing arrows from their smaller bows right in amongst the enemy line. As the columns crossed each other and cantered away, the main body of horsemen was already galloping down the centre of the practice area, a *lana-dan* formation in the centre with two *lana-din* formations either side. She was momentarily dazzled as their axes spun, glittering in the bright sunlight, before splitting open the shields just as the riders hurtled through with lances lowered. The mounted archers poured in behind them loosing arrows amongst the shields as they passed, while the longbowmen followed up in their *offset-box formation* and loosed arrows in amongst the shattered shields at a sickening rate.

The feast day had displayed the separate warrior-skills of

riding and throwing and archery. What they witnessed just now, with all those skills melded together into one cohesive attacking thrust, was utterly devastating.

'Whew,' Lenyé let out a long breath. 'What sort of army could ever withstand that kind of attack?'

'I don't know,' Kyros grabbed her by the hand and started pulling her back towards their own horses. 'We mustn't breathe a word about this to Uncle Morthrir. I'm sure he never intended us to see that. We have to get home and warn our Fathers. If he ever used his warriors against the Royal Garrison, we wouldn't stand a chance.'

Whether their Uncle found out what they'd been up to that day, or not, they never knew; but later on at dinner he said he had organised an escort for the morning to ride back to Terrazarema with them.

The more she thought about the impact of a warrior charge the more she struggled with how to advise Captain Turvil. The Nastârs had to withstand those formidable tactics. Even if the new longbows eliminated the warrior longbowmen early on, they still needed to counter the *lana-dan* and *lana-din* threat.

A plan was forming in her mind, but it all depended on the Nastârs learning to loose arrows fast enough in battle, while she used Chuah-te-mok to signal the direction and range. At least she could do that while chained to the Execution Rock.

She focused on Captain Turvil just as he was explaining how quickly his soldiers had become experts with a longbow.

Lenyé smiled. 'You've made good progress. I just need Chuah-te-mok as a spotter for the archers to signal the range.'

Captain Turvil frowned, 'Who is Chuah-te-mok?'

'One of my most trustworthy friends.'

Chapter Sixty Four

Quinn used the second horse to keep up with Rafé and followed him through the Woods of Rosantyre to a tiny cottage. He tethered the horse and climbed up under the eaves and into the roof to find a chink in the plaster of the ceiling where he could watch and listen as Rafé and his host sipped what smelled like an infusion of herbs. He was fascinated by the old man's face. The eyes showed the man was unable to see properly, but he gave no impression of any disability as the two of them talked. Despite the gentle voice, Quinn sensed Rafé was being tested.

The old man was talking, 'I know you as Rafé for I never forget a hand once I've shaken it. You were at Druis-cyf-rin.'

Quinn stifled a gasp of surprise. So Rafé *was* there after all.

'How did you join the Ten Priests?' the old man continued.

'Eawen, my friend, I can only say that I feel drawn to these events by a strange power and I see it as my duty to obey.'

'The call seems to be strong enough,' Eawen paused, his jaws working as if chewing on something, and Quinn wondered if the old man was ever going to finish his sentence. 'And you were standing in the middle of the arc when the Hidden Power hit us. That emanation you channelled proves you are able to make a strong connection with spiritual forces.'

Quinn clenched his hand into a fist. So that figure in the middle of the arc of Priests was Rafé. He's right in the thick of it.

'Thank you,' Rafé's voice was little more than a whisper. 'I've never felt anything so powerful before.'

'So why didn't you point directly at Morthrir? After all, he ordered the convocation.'

Rafé frowned, 'I couldn't bring my hands down any further.'

'Did you receive the answer to Lenyé's whereabouts?'

'Not exactly. The intermediary turned out to be a cobra.'

Quinn thumped his fist against the rafters as quietly as possible. So Beth was right about a snake.

'Its vision was so poor,' Rafé continued. 'All I had was a glimpse of rocks and flares and felt curious vibrations through its jaws.'

The old man chuckled, 'You should have gone for a lioness or even an eagle: something with good eyesight. But it wasn't bad for a first attempt. What was the snake's name?'

'All I could get out of it was, "Ra-Na".'

'That'll do.' The old man coughed. 'Come. Kneel before me.'

Rafé did as he was told.

Eawen leaned forwards in his chair and laid both hands on Rafé's head, muttering words that Quinn couldn't hear properly from his vantage point.

Then the old man spoke out loud. 'Rafé. I confirm over you the unity of our brotherhood. Receive this impartation. All you have to do is calm your mind and enter in on yourself and think, "Ra-Na, Ra-Na" and the snake will do want you command.' The old man relaxed, removed his hands and sat back in his chair, while Rafé returned to his own.

'There. At least that gives you a spy so you can keep track of Princess Lenyé. You should get a clearer answer next time.'

There was more discussion but Quinn had enough to think about already. Clearly Rafé was deeply involved with people wielding incredible power, and Uncle Morthrir was trying to use it for his own ends. He focused back on the two men as Eawen leaned forwards and whispered to Rafé. Quinn had to concentrate to hear what he said.

'This is for your ears alone, my friend. Morthrir is being prepared.'

'What do you mean, *"prepared"*?' Rafé was clearly startled.

'There is tremendous spiritual potential locked up in everyone, but at certain key moments particular individuals are called forth to reclaim their spiritual power and control the destinies of others. I believe Morthrir is such a person and his time is fast approaching. He will stand and speak a word of power that will echo through the Waking World and call into being a new spiritual order to direct the future course of our existence.'

'When do you think this will happen?'

'I believe it is imminent. There is a Grand Convocation called for the Summer Solstice on Mount Malkamet. That is where it will happen. I'm certain of it. Make sure you're there.'

As the two men shook hands in parting, Quinn slipped out of his hiding place and raced back to his horse. He had to get away before Rafé spotted him. More importantly, he must get back to Beth with his news and decide what to do.

Chapter Sixty Five

'Ra-Na-Jiri', Lenyé sat up on the bed. 'You made me jump. 'Where did you come from?' She looked hard at the cobra and was startled again by Ra-Na-Jiri's staring eyes. This time his long body formed a rigid wiggly line on the floor with his head raised up above the edge of her bed, but the hood wasn't flared.

'Ra-Na-Jiri. What's the matter with you?' Lenyé snapped her fingers almost in the cobra's face. 'You really frightened me.'

'Huh?' The cobra shook his head, relaxed into his coils on the floor and then reared up so he could see her better.

'How did you get involved with me in the first place?'

Ra-Na-Jiri hesitated slightly. 'I felt powerful vibrations telling me to find you, and I came. That's how snakes behave.'

'And why do the Nastrim know part of your name?'

'My family has always been called Ra-Na, right back to the Beginning. Maybe that's how the Nastrim named their god.'

'But Yanantha didn't send you, did she? You never had any words from her like the others.'

'I've got some now. That's why Chuah-te-mok grabbed me.'

'Really?' Lenyé felt relieved that she'd misjudged him. She pulled her parchment and writing things from her satchel.

He waited for her to ink her pen and then started:

> *Two Swords in splendid jewels bound*
> *Reflecting moonlight on their shimmering blades*
> *The haft of one is secret marked*
> *And only one of twain is sacred true.'*

'But there's no way I'm ever going to get my hands on those Swords.' Lenyé frowned as she puzzled over the words. 'Not with Acwellan keeping watch over them.'

'Have the other words from Yanantha come to pass?

'Most of them.'

'Well, then. You just have to trust.'

'Thanks, Ra-Na-Jiri,' Lenyé glanced up and saw the cobra was about to turn away. 'Anything else you want to tell me?'

Ra-Na-Jiri raised his head. 'The others are planning a rescue.'

'How are they going to do it?'

'Next time you're on the outside of the mountain, make sure you're alone somewhere and they will whisk you away.'

Lenyé pulled a wry face. 'There won't be a next time,' she slumped back against the headboard. 'The Executioner doesn't believe I'm The Mighty Huntress. He's keeping me locked up in here all the time until the day after tomorrow. Then I get chained to the Execution Rock and if Youdlh's warriors can free me, I get hauled off to become my Uncle Morthrir's bride. If they fail, I get to be the bride of some spiritual being that's just about to break back into the Waking World. Either way, he's not going to let me out of his sight for a moment.'

'Can't you plead your complexion will suffer for your new husband if you don't get out and have some fresh air.'

Lenyé thumped the bed with her hand. 'Two days won't make any difference and he knows it.'

'Well. Think of something. Not even the intrepid three can break in here and get you out. You'll have to come to them.'

'I'll see what I can do,' Lenyé flashed a quick smile at him. 'Oh. And watch out for yourself as you glide around the palace. The Executioner is certain you're not the god Ra-Na after all. If he catches you he'll chop you up for his cooking pot.'

Chapter Sixty Six

Rafé sat on his blanket in the woods. He had to get some clear answers from the cobra and try to work out what Lenyé intended to do, and how best he could advise Morthrir.

He started breathing slowly and deeply to calm his mind and began to concentrate his thoughts.

Almost immediately he made the connection and could see Lenyé part-sitting, part-lying on a bed. She was in some sort of bedroom, and clearly the snake had just entered the door for she whipped round and stared at him as though he had startled her.

But then he heard a sharp sound, like someone snapping their fingers, and the connection was broken.

He thumped his fist on the ground in frustration. Even with Eawen's impartation he realised this was going to take time. But he didn't have the time; he needed to know now!

Chapter Sixty Seven

Lenyé sat at the writing bureau in her apartment, unrolled her parchment and read through all the words she had written down. Then she sighed. When would all this be fulfilled?

She knew she was the one to regain the Blade. It was so near, but how was she to get it from Acwellan? And what did the "*Not by might or human strength*" bit mean? What was the point of having a Sword if you couldn't use it as a powerful weapon?

Then there were the three animal quatrains. Had she really developed a vision like the eagle? It was all very well for him to soar beneath the heavens and look down to discern all things, but she couldn't do that. But then Chuah-te-mok said "*You don't need wings on your arms, but in your spirit: you must learn to rise up and see in the spirit realm, and then all things on the ground will fall into place*". What did he mean by that? How could she make it happen? Then he said, "*Learn to do that, and you shall indeed be a maid of honour, and wherever you go, you will bring new life*". The more she thought about what he said the more despairing she became of ever fulfilling those words.

At least Ariella called her a true lioness after that battle with Youdlh's warriors. She wasn't so sure about the courage bit. She just recognised at the time she had to do it or they would get her instead.

The words about Mamma Uza-Mâté were a bit of a puzzle: waiting and incubating. Maybe her desire to find the Sword and get back to rescue Beth and the others was the driving force that kept her going at the moment. That was certainly guarding offspring or loved ones fiercely: at least, that's how she understood it.

But the words Mamma Uza-Mâté gave her proved that one of Acwellan's swords was the one she was after. But what did they mean by *"pierce his last defences"*, she didn't even have her longbow any more, let alone a sword.

Then there were the words from Ra-Na-Jiri. The *"two swords in splendid jewels"* was fairly obvious: they were strapped to Acwellan's back. But she still to get them and find the secret mark to work out which was the right sword. How was she going to do it? That was the real question.

Chapter Sixty Eight

The morning after his terrifying dream, a package was delivered to Morthrir as he sat at his desk. He broke the seal, removed the wrapping and found two identical parchments enclosed. He unrolled one and skimmed through the important points:

I, Abbérron…draw up this contract to appoint Morthrir…as my Regent in the Waking World… in consideration for the sum of his life: to fall due by the signing of this contract… If you fail me, I will seek you out and exact a terrible revenge upon you.

Both copies were already signed.

Morthrir shuddered. So it had come to this at last. All that was necessary to complete the contract was his own signature.

Chapter Sixty Nine

Lenyé sat on the Execution Rock fingering the chain and its huge staple imbedded in the rock. She was allowed out at dusk for some fresh air, and already it was nearly dark. Acwellan supervised as the manacle on the free end of the chain was replaced with a smaller one. 'I don't want your dainty little foot slipping out by mistake.' Now he stood alone on the other rock looking out over the plain to the warrior army camp. Lenyé could just discern the gaps in the "D" forming the semi circle that thrust out into the plain as her eyes were drawn beyond it to the twinkle of flames; and she could smell wood smoke from their campfires on the night breeze. She glanced down at the detachment of guards surrounding her rock, and watched as Captain Turvil climbed up the steps to join her.

'So this is what I'm going to be chained to when the time comes,' Lenyé tugged at the manacle. 'Like bait for ravening wolves. What are Acwellan's tactics to stop them?'

Captain Turvil turned to her and kept his voice low. 'He'll fill that semicircle of rocks with soldiers and have a large detachment outside with those new shields. He'll expect to soak up all the shock of their first few charges and then pour his soldiers out through those gaps in the rock for a counter attack to catch the warriors on the run.'

'I don't think that'll work.' Lenyé explained to him what she knew of the *lana-dan* and *lana-din* formations with the throwing axes and lances to follow up. 'Not even those new shields will stand up to the axes for long. Besides, their longbowmen in the *offset-box formation* will just loose their arrows over the tops of the shields and bring your soldiers down.'

'He will use his javelin throwers to counter that and attack the front row of horsemen.'

'That's still not enough.'

'What do you suggest then?'

'If you stood those new shields on the ground, they would totally cover the front of a Nastâr soldier, wouldn't they?'

'Yes.'

'That's what the front rank has to do: create an impenetrable shield wall. Then the rank behind them must hold their shields over the heads of their comrades in front, and so on, all the way to the back line. That means no arrows can get in at all.'

'Not sure Acwellan will listen to that.'

'When the *lana-dan* and *lana-din* formations appear at the front of their attack, position your javelin throwers under the shields, in-line with their formations. At the last minute, slide the front shields away, and the warriors will be impaled on the javelins.'

'Yes. That might work.'

'I suggest you run the shield wall across the plain between those two spurs of rock, and concentrate the main body of soldiers at the centre, like a giant crab. That will take the brunt of the warrior charges and allow you to counter-attack from the wings.'

'Yes. I agree. But at some point I will have to order the archers into position regardless of what Acwellan is up to. I'm convinced it's our only hope of driving the warriors back.'

'When you do,' Lenyé craned her head round and studied the base of the mountain where it came down to the "D" of rock, 'make sure they are a good twenty to thirty feet up amongst those rocks that go along the ridge. That'll give them the best range out over the plain and also allow them to loose their arrows down into the "D" if your positions get over run.'

Lenyé heard a disturbance behind her and twisted round to see what caused the commotion. 'Ariella,' Lenyé was too surprised to even move.

The big cat leaped onto the rock, hurling Captain Turvil onto the plain below and dislodging two of the guards before anyone else became aware of the attack. Then Mamma Uza-Mâté's head appeared above the edge of the rock as she hauled herself up and Chuah-te-mok dropped out of the night sky.

'Over here, Lenyé,' Mamma Uza-Mâté whispered. 'We must get you away.'

But they'd reckoned without Acwellan.

He spun round, jumped down off his rock and came racing across, bellowing for guards. He leaped up onto the rock and grappled with the she-bear. Acwellan was a good two feet taller, but Mamma Uza-Mâté was far heavier. She planted her feet apart and seized him in a hug that would break a man's ribs; but he was too strong, thrusting against her and toppling them both over. Then Chuah-te-mok was on him, flying at his face with his talons outstretched while Ariella bit his neck and clawed at his shoulder. With a yell, Acwellan heaved himself off the she-bear as soldiers ran up with ropes. But Mamma Uza-Mâté and Ariella were too quick, diving off the edge of the rock and running for a gap in the "D" of rock before anyone could catch them. Chuah-te-mok rose in the air and called down to Lenyé, 'We won't leave you. We'll get you out somehow.'

'So,' Acwellan thrust his face close up to Lenyé. 'An attempted rescue. Your request for fresh air was just a ruse to get you out of the mountain.' He turned to the guards. 'Escort the Huntress to her apartment and mount a guard. Tomorrow she will be chained to this rock.'

Chapter Seventy

Beth was up and fully dressed while Ishi-mi-réjá pottered about in the kitchen brewing something with herbs.

'Did Quinn say how long he would be?' Beth had to raise her voice slightly over the clatter of pans.

'No. But he'll be back for supper.'

Ishi-mi-réjá came into the living room with a small steaming bowl on a tray. 'Here. Drink this,' and she held the tray towards Beth. 'It'll help you get your strength back.

Beth took the bowl and sniffed at the contents. It smelled of freshly mown hay. She took a sip. It was very hot in her mouth, and tasted quite bitter.

'Your Uncle Morthrir has caused a lot trouble for a great many people: your families especially,' the old woman continued. 'The stone of Ishi-mi-réjá never lies. This is between you and me and no one else, except your cousin.' She leaned over and whispered in Beth's ear, 'You are going to uncover the secret behind your Uncle's rise to power.'

'I don't understand.'

'When you do, you will play a significant part in bringing him to justice.'

Beth looked startled. 'I still don't understand. Why me?'

'Well. Not just you. Your cousin as well.' Ishi-mi-réjá held her gaze for a few seconds before continuing. 'Look for me by moonlight at the Summer Solstice and I will be there.'

Chapter Seventy One

'You ask a great thing, my friend.'

Kyros lay panting on the left bank of the River Lammista-ké, relieved to be out of the water and in command of his faculties once more. He looked expectantly at Osâcah, before replying. 'But it must be possible. Stellatus would never have sent me here otherwise.'

'To raise all the Sacred Pilgrims? It cannot be done.'

'Why not?'

'No one has ever tried before,' Osâcah shrugged. 'Besides. They are at rest from all their labours in the Waking World, awaiting the summons of the True King for the Restoration.'

'I'm not asking you to re-enter the Waking World. I need you to pull down a fortress of the Dé-monos in the Realm of Travail.'

'That is very different. Does the True King command it?'

'The True King, you say. Is that the only name you know him by?'

'Yes. Of course,' Osâcah sounded puzzled. 'For by that name we honour him and stay faithful to his memory.'

'That is good. I am here on his business.'

'In that case, come with me.' He led Kyros away from the river till they reached an area where a number of figures, dressed in white, were walking around and stretching up, as though to the branches of numerous trees, and then moving their hands to their mouths.

'What are they doing?'

'Forgive me,' Osâcah looked into Kyros' eyes. 'You may not

be able to see what I see.'

'Which is?'

'We dwell in a place only one stage removed from the Realm of the Blessèd Throne. We ever behold the True King and live in the light that flows from him. All that we need is easily available. This is the time of feasting.' Osâcah raised his hand as though to pluck something Kyros couldn't see. Whatever it was, he offered it to Kyros. But when Kyros reached out to take it, there was nothing there. 'I'm sorry, my friend,' Osâcah's voice was full of concern. 'You have not yet passed over to the Realm of the Departed. These things are still hidden from you.'

'You're right. I only see a dull greyness and people in white plucking things out of thin air.'

'Do not be troubled, but rather, rejoice. For the favour of the True King must rest upon you if you have been able to come this far and not suffer any loss of your faculties. Now I know you have been sent to me.'

Kyros frowned, 'What makes you say that?'

'We regularly petition the True King to avenge us against those who stripped us of our lives in the Waking World. But he always tells us to be patient and wait a while till all things are ready and he sends us his messenger. I was on the bank of the River Lammista-ké, musing on these things, when I saw an arm part the surface and I gripped the wrist and pulled you ashore. By that token, I know the time is ripe.'

'My friends,' Osâcah turned and cupped his hands to his mouth as he addressed the other Pilgrims. 'When we arrived here, we took an oath to come to the aid of the True King if ever we should be called upon to do so. This brother has come from the Realm of Travail asking for our help to free his companion from a fortress of the Dé-monos. Are we willing to undertake this task?'

A voice called out from the crowd, 'What surety do we have that once this task is completed, we can return here unharmed?'

'I can offer no surety except the word of my friend.'

'How do we know we won't get pulled back into the Waking World?' another voice shouted.

'The way from the Realm of Travail is sealed,' Osâcah replied.'

'Then how did your friend get there? He has the mark of the Waking World upon him?'

'I came through the Spiral from the Eye of Hoffengrégor,' Kyros answered. 'But only with the express permission of the True King himself. The one I am trying to rescue came through by mistake, and I am charged with returning him safely to the Waking World.'

'And you're certain we cannot be drawn up though this spiral?' the questioner continued. 'For it is not clear how we would appear in the Waking World. Surely we would be as mere phantoms of our former selves, and who knows what will become of us then?'

'The way is barred by the Guardians of the Spiral,' Kyros replied. 'I have seen them for myself. There is no possibility of them allowing any unauthorised departure from the Realm of Travail, I can assure you.'

'Very well,' the first voice resumed. 'We accept this task.'

'Good.' Osâcah took control again and turned to Kyros. 'The Sacred Pilgrims of Lohr cannot return by using the ferry, even if you can. There is only one way for us that leads out of here. Follow me.'

Chapter Seventy Two

'Ra-Na-Jiri,' Lenyé sat at the bureau reading her parchment as the cobra slithered through the partly opened door. 'You startled me. What news of the others?'

'They managed to escape from the Executioner.'

'Will they attempt another rescue?'

'Yes. They're planning one now.'

Before she could respond there was a bang on the door and Acwellan barged in. 'I want to make sure...' He stopped and focused on Ra-Na-Jiri. 'Just what I need for the illusion.' He strode over to the cobra, feinted a distraction with his left hand, and, as Ra-Na-Jiri struck at him, caught the snake behind its head. Acwellan stood up with the cobra lashing and coiling around his arm. 'Tell your snake friend I want him in his golden dish on the other rock tomorrow morning or I will slit him open and remove his poison sac. Is that understood?'

Lenyé nodded and spoke to Ra-Na-Jiri.

'Tonight I keep him in a lidded basket. If he escapes, it'll be your neck on the block.' With that he strode to the door.

Ra-Na-Jiri called over the Executioner's shoulder, 'Lenyé. Don't let him chop me up for the pot.'

Chapter Seventy Three

Beth and Quinn waved goodbye to Ishi-mi-réjá and trudged up the slope towards the woods where Rafé had shown Quinn he would be camping. They'd stayed at the cottage for two nights and the day in between and now Beth felt fully rested and refreshed.

'She's such a lovely person,' Beth hitched her bedroll further up on her shoulder. 'I almost hate to leave.'

'Come on.' Quinn turned back and waited for Beth to catch up with him. 'Rafé said something about going a shorter way to Onadestra.'

'Before we meet him, I want to be clear what happened back at our old campsite near the Great Oak Tree. Did he suspect we followed him?'

'I don't think so.'

'And did you see if he was one of those robed figures?'

'No,' Quinn glanced at her. 'I was so desperate to get you back before he arrived. I only just made it. That old man I was telling you about confirmed Rafé was there. So he is definitely involved with all this power business.'

'I couldn't get the picture of that snake out of my mind till Ishi-mi-réjá sang over me.'

'I know,' Quinn winced at the reminder. 'The old man confirmed Rafé conjured up the snake in the first place; and now Rafé can use it to find Lenyé.'

'But it's four nights since we were at Druis-cyf-rin. If that snake's been messing around for so long, Lenyé must be in real danger. We've got to go and help her. Or maybe we split up. You go on to Onadestra and I'll try and find Lenyé myself.'

'Beth. Don't be ridiculous. We have to stay together, and we have to concentrate on one thing at a time.'

'But the more we head for Onadestra, the further away from her we're getting.'

'I can't help that.'

'She's my sister,' Beth rounded on him. 'Someone's got to find her and help her.'

'Listen, Beth. We either rescue our parents, or try and stop Uncle Morthrir from getting this mysterious power, or find Lenyé. We can't do all three!'

'I'm just so worried about Lenyé. She's in danger somewhere.'

'But we've no idea where she is,' Quinn shrugged his shoulders. 'And what about our parents? If Rafé's right, Uncle Morthrir's going to have them executed. We've got to stop him.'

'Ishi-mi-réjá said something about me uncovering the secret behind Uncle Morthrir's rise to power and bringing him down. That would solve everything. Maybe we should go after him.'

'But we can't keep track of Uncle Morthrir without Rafé interfering.'

'I don't know. How are we ever going to decide what to do?'

Quinn looked Beth full in the eyes. 'I'm convinced we have to keep going as we are and find our parents and get them released. What do you say?'

'All right, then,' there was a reluctant tone in Beth's voice.

Quinn smiled at her gratefully, 'Besides. Father will know what to do.'

'But if anything happens to Lenyé in the meantime, I'll never forgive you.'

They were well in amongst the trees by now and before Quinn could answer, Beth pulled him down into the

254

undergrowth and put her finger over his mouth. 'Shhh,' her whisper sounded loud in the silence of the woods. 'Look.' She pointed between the trunks to their right.

Quinn looked to where she was pointing and saw a figure with its head bowed, dressed in a brown hood and robe sitting cross-legged under an oak tree. The hood drooped down over the face and hid all his features.

They crouched in the undergrowth watching for some time until the figure stirred. Then he knelt up and looked around before disappearing behind the tree. When he emerged a few minutes later he was minus one cloak and hood and busy doing up the clasp of a familiar looking bag.

'Rafé,' Beth clenched her fist. 'What's he playing at? Was that him trying to control the snake? How can we ever trust him if he's responsible for that snake interfering with Lenyé?'

'I know,' Quinn frowned. 'Despite what he said back at the palace about being loyal to our Fathers, we're going to have to watch his every move.'

They saw him walk off into the forest and return with the two horses.

'Let's get back on the path and make a bit of noise so he thinks we've only just entered the woods.' Beth scrambled out of their hiding place and pulled Quinn with her.

'All right.'

They hadn't gone far when they heard a, 'Hsst!' from amongst the trees and saw Rafé beckoning them over. 'Get down out of sight,' he whispered as they joined him. 'Someone's following you.'

They waited for several minutes huddled behind a cluster of young trees, the horses standing patiently with Rafé's hand on both reins.

'You must have been mistaken.' Quinn was about to get up when they all heard the faint melody of somebody singing. He peered round one of the trunks and started as he saw a figure approaching in a brown cloak with the hood up, and the face completely concealed. Then he relaxed. The figure was too small and too bent over to be one of the figures from Druis-cyf-rin. He glanced round at the others and saw that Rafé was watching him closely.

'What is it, boy?'

'Nothing,' he hesitated. 'Whoever it is looks vaguely familiar. That's all.'

The figure came on carrying a wicker basket with a cloth hanging over one side, and walked past their hiding place. They caught a glimpse of the face.

'It's Ishi-mi-réjá,' Beth was about to break out of hiding, but Rafé gripped her arm and stopped her.

'Don't move.'

'She's only going mushroom picking,' Beth tried to wrench her arm away, but he tightened his hold. 'She told me that's what she'd be up to after we'd gone.'

'Then why didn't she walk up the hill with you? Give her a few more minutes and we'll head across the woods away from the road altogether and pick up a path that will take us up into the mountains. She mustn't see us together or which way we've gone.'

Chapter Seventy Four

Lenyé sat on the edge of her bed, slumped forwards, elbows on knees and her head in her hands. Her eyes were hot, but no tears would come.

What am I supposed to do? She whispered to herself.

None of my friends can get to me, except Ra-Na-Jiri. I can hardly send one cobra against the entire Nastrim army. All those words from Yanantha have come to nothing. I'm Acwellan's prisoner and will either be captured and taken to Uncle Morthrir or kept here for Acwellan's Father to suddenly appear.

The Nastrim all believe I'm a goddess, except Acwellan, and he's keeping quiet about that. Presumably it suits his purpose to maintain the pretence.

The Sword is so close.

How am I supposed to get it, though? I would have to kill Acwellan, but there's no chance with so many guards around. Even if I do kill him and get the Sword, there's still Youdlh's army. I would have to use the Nastrim to destroy that threat.

But I would be deluding them. I'm not a goddess. I don't have any divine powers. I'm only a girl. What will they do to me if they ever find out? I can't keep it hidden for much longer. They're bound to guess the truth at some point.

Oh, Kyros. If only you were here. This is too much for me to take on and think about and carry through in the right way. What am I supposed to do?

I feel so lost and alone. Not even my closest companions can help me.

But you said, *"One of us has to bring Uncle Morthrir to justice, whatever it takes"*.

He's ruthless, Kyros. Utterly ruthless. You've seen that.

They loosed their arrows at you as you dived off the Dangst Rock. They weren't doing that for fun. They want you dead, Kyros. Dead. Do you realise what that means?

If I don't fight and defeat his army, they'll come and get me and force me to be his bride.

Is that what you want?

Well. Is it?

Where are you when I need you most? You can't have completely disappeared.

Why don't you come back to me and sort all this out? Or, at least, let us sort it out together.

I can't face being on my own any longer. I need you.

Then all her anguish over Beth came pouring into her mind again. She hadn't changed towards her sister at all; she was fooling herself. No one can change themselves that much.

A knock at the door interrupted her.

Lenyé wiped her eyes on the back of her sleeve. 'Yes.'

The door opened.

'Captain Turvil. I wasn't expecting you.'

'I came to see if you were all right about tomorrow morning.'

'Not really. Is everything prepared for the archers?'

'They're still working on the ribbons for the fire arrows, but everything else is finished.'

'Make sure they're ready. Fire arrows are absolutely crucial.'

'I'm sorry. I have to go.'

But Lenyé stopped him with one last plea. 'Captain Turvil. There's something I need to tell you.'

'Oh?'

'I'm not the Mighty Huntress. I'm only a young woman. A Krêonor. Of the Royal House. My real name is Princess Lenyé.'

Captain Turvil staggered slightly as though he'd been

258

wounded, and stretched out a hand towards a chair back so he could sit down. 'Do you realise what this means?'

'I have deceived you all along. You must hate me.'

'No. No. It's the best news I've heard in a long time. If what you say is true, you are the rightful keeper of the Sword of Justice. Now is the time to be freed from Acwellan's tyranny. That Sword, in your hands, will release us all from the *Death of the Undying*. If you will use it to that end, we will serve you as our true leader.'

'What?' Lenyé was utterly astonished at his response.

Later, as she fell asleep, Lenyé felt herself clinging on to the edge of a window sill. She knew exactly where she was: the window of the playroom in the palace at Terrazarema between Kyros and Quinn's bedrooms. Uncle Morthrir chased her right through the top floor and she rushed into this room to hide, but the room was completely empty. In her despair she flung open the window and scrambled out onto the sill to try and climb down, but slipped and only just managed to grab the window ledge before she fell.

But as she clung there, she felt a great weight dragging at her ankles. When she glanced at her feet, there was Acwellan trying to pull her down.

She kicked and thrashed her legs till finally he let go and went crashing to the ground three stories below, but then Uncle Morthrir poked his head out of the window and caught hold of her wrists and started pulling her back into the room.

She jerked one hand away and swung outwards, pivoting on her other wrist. Then she shoved both feet against the wall and thrust with all her strength till Uncle Morthrir let go and she felt herself falling. She would rather be dead than marry her Uncle.

But instead of hitting the ground she began to float down slowly, and she could determine her own direction. She tried going sideways, and that was all right. She tried moving away from the palace, and that was interesting. She tried going up, and that was fun. As soon as she thought about where she wanted to go, she found herself soaring way up into the sky with such a sense of freedom and joy she didn't want it to stop.

As she flew she looked down and saw pin pricks of light in a huge plain, and could make out the campfires of Youdlh's army; but they looked so small and insignificant that she found herself laughing. Then her eyes were drawn to Captain Turvil as he commanded the Nastrim and she was at the head of his army with a Sword in her hand.

Suddenly she doubled up in pain, clutching her stomach, unable to move, until gradually she was able to stand up again and shout: 'I defy you, great army of Youdlh's warriors. For you seek to do my Uncle's bidding; but I stand against you.'

Lenyé knew at last that she was no longer doing this because she had to, or to free her sister or because Yanantha told her to. She was doing it because she wanted to. Mamma Uza-Mâté was right: the time of incubation was over. This desire had been growing inside for so long now that it was ready to come out into the real world.

Uncle Morthrir could no longer threaten her.

Acwellan's Father had no hold over her.

Whatever happened now, nothing could touch her. No one was going to force her to marry against her will.

She was completely free.

Chapter Seventy Five

Kyros and the Sacred Pilgrims of Lohr stood at the edge of the River Lammista-ké. Osâcah brought them to a point much further away from the ferry than the place where Kyros had been rescued.

Osâcah turned to face him. 'You may be able to swim this river, but we cannot, for we are subject to the laws of the Realm of the Departed.'

'Then how are you to get across?' Kyros sounded dismayed. 'Even if there was a boat, I cannot row all of you to the other side. It would take too long.'

'The way is simpler than that. As a living representative of the Waking World, you have an authority here that we do not. Call on the name of the True King and step into the river. He will hear and answer you. And that will be proof that you are his messenger.'

Kyros studied Osâcah's face trying to decide whether to speak the True King's real name. Eventually he decided not to, as the time had not yet come, and so he did as he was asked. He faced the river and lifted up his right hand, as though taking an oath. 'Be opened in the name of the True King!' Then he stepped into the water.

As soon as his foot touched the surface, the river stopped flowing. Everything downstream of him cleared so that not even a trickle remained. Kyros continued walking till he was standing in the middle of the riverbed with a huge wall of water upstream to his right.

He turned back to Osâcah and the others. 'Cross now while I hold back the waters.'

All the Sacred Pilgrims of Lohr walked over dry-shod. It took some time and Kyros grew increasingly astonished at their numbers as they filed over. He thought there would be only a few hundred, but there must have been several thousand.

When they had passed him and were assembled on the further side, Kyros followed. As soon as he was on the bank, the river surged back to its original state.

'Praise be to the True King,' Osâcah slapped him on the back, 'for he has conferred on you the power to release us from the Realm of the Departed.'

At that instant there was a shout from in front of them, and a blinding light flooded the bank.

Kyros raised his hand to shield his eyes, but Osâcah darted forwards.

'It's all right, Kyros,' Osâcah called back. 'It's Stellatus come to meet us. I am so delighted to see him again. When all the Sacred Pilgrims of Lohr were martyred, Stellatus and his company escorted us to the Realm of the Departed, and we were able to walk across the River Lammista-ké on the bridge of their song.'

Kyros' eyes focused on his friend, but Stellatus waved away all greeting.

'Quick. There isn't a moment to lose. We cannot contain the Dé-monos in their fortress any longer.'

Chapter Seventy Six

Lenyé stood on the Execution Rock and gazed out over the Nastrim army packed into the "D" of rock and the advanced guard of warriors on the plain facing them. The mid-morning sun was hot on her face, and gusts of wind stirred up eddies of sand and rippled through the parched grass between the Nastrim ranks and the campfires of Uncle Morthrir's army.

She glanced across to Ra-Na-Jiri on the other rock, coiled in his golden dish, and supported on the shoulders of four guards. The fire on the metal dish between their two rocks burned a dull red in the bright sunshine. As Acwellan cast a handful of incense into the flames she could smell the sudden waft of fragrance.

Acwellan looked immense in his chainmail hauberk and plumed helmet, and the polished greaves on his shins sparkled in the sunshine. Lenyé thought of her first encounter with Nastâr soldiers and her analysis of their weak spots: eye, throat or thigh. But that was with the accuracy of her longbow. If she had to fight Acwellan with a sword, she would have little chance of hitting those parts. But it was never going to happen: firstly, she was about to be chained to a rock, and, secondly, she had no sword.

Lenyé watched Acwellan as he knelt towards Ra-Na-Jiri on the other rock. 'O great god, Ra-Na,' he intoned. 'Receive our humble offering and grant us victory this day.' Then he stood up and turned to the soldiers with his arms outstretched. 'Hear, O fellow Nastârs. We are fighting today to preserve the honour of the Mighty Huntress amongst us. Those dogs before us seek to capture her for their King. Let us put off the fear of the *Death of the Undying* and put on courage that we might prevail. For, beyond our hope, the great god Ra-Na has returned amongst us to grant us certain victory.'

A great shout erupted from the Nastrim soldiers and they beat their swords on their shields: 'Ra-Na', clash-clash-clash; 'Ra-Na', clash-clash-clash.

Acwellan waved his arms for silence. 'For Saida's protection, I will chain her to the Execution Rock. Defend her with your lives.'

Lenyé winced at his use of that name for her, knowing full well that the deception couldn't last for much longer.

The chant changed to: 'Saida', clash-clash-clash; 'Saida', clash-clash-clash.

Then Acwellan strode over to her rock, reached up and grabbed the end of the chain, while two guards held her from behind and another pulled one of her feet forwards. She felt the manacle close around her ankle and heard the snick of the key in the lock. She pulled hard with her leg, but the chain attached to the manacle merely clanked against the rock and went taut with the other end fastened to a staple drilled into the rock.

'Acwellan,' Lenyé moved her leg back and the chain went slack. 'You're making a big mistake. Those warriors will decimate your soldiers. Then what?'

'Ah. But you are chained to the rock and I have the key. I don't think they will carry you off that easily. Besides. The Dé-monos are very close to breaking into this world. What better gift could there be for Vashtani than his son to present him with a new bride from the Waking World.'

He signalled to the bugler to sound the start of the battle, but Lenyé could see, from her vantage point on the rock, that the warriors were already advancing in two columns to outflank Acwellan's soldiers. A greater force was massing in the centre to hit the front ranks of the Nastrim.

Before the bugle sounded, the warriors broke into full gallop. Under an arc of covering arrows from their longbowmen, they hit the front line of the soldiers, the throwing axes splitting the Nastâr shields wide open to be followed up by an onslaught of lances. Outriders swept down both flanks effectively surrounding the mass of Acwellan's soldiers, and still leaving warriors to pour through the gaps in the "D" and surround her rock and cut their way through the defending guards.

With the constant assault of axes and lances, the ranks of guards thinned, and warriors were able to swarm up onto her rock and hack at the chain with their axes. One of them pushed the others aside and shoved the spike of his axe through the staple and heaved backwards using the head as a fulcrum against the rock. Nothing happened. But then two others thrust their spikes under his where it protruded through the staple and heaved as well.

There was a screeching of metal against rock and the staple jerked upwards bending over towards the original axe. The men kept heaving and grunting as inch by inch the staple started to come out of the rock.

Lenyé kicked and punched the warriors and smacked the chain against their legs as hard as she could, but two of them pulled her away from the staple and pinned her arms behind her back.

A man squatted down by her head, and spoke urgently into her ear. 'You're coming with us, my pretty one.'

She knew from the blue horsetail on his helmet that he was a Field Commander, and the authority in his voice confirmed his message was straight from her Uncle.

'These are Morthrir's orders. If you're not back at the palace within seven days, he will execute the rest of the Royal youngsters; one a day, starting with Beth, then Quinn, then the next youngest. Better give yourself up now and come quietly.'

'Never!' Lenyé felt his words piercing her heart like a hot knife. She writhed this way and that trying to get her hands free. 'Acwellan,' she shouted, 'Help.' But she could see he was well away from her rock now as the battle raged around the soldiers, and he didn't hear her cry.

Lenyé threw back her head and let out an ear-piercing scream. She saw Acwellan's head whip round and the look of alarm on his face when he registered what was happening.

With a bellow he rushed forwards, grabbed a double-handed sword from another soldier and scythed his way through the warriors that blocked his path. Then he was up on her rock and laid into the warriors before they could drop their axes and defend themselves. The hand-to-hand fighting forced the warriors back down onto the ground between the two rocks. Acwellan jumped down and waded into them with his massive sword. In the confusion the tripod supporting the metal dish with the sacred fire was upset, and all the red hot charcoal fell out into a heap on the ground.

Once he'd dealt with the warriors, Acwellan climbed back onto the rock and examined the staple, giving it a couple of hefty tugs. 'That should still hold.' Then he stood up and roared to his javelin throwers to lead the counter attack while the soldiers came behind with their double-handed swords.

They cleared the warriors out of the "D" and were beginning to press them back, gaining momentum and chasing the horsemen. Many soldiers threw their bolas to bring down the horses while others finished off the riders with their swords. As Acwellan moved back to the edge of the "D" to direct the battle, Lenyé was startled to hear familiar voices behind her.

She whipped round and glanced down from the height of her rock. 'Ariella. Mamma Uza-Mâté.'

'Hush, Lenyé. Keep you're voice down.' Mamma Uza-Mâté climbed up the steps onto the rock

Ariella sprang up alongside her. 'We're going to get you out of here this time.'

The she-bear began tugging the chain away from the staple. 'It won't budge.'

'You need something to lever it with,' Lenyé whispered. 'I've just seen warriors using the spikes on their axes.'

Mamma Uza-Mâté grabbed a discarded double-handed sword, jammed the point through the staple, and began levering.

'It's coming,' growled Ariella.

The more the staple came out of the rock the further the she-bear could shove the sword blade through, till it was up to the hilt guard.

She kept levering till there was a sound of cracking metal.

'You've done it,' Ariella was exuberant.

'No I haven't.' Mamma Uza-Mâté pulled part of the sword out and the rest of the blade slid off the rock. 'I've broken the sword.' She flung the useless hilt away, grabbed the chain and started heaving. There was a rending screech of metal against rock and the whole thing jerked out sending her flying over the edge of the rock.

Lenyé felt her foot yanked forwards, but Mamma Uza-Mâté let go and Lenyé was able to haul the chain up.

'Quick.' Ariella started pawing at the loose chain. 'We have to get you away.'

Just then Acwellan glanced behind him, saw what was going on, and, with and angry bellow, rushed back towards the rock.

PART VI

_____

THE SECRET MARK

Chapter Seventy Eight

Lenyé saw Mamma Uza-Mâté sit up and shake her head as though still dazed from the fall. Then the she-bear staggered to her full height and swung her paw to punch the Executioner. Lenyé winced as Acwellan side-stepped, grabbed the she-bear's arm and used her own momentum to throw her to the ground.

Before Lenyé could do anything to help, Ariella leaped from the rock and landed on Acwellan's chest, her claws obviously penetrating through the rings of his chainmail as he cried out in pain. But Ariella couldn't make any impression against the chainmail with her teeth. Her momentum spun Acwellan round. Lenyé gasped as she saw Ariella reach up and cover the Executioner's nose and mouth with her powerful jaws. She had heard of a lioness giving a buffalo the kiss-of-death, blocking the animal's nose and clamping its mouth shut, to suffocate it, but had never seen the tactic in action till now.

Acwellan steadied himself from the impetus of the lioness' spring and ended up with his back towards Lenyé. As Lenyé prepared to jump on him, she kept saying to herself, 'Which sword? Which sword?' The one protruding over his right shoulder was easier for her. She landed on Acwellan's back, swept the sword out of its scabbard, and slithered to the ground. She grasped the hilt firmly in both hands, as she backed off, holding the point of the sword out towards him and taking care not to trip over the chain still clamped to her ankle.

Acwellan punched upwards catching Ariella in the belly, knocking the wind out of her and loosening her grip over his mouth and nose. The power of his punch threw the lioness wide and he whirled round wiping the blood off his face with the back of his gauntlet. Then he laughed. 'So? My pretty little bride-to-be fancies taking me on at sword play. Did you not see how easily I despatched Decatur, the other night? And he was a seasoned veteran.'

Lenyé registered a blur of movement and the remaining sword was in his hand. But even as he moved to strike, she saw the familiar shape of the eagle dropping on him like a stone.

'Chuah-te-mok,' Lenyé waved her sword in the air to attract his attention. 'Look out.'

Acwellan glanced up. Slowly, deliberately, he changed the position of his sword as though he was striking upwards with a bat.

Lenyé hardly saw the blow the speed of the blade was so fast.

With a shriek Chuah-te-mok broke out of his dive, the flat of the blade glancing across the backs of his wings as he went tumbling across the ground in a flurry of feathers.

Lenyé braced herself as Acwellan turned back to her, but was momentarily distracted by the odd movement of his thumb along the cross-guard of his sword. Why would he do that?

Then his face lit up with a long, cruel smile as he settled the hilt back into an attacking position in his grasp. 'Let us see if you chose the right weapon. Which one of us will use the Sword of Justice to despatch the other to their final resting place?'

He lunged at her, but she parried the stroke and flicked it off her blade quite easily.

'So,' there was a hint of respect in his voice. 'The maiden's arms have a little strength and skill after all.' He tried another stroke, and she parried him again. 'But not enough.' His face contorted with rage and he waded in with stroke after stroke, forcing her back. She parried and deflected each stoke easing her way towards the fire. It was her only hope.

She could feel the heat from it on the back of her thighs just above the tops of her boots. Next time, she muttered to herself. Lenyé continued to parry the blows as they rained down on her, but tripped on the chain and stumbled catching the full force of his sword on the hilt guard of her own. As his sword swept up for the final stroke, she turned and scraped her own blade along the ground thrusting it deep under the fire. Then using her legs as springs, she twisted her hips and back together shovelling as much hot ash and burning embers as she could straight into his face.

With a howl of agony Acwellan dropped his sword and scratched at his eyes.

Lenyé had to get above him to gain any advantage. Ra-Na-Jiri's rock was closest, but the steps were too far away to her left. She grasped her sword in one hand and leaped for the rock, caught hold of a rough edge, shoved the toe of her boot into a crack and thrust herself upwards. She jammed the sword between her body and the rock using her freed hand to catch hold of another crack. She was nearly there. Lenyé heard the shim of steel against rock as Acwellan retrieved his sword. She scrabbled with her foot for a purchase hold, grabbed an old tree root with her other hand and heaved herself onto the flat top of the rock, snatching at her sword as it began to slip away from her.

She jerked her legs up under her and spun round in a squatting position grasping the sword hilt in both hands to face her opponent. But the chain on her leg was dangling down within the Executioner's reach. In the split second remaining, she lashed her foot across her other leg and the end of the chain with the heavy hasp swung across and caught Acwellan on his cheek. With a yelp of pain he grabbed the manacle and began dragging her towards him. She thrust herself further back on the rock using her free foot; scrabbling for a hold with one hand and hanging on to her sword with the other.

Lenyé heard a deep roar and saw Mamma Uza-Mâté wrap

her furry arms around Acwellan's neck as she leaped on his back and began tearing at the side of his helmet with her teeth. Lenyé felt the chain go slack as the Executioner released it; but gasped in amazement as he whipped round, throwing Mamma Uza-Mâté off-balance so that the she-bear's hind legs swung out to one side. Using the momentum, Acwellan lunged with his arm up under the she-bear and flung her off.

Lenyé yanked the chain out of reach and backed up the rock, but Acwellan was after her. She jerked her foot away just in time before his sword stroke fell. There was a shower of sparks as it glanced off the rock and the ringing of steel jarred in her ears.

Again and again Acwellan tried to get at her, but was totally hampered by her height above him. 'Guards,' he roared. 'To me. Rally to me. Drop that stupid snake and grab her.'

'Don't let them chop me into little pieces, Lenyé,' Ra-Na-Jiri's hiss startled her. 'Save me.'

Lenyé blocked his cry from her mind and focused on the task. There was no way she could strike Acwellan in any of his weak spots with her sword, not even his throat. What was it the warrior said to Beth when he was showing her the spike of his axe? *"That'll go through chainmail as easy as anything and wound or even kill them. You could do it with the point of a sword rather than slashing across the mail rings with the blade, but you would have to be incredibly accurate. Or just plain lucky."* She would have to do this with the point of a sword after all and aim at his chest. Maybe that was what Mamma Uza-Mâté's words meant: *"You must pierce his last defences"*. She was taking an awful risk: if she failed, he would be on her straight away.

The crash behind her as the guards dropped the golden dish distracted her for an instant.

Acwellan backed off to give himself more room to swing his blade. Lenyé saw her chance and edged towards the front at the top of the rock. She squatted down and held her arms above her head with the sword pointing straight out in front of her.

Lenyé could see the lioness had recovered from that terrible blow and was preparing for a spring. 'Ariella, no,' she screamed. 'You cannot fight his chainmail with teeth and claws. He's mine.'

She could feel the hands of Ra-Na-Jiri's guards grabbing at her from behind.

As the enraged Executioner charged towards her Lenyé launched herself at him, thrusting off the rock with all the power in her thighs and straightening her body like a human javelin: the sword held in-line with her outstretched arms.

The impact nearly wrenched the sword handle from her grasp, but she felt the tip of her blade penetrate between the mail rings. She held on and her momentum carried her forwards till the point pierced through the chainmail on his back and the hilt guard thudded into Acwellan's chest right over his heart. With a terrible cry the Executioner toppled over backwards, the tip of her sword hitting the ground before his body, and thrusting the blade back through him before stopping with a jerk that tore the hilt out of her hands. Lenyé fell forwards on the enormous body, and caught his final words as the life ebbed out of him.

'You had the wrong blade all the time and now you have despatched me to the *Death of the Undying*.' He paused, labouring for breath. 'But the great Breaking-in of our Sires of old is at hand.'

Lenyé started as Acwellan's eyes snapped open and he held her gaze.

'When the Dé-monos return, we come with them.' He paused, his breath wheezing and blood trickling from the corner of his mouth. 'You and I will meet again. Then I shall have my revenge.'

Chapter Seventy Nine

Kyros grabbed Stellatus by the arm. 'How are we to come to the fortress? Your song cannot lift and carry this whole company.'

'You will have to run round by way of the plain.'

'Surely we will never be in time?'

'Have faith. You can only grow in strength and power as you continue to trust. Come. I will lead you.'

Kyros scrambled down from their vantage point and glanced over his shoulder to see all the Sacred Pilgrims of Lohr streaming out behind him. Stellatus hovered in the air above, leading the way. Kyros began the long slow trudge across the plain towards Malvi-Quîdda, the stronghold of the Dé-monos. As he walked he rehearsed in his mind all that he knew of the True King and the use of that name in the overthrow of his enemies. Still he felt a check in his inner being about revealing the real name of the True King to others, even Stellatus. He began to feel his breathing deepen and his stride lengthen into a run that would out-sprint even the steeds of the Dé-monos as he raced across the desert plain, the distant fortress rushing towards him. He glanced over his shoulder again and saw the whole host keeping pace with him.

He called out to Stellatus, 'Surely, as soon as they see such a huge company they will unleash a hail of arrows and rocks that none of us can withstand?'

'For the moment I have blinded their eyes to your presence and their peril,' Stellatus paused in his forward flight and hovered some distance above Kyros' head. 'But it won't last for much longer. That is why we have to work quickly.'

Kyros stopped with him, guessing this was the furthest range of any trebuchets, the assault engines he could see mounted on the walls of the fortress.

'It's up to you now, Kyros,' Stellatus called down to him. 'The fourth test is before you: to overturn the power of the Dé-monos and free Harbona. Do not waver at what comes against you, for the True King has equipped you to prevail against the gates of Malvi-Quîdda. Abbérron has been conspicuous by his absence. Something is be brewing but I don't know what. I must seek out my scattered company and return with them as soon as I can, and so come to your aid. For even now the Dé-monos are deadly foes. I bid you farewell, for a time.'

Kyros turned to the Sacred Pilgrims of Lohr, and, with Osâcah's help, formed them into divisions. Then he led the way and started to walk around the fortress. Every hundred paces they stopped, faced the walls and shouted, 'We come against you in the name of the True King!'

The only answer was the clang of a bell from a squat tower located just above the main gates; but there was no sign of any creature appearing on the parapets or preparing any of the armaments to challenge his assault. Stellatus had done his work well. Apart from the bell-ringer, it was as though the entire fortress was empty.

Kyros had no illusions about what they were doing. It was clear that their voices did not carry to the fortress itself. Nevertheless, he could sense the raw power released through his company at the speaking of the True King's name, and wondered at the final outcome. Even if the Dé-monos could see him, perhaps the power of the name of the True King was making them cower away as they had done when he tried to defend Harbona earlier by himself.

Kyros began to climb as their circling brought them further up the mountain so that within a few paces they were shouting down over the fortress itself.

Still no response.

Their height above the fortress, and the constraints of the rocky terrain forced them nearer to the walls, so that as they descended and began walking round towards the front, Kyros realised they were now closer in than he intended.

Still nothing happened, except a second clang of the bell.

The lack of response gave him greater courage, and spurred him on to draw even closer to the fortress. He began cutting across the loop they had already traversed on their previous lap.

Again the pause and the shout. Still no response.

The bell clanged for a third time, as though the bell-ringer was recording each of their laps.

Surely they must be within range by now?

He carried on lapping the fortress, deliberately drawing closer on this circuit till they were well within arrow range. Stellatus' blinding of their eyes was working for longer than he expected. This was going to be easier than he thought.

They were only a quarter of the way round the next lap when Kyros felt a chill breeze on his face. The wind picked up till it howled around him and he could see, overhead, vast clouds billowing down from the North and filling all the sky. Then came the rain. In seconds it had changed from a few lancing needles to a heavy deluge, slanting at a steep angle towards him in the strong wind. The temperature continued to drop until Kyros was shivering. The path he was climbing became a boiling torrent of pale-cream water surging around his ankles; the ground underfoot churning into heavy clay that clung to his boots and hampered his movements as he tried to wade against the power of the water.

He turned to see the Pilgrim's faring no better, some had slipped to their knees already and one or two had been swept away.

Kyros roused them for one more shout in the name of the

True King. He managed to breast the summit of the path and turn the corner and begin to half-slither, half-wade along the path at the back of the fortress. As he did so, the raindrops changed to hail as the storm lashed and raged around him, the tiny balls of ice stinging his hands and face. By the time he'd turned the third corner and was sliding down the path at the side of the fortress, the hail had changed to huge lumps the size of a man's fist. He tried covering the top of his head with his arms for protection but the weight of the hail forced him to the ground and he was only able to crawl on hands and knees. By the time he turned the fourth corner all his energy was spent and he slumped forwards, unable to reach ahead with his hand.

'O, My King,' he called out. 'Come to our aid.'

As he crumpled to the ground he heard Osâcah's voice behind him: 'Wait patiently for the True King, for he has heard your cry.'

Kyros turned to see his comrade, but Osâcah had slipped forwards on his hands and knees and was now lying face down in the mud.

Then Kyros' thoughts were raised to contemplate the True King and strong words coursed through his mind as if someone else was thinking on his behalf: You are my rock, not only above my head when you pulled me out of the crevasse to safety; but now, also, below me. For the clay that sticks to my boots and makes me flounder in weakness is no match for the rock beneath that lifts me up and makes a secure path for my feet!

Then the voice he had come to love whispered in his heart, 'Have courage, Kyros. This is but a trick of your enemies. Remember. You will prevail *with* me.'

Kyros staggered to his feet and looked back at the rest of his companions. 'Up,' he shouted against the violence of the wind. 'On your feet, all of you. It's our only chance.'

He saw them lurch to their feet in response.

'Now shout together.'

They all turned towards the imposing wall of the fortress and shouted: 'In the name of the True King, we come against you!'

As they neared the main gates, the wind faltered and then dropped altogether, the hail ceased and the clouds melted away.

Kyros was utterly exhausted, half-caked in mud; but a fire of determination burned in his eyes.

'We have to keep going,' he shouted to the company following behind.

As they passed the gates, the bell clanged for a fourth time.

They made good progress, pausing to shout their cry against the walls at regular intervals.

Gradually Kyros became aware of a curious buzzing sound that followed them and caught up with them at the back of the fortress. He looked round in alarm, and saw a dense black cloud overwhelm the rear ranks of his host and surge forwards till they were all enveloped.

At first he thought they were tiny insects and tried to wave them away with his hands, but he soon heard Voices in the dense cloud, speaking against all the things and people he held dear, goading him to abandon Harbona, return to the Waking World and surrender to his Uncle. His last thought was that Lenyé no longer cared for him; he'd be gone so long she had found another, and would reject his love if she ever saw him again.

Kyros laughed to himself despite the dark cloud around him, for these thoughts were absurd. How could he ever consider them? They were completely opposed to all his desires and intent. But the mere repetition of them, endlessly consuming his mental strength and redressing the arguments in more and more of an attractive light, was beating down his resistance and weakening his will. Just think: he would be free of all this pain and suffering, he could return to his own world and no longer interfere in business that wasn't his responsibility, he could lay down the burden of ever becoming a King himself in the Waking World, and he would be free to chose another woman for his wife, rather than endure the naïve tenderness he experienced from Lenyé.

'Kyros.' He thought it was Osâcah speaking again and whipped round to look at his companion. But it wasn't Osâcah. It was the True King whispering to his innermost being. 'You have to resist these Voices. Evil crouches at the door of your heart. But you are able to master it.'

Kyros shook his head. Then he spoke aloud. 'No one can influence my thoughts. Be gone!' He turned and shouted to his companions, 'This evil is now spent and the bright day is at hand. Let us cast off these works of darkness, and put on the armour of light; for the True King will defend us against our enemies!'

This time, their shout of, 'We come against you in the name of the True King,' reverberated against the walls and set up a tremor in the ground that subsided after a few seconds.

They completed the lap and passed the main gates, and as they did so, the bell clanged for a fifth time.

Then a voice came from the battlements. 'You have spoken against darkness, but that was not darkness at all. Let the real darkness come upon you!'

Chapter Eighty

Lenyé pulled the sword out of the Executioner's body and wiped it clean on the plume of his helmet. Then she rolled him over and unbuckled the scabbards, but jumped back with them in her hands as his body began sinking; the hand grasping his sword being the last part of him to remain above ground. With a clatter, the sword fell away as his hand finally disappeared.

Now she understood what he meant with his last words: that she had the ordinary sword and he had the Sword of Justice. But how could he tell them apart? She retrieved the other sword and examined them both. Identical, except…Yes, she'd found it. A tiny V-shaped nick carved into the cross-guard where the blade met the hilt of the sword she had used. Her mind flicked back to the words of Yanantha that Ra-Na-Jiri brought her:

The haft of one is secret marked
And only one of twain is sacred true

So that odd little movement the Executioner made with his thumb showed that he was feeling for the nick. When he didn't find it, he knew he had the Sword of Justice in his hand. No wonder he smiled like that: he must have assumed he would win. She dried the blade of her sword with some loose dusty sand from the ground and made sure to sheath it in the scabbard that had protruded over his right shoulder.

Then she held the other Sword in her hands.

This must be it: the Lost Blade of Zerigor.

Why her?

Why was she the one to find and wield this Blade?

What was it Yanantha said? *"It is an instrument of justice and peace"*. If ever there was a need for justice she needed to be free of this manacle and chain. She stooped down and held the blade against her boot, just in front of her shin, and right at the top of the manacle: then sliced downwards. The Sword cut through the metal as easily as if she was slicing vegetables for a campfire hotpot. She pulled the manacle open and slid her ankle out.

There must be something else special about it.

She slid the Sword into its scabbard, then held the scabbard firmly in her left hand and pulled hard at the hilt with her right, expecting it to be tight and require a lot of strength. But no. It slid out so easily that she nearly dropped it, and only just managed to grip tighter on the handle in time.

So it wasn't a matter of strength after all. Originally she thought only someone as strong as Acwellan could pull the Sword out.

What then?

She placed the scabbard carefully on the ground, and held the Sword aloft in both hands, sweeping it back and forth above her head. It felt as light as a feather. She pulled the other sword out to compare. Both had exactly the same balance point, but the sword with the nick had the weight she would expect from a weapon that size, but not the Blade of Zerigor: it was so much lighter. Why the nick if you could tell them apart by weight alone? Surely she couldn't be the only one to notice the difference? But obviously Acwellan couldn't. That's why he had to rely on the nick in the cross-guard.

Suddenly she remembered Yanantha's words to her at the House of Consolation: *"Unless the Blade is recovered, you can never free Beth and the others. For behind Morthrir there sits a far greater power than any mortal can ever challenge unaided. That power is what you have to bring down and vanquish. But it is beyond mere human wisdom and strength to ever master. Without the lost Blade, even Kyros' return will avail little"*.

Maybe the Sword was meant for her, or she was meant for the Sword in a way that she didn't fully understand. Not yet. But clearly it had come to her in order to fulfil Yanantha's words.

She buckled the scabbards in place across her back, just as the Executioner had done, and was about to slot the swords in when she was startled by a voice from behind her.

'Lenyé.'

She whipped round, dropping the ordinary sword and holding the real Blade out in front of her, hearing afresh the roar of battle around her as though for the last few minutes she had been wrapped in a pocket of silence as she contemplated the significance of the Sword in her hands. Then she relaxed. In the heat of the moment and the revelation of her find, she'd forgotten about the others.

'Chuah-te-mok.' She watched him lift off the ground and hover above her before dropping down again. 'You can fly.' She turned to the others. 'And Ariella.' The lioness bounded over and rolled onto her back, patting at Lenyé with her paw. Then Mamma Uza-Mâté was giving her a big hug. 'Mamma. You had some nasty falls back there.'

'I've taken worse and survived. I'm so glad you're all right, too. And you've captured your fancy Sword.'

'Do you know if the crafters finished the fire arrows?'

'No,' Ariella patted at her again. 'But we saw hundreds of Nastâr archers take up their positions earlier.'

'Good,' Lenyé sounded relieved.

'I managed to grab these when no one was looking,' Mamma Uza-Mâté held up Lenyé's longbow and a quiver of arrows.

'Thanks,' Lenyé smiled at her. 'Keep them for a bit longer.'

There was a hiss from behind. 'What about me?'

Lenyé spun round and saw Ra-Na-Jiri, hanging over the edge of the rock, his tongue flicking in and out.'

'At least they didn't chop you up for stew,' Lenyé clapped her hands with delight. 'I've got all my friends safe around me.'

'Excuse me,' Ra-Na-Jiri cut in. 'Can I have my guards back.'

'Your guards?' Lenyé glanced up at him with a puzzled frown on her face.

'Take a look.'

Lenyé was suddenly aware of the guards who bore the golden dish, kneeling before her and bowing to the ground.

'What is the meaning of this?'

'Most Noble Huntress,' the chief guard spoke up. 'Acwellan ordered us to drop the golden dish and aid him. We obeyed his command, but fear we have incurred the wrath of the gods. By slaying the Executioner you have proved you are indeed divine, and more worthy to bear those swords than he was.'

'I see. Very well. You may resume your duty of upholding Ra-Na's golden dish and restoring him to his rightful place of dignity. We will need all his powers if we are to win this battle.'

The guards climbed the rock and Ra-Na-Jiri slithered back onto his golden dish.

'Lenyé,' Ariella rolled back onto her paws and stood up. 'You're not thinking of getting involved in this battle are you?'

'Why not?'

'Yanantha sent you to find the lost Blade,' there was a faint growl in the lioness' voice. 'You've done that. It's your duty to escape with it and use it properly.'

'But I will be using it properly. Listen.'

Ra-Na-Jiri's guards were crying out: 'Acwellan is dead. The Huntress rules the Sword. Let her lead our army.' The shout was taken up by the rest of the Nastrim soldiers.

Chuah-te-mok fanned his wings. 'Let me remind you of the words from the Lay of Hoffengrégor:

> *… not by the hand of any man*
> *shall the Ancient Blade be regained.*
> *Not by might or human strength*
> *shall the final victory be won…*

Lenyé frowned. 'The Nastrim are not human.'

'But you cannot use that Sword as a weapon of war,' Mamma Uza-Mâté insisted. 'That was Zerigor's mistake.'

'I don't understand these words. None of us do. This is a battle field not a classroom, and victory hangs on a thread.'

'We know how you feel,' Ariella paced towards Lenyé. 'We're here to help you. But you need to learn how to use the Sword.'

'Look. The Executioner had absolutely no idea what Youdlh's warriors will do to them. He's left them walking blindly into a trap. At least I know what to expect and how to counter it.'

'You cannot ally yourself with the Nastrim,' Mamma Uza-Mâté growled softly. 'This is madness.'

'I'm sorry,' Lenyé sighed. 'I'm trying to fly like an eagle, have the courage of a lioness and the power of a she-bear and you're all trying to stop me. I'm not going to argue any longer. Kyros charged me to, *"bring Uncle Morthrir to justice, whatever that takes. Otherwise he will destroy the Krêonor and ruin all that we stand for"*. And I'm not about to let Uncle Morthrir's army snatch me away to be his bride. If I don't destroy them now, they'll hunt me down till they've caught me this time. Is that what you want?'

She glared round at them. 'Well. Is it?'

They were all silent.

'I have the Sword and an army that he fears. That's enough, isn't it? You might disagree with me, but at least you can show your friendship by sticking with me. Are you in?'

'Yes, Lenyé,' all three of them responded together. 'We're in.'

'And you, Ra-Na-Jiri?'

'As long as no one chops me up for the pot, I'm in.'

Chapter Eighty One

Rafé sat in his campsite and focused on the cobra. The connection was instantaneous and the snake appeared to be on a rock overlooking a plain. This time its eyesight was much clearer and he could see further and sense other things through the cobra, like strong sunlight and a curious drumming sound and the clash of metal against metal, or the thudding of heavy objects against wood. There were screams and shouts and frequent sounds like a bugle.

Clearly a battle was in progress.

Then he saw Lenyé on the ground well below the cobra.

She had a sword grasped in both hands and was sweeping it backwards and forwards above her head.

It was the right size for a human, so maybe she wasn't with the Nastrim after all. Surely they would have much bigger swords? But how could she have a sword that size unless she'd taken it from one of Youdlh's warriors?

How could she have done that unless the warriors had been defeated?

The sword was too much of a puzzle to resolve just by using the snake. He had to have more information. He had to...

But the cobra moved off his rock, slithering down towards Lenyé and the connection was broken.

Chapter Eighty Two

'Chuah-te-mok,' Lenyé slotted the swords into each scabbard. 'You get up in the air and see what's going on. Mamma Uza-Mâté, find me a bolas I can use.'

'Is this any good?' Ariella pawed at a stone close to the hind legs of a dead horse.'

'Is it attached to anything?' Mamma Uza-Mâté came over to investigate. 'You pull it out while I heave the horse and its warrior over.'

Between them they recovered the bolas from under the fallen warrior, and Mamma Uza-Mâté handed it to Lenyé.

'Thank you. Now grab my longbow and arrows and follow as quickly as you can. Ariella, you come with me. I need to trap a horse.' With that, Lenyé was off, sprinting towards the end of the battle-line with Ariella close on her heels.

She ran after a group of warriors. The horsemen had cantered down the flank of the Nastrim soldiers, harrying them with their small bows, and now turned to ride up the line and rake them with more arrows. Lenyé was just in time to catch up with the tail-ender as he turned. She swung the bolas above her head, let fly as the horse picked up speed, and watched as the momentum of the weights wrapped the cords around the horse's hind legs, bringing the creature down and toppling the rider. Ariella leaped on him while Lenyé grabbed the horse's reins. She whipped out her dagger, cut through the cords of the bolas, and sprang on the horse's back as it staggered up and started to move off before she could fully control it.

She glanced up and saw Chuah-te-mok drop towards her. 'The Nastrim have the warriors on the run, forcing them back in disarray.'

'Yes. But for how much longer?' Lenyé, sheathed her dagger, pulled on the reins and brought the horse to a standstill, before leaning forwards in her stirrups and stroking its mane and patting its neck. 'I have to get to the front and stop them before the warriors turn or else we're done for.'

'I think you were waiting for these, Lenyé.' Mamma Uza-Mâté lumbered up and handed her the weapons just as Ariella finished with the fallen rider.

'Thank you.' Lenyé fastened the quiver onto the saddle behind her left leg and held the longbow in her hand. 'Now. All of you, follow me.' With that she dug her heels in and spurred the horse into a fast canter, Chuah-te-mok hovering above her, Ariella running easily alongside and Mamma Uza-Mâté loping behind. 'Faster, faster,' Lenyé spurred her horse to a full gallop and began overtaking the flanking riders. 'We've got to stop the Nastrim marching straight into a trap.'

Her longbow was awkward to use on horseback, but she needed to clear these riders out of her way. She jammed the reins under her thigh, held the longbow horizontally so she could aim over the horse's head and loosed her first arrow, bringing down the nearest rider. Then she was in amongst the tail-enders, picking them off as fast as she could notch an arrow. The front riders wheeled round to counter this new threat, but Chuah-te-mok and Ariella were on them immediately, tipping them out of the saddle for Mamma Uza-Mâté to deal with.

Lenyé tried to wipe the sweat from her face with the back of her hand, but the dust kicked up by the riders was already caked on her cheeks and up her nose, making her cough and retch as it hit the back of her throat.

Lenyé was now level with the front of the Nastrim line and rapidly overtaking them. She galloped in a loose curve right across the line of soldiers, startling them by her speed and waving her longbow at them.

The line faltered with the ranks behind jostling and shoving as the entire company halted.

Lenyé galloped to the centre of the line, pulled her horse up, wheeled it round and stood up in the stirrups to address them. Then her voice was lifted up like a trumpet and her words rang out for all the Nastrim to hear.

'Listen to me. Acwellan is dead, and I am now keeper of the Sword of Justice.'

They clashed their swords against their shields and shouted, 'Saida! Saida!'

'And I'm not the Mighty Huntress.'

There was a pause in the clashing of swords.

'I am a woman, of the Royal House of the Krêonor, your ancient enemies. My real name is Princess Lenyé.'

There was a deathly hush.

'But I come amongst you today as a friend. For the man who controls that army,' she jerked her thumb over her shoulder, 'is my enemy as well.'

'How do we know you will be true to us?' a voice shouted.

'I could have made good my escape once I'd recovered this Sword, but I chose to stay, for I cannot bear to see you annihilated by those warriors.' She paused to let her words sink in. 'Without me, you cannot defeat this army that sits at your gates. With me, we can achieve a great victory together. Will you trust me?'

There were a few shouts of, 'Lenyé, Lenyé,' but it didn't sound very convincing.

'Ra-Na is my friend,' she continued.

The host erupted into, 'Ra-Na, Ra-Na.'

She spread her arms out to quieten them. 'But he is not divine.'

Again a deathly hush.

'He is an ordinary cobra. So there will be no visitations from the heavens to rescue you from your enemies. Neither will your Sires appear, as Acwellan promised you, to claim me for a bride.'

Lenyé knew she was telling them things they didn't want to hear and could feel the beginnings of a hot wrath coming from the Nastrim in response. She needed to redirect this before it was unleashed on her and they went berserk and were mown down by Youdlh's army. She glanced over her shoulder and could see that the retreating line of warriors had already turned and a great press of horsemen was gathering behind them. She didn't have much time.

'The only way to defeat your enemies is by your own courage and strength. Listen to me. I want you to move back in the field to those two outcrops of rock and form a line across, with the main company of your soldiers concentrated at the centre, like a giant crab.'

Someone at the front shouted out, 'We have never retreated in battle before.'

The cry was taken up, 'Never retreated, never retreated.'

She silenced them with her arms. 'I'm not asking you to retreat. I want you to set a trap.'

Dead silence. She had their attention now.

'Fall back to that crab position and use the tactics Captain Turvil has drilled you in. Forget everything Acwellan demanded of you. You can defeat those warriors if you really want to.'

A ragged cheer broke out from the front and then changed to, 'Lenyé, Lenyé,' while they clashed their swords on their shields.

She ducked as a volley of arrows whistled overhead and rained down amongst the Nastrim. Several soldiers fell.

'When you withdraw, cover your backs and heads with those new shields, otherwise their longbowmen will pick you off.'

'We will only fight for you,' a soldier shouted. 'If you stay and lead us and do not go and hide in the mountain.'

'Very well. I promise to lead you.'

They stood there gazing at her, no one moving, so she shouted out, 'Company. About turn. Shields raised. Forward march.' To her surprise, the whole army obeyed, moving as one, and hurrying back to the outcrops of rock.

Lenyé glanced behind, ducked another hail of arrows, and was horrified to see the front division of warriors riding hard after them. She galloped to and fro across the back of the retreating line urging them on, while Ariella and Mamma Uza-Mâté kept pace with her and Chuah-te-mok hovered overhead.

She was relieved to see the soldiers were in amongst the rock outcrops and to hear Captain Turvil commanding the drill for them to turn and take up the crab formation.

'Open up and let me through,' Lenyé glanced over her shoulder to check on the position of the pursuing warriors, and then realised her awful mistake.

Chapter Eighty Three

Rafé led them at a fast pace through woods and across occasional open meadows, till, by late evening, they reached the banks of the River Rubichinó at the foot of the mountains.

'We'll use the ford to cross tonight and camp on the other side,' Rafé pointed at two white markers on the further bank.

'The water seems very high to me,' Quinn narrowed his eyes and gazed over the swirling water in alarm. 'The horses are going to struggle in that.'

'I know,' Rafé's voice grated with tension. 'But we have to get across while there's still some daylight left.' Without waiting for an answer, he kicked his horse forwards and let him wade out into the river. Quinn insisted Beth dismount while he laid a cloak across the pommel of the saddle, so she could ride in front of him for added safety. Then he urged the horse into the river.

Beth could feel their horse pick its way with care as it entered the ford. Two or three times its forelegs slithered as it tried to transfer its weight forwards. She screamed as the horse stumbled altogether and plunged into the water, soaking her legs to just above her knees, before recovering its footing. The horse hesitated.

Rafé turned back and shouted, 'Quinn. You'll have to kick him hard and make him swim. You're at the pool where he'll be completely out of his depth.'

Beth felt Quinn's thighs tense and relax behind her as he kicked with both legs. The horse snorted and tried to turn back, but Quinn pulled his head round and kicked again and the horse launched out into the water. Beth winced at the current swirling around her knees as the horse thrashed with its legs and swam towards the further shore, the current carrying them out of their course for the white markers. She watched as Rafé's horse started rising up out of the water and breathed a sigh of relief as their own horses' hooves struck firm ground again and with a rasping of stones under each stride, the horse was climbing up the causeway to the bank.

They found a sheltered place in the woods to camp for the night and discussed their plans.

'We've made good progress today,' Rafé took a swig from their water skin. 'Tomorrow we'll have to walk and lead the horses. The path up into the mountains is far too steep to ride.'

'How long will that take?' Beth passed Quinn some dried fruit.

'A day and a half. Two at the most.'

'And then we get to the castle?' Quinn held out his hand for the water skin.

'When we get to the pass at the top, we turn left and it's little more than half a day's steady canter to Onadestra.

'And we just ride up to the main gate?' Beth watched Rafé's face closely in the light from the fire.

'When we get to the edge of the woods, just before we see the castle walls, I'll leave you in hiding and go and see what's happening inside. I'll either come for you or send a message if it's safe for you to show yourselves and enter. Remember. This is your Uncle's stronghold. As I understand it, the troops he left here are likely to be under strict orders to destroy your two families.'

Chapter Eighty Four

Kyros saw the darkness coming. There was no sound like the approach of the Voices. It was as though light just disappeared. As the darkness hit him everything he knew disappeared with it. This was far worse than the River Lammista-ké in the Realm of the Departed, or the Voices earlier, for then he had something to fight against or precious thoughts to cling on to.

It was more like Hoffengrégor's description of the Dé-monos: *"Do not look into their eyes, for they will suck the very life out of you"*. Everything he had learned about using the name of the True King seemed to vanish from his mind in an instant, and it was a struggle to recall anything that would help him. He felt no strength or power to resist.

Kyros sank to his knees, muttering, 'Come to my aid, Oh My King. Be a light to me and enlighten my darkness.'

Then he heard again the reassuring whisper to his heart: 'Kyros. You have been chosen by the True King. You are to return to the Waking World and fearlessly proclaim the knowledge of him.'

'Who am I,' Kyros cried out in response, 'that My King should come to me? Rather, let me come to You, that I may serve You, and You alone.'

Again strong words arose in his mind: For the True King has called you out of darkness into his marvellous light!

Then Kyros laughed for joy: In Your Name I can run against a troop, and in Your Strength I can leap over a wall and prevail against these enemies.

He rose to his feet. 'Enough,' he cried aloud. 'For the light of the True King has blazed in my heart and your darkness cannot put it out. Stand back you evil Dé-monos. You think you can oppose me and delay the fate that is to come upon you. Enough, I say. For you cannot prevail against me!'

There was a roar from the Sacred Pilgrims as the darkness lifted. They surged around Kyros, lifted him on their shoulders and ran him around the fortress, shouting their cry of "the True King, the True King!" against the silence of those towering walls.

As they approached the main gates again the bell clanged for the sixth time.

Then came the response.

First a hail of arrows was loosed from the battlements and fell amongst his host. Kyros raised his arms and shouted, 'Stand firm, my friends. These arrows cannot hurt you. Have faith in the True King, for he will protect you from all harm.' But even as he spoke, another wave of arrows was loosed, this time their tips flickered with fire. Some of the Pilgrims fell, screaming, as another volley of arrows burst in amongst them.

Before he could rally them again, he heard a whistling sound and looked up in time to see huge boulders being released from the trebuchets, the assault engines on the parapets. The boulders crashed in amongst them, knocking swathes of Pilgrims to the ground. He heard the creak of tackle and the swish of many more boulders being released as the assault engines hurled their missiles amongst them.

Then the barrage ceased as quickly as it had begun. But even as Kyros stood up to survey the scene of devastation he heard a shrill cry as a dense flock of Maljaros, the evil birds that had stolen Hoffengrégor's roll from him earlier, burst over the battlements and swooped down on them. Kyros saw six dive straight at him and raised his arm to protect his eyes, but the sheer weight of numbers bowled him over as they harried and pecked at him. He lurched to his hands and knees trying to keep his face away from their ravening beaks, and saw the whole of his company down on the ground being assailed by the terrible birds.

He staggered to his feet and shouted to his followers to stand with him. 'Remember. We are clothed in the armour of light. There is nothing these foul Maljaros can do to us.' He raised his hand against the birds, 'In the name of the True King, be gone!'

With a piercing shriek the birds broke away from him, rising in a dense flock as they fled back behind the battlements. But even as they did so the main gates crashed open.

A division of Dé-monos appeared mounted on their huge steeds and armed with swords and lances. Their horses paced slowly through the gates and fanned out on either side till they were drawn up in a long line just in front of the wall. A faint light emanated from the Dé-monos but it didn't last for long before it flickered and went out. Then they were revealed to Kyros in their real form: manifestations of darkness. For they were cloaked in a black pall that engulfed them and hid their features, while the true horror of their hatred for all living creatures broke in upon Kyros' mind and tried to destroy him.

Kyros reeled as though struck by a physical blow.

Without warning the Dé-monos lowered their lances and charged.

The thunder of hooves was deafening in Kyros' ears and he realised the steeds were galloping on the plain rather than flying. 'Stand firm, my friends,' he yelled to his companions as he stood up straight. Kyros raised his right hand towards the advancing Dé-monos and shouted above the sound of the onrushing steeds. 'In the name of the True King, stand firm. This is all they have left, my friends. No weapon of our enemy can touch you. Stand firm and the fortress is ours!'

The massed weight of the charging Dé-monos crashed in amongst them hurling Pilgrims aside as the onslaught swept through. But Kyros rallied his host and they turned to face the next charge as the Dé-monos completed a tight curve and galloped back towards them.

Kyros sprinted through his own ranks so that he was between them and the charging Dé-monos. This time, as he raised his right hand against them, he cried out in the name of the True King.

Still the massed ranks charged straight at him.

'Do not fear,' Kyros glanced over his shoulder. 'Hold your places.'

The Dé-monos were almost upon him when Kyros spoke, his clear voice lifted up so the entire host could hear him. 'Be gone in the name of the True King, Luchianó-bé, Lord of Light!'

Instantly the ground shook and split open to reveal a bottomless chasm right at Kyros' feet and just in front of the charging Dé-monos.

The first horses stopped abruptly and their riders were catapulted over their heads into the abyss. Then the weight of numbers from behind forced the steeds over the brink, followed by wave after wave of riders till the whole cavalcade had crashed over the rim.

Kyros watched the Dé-monos writhe in anguish. As the darkness was stripped from them, he could see expressions of utter despair etched on their faces as they fell away into nothingness. A cloud of darkness accumulated right in front of Kyros and began spreading out threatening to engulf him.

Kyros still had his right hand raised. 'Be gone,' he cried.

The jaws of the chasm snapped to with a bang that reverberated against the mountains behind him, and the darkness of the Dé-monos was blown away by a gust of wind.

'Come, my friends,' Kyros turned to his companions and was startled to see their stunned expressions. They were staring at him as though they were about to fall down and worship him. He stooped to help raise those who had been thrown to the ground by rocks and arrows, or Maljaros or Dé-monos charge.

As the Pilgrims gathered around him he decided the time had come to declare the name of the True King to them. He lifted his arms for silence before speaking. 'We have used the name of the True King so far and only just beaten off the strength of the Dé-monos until now, when you saw the effect of using his full name and the power that released. When I was drowning in the River Lammista-ké, the True King appeared to me at my time of greatest need and revealed his name to me. He is, "Luchianó-bé, Lord of Light". Using his full name will release far greater power through us. We are not just going to break into this fortress, we are going to utterly destroy it and raze it to the ground.'

He looked around at their faces. 'Will you join me and use his full name?'

Osâcah spoke up for his comrades. 'Clearly you have been sent to lead and inspire us. Did I not say to you: "*We ever behold the True King and live in the light that flows from him*", but we never knew his full name. Now we are complete, for you have revealed it to us and we understand. We will do all that you tell us to.'

Kyros set his face grimly for the last lap; but this time, no pauses and no shouting: just total silence. Also, he commanded some of the Pilgrims to stay in position as they went, rather than carry on walking, till at the completion of the lap the whole company formed a ring encircling Malvi-Quîdda.

As he led the Pilgrims around the walls of the fortress, he could see hurried activity high on the battlements: archers preparing to loose arrows and others lifting rocks into slings to cast from their trebuchets.

Kyros heard the seventh clang of the bell as he completed the final lap. He turned and faced the main gates, glancing either side to check that some of the Pilgrims were spread out in a line along the front of the fortress. As he lifted his hand, the Dé-monos released a hail of arrows and a barrage of rocks. When he shouted the whole company raised their voices in unison, 'In the name of the True King, Luchianó-bé, Lord of Light, we come against you!' Then they all ran straight ahead at the forbidding walls.

At the sound of the name, "Luchianó-bé", the arrows fell to the ground as though they had struck an invisible barrier, and the rocks dropped out of the slings of the trebuchets and crashed around the base of the walls.

By his third stride Kyros felt a shudder run through the rock of the mountainside, imperceptible at first, but gaining in strength as he ran. Then it was shaking violently till finally the whole ground was rocking. He was within a few paces of the gates when, with a roar of falling stonework, the front wall of the fortress buckled and collapsed outwards.

Kyros was well ahead of the company and sprang forwards into the gap of the gates as the wall crashed to the ground around him. He peered through the rising dust cloud into the main courtyard and saw all the other walls and towers tottering and falling outwards. He glanced over his shoulder at the rest of his company surging over the fallen masonry and pouring in behind him.

With a shriek a swarm of Maljaros rose screaming into the air, their wings beating around Kyros' face; but they weren't attacking him this time, rather, they were trying to escape from the crumbling masonry that rained down upon them.

But even as he thrust them away with his arms, Kyros froze in horror.

Chapter Eighty Five

Lenyé knew instinctively she wasn't going to make it in time.

The warriors immediately behind her had taken up an inverted-wedge *lana-din* formation, the two leading arms of warriors already beginning to draw level with her while the central riders closed in on her tail. As the line of Nastârs opened to let her through, a volley of throwing-axes cut into them and the *lana-din* formation hit the soldiers on both sides of the gap. She was dimly aware of Ariella and Mamma Uza-Mâtê being tossed aside as the central riders hurtled through, their momentum thrusting her forwards into the area behind the crab.

Her longbow was far too unwieldy to use in the ensuing confusion of jostling riders around her; each time she tried to aim, one or other end would be knocked askew. She was about to cast it aside when a rider grabbed her from behind, almost wrenching her out of the saddle. She struck out with her elbow, but he twisted to one side and continued yanking at her.

'Down, Lenyé.'

The shrill cry from above startled her.

She threw herself forwards onto her horse's neck as the eagle dived straight at them, catching the rider full in the chest and hurling him to the ground.

Lenyé reined in her horse to a walking pace. 'Chuah-te-mok. Get back up in the sky. We have to gain time. When I give the signal, alert our archers.' She cantered away from the pursuit to find out what was going on elsewhere. Lenyé could see horsemen pouring in through the gap in the crab, and a huge wave of riders following them across the plain. She raised her left hand and looked up to make sure the eagle was watching her. She glanced back at the advancing riders judging their speed, then dropped her hand. Chuah-te-mok dipped his left wing in response. There was a slight pause before Lenyé heard the shrill singing of a thousand arrows loosed in the air from behind her. She ducked instinctively as the sky overhead darkened with their passage, and shielded her eyes with her hand at the sudden bright sunlight after they passed, to watch the effect. Several seconds later she heard the dull staccato drumming, like heavy hail on a tiled roof, as the arrows rained down on the advancing warriors piercing their helmets and chainmail. The impact was astonishing: the first few rows of charging horsemen went down and the ranks behind stumbled on their fallen comrades. She raised and dropped her hand twice more and the successive volleys of arrows cut through the riders. The remainder wheeled away and fled.

'Close the gap.' She heard Captain Turvil's voice ring out.

But still there were riders behind the crab to deal with. Before she could shout for help, Nastârs from within the "D" ran out whirling their bolas and bringing the horses down, then swept out their short swords to finish off the warriors. As Lenyé turned to ride back to the crab, two horsemen galloped up from behind, one on either side, and seized her by the elbows. She felt herself being lifted out of the saddle as they accelerated to go past her, but was surprised by a tawny blur leaping over the necks of the horses and crashing into the rider on her left and hurling him from his saddle. She tried to break away from the other rider, but was shocked to see a black shape rise up in front of them. Both horses veered either side as a huge furry paw smashed into the other rider, knocking him over the rump of his horse.

Lenyé panted with exertion as she slowed her horse and turned to see what was happening in the unfolding battle, feeling the sweat trickling down between her shoulder blades.

'We've got to get you out of here,' Mamma Uza-Mâté shuffled over to Lenyé and laid a gentle paw on her thigh. 'That was too close for comfort.'

Ariella joined them. 'Mamma Uza-Mâté's right. We've got to get you back inside the mountain to defend you properly.'

'They won't fight without me. You heard me promise them.'

Chuah-te-mok dropped down, hovered above her head and called out, 'You could stand on your rock with some guards around you.'

'That makes me an even easier target. At least I can keep moving on a horse.' She glanced out over the plain. 'Get back to your positions everyone. Here they come again.'

Lenyé watched the warriors as they approached the crab under a hail of arrows from their longbowmen, their front line changing into the *lana-dan* and *lana-din* formations. She was startled by one short blast from Captain Turvil's bugler. At strategic places along the curve of the crab, the Nastrim slid their shields to one side and left gaps bristling with javelins like teeth in some many-mouthed monster. A final hail of arrows thudded on the roof of Nastâr shields as the impetus of the horsemen thrust the *lana-dan* and *lana-din* formations straight onto the javelins.

Lenyé tried to shut her mind off from the horror of seeing men lifted out of the saddle on the point of a javelin or a Nastâr's short sword and hearing the wild screams of terrified horses.

She watched the next wave of warriors, under an arc of supporting arrows, veer away from the javelin sections at the last moment. A volley of throwing-axes sliced into the Nastâr shields and the *lana-dan* and *lana-din* formations crashed into the line penetrating through several ranks, before being thrown back as the Nastârs recovered.

'More javelins,' Captain Turvil bellowed. Carriers ran out from the "D" of rock distributing dozens of javelins along the line.

Lenyé shouted up to the eagle to attract his attention. 'Chuah-te-mok,' Lenyé raised her arms out wide and then swept them together in front of her. 'Signal to Captain Turvil.'

Chuah-te-mok dipped his head in response, glided over to Captain Turvil, and swept his wings together.

The Captain looked up, glanced over to Lenyé and nodded.

A greater press of horsemen came charging in for a third attack to try and smash through. This time, every second shield in the crab slid sideways to reveal javelins all the way along the line. It was too late for the horsemen to veer away, and, as the *lana-dan* and *lana-din* formations hit the line of Nastârs and were impaled on the javelins, Captain Turvil ordered two blasts from his bugler. The claws of the crab whipped round in a running march to totally surround the riders. Nastârs in the body of the crab flung down their shields and hauled out their massive double-handed swords from the scabbards on their backs. Then they thrust past their comrades in the front ranks and fell upon the warriors like dozens of harvesters scything their way through a field of corn. As the riders went down the claws of the crab tightened, as though the many-mouthed monster was digesting its prey.

When the claws of the crab opened and the Nastârs began to march back to their positions, the swordsmen wiped their blades clean, sheathed them and resumed their places in the body of the crab. A few horses scrambled up and cantered away. Not a single rider stirred.

The Nastârs shouted and beat their swords on their shields in a war-chant: 'Lenyé', clash-clash-clash; 'Lenyé', clash-clash-clash.

But Lenyé was watching the main body of horsemen in the distance. Surely, after such a decisive rout, they would pull back and change their strategy? But as the dust cleared, she could see two lines of warriors sweeping down the outer flanks to reach the outcrops of rock before the claws of the crab could reform. At the speed they were going she saw they would just do it.

Chapter Eighty Six

Morthrir fumed at his escort leader as the carriage wheels stuck fast yet again. The sudden storm had caught them completely by surprise. He thrust his head out of the window into the howling wind and driving rain. 'Can't you make your horses go any faster?'

'No, Sire. The highway is so muddy they would tire too quickly if I forced the pace.'

'But I have to be at the head of the pass by tomorrow night. If not, I'm holding you personally responsible.' Morthrir slumped back into the comfort of his padded seat and drummed his fingers on the window ledge as the repeated crack of the whip cut through the sound of the downpour. He kept telling himself that the spare horses attached to their company were only for use when they started climbing up into the mountains and would have to leave the coach behind, but already Morthrir was toying with the idea of ditching the coach and riding the rest of the way. Curse this abominable rain! Why haven't the Priests done their job properly this time, and made sure the weather conditions are suitable for such an auspicious occasion?

Chapter Eighty Seven

As the last walls of the inner citadel collapsed, Kyros fanned the air with his hands to clear away the dust and make sure he wasn't mistaken. There, revealed in front of him, was Harbona, kneeling towards him, his elbows and hands tied behind his back and his outstretched neck laid on a block of wood. Beside him, its scimitar poised to strike, stood a hooded Dé-monos. In front of the wooden block a fire was burning.

Vashtani stood amongst another group with his hand raised. He was no longer clothed with light and Kyros was able to discern the darkness of utter hatred at the core of the Dé-monos.

'Come no further, Kyros,' there was a menacing note in Vashtani's voice. 'You may have destroyed Malvi-Quîdda, but I still have power over two things you value highly. The wretch you see here,' Vashtani indicated Harbona with his foot. 'And this,' he held aloft the roll. 'The infantile scribbling of your Prophet-friend. We have searched many centuries for this parchment that we may destroy it and so rid all Realms of the lies contained in it.' Calmly he tossed the roll into the fire.

Kyros lurched forwards, but the harshness of Vashtani's tone stopped him in his tracks. 'One more step and I give the command to strike off your friend's head!'

With a shout Kyros was amongst them, his voice lifted up as he cried out to Luchianó-bé, Lord of Light. Down came a blaze of living flames, its various tongues darting this way and that amongst the Dé-monos, throwing them to the ground and overpowering them. Kyros dived at Harbona, rolling him off the block and pushing him to the ground. As he heaved himself up he could see the tongues of flame settling out into the familiar shapes of Stellatus and the other En-luchés. Kyros whipped out his dagger and cut Harbona's bonds, then hurled himself at the fire, snatched the roll from the blaze, and staggered to his feet. He dropped the bundle on the ground and stamped out the smouldering embers that had caught in the cloth.

But even as he did so, Stellatus' voice rang out, 'The battle is won, Kyros. What would you have us do with Vashtani and his underlings?'

'Do? Why ask me to speak their fate?'

'Are you not a Prince amongst the chosen of the True King? Clearly he has revealed his full name to you, otherwise you could not have prevailed against the gates of Malvi-Quîdda like you did. This is your rightful office, to pass judgement on the True King's foes. Not even Abbérron has appeared to contest your victory.'

'Very well,' Kyros felt a new surge of power run through him. 'Bind them and cast them into the everlasting fire reserved for them in the Realm of Consumption.'

A terrible cry went up from Vashtani. 'You cannot do that! Not ahead of the appointed hour.'

With a sudden clarity of insight Kyros spoke out and his voice rang with a new authority. 'This is the appointed hour! Now the judgement of Luchianó-bé, Lord of Light, has come upon you.'

307

Chapter Eighty Eight

'To me, Nastârs,' Lenyé yelled, and spurred her horse to the right hand side to counter the threat of the approaching warriors. She signalled to soldiers on the ground to follow her, and ordered some over to the other flank.

She reached the outcrop of rock as the warriors poured through and was caught up in a galloping mêlée, using her longbow as best she could, but being herded by the warriors back behind the centre of the crab. The warriors chased her down, loosing arrows into the unguarded rear of the crab as they went, bringing down scores of Nastârs before Captain Turvil realised what was happening and could order more soldiers over to deal with them.

Lenyé sped through a gap in the "D" as warriors from the other flank raced down towards her. She galloped over to the Execution Rock and leaped onto the steps from her saddle and raced up to the flat top. Nastâr soldiers surrounded her as a defence shield, but warriors poured in after her and rode past them from every angle, loosing arrows and throwing their axes. As the ranks of Nastârs thinned, some of the warriors leaped onto the steps and clambered up onto the Execution Rock.

Lenyé found herself in a circle of enemies.

She dropped her longbow and put both hands up to her shoulders to grab the handles of her swords and pulled hard to sweep them out of the scabbards on her back. But only one sword came away in her hand. She knew immediately by the weight that it was the ordinary sword, but involuntarily checked by running her thumb down the cross-guard to find the nick. Why had the Sword of Justice let her down when she needed it most? She was so distracted by her thoughts that she missed seeing the first blow from one of her assailants, and only just blocked it with her sword in time.

She glanced upwards and saw the eagle circling and decided to gain time by bluffing. 'This is the Sword of Justice,' she whirled round to make sure no one was getting any closer. 'The one stolen from Zerigor. Any man touched by this blade will...'

'Don't make me laugh,' one of them sneered. 'A sword is sword. And it's only as good as the swordsman.' He lunged at her just as Chuah-te-mok dropped out of the sky. The eagle hit the man in the chest and thrust him off the top of the rock. Then he was hovering over the next man and clawing at his eyes. With a snarl, Ariella sprang onto the rock in between Lenyé and her next attacker and Mamma Uza-Mâté bounded up the steps and waded in throwing warriors out of her path. The rock was soon clear of enemies.

Lenyé sheathed her sword, but, as she looked up, the words of thanks died on her lips.

The rest of the warriors on the plain trotted forwards and were now fairly close to the crab. They were still a huge army, despite those already slain. Even their longbowmen followed in behind, clearly sensing the end was in sight. Now they were able to loose their arrows beyond the crab, right into the body of Nastâr soldiers around the Execution Rock.

It was time to reveal the extraordinary range of her own longbows.

'Chuah-te-mok,' Lenyé cupped her hands around her mouth and shouted up to the eagle. 'Get ready to signal.'

The horsemen began to canter, covering the distance swiftly before they wound up to a full gallop, a storm of arrows arcing over their heads to protect them. They obviously expected that such a press of tightly packed horsemen would carry all before it.

She raised her right hand in anticipation of the longer range and called to Chuah-te-mok as he hovered above her. She was measuring distances and estimating times. When the front ranks of horsemen were just within the outstretched claws of the crab, she dropped her hand.

The volley of arrows took out most of the enemy longbowmen in one go, but she loosed off two more to make totally sure.

She saw the charge falter as their covering arrows ceased. Then she raised both hands as the riders tried to turn their horses and retreat. She dropped them together and Chuah-te-mok dipped his wings to left and right in quick succession. There was an agonising pause and Lenyé watched in frustration as the retreating riders picked up the pace. 'They're going to escape.' she muttered to herself.

At last she heard the sing of arrows from behind her, and this time, as she looked up at the darkening sky, she could see telltale wisps of smoke. She breathed a sigh of relief: the crafters had done it. The fire arrows fell way beyond the retreating warriors, setting the dry grass ablaze and creating dense smoke which blew back towards the riders.

She could hear the screams of terrified horses and see them bucking and plunging and trying to throw their riders, or turning and running away from the flames, until the whole host was in confusion, all formations broken, every horse running out of control straight back towards the crab. She signalled for more fire arrows on a shorter range to keep harrying and pressing the horses back towards them.

Lenyé saw the skill and courage of the warriors prevail as they regained control of their mounts, and regrouped in yet another wave to hit the crab. This time Captain Turvil's bugler blew three blasts, and the crab opened in many places with no javelins to hinder progress. The Nastârs at the edge of the gaps held their shields to the side so that each gap was shaped like a

310

funnel and all the horsemen shot through into the open space behind. Then the crab turned on the warriors and the Nastâr soldiers drove them forwards through the gaps in the rocks of the "D" and sealed them in.

Lenyé pointed to one of the gaps in the "D" and shouted at the Nastârs as she could see a press of warriors bunching in a concerted effort to break out.

Then she ordered the Nastârs in the rear ranks to enter the "D" itself. They flung down their shields and thrust between their comrades wielding their double-handed swords, while the archers, part way up the mountainside, loosed their arrows directly into the packed ranks of horsemen.

Even as the Nastârs cut down the warriors around them, one man scaled the rock behind her. She whirled round at the sound of his boots scrabbling for a foothold, noticed his blue horsetail and recognised the Field Commander from earlier. She swept out the sword to attack even as he jumped onto the flat top.

Lenyé parried his blows and kept him trapped at the edge of the rock. 'Your army is practically wiped out,' she shouted at him. 'There's no way you're taking me back to my Uncle.' She feinted to the left, almost squatting to get low enough, before thrusting up right under the edge of his chainmail and running her sword through his stomach. With a cry of agony he clutched at the blade, staggered backwards and toppled off the rock. A roar of victory arose from the Nastârs and Lenyé looked up to take stock of the rest of the battle.

If the earlier destruction when the crab claws whipped round and encircled the warriors was terrible to behold, the carnage now was utterly horrendous: the shouts and cries of men, the screams of terrified horses and the unrelenting chant of 'Lenyé,' clash-clash-clash; 'Lenyé,' clash-clash-clash.

Most of the Nastâr soldiers were withdrawing from the "D". Only a few still kept guard as they surrounded her on the Execution Rock. Of Youdlh's warriors, not a man was left alive:

only riderless horses, running around, neighing with terror, their reins trailing in the dust and tripping them when they tried to jump over the heads of the Nastrim who still stood in the gaps.

For the first time Lenyé felt the blaze of the sun on her face. She glanced up and realised it was still only mid-afternoon. In less than six hours since Acwellan ordered his bugler to sound the start of the battle, it was all over; except for the reek of burning grass and the stench of the dead in her nostrils, and the shrill screams of horses ringing in her ears.

She slumped to her knees utterly exhausted, but glanced up as Chuah-te-mok brought news that about thirty horsemen had escaped and were heading back over the plain towards Terrazarema.

'Let them go,' Lenyé was too tired to care any more. 'News will get back to Uncle Morthrir soon enough, even if we chase after them. We've more important things to do here.'

Dimly she was aware of Ariella and Mamma Uza-Mâté climbing up the steps of her rock. But before they could get to her, Captain Turvil swung himself up, lifted Lenyé to her feet by the shoulders and hugged her, crying, 'Long live Lenyé, for you have gained us this great victory over our foes.'

A dozen Nastârs swarmed up on the rock, hoisted them both onto their shoulders, hustled them down the steps and ran them out through a gap in the "D", singing as they went:

> *'Turvil is our Captain*
> *But Lenyé is Victorious.'*

The song was taken up by the rest of the Nastârs as they surged in behind. The whole procession ran out past the line where the crab had been, singing their anthem of victory and accompanied by those still bearing shields breaking into shouts of, 'Lenyé,' clash-clash-clash; 'Lenyé,' clash-clash-clash.

PART VII

WORD OF POWER

Chapter Eighty Nine

'What is it, man?' Morthrir leaned out of the coach window and swore at the escort leader.

'The River Rubichinó is too swollen to cross at the ford, Sire. We'll have to go back to the road and use the bridge.'

'Rubbish. Untie the spare horses and let them swim. We'll leave the coach here. There isn't time to go the long way round.'

'How will you get across, Sire?'

'I can ride a horse. Now get your men moving!'

The horses plunged into the swollen river and were struggling against the current when a surge of water from upstream hit them. Morthrir yelled to his men to keep their horses swimming across, but they were all swept downstream and scattered.

He cried out against the sound of wind and rain, 'I call upon the Hidden Power to come my aid!'

Morthrir clung to his horse's mane and gripped with his knees, but the horse was thrashing its legs so wildly in the water that he was flung from the saddle. He felt himself going down in a rolling mêlée of turbulent water and clinging weeds. His lungs were on fire as he fought for his next breath. When his head broke the surface he could see his horse a dozen yards down-river being swept further from him by the strong current. He grabbed hold of a log as it careered into him, and kicked with his feet steering it towards the further shore. Eventually, battered, bruised and half drowned he thrust out a hand and clung to the reeds on the bank, but they tore away in his hand and he could feel himself being dragged away by the river.

Then his flailing arm was caught by another hand.

He opened his eyes in surprise and gaped at his rescuer. That aged face, and those blank staring eyes, and the haunted look of a man who spent most of his time alone in the mountains. Where had Morthrir seen him before? Suddenly recognition dawned. It was Eawen the Henosite.

'I came in answer to your cry for help, Sire.'

With the recollection of the man's identity came the reminder of the day Morthrir received his new name; and then the shock of seeing the Henosite seated at his desk in that terrifying dream.

'Eawen,' Morthrir's breath was short from fighting against the river and he struggled to get his words out. 'I must talk to you.'

With his other hand Morthrir grasped the trunk of a small tree that leaned out over the water, and hauled himself ashore.

He lay gasping and panting on the boggy ground till he felt rough hands seize him and drag him further from the raging waters.

'Are you all right, Sire?'

Morthrir rolled over and gazed at the man for some time. The question he most wanted to ask Eawen was forming slowly in his mind. But now that he focused on the speaker, the face was all wrong. This man was young and strong and had eyes that could see. Where was the Henosite? He shook his head and blinked several times before recognising his escort leader. 'Of course I'm all right. Where are the rest of the men?'

'There are only four of us left, plus yourself, Sire. All the horses were swept away.'

'Then round up some more. We have to go on. There isn't a moment to lose.'

316

Chapter Ninety

Lenyé touched the hilt of the Sword of Justice in its scabbard on her back: the Sword that had become part of her destiny.

Why wouldn't it come out earlier?

She pulled the handle and it slid out easily. That's odd. It's almost as though some power was preventing me from using it to take life in anger.

Maybe now was the time to re-establish its proper function.

Mamma Uza-Mâté said, "*...the Sword of Justice...is the very Sword you're looking for. It was given to the Krêonor by the True King. It's his Sword. Don't you understand? Justice is locked up in that Sword, not for this world only. The Waking World is the proving ground of Justice for the entire Universe*".'

Despite her affirmation to Yanantha that she could identify with those "*who ever live to hear the voice of the True King and walk in his ways*", Lenyé only knew of the True King as some distant figurehead presiding over the affairs of the Waking World. If it was his Sword, then she would have to know him for herself?

What was it Yanantha said? "*It is not a weapon of war, but an instrument of justice and peace. If you are truly the one, then once you find the Blade, it is down to you and you alone to use it for its rightful purpose*". I'm not sure I understand what that means.

Mamma Uza-Mâté had said much the same thing: "*That was Zerigor's fatal error: using the Sword as a weapon of war*".

Who is there to help me work it out if Yanantha didn't know?

Maybe the Sword had restrained her from repeating the same mistake. Was she going to learn anything more from the Sword

317

itself? She would have to remain alert…

Lenyé was distracted in her musings by movements around her. Ariella and Mamma Uza-Mâté were out on the plain, chasing stray horses back towards the mountain where they were corralled in the "D" of rock.

Ra-Na-Jiri was basking in the sun on his rock, having asked her to send away the giants with his golden dish. She smiled to herself. He hadn't actually taken part in the battle, but as long as he helped to inspire the Nastrim, he had served his purpose well.

Lenyé shielded her eyes from the glare of the sun. She blinked hard, re-focusing on Ra-Na-Jiri. For a moment she thought she'd seen the cobra rise up from his rock, thrashing and coiling in mid-air and then hang limp and straight for several seconds staring at her with fixed eyes, before falling back in a heap onto his rock and slithering round in his coils and rising up with his hood flared. She watched his head dart this way and that as if searching out any immediate threat before he settled back down and the hood deflated. She blinked again. Maybe the sun had played tricks with her eyes and she had been dreaming.

Then she saw movements elsewhere, and watched the Nastârs where they were busy gathering the weapons of the dead warriors and recovering as many spent arrows as possible. Others were hauling the bodies of the warriors in wagons to a spot far out on the plain where they could dig a pit and bury them. Lenyé's thoughts flitted back to that other burial site in the foothills where she killed her first man. What was it she said? *"Here let these fallen remain in peace, and let this be the beginning of the end of all enmity between the peoples and creatures of this world. So let it be."* Were those only token words, or did she really mean them? Now she was caught up in the aftermath of a great slaughter in which she played a significant role.

If she was inwardly distraught over the dead warriors, a people not even related to the Krêonor, then the grief of the Nastârs over those recently banished to the *Death of the Undying*

318

was palpable. Most of the Nastâr bodies slipped through the ground unnoticed during the battle as they fell to the thrust of a sword or a lance, which was then pulled out by the warrior. But those brought down by arrows or axes that remained in the body were only released when the weapon was finally pulled from them: a sore trial for those left alive, who had to perform the task. But she sensed there was more to it than that: the overwhelming grief at their greatly reduced numbers. She heard some mutter against Acwellan's futile tactics, for most of the Nastârs were brought down while he was still alive and in command. But the rest murmured their fear of what would happen now to their dwindling race. They kept looking at her as though she held the key.

Lenyé rode on horseback around the various groups pointing out things still needing to be done and trying to lift their spirits. The Nastârs burst out in their victory song as she passed, praising her as their great heroine, but she noticed the spark go out of their eyes as they turned back to their tasks. How could she rouse them for one final battle to gain complete victory over her Uncle and rescue Beth and the others in time?

Chapter Ninety One

Rafé sat cross-legged on the floor of his private room in the castle at Onadestra and concentrated his mind. He was successful at last. His power over the cobra was extraordinary. Eawen's words were having effect after all. He was able to raise the cobra off a rock, make it hang in the air, and feel the lashing of its body as it tried to curl around a support. But more importantly he forced it to focus specifically on Lenyé and he could ask questions: where was she, what had she been doing, and what did she intend to do next?

He was able to read the cobra's mind as well as sense what was going on around it. Lenyé was at Mount Nastâri with the Nastrim soldiers and had just won a great victory against her Uncle's army. And now she was planning to march on Terrazarema and capture the city.

But he was still troubled by the image of the sword from last time. Was it a warrior's sword or one the Nastrim had given her? Or did it have special powers that gave an advantage in battle?

For an instant he let his guard down and the snake rounded on him, probing his mind for its own purposes. Rafé panicked and broke the connection before he totally lost control.

But at least he had found out what he wanted to know, and could now use this to push Morthrir into taking the final step. He assumed Morthrir was heading for Mount Malkamet. He would have to deliver the message in time without Morthrir suspecting it came from him.

Chapter Ninety Two

Beth and Quinn finished their meal under a rocky overhang that sheltered them from the wind and rain. Rafé had met them earlier to discuss entering Onadestra and the news was not good. The captain was clearly hostile towards him, let alone anyone from the Royal Family. Their parents were not in the castle after all, but had been moved to Fantrios, the Royal Hunting Lodge. Rafé brought his horse for them so they could have one each to ride, a supply of food and water, and fur-lined hoods and cloaks for the colder weather in the mountains. He wished them well on their journey, and returned to the castle.

'I don't think we should be doing this,' Quinn packed away the remains of the food Rafé gave them into his saddle bag.

'What do you mean? We have to get to Fantrios as quickly as possible and rescue our parents.'

'Slow down and think, Beth. Do you really trust Rafé?'

'If our parents aren't in the castle, then where are they?'

'How do we know Rafé isn't trying to get us out of the way?'

'Why would he do that?'

'If something extraordinary is about to happen on Mount Malkamet,' Quinn finished doing up the buckle on the saddle bag. 'Like that old man said, then maybe Rafé doesn't want us around and have a repeat of Druis-cyf-rin.'

'I don't want to be around for a repeat of that dreadful place.'

'Beth. We have to choose between rescuing our parents and stopping Uncle Morthrir getting this power.'

'Just how do you propose we do that?'

'Something will turn up.' Quinn strapped his saddle bag in place and turned to Beth. 'What did Ishi-mi-réjá say to you?'

'She said: *"Look for me by moonlight at the Summer Solstice and I will be there"*.'

'But it's the Summer Solstice today. That old man said something about a Grand Convocation. I bet it's going to be at midnight tonight.' He grabbed Beth by the hand and pulled her to her feet. 'We have to get to that mountain in time.'

'Quinn, you couldn't have a night with less moonlight. It's pouring with rain out there. I think we should head back to Onadestra and find some proper shelter. There must be a secret way we can get in. We can check if our parents are still in the castle and try riding again when it's a bit clearer.'

'All right,' Quinn didn't sound too convinced. 'But we mustn't waste any time. We have to get to Mount Malkamet before Uncle Morthrir and stop him.'

They rode quickly most of the way, but slowed down to a walk as they approached the walls of Onadestra. Their hoods and cloaks were soaked, and Beth began to shiver with cold.

As they drew level with the Eastern Gate there was a shout from the parapet.

'Look out,' Quinn kicked his heels into his horse's flanks. 'We've been spotted.'

Even as they veered away from the wall and began to canter, the gate was thrown open and half a dozen riders in chainmail armour and cloaks billowing behind them, came clattering out over the cobbled threshold and began chasing after them.

'Quick, Beth. We've got to out distance them.'

'Where can we go?'

'Down towards the head of the pass. Ride, Beth. Ride,' Quinn shouted back to her as his horse picked up the pace. 'They mustn't catch us. Ride like you've never done before.'

Chapter Ninety Three

After the battle Lenyé talked with Captain Turvil. She was afraid he might resent the soldiers' victory song about her when he played such a valiant role himself. But he gave nothing away.

'You do realise we can't stop here,' Lenyé was keen to press her case. 'My Uncle has another army based at Terrazarema greater than the one we've just destroyed. He will be swift in taking revenge and catching us unprepared.'

'What do you suggest?'

'We can either sit here and wait, or go out to meet him.'

'If we wait here, he will come knowing about your longbows.'

'Correct.' Lenyé looked Captain Turvil directly in the eyes. 'We could lure him into another trap.'

'Your tactics with the crab worked very well.'

'I don't mean repeating the same thing. They're plainsmen warriors. Away from this mountain they're in their natural element and will run rings around us.'

'So how can we take advantage of that?'

'You march the soldiers across the plain to entice them out. Use the captured horses to pull wagons of gear for scaling walls, as though attempting a siege at Terrazarema. When the warriors attack, draw the wagons into a circle. Take some archers and they can loose their arrows from behind the protective ring.'

'And the rest of the archers?'

'They will come with me. While you draw their army out and keep them focused on attacking your ring of wagons in the plain, we will march through the forest and take Terrazarema.'

'That could work, but you will need some companies of soldiers to go with you.'

'The question is,' Lenyé was probing for the truth. 'Will they do it?'

'If we strike while the afterglow of victory is still fresh.'

'Yes but are they willing to fight after losing so many comrades? I don't see any enthusiasm for risking another battle.'

'They look to you, Lenyé, not only for inspiration, but also their hope. I meant what I said in your apartment before the battle, *"You are the rightful keeper of the Sword of Justice"*. Decatur believed it so strongly that he predicted one of your Royal line would arise to free us from our fate. That person is you. I've been talking to my soldiers. They now believe it and will follow you anywhere and obey your every command if you will lead us.'

'Very well,' Lenyé answered. 'But we must march tomorrow or we'll be too late.'

'We will be ready for you.' Captain Turvil turned away to resume the instructing of his soldiers.

Lenyé remounted her horse and sat thinking. Despite all that had happened and still lay ahead of her, she felt curiously at peace. She searched her mind for the answer and realised it was when the Field Commander delivered the ultimatum from Uncle Morthrir about executing Beth and the others. In that moment of shock she knew that all her angry thoughts towards Beth had evaporated as though they never existed, and all she could feel instead was a strong sense of love towards her sister.

Suddenly all Yanantha's words to her fitted into place and she knew she could see ahead like an eagle, the time of waiting to recover the missing Blade was over and she was ready to use it, and she felt strong in a way she had never done before.

Chapter Ninety Four

'All I can find, Sire, are mules.' Morthrir's escort leader gestured helplessly.

'Hmmph!' Morthrir sat in the fisherman's hut with a blanket wrapped round him while his clothes dried out by the fire. 'Not as fast as horses when we get to the upper grassland plateau, but better for the mountain trail. How soon can we ride out?'

'Within the hour, Sire. Also, the fisherman's wife has a warning for you. Whether awake or dreaming she couldn't tell, but a man with unseeing eyes held her hand and whispered, "If Morthrir goes up into the mountains he will encounter terrible destruction." Should we head back and prepare the army?'

'No.' Morthrir turned away from his escort leader and continued speaking, as if to himself alone. 'The struggle in the water was sent to me as a sign.'

'I beg your pardon, Sire.'

Morthrir paused as he recalled the image of the Henosite's face and the surprising vigour in the old man's grip on his arm. 'The army is no longer the answer. Everything I have ever trusted in for strength and protection has been washed away and I am cut off from what lies behind me. I cannot go back as I am. The struggle at Rubichinó will go down in history as confirmation of my destiny. No one can defy me now.'

'What are your orders, Sire?'

Morthrir frowned as he turned back to his escort leader. 'Get the mules saddled up.' He smacked his fist into his open palm. 'I must go on. I have to be there in time.'

Chapter Ninety Five

Quinn slowed his horse as the ground began to dip down in front of them.

'What's the matter?' Beth yelled at him against the wind.

Quinn pointed ahead and to their right. 'Lanterns. Someone's coming up the Pass.'

Beth slowed her horse to a walk and waited for Quinn to catch up. 'Who do you think it is?'

'It has to be Uncle Morthrir. That would fit with what the old man said.' He kicked his horse back up to a canter and made for a scattering of rocks and large boulders to their left. 'Let's hide in here. I want to see what's going on.'

They dismounted and ducked down behind the rocks, holding onto the reins to stop their horses wandering off.

Sure enough as the clouds parted and the moonlight began to shimmer through, they could see a number of mules making their way up the last steep incline to the head of the pass.

'There's Uncle Morthrir, towards the back, shouting at them,' Beth whipped round to Quinn, but he clamped a hand over her mouth.

'And here come the soldiers from the castle.'

Even as he spoke, a lone rider, muffled in hood and cloak, and shadowing the soldiers some distance back from the company, rode over towards their hiding place and ducked down behind a row of rocks in front of them.

'Who's that?' Beth whispered.

Quinn merely shrugged his shoulders and turned his

attention to the mules.

There was a shout of command from the leading mule rider, 'Who goes there?'

'Guards from Onadestra. We're chasing two horsemen we saw on the plateau. Rafé ordered us out.'

'Then you can escort me to Mount Malkamet,' Quinn heard his Uncle shout back, and saw Uncle Morthrir urge his mule to the front. 'And one of you can give me his horse. I'll never make it in time on this mule.'

Quinn and Beth watched as Uncle Morthrir galloped away on horseback surrounded by the rest of the mounted guards, while the mules and their riders turned and headed for Onadestra. When everyone else had gone, the lone figure cantered out from his hiding place and headed off in pursuit of Uncle Morthrir.

'It was Rafé. I saw his face as he turned,' Quinn mounted his horse and held Beth's by the reins for her. 'With Rafé between us and the mountain, we'll have to be careful not to be seen.'

They rode for a while in silence, the keen wind blowing the clouds and revealing intermittent patches of moonlight.

'What's that up ahead?' Beth slowed her horse from a canter to a walk as Quinn caught up with her.

'Where? I can't see anything.'

'Over there,' Beth pointed to a tumble of boulders where the grass on the plateau began to give way to bare rock as the path climbed to the final heights of Mount Malkamet. 'I wish the clouds would blow right away and give us some clear moonlight. I'm sure I saw something move.'

'At least it's stopped raining.' Quinn pulled his horse to a complete halt so he could scan the ground ahead better. 'There's more to come though,' he sniffed the night air. 'Those clouds are building up again. We need to get under cover soon.'

'There it is again.'

'I see it now.' Quinn dismounted and crouched down before creeping towards the boulders. Then he stopped and laughed.

'Hey, Beth. Come and see,' and he ran forwards still laughing with delight.

As Beth dismounted the clouds parted, and, in the sudden bright moonlight, she saw a figure rise up from the boulders. Immediately she recognised who it was. As she ran over, Quinn threw his arms around the dark figure. Then Beth was up with them and hugging and kissing the old woman. 'Ishi-mi-réjá. I thought it might be you, but I didn't know where to find you.'

'Did I not say: "*Look for me by moonlight at the Summer Solstice and I will be there*"?'

'Yes, but…'

'Come. We have much to do tonight, and we need to find the right place in time.'

Ishi-mi-réjá walked at a surprisingly fast pace while they followed behind, their horses picking out the line of a path as it began to climb in a long zigzag up the mountain. Soon they had to dismount and lead their horses as the path became steeper. The rain began again and Beth was stumbling with fatigue by the time they reached their goal and were able to picket their horses. They unbuckled the saddles and stashed them under a small overhang of rock to keep the worst of the rain off, and left the horses feeding on tufts of grass. Ishi-mi-réjá led them to the very rim of a shallow ravine where they were able to look up to the flattened summit above them and down into the ravine itself.

Quinn gripped Beth's arm. 'Look,' he pointed to a group of figures about two-thirds of the way up the ravine towards the summit. 'They're building an altar. Like the one at Druis-cyf-rin.'

'This is nothing like Druis-cyf-rin,' Ishi-mi-réjá's words startled him and he jerked his head round to look at her. 'This is much darker. That altar is only for human sacrifice.'

'Why have you brought us here?' there was a tremor of fear in Beth's voice. 'This is much worse than Druis-cyf-rin. I don't like this place. I want to go back.'

'For goodness sake, Ishi-mi-réjá,' Quinn let go of Beth's arm and turned to face the old woman fully. 'If Druis-cyf-rin put Beth into that trance, what's this place going to do her?'

'It's not the place that's the problem,' Ishi-mi-réjá frowned at him. 'It's the power that's released. 'Something terrible is about to happen here tonight. We have to stop it.'

'But I felt it as well, last time,' Quinn persisted. 'It almost squeezed the life out of me.'

'I wasn't with you then. And neither was my stone.' She dipped her hand in her shoulder bag and pulled out her *ishi-mi-réjá*.

'Can I hold it?' Beth's eyes sparkled as she turned to the old woman. 'I think that would help overcome my fear.'

'Indeed it will. In fact, you are the very one to hold it tonight and go on holding it whatever happens.'

'What do you mean?'

'As long as you hold that stone aloft, no power can be released in the ravine below us.'

'How long must I do that for?'

'As long as it takes.'

'But suppose my arms grow tired and I can't hold it up any longer?'

'Then your cousin and I will have to help you: one on either side.'

Beth took the stone and caressed it in her hands and then suddenly thrust her arms up holding the stone above her head.

'That's right,' the old woman smiled at her. She put out her own hand to help steady Beth's left arm. 'Come and help us, Quinn.'

But Quinn was a few paces away, squatting down and peering over the edge of the ravine. 'It's working,' Quinn's voice was whipped away by the wind as he spoke from his vantage point. He could see four figures in cloaks and hoods: white, black, red and grey around the altar with a ring of ten figures in brown robes and hoods surrounding them inside an oval of torches. He smiled grimly to himself. One of them must be Rafé, but he couldn't tell which. The wind billowed the cloaks and cowls of the figures and fanned the dancing flames of the torches. He turned back to the others and yelled, 'Hold it up, Beth.'

'I can't. My arms are aching already.'

Whenever Beth dropped her arms he noticed the flames of the torches begin to straighten and the billowing cloaks fall limp. But as soon as she raised the stone again, the wind picked up to a greater fury, surging in amongst the torch flames and ripping through the tufted grass. As she dropped her arms this time, a lone man emerged, walking up the ravine towards the figures at the altar. The man was bareheaded, with his cloak swirling around him in the wind. Quinn wasn't particularly surprised when he recognised Uncle Morthrir. His Uncle cupped his hands round his mouth and shouted something, but Quinn couldn't hear the words. Then Quinn gasped in surprise. His Uncle checked his pace briefly then strode in between all the figures, drew his cloak tightly around himself, climbed onto the altar and lay down on his back, clasping his hands together on his chest.

Quinn dashed back from the edge of the ravine and caught hold of Beth's sagging arm and helped her lift the stone again. On the other side, Ishi-mi-réjá was holding up Beth's left arm, but clearly tiring.

'How much longer must we go on like this?' Quinn gritted his teeth as his own arms began to ache.

'I don't know,' Ishi-mi-réjá nodded her head. 'We're not through yet. I can feel something momentous is about to happen.'

Chapter Ninety Six

Morthrir strode up the ravine towards the waiting figures. The wind tugged at his cloak and howled past him. He glanced at the familiar time-candle and was relieved to see the flame just burning through one black line, leaving another about an inch lower down. It must be about twenty-five minutes to midnight. He'd made it in time.

What surprised him most, though, was how much the wind continued to whip around the figures by the altar, and the flames of the torches flared away from him. Surely by now that pocket of absolute stillness should have gathered around the ring of Priests to protect them all for what was to come next.

He still held the small piece of parchment handed to him by a soldier as he skirted the outcrop of rock to enter the ravine. The man said it was from one of the Priests. His mind recoiled at the message: *Half your army has been destroyed at Mount Nastâri. The Nastârs have a secret weapon and your niece is leading them as they march on Terrazarema.*

He hesitated briefly before thrusting the parchment into a pocket under his cloak. Armies and battles didn't matter to him any more; it was the ceremony here tonight that would decide the final outcome. He had to make it happen.

Morthrir strode in between the figures not even waiting for their bidding this time. When he reached the altar he held his cloak tight to stop it billowing in the wind, climbed onto the top, lay down on his back, clasped his hands on his chest and waited.

The Four Summoners approached him, the figure in white bearing the same silver chalice as before. Morthrir sat up, swung his legs over the edge of the altar and grabbed the chalice. Very slowly, very deliberately, he tipped it up so that the contents poured out and were whipped away from him by the wind, splashing all four of the Summoners with red wine before reaching the ground.

He flung the chalice away and settled back on the altar.

There. That would show them he meant business this time: no longer a reluctant victim bound against his will to the altar or half-stupefied by drugged wine, but a willing sacrifice making a voluntary offering. No more the fear of what the Summoners' knives could do to him. He was beyond them now. Had he not been called back from death for this very purpose? He would utterly confound them. What power his commitment would now release!

As Morthrir lay back on the altar he felt the rain lashing down, stinging his face and the back of his hands, and drenching his already soaked clothes. Where was the preparation of the Priests? Surely they could control the elements and command the weather to be propitious for such a solemn and significant occasion. It was almost as though another power was ranged against him, seeking to divert him from his goal.

But no.

Nothing could do that now.

He had come this far.

He had to have absolute power.

Morthrir watched as the flame on the time-candle burned through the remaining black line: a quarter to midnight. He started breathing slowly and deeply to calm himself in preparation for what lay ahead.

Gradually he became aware of another conflict raging beyond the reach of the torchlight. Imperceptibly that pocket of stillness would descend upon them. He glanced to his left and saw the flames of the torches begin to steady and burn more upright while the cloaks and hoods of the Priests hung limp around them, and he felt the tug of the wind against his own robe lessen. Then suddenly it would shift and the full force of the storm was ragging around them again. He could feel the combined will of the Priests and the Summoners extend out beyond their ring and probe the surrounding darkness seeking where the point of resistance was coming from. Whatever it was, it occurred to Morthrir that it must be extremely potent if it could interfere with the activities of this group.

He felt the focus shift up the edge of the ravine and stop just before the summit of the mountain. He tensed his muscles ready to spring up and run if things went amiss, but something like a huge hand pressed down on him and kept him firmly in place on the altar.

Then he heard a great cry from the Four Summoners. 'Lord Abbérron. We have a willing victim this time. Come to our aid.'

As if in direct response the mountain top was lit up by a dazzling flash of lightening, followed by a long rolling peel of thunder.

At the second cry, great forks of lightening flashed and the thunder rolled over them.

At the third cry, the lightening hit the flat top of the mountain above them with a great crack of thunder right overhead.

Chapter Ninety Seven

Kyros watched the En-Luché bind the Dé-monos in chains of light and drag them away.

'Well done!' Stellatus clapped him on the shoulder. ''You have won a great victory.'

Kyros frowned. 'There's one thing I would like you to clarify. Three times I have heard about the Blade of Zerigor: firstly from Hoffengrégor, then Vashtani, and finally a Nastâr in the Realm of the Departed. I thought it was lost forever. Why is it suddenly so important?'

'The Blade of Zerigor was forged in the Realm of the Blessèd Throne by the True King himself,' Stellatus began. 'It is His Sword and has power in all Realms over every being. He presented it to Zerigor to use wisely; the first task being to despatch the Nastrim to Elasis, their resting place, and so rid the Waking World of the curse from their Fathers.'

'What happened?'

Zerigor was defeated and the Sword stolen from him. If it is ever found, that is the first task of the new keeper. Otherwise the keeper will suffer the same fate as Zerigor. My heart tells me your victory here has triggered the finding of the Blade. You must return to the Waking World with this warning and seek out the new keeper in time.'

'What about Abbérron's counter stroke?' Kyros queried.

'That is what concerns me the most. I told you I felt something was brewing. I feel it even more strongly now and fear something terrible is about to happen.' Stellatus gestured for

Kyros to walk ahead of him. 'In the meantime, I must escort you and your comrade back to the Guardians of the Spiral. Remember. Your final three tests await you in the Waking World.'

Chapter Ninety Eight

That night Lenyé couldn't sleep. She paced up and down in her apartment thinking over what Captain Turvil said. She had to seize the opportunity and use the Nastrim army against her Uncle Morthrir as soon as possible.

But the apartment was so hot and stuffy. She longed for the feel of the night air on her face. Finally she could bear it no longer, flung open the door and hurried down to the main entrance of the Nastrim fastness. Once out on the lower slopes of the mountain she breathed deeply and felt the welcome chill against her face. Far away to the South-East she could see a thunder storm raging, the bright flashes of lightening flickering in the night sky, although the thunder itself was too far away to be heard.

Other thoughts kept tugging at her mind. She recalled Acwellan's words about the Dé-monos breaking back into the Waking World and Vashtani leading them.

Surely with Acwellan despatched to the *Death of the Undying*, there was no way she could be forced against her will to be the bride of Vashtani? And with one of Youdlh's armies wiped out, she wasn't going to be Uncle Morthrir's bride either.

So why the nagging doubts now?

A stab of lightening made her look up expectantly, but it died away just as quickly.

Was the Breaking-in dependant on Acwellan still being here or not? If the Dé-monos really were beings from another Realm, then they must have a power of their own to force a point of entry. Supposing the seals set in place by the True King, that Mamma Uza-Mâté mentioned, were broken and the Breaking-in happened after all? Would the Nastrim join forces with them claiming the Dé-monos as their Sires? If they did, where would that leave her? Would they still fight for her against her Uncle?

With a sudden shock, Acwellan's final words surged back into her mind: *"When the Dé-monos return, we come with them. You and I will meet again. Then I shall have my revenge."*.

What did he mean by that?

A second lightening flash seared the blackness of the night and died away.

Then she remembered Acwellan's words over dinner with King Ogandés: *"All it needs is a word of power from a human being with the right authority in this world, then the Breaking-in will begin"*. But who was there with that kind of authority, to defy the True King himself and break those seals?

She didn't know the answer to any of these questions. Especially the last one.

She shrugged her shoulders. With Acwellan out of the way, none of this was going to happen. Besides, she could only handle what she could see and understand.

A third flash of lightening made her jump, and she looked across the night sky wondering about the significance of such a fierce storm.

Her thoughts flicked back to Captain Turvil as she made up her mind. She had to destroy her Uncle Morthrir's threat before tackling anything else.

Lenyé smacked her hand against a rock beside her. 'Uncle Morthrir,' she muttered to herself. 'Half your army is wiped out, we have a strategy to destroy the rest of your warriors and seize Terrazarema, and I hold the Blade of Zerigor that will motivate the Nastrim against you. If you harm so much as a hair on Beth's head you will regret it. You're not as invincible as you think!'

Chapter Ninety Nine

As Ishi-mi-réjá spoke the dark clouds and the mountain top were lit up by a dazzling flash of lightening, followed by a long rolling peel of thunder. At the second flash, Beth stretched up as high as she could go, trying to use the stone to quell the very violence of the storm, even as the thunder rolled in the night sky. The third flash hit the flat top of the mountain above them with a great crack of thunder right overhead.

Beth screamed, but her voice was drowned out by the following thunder. Her hands began to shake as she felt the stone heating up to an intensity she could hardly bear. She screamed again as, still clutching the stone, she stumbled, the stone disintegrating in her hands and trickling out as fine dust through her fingers. On her third scream she pitched forwards onto the rocks and lay still.

Quinn felt that awful grip surge over him, this time crushing the breath out of him in a matter of seconds, as though his chest had crumpled until there was no air left in his lungs and he fell prostrate next to Beth.

Of Ishi-mi-réjá there was no sign.

Chapter One Hundred

The metal cross-piece fell away on the time-candle: midnight.

As Morthrir sensed the resistance melt away, and saw the flames burn straight up on the torches, he felt a jarring sensation through the altar under his back. Then he was on the flattened peak of the mountain, standing before the image of the Lord Abbérr...; even now he couldn't fully form that name in his mind. The Summoners and Priests formed a horse-shoe shape behind him and were bowing low.

The wind continued to howl and the rain poured down in torrents, but around the awe-inspiring image there was a pocket of absolute stillness that covered Morthrir and the others.

The image spoke, 'What is your answer, Morthrir?'

He had been rehearsing in his mind all the conditions he would impose, but his tongue stuck to the roof of his mouth.

'Yes or No?' the voice penetrated down into his inner being.

There was nowhere to hide from such a gaze.

'Your Kingdom is about to slip from your grasp. Only I can help you. But I must have your answer. I repeat, "*Yes or No?*".'

Morthrir shook from head to toe. He tried to open his mouth, but his dry lips were stuck fast together.

'I can't wait all night. I grow impatient.'

Then something entered into his mind and broke the reluctance of his will. His cracked lips parted and a voice came from deep down inside him that spoke in a far lower register than he was normally capable of, and answered: 'Yes!'

'Swear on oath.' Abbérron's voice was scarcely more than a

whisper, but it went right through Morthrir like a spear of ice.

'I swear.' Morthrir's hand trembled as he held out the parchment. 'And here is the signed contract to prove it.'

'Fool,' Abbérron threw back his head and laughed. 'As is if a piece of parchment with signatures on it has any real value. All I needed was for you to believe in your deepest being that I can give you whatever you ask of me, and, in return, you can give me what I demand of you. And you have sealed it by oath. Nothing can break that. I will call on the Summoners and Priests as witnesses should you ever try to go back on your word.'

Abbérron leaned forwards and snatched the contract out of Morthrir's hand. 'But I'll take this anyway.'

The mountain top shook and the Lord Abbérron appeared to shrink, while Morthrir grew in stature. The vision of the Lord Abbérron began to fade, but before it totally disappeared Morthrir distinctly heard the image give an urgent command.

'Turn and face West towards Lake Sanchéso, and the Eye of Hoffengrégor, and the cursèd spot on the Dangst Rock where the Seer stood and prophesied the Restoration of the Krêonor. Speak my words against him.'

As the command died in Morthrir's ears a power welled up within him as though he'd just drunk a tankard of hot fire-juice, the spiced alcohol running through his veins to his very finger tips. He felt new and alive and full of power to make anything he desired happen. Then he spoke aloud using unfamiliar words and names that came to him as if some other being was using his voice, and the mountain reverberated to his command. 'Let the Guardians of the Spiral be thrust aside and the seals broken. Let the Spiral itself be opened from the Realm of Travail. Let the Dé-monos be released again into the Waking World.'

Morthrir's voice rose to a final crescendo, and, without any hesitation or stumbling over the name, he cried out: 'Let the Hidden Power of My Lord Abbérron come to me!'

END

OF

BOOK I

IN

THE RESTORATION

OF

THE CROWN OF LIFE

A COLLECTION OF WRITINGS

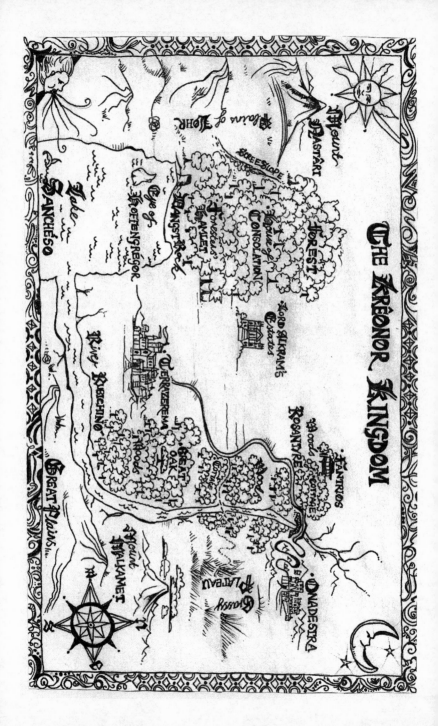

THE KRÊONOR ROYAL FAMILY

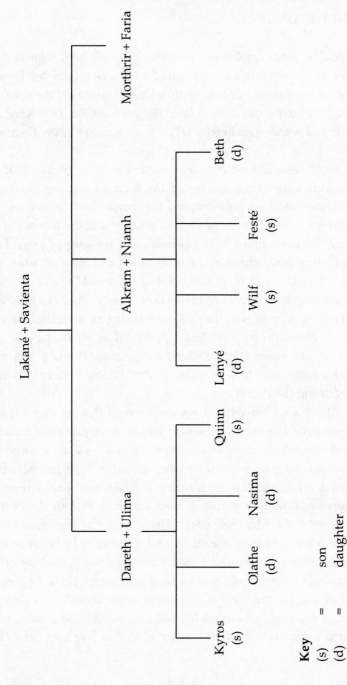

Lakané + Savienta

Dareth + Ulima

Kyros
(s)

Olathe
(d)

Nasima
(d)

Quinn
(s)

Alkram + Niamh

Lenyé
(d)

Wilf
(s)

Festé
(s)

Beth
(d)

Morthrir + Faria

Key

(s) = son
(d) = daughter

The Comings

I, Hoffengrégor, called by the True King himself, who is Lord over all the Realms, and appointed by him to receive the Peoples and instruct them in the way they should go; to all the sons and daughters who ever live to hear the voice of the True King and walk in his ways; do hereby set forth an account of the Comings.

For I observed all that was around me: the grandeur of the mountains and the crashing of the waves upon the shore, the beauty of the trees and flowers, the warmth of the sun and the soft breeze on my face, the chill of evening and the wonder of the stars, the companionship of animals and the song of birds. For I was given understanding of their voice and they of mine, and birds would come to my finger and we would sing harmonies concerning the marvels of the Waking World. And the food that was to hand and easy to pick and tasted so delicious, and all things bountiful for life. And I delighted in all that I saw and beheld and entered into understanding thereof and I perceived that wisdom was born that day. But one thing it lacked for utter perfection: the Peoples.

And then I looked and my eyes were lifted up and I beheld beyond the Westering waves an island more fair even than the land in which I walked. And in its midst I saw the Bara-mâla-ké, the blessèd Peoples, dwelling in perfect harmony. Then I perceived Zerigor, wearing the Krêon of Tulá-kâhju, the Crown of Life, that blazed around his head, and all the Peoples radiated light from their heads, like a circlet of fire around their brow when seen from one angle, or a flat disc of light above their heads from another: and I saw from afar the Perfection of the Peoples. For the island had no need of light by night, or even on a dull day, for the Light of Life shone about them. And I thought, surely when they have multiplied and filled their island, some brave seafarers would seek other places to live and raise their offspring and so venture to my shore that I might welcome them in the name of the True King, for it was not permitted that I should take the wings of the seas and go to them.

But alas, as I looked and beheld I observed over a period of some time that the light about their heads flickered and went out, one by one, and the blaze from the Krêon of Tulá-kâhju was diminished and there arose a terrible conflict between the Peoples. As I cried out to the True King for understanding it was revealed to me that the Tsé-shâmé had sought after a secret knowledge to give them power to overcome Zerigor and place their own ruler in his stead. Many were cast down and breathed no more. And there was a dividing between those who remained in the Waking World and those who perished and went down to the Sleeping World, and I perceived that the span of life for those left in the Waking World was reduced to no more than one hundred and twenty years before they, too, went down to the Realm of the Departed. And it grieved my heart that this should be, and I sought in my reason what manner of Peoples are these who paid such a terrible price for not persevering in seeking to live together in harmony and resolving their differences without recourse to bloodshed. And I knew not.

So I walked some time, bowed in grief. For surely these Peoples tarried overlong in their blessèd isle and failed to go forth and make landfall with the rest of the Waking World, and so at an early stage may have come under the wisdom and teaching of the True King, and thereby preclude this disaster. It is one thing to encounter the True King for a brief moment as they did on their island; it is quite another to embrace his teachings and sustain the reality of that encounter over an entire lifetime. For I perceived that these Peoples had given heed to the Voices that whisper in all men's hearts and breed thoughts of dissatisfaction and overlay the foundations of a harmonious disposition with the desire to put down others and be first in all

ii

things. And so, as I mused, it seemed clear to me that by provision of the True King himself, the seeds already sown in their hearts were come to fruition and we might behold what manner of Peoples these are: whether they regard each other more highly than themselves and treat each other as they would have others treat them and so fulfil the earnest desire of the True King, or become selfish in their ways and want the best for themselves to the exclusion of others. For which is more precious in the eyes of the True King: another person in all their beauty or the accumulation of wealth at the expense of others. And so their deepest intent was no longer hidden and the taint of the Voices they harkened to was finally exposed.

So I considered how best to greet such Peoples should they venture to my shore. For it appeared to me, even from such a distance, according to the eyes of discernment given to me by the True King, that they had descended into the arrogance of ruling without mercy, the idleness of wanting without working and the resentment of serving without appropriate reward. And it seemed a great folly to me that these Peoples could not excel in their separate giftings for the common good. But no counsel arose in my heart to instruct me, and I deemed that matter to be beyond the extent of my wit.

Who, then, would arise to heal the rift that came about in the Beginning?

Then I looked and beheld, and lo a mighty ring of waves surrounded the island and rushed inwards and crashed upon its shores in a vast inundation that carried away all things and hid the island in a great mist. And out of the deluge came fleeing, boats and crafts of all kinds and people clinging to whatever floated, and they were borne upon a great wave that swept them to my hither shore. So I hastened to come down to them and make what provision of food and clean water to drink and shelter that I could contrive, for they were exhausted; and I thought surely they will put away all animosity from amongst themselves and fall in with a considered plan to fortify their spirits and rebuild some semblance of a settlement for themselves where they could gather sufficient food for many hungry mouths and so prosper together in spirit and in health.

For out of the flood came three Peoples: firstly, the Krêonor, tall and long-limbed and pale to golden skinned, with striking features and brightness of eye, and hair ranging in colour from fair to dark; secondly, the Tsé-shâmé, who were shorter and broader and of a swarthy countenance and darkness of eye and hair, except for some dark-haired Krêonor who stayed close by them and refused to look me in the eye and seemed at variance with their own brethren; and thirdly, the Harmoth, of much darker skin than the others and a blackness of hair and a stature in height and girth somewhat between the other two.

The Krêonor accepted my help and counsel gratefully; but the Tsé-shâmé refused, saying they would never serve another again, and took themselves off in their war boats some way down the coast and were lost to sight; while the Harmoth, full of anger at the Krêonor for failing to protect them against the onslaught of the Shâmé army, spurned my aid and wandered away inland.

A cloud of anxiety covered my meditations for I had forebodings of evil yet to come. Through the vision and discernment given to me I was able to see from afar and discover the intent of the Tsé-shâmé, and it was after this fashion.

Lenyé's Scroll

Sung: *...not by the hand of any man*
shall the Ancient Blade be regained.
Not by might or human strength
shall the final victory be won...

Birds: *If for vision, be an eagle*
Soar beneath the heavens above
Looking down, discerning all things
Maid of honour, bring new life.

Chuah-te-mok: *If for ruling, be a lioness*
Bright the huntress, crowned in splendour
Let your courage match your virtue
With great strength now be endowed

Ariella: *If for waiting, be a she-bear*
Incubate from death to life
Guard your offspring, guard them fiercely
Use your power, rich in mercy

Mamma Uza-Mâté: *Beware the Executioner*
Sword of Justice is his prize
You must pierce his last defences
Seize the Sword as you arise

Ra-Na-Jiri: *Two Swords in splendid jewels bound*
Reflecting moonlight on their shimmering blades
The haft of one is secret marked
And only one of twain is sacred true

ABBÉRRON'S CONTRACT

I, ABBÉRRON,
   Lord of the Realm of Dominion,
   Prince over the Realm of the Waking World, and
   Ruler of the Realm of Travail,
Hereby draw up this contract to appoint MORTHRIR,
   Lord of Onadestra, and
   Crown Prince of the Kingdom of the Krêonor,
As my Regent in the Waking World
   To reach out his hand and take all that he desires
 In consideration for the sum of his life:
   To fall due by the signing of this contract.
I confirm upon the said MORTHRIR three things:
   1.   I have called you from birth and given you your name
   2.   As heir to the throne of the Krêonor you have authority
        to act, and
   3.   You are mine and will walk in my ways and know my
        power.
If you fail me, I will seek you out and exact a terrible revenge
upon you

Signed: Abbérron   *Signed: Morthrir*

CUSTOMS OF HONOUR

The inhabitants of the Waking World have a very highly developed sense of honour for their older generations which is reflected in their grammatical rules. Therefore, all descriptors of an older generation are capitalised, such as Father, Mother, Uncle, Aunt, Grandparents, Grandfather and Grandmother; whereas descriptors for the youngest or same generation are not, for example cousin, brother, sister, son or daughter.

Also the main points of the compass, North, South, East and West are capitalised as travelling long distances is a serious undertaking and those who come from afar are equally venerated.

PRONUNCIATION

All who dwell in the various Realms speak a common language, but it may help to know the sound of accented letters.

The most common one is "é". At the end of a name, the accent is there to force the pronunciation of the "e", rather than allowing it to remain silent, so Lenyé would sound as Lenyay.

Where "é" appears within a name, it sounds similar, for example, Hoffengrégor would sound as Hoffen-gray-gor.

Abbérron is a complete exception as his name comes from a former era, so it sounds as Ab-ber-ron rather than Ab-bay-ron.

An "á" would be pronounced "uh" as in Ishi-mi-réjá. The regional dialect is dominant here, so the "j" disappears in "ray/uh", and her full name sounds as Ishi-mi-ray-yuh

An "ó" would be pronounced as "o" in "no", so Rubichinó would sound as Rubi-chi-no, and Luchianó-bé as Luchia-no-bay.

Generally an "â, ê or î" lengthens the vowel sound as in Tsé-shâmé which would sound as Tsey-sharmay, Krêonor as Kree-on-or, Malvi-Quîdda as Mal-vi-keed-da, and Nastâr/i as Nast-ar/i (â + r creates only one long "a" sound).

Names with Accents	Pronunciation
Abbérron	Ab-ber-ron
Bara-mâla	Bar-a-marla
Bara-mâla-ké	Bar-a-marla-kay
Dé-monos	Day-monos (retains the "s" for the singular)
Dé-mono-chromés	Day-mono-chromez (é + s = "z")
En-luchés	En-luchay (silent "s" for the plural)
Hoffengrégor	Hoffen-gray-gor
Ishi-mi-réjá	Ishi-mi-ray-yuh
Krêon	Kree-on
Krêonor	Kree-on-or

Names with Accents	Pronunciation
Lammista-ké	Lammis-ta-kay
Lenyé	Lenyay
Luchianó-bé	Luchia-no-bay
Maliché	Mali-cay
Malvi-Quîdda	Mal-vi-keed-da
Mamma Uza-Mâté	Mamma Uza-Mar-tay
Nastâr/i	Nast-ar/i ("i" is their mountain)
Ogandés	Ogan-dez (é + s = "z")
Osâcah	O-sar-ca
Rafé	Rafay
Rubichinó	Rubi-chi-no
Sanchéso	San-chay-zo (é + s = "z")
Tsé-shâmé	Tsay-sharmay
Tulá-kâhju	Too-luh-car-ju

Names without Accents	Pronunciation
Chuah-te-mok	Chew-a-t-mock
Druis-cyf-rin	Drew-iss-sif-rin
Eawen	You-wen
Ibarno	Ib-ar-no
Maljaros	Mal-jar-oss
Malkamet	Malk-am-et
Nastrim	Nast-rim
Onadestra	Owna-des-tra
Terrazarema	Terr-atza- rema
Youdlh	Yoo-dle

LIST OF CHARACTERS

Name	Description
Abbérron	The Hidden Power that appears to Morthrir
Acwellan	Lord High Executioner of the Nastrim
Alkram	Morthrir's second elder brother and Lenyé's Father
Ariella	The lioness who rescues Lenyé
Beth	Lenyé's sister
Chuah-te-mok	The eagle sent to Lenyé by Yanantha
Daivat	Lenyé's horse at home
Dareth	King of the Krêonor, eldest of the three brothers: Dareth, Alkram and Morthrir, Father of Kyros and Quinn, and Uncle of Lenyé and Beth
Decatur	Self-appointed liberator of the Nastrim; seeks to overthrow Acwellan
Eawen	The Henosite and Chief Priest of the Hidden Power
Elskin	A captain in Morthrir's army
Faria	Morthrir's wife
Harbona	A captain in Morthrir's army
Hoffengrégor	The Ancient Prophet
Ibarno	Morthrir's original name
Ishi-mi-réjá	Lady of mystical powers who helps Beth and Quinn
Kyros	Prince of the Krêonor, older brother of Quinn and cousin to Lenyé and Beth
Lenyé	Princess of the Krêonor and Daughter of Lord Alkram
Luchianó-bé	The True King
Mamma-Uza-Mâté	The She-bear who comforts Lenyé

Name	Description
Morthrir	Uncle of Kyros and Lenyé
Nostrea	Apothecary referred to by Quinn
Ogandés	King of the Nastrim
Osâcah	Leader of the Sacred Pilgrims of Lohr
Quinn	Younger brother of Kyros and cousin of Beth
Rafé	Personal counsellor to King Dareth and then Morthrir
Ra-Na-Jiri	Cobra who comes to Lenyé's aid
Stellatus	A Leader of the En-luchés and Herald of the Eastern Principality
True King	Lord over all Realms
Turvil	A captain in the Nastrim army
Vashtani	A powerful Lord of the Dé-monos and Acwellan's Father
Yanantha	Prophetess who sings over Lenyé
Youdlh	Commander of Morthrir's army
Zerigor	First King of the Krêonor

For Further Details of the Trilogy

visit

www.crownoflifelegend.com

info@crownofliflegend.com

For Further Details of the Trilogy

visit

www.crownoflifelegend.com

info@crownofliflegend.com